# CHOOSERS OF ★THE SLAIN★

JOHN RINGO

CHOOSERS OF THE SLAIN

This is a work of fiction. All the characters and events portrayed in this book are fictional, and any resemblance to real people or incidents is purely coincidental. This book and series have no connection to reality. Any attempt by the reader to replicate any scene in this series is to be taken at the reader's own risk. For that matter, most of the actions of the main character are illegal under US and international law as well as most of the stricter religions in the world. There is no Valley of the Keldara. Heck, there is no Kildar. And the idea of some Scots and Vikings getting together to raid the Byzantine Empire is beyond ludicrous. The islands described in a previous book do not exist. Entire regions described in these books do not exist. Any attempt to learn anything from these books is disrecommended by the author, the publisher and the author's mother who wishes to state that he was a very nice boy and she doesn't know what went wrong.



A Baen Book

Baen Publishing Enterprises
P.O. Box 1403
Riverdale, NY 10471
www.baen.com

ISBN 10: 1-4165-7384-4
ISBN 13: 978-1-4165-7384-5

Cover art by Kurt Miller

First Baen paperback printing, November 2007

Distributed by Simon & Schuster
1230 Avenue of the Americas
New York, NY 10020

Library of Congress Cataloging-in-Publication Data: 2006007458

Printed in the United States of America

10 9 8 7 6 5 4 3 2 1

## ★ HAMMERING THE POINT HOME★

"Good morning, Yuri," Mike said pleasantly as the man's eyes flew open from the ammonia capsule. "Did you have a good rest? I'm sure you recognize the after-effects of chloroform; you've used it a time or two."

Yuri Smegnoff was taped to a chair that was firmly bolted into the middle of the floor of an abandoned factory.

Mike drew out a folder and pulled out a picture, flipping it in front of the man's face. "Now, I know you see a lot of young women," Mike said nicely. "But I'm really hoping you recognize this one. Because if you don't, I'm going to have to improve your memory."

"I . . . I do," Yuri said, licking his lips. "Yes, I remember her. One of my catchers picked her up near that town square. She said she was Ukrainian, that she was looking for work."

"Go on," Mike said.

"Can I have some water?" Yuri asked, carefully. "I am very parched."

"It's an effect of fear," Mike pointed out. "It comes from the adrenaline. I'm sure that many of your little girls had very dry mouths. Did you give them water, Yuri? No, I thought not."

"This is who you look for? She had no friends!"

"We'll get to that later," Mike said, smiling. "And then what, Yuri? She's not walking the street for you. We've checked rather carefully. So, where'd she go, Yuri?"

"I did what I always do," the slaver said with false bravado. "I sold her. I don't remember to whom."

"Ah, Yuri, Yuri," Mike said, reaching back and accepting a large sledge hammer from the Keldara. "Bad answer."

## Baen Books by John Ringo

*The Legacy of Aldenata Series*
*A Hymn Before Battle*
*Gust Front*
*When the Devil Dances*
*Hell's Faire*
*The Hero* (with Michael Z. Williamson)
*Cally's War* (with Julie Cochrane)
*Watch on the Rhine* (with Tom Kratman)
*Yellow Eyes* by (with Tom Kratman)
*Sister Time* (with Julie Cochrane) (forthcoming)

*There Will Be Dragons*
*Emerald Sea*
*Against the Tide*
*East of the Sun, West of the Moon*

*Ghost*
*Kildar*
*Choosers of the Slain*
*Unto the Breach*
*A Deeper Blue*

*Princess of Wands*

*Into the Looking Glass*
*The Vorpal Blade* with Travis S. Taylor
*Manxome Foe* with Travis S. Taylor (forthcoming)

*Von Neumann's War* with Travis S. Taylor

*The Road to Damascus* with Linda Evans

**with David Weber:**
*March Upcountry*
*March to the Sea*
*March to the Stars*
*We Few*

# ★ DEDICATION★

As always

For Captain Tamara Long, USAF
Born: May 12, 1979
Died: March 23, 2003, Afganistan

*You fly with the Angels now.*

# ★ Chapter One ★

"Colonel Kortotich," Mike "Jenkins" called out as the unwounded Chechen prisoners were being unloaded at a Georgian military prison.

Mike Harmon had been a college student at the University of Georgia when he'd witnessed the kidnapping of a coed. Most college students would have picked up their cell phones, or run to someone who had one, and called 911. But before he was a college student he'd been a SEAL and a SEAL instructor. So he just jumped on the kidnapper's van and rode it to its destination.

That move, and a series of similar decisions, had led him to an underground bunker near Aleppo where terrorists backed by Syria had brought American girls to be used as hostages. And their plans didn't just include holding them, but torturing them for the cameras to force American units to leave the Middle East.

Mike had lost one of the hostages before he realized what the plan was, but he'd fought his way through to the rest and held the position until relieved, along the way wiping out a chemical weapons factory, the Syrian president and Osama Bin Laden.

This had earned him the grateful thanks of a nation, quite a bit of money and a price on his head from every Islamic terrorism group on earth. "Mike Harmon," Team Name "Ghost," had quietly disappeared, maybe alive, maybe dead, and "Mike Jenkins" had reappeared in his place.

After being the wrong place at the wrong time too many times, Mike had settled down in the Republic of Georgia, using part of his reward money to buy a pleasant little farm with a group of tenant farmers already in place. However, the security situation in the area being what it was, he'd taken the opportunity to train the retainers as a local "militia."

The retainers, called the Keldara, had taken to it like so many ducks to water. A little digging turned up the fact that the Keldara were anything but simple farmers. According to his interpretations, they were, in fact, the last remnant of the Varangian Guard, the Viking guards of the emperors of Byzantium. The group had apparently descended from a small force of mixed Norse and Scots-Irish that had drifted down through the Mediterranean until encountering the Byzantine Empire.

They farmed quite well but at heart, like the Kurds and the Gurkhas, they were warriors first and foremost. A couple of million dollars in equipment and a similar amount in payroll for trainers and training had turned them into a formidable, if small, fighting force. They had taken on a Chechen "battalion" at nearly three-to-one odds and the prisoners and dead now being loaded into the Georgian military trucks were the result.

Mike suspected it wouldn't be the last such battle for the group called "The Tigers of the Mountain."

"Mr. Jenkins," the Russian attaché replied, nodding. "Quite a battle for a little militia."

"Untrained militia," Mike pointed out. "They were only in their third week of training. The teams fought them straight off of their first days of range training."

"How many did you kill?" Kortotich asked.

"One hundred and three KIA," Mike replied. "Including some who got froggy when we were in the capture phase. Forty-two WIA, including some the doctors don't think will survive. And twenty-one prisoners, unwounded."

"And Breslav?" the Russian asked.

"He, unfortunately, did not survive the encounter," Mike said, slipping a picture out of his jacket pocket and handing it over. Breslav had, apparently, been directly in the area of effect of a claymore, since his torso and right arm were missing. However, his head was still attached and the expression of surprise was clear on his face. As was the expression of satisfaction on the face of the Keldara who was holding his head up by its hair. "I would have liked to capture him for intel purposes, but you can't always get what you want."

"We are glad enough that he's dead," Kortotich replied, smiling at the pic. "Can I keep this?"

"Certainly," Mike said. "It's a photo quality printout, anyway. We only use digital cameras."

"Three weeks of training, you said?" Kortotich asked. "I think that my bosses will be impressed. Very impressed."

"And, of course, the intel we forwarded you," Mike pointed out. "That stopped his team from entering Chechnya. Can I take it we might be able to avoid a border war?"

"There is still the matter of the Pankisi Gorge," Kortotich pointed out. "That is where their main bases are."

"I don't think the Keldara will be up to taking that on any time soon," Mike replied. "But we'll start interdicting their movements as soon as our training is complete. The Gorge will be a matter between you and the government of Georgia."

"I'll pass all of this on," Kortotich said, pocketing the picture. "And I give you the thanks of Russia, for what it's worth."

"Oh, I'm sure it will have some use in the future," Mike said, smiling faintly. "You scratch my back, I scratch yours. Take care, Colonel."

"Back into training again," Nielson said in a satisfied tone. "Nothing like a little live-fire exercise to get the blood pumping and the troops motivated, but now they're going to think they know it all."

Colonel David Nielson was the senior officer of the group Mike had hired to train the Keldara. The colonel's field credentials were impeccable but he was, at heart, a trainer. He loved taking soft clay and molding it into soldiers. As such he'd been a very good choice to lead the training, although some of the trainers, notably the SEAL and Marine Recon members, had questioned having a regular Army guy in charge. That was until they started to see the results.

Mike had been flown back to the serai, courtesy of the Georgian government, which was being remarkably friendly at the moment. He'd consistently tried to downplay the

Keldara, but having a fraction of their force wipe out a Chechen "battalion" was, he was told, being discussed at the highest levels. It had also made the international news, although the story for press consumption was a special Georgian commando group. Which, in a way, they were.

"Get that out of their system with a good, solid after action review," Mike said. "I'll be on the grill, too."

"Everyone was involved," Nielson pointed out. "Who conducts it?"

Mike started to answer when his sat phone rang.

"Jenkins," he said.

"Pierson, go scramble."

"Scrambled, how's it going, Colonel?" Mike replied when the system was in place.

"I thought it was going to be a year before you were fully in the groove," Pierson said. "What's with making network news?"

Colonel Robert Pierson had been Mike's "control" ever since his first mission in Syria. The colonel just happened to be the guy picked to talk on the phone with some madman who had traced the kidnapped coeds halfway across the world. Since then he'd received similar calls from Mike and made a few in the other direction. He never ordered Mike, who was after all a free agent, he just suggested or in a few cases pleaded. He was less a "control" than an information conduit. And in a way a friend.

"We did?" Mike asked, frowning.

"Slow news day," Pierson pointed out. "And the Chechens are still a bugaboo after Breslan. Apparently the guy you wacked had a small piece of setting that up. At least, according to CNN."

"Nice of them to tell us," Mike said, rolling his eyes at Nielson.

"Seriously, what did you do, use all the trainers?" Pierson asked.

"No, it was mostly Keldara," Mike replied. "Their first FTX. Right off of their first two days on the range. The mortar girls had had more range time, but not much."

"Jesus Christ," Pierson said, wonderingly. "How far are you into training?"

"Three, four weeks," Mike said. "Depending upon whether you consider that training. Colonel Nielson doesn't."

"I didn't say that," Nielson said with a sniff. "Just that it's interfered a bit."

"Well, the boss man said 'Good job' followed by 'next time, try to avoid the papers.'"

"Tell him I said thanks," Mike replied. "Anything else?"

"Just that," Pierson said. "I'll add my own 'good job.' Take care."

"Will do," Mike replied. "See ya."

"We were talking about an after action review," he continued, looking at Nielson.

"I was thinking it might make sense to ask D.C.," Nielson replied, gesturing at the phone with his chin.

"Thought about it," Mike said. "Too many fingers in the pie. You'll work up the AAR. Include me in the review as well as yourself. Get Adams and a couple of the instructors to do a forensic of the shoot site. I want a count of every round expended and a probable of who shot who. Work them all down and show them exactly what they did wrong. And I did wrong. Start with my forgetting to bring the mortars; I'm not used to having to think about integral heavies. And we had a major problem at one point with commo control. I want that hit heavy, along with the fact that it slowed down the pursuit, and I want Vanner to get started on what we can do about team freqs and sub-freqs. When Oleg told them to move by odd and evens, the security guys wanted to get out and pursue. That has to be covered, too."

"Will do," Nielson said, sighing. "Can I have Kat to assist?"

"Go for it," Mike replied. "Hot-wash tomorrow, full AAR with all teams by the end of the week."

"Got it," Nielson said. "I'll get started."

"Vanner," Mike said, sticking his head in the radio room. Vanner was pointing to something on one of the computer screens with his head nearly touching that of the Keldara female working the computer. Mike wasn't sure who she was, but he was pretty sure she was from the Makanee clan.

"Kildar?" the intel NCO said, spinning around.

The term "Kildar" was what Mike was called by the Keldara but it had caught on with others. It was a unique name for the local warlord, translating as something like "baron." What it meant, simply, was leader of the Keldara and that was enough for those who had come to know them.

Patrick Vanner was a former Marine, but Mike tried not to hold it against him. The guy was plentiful hardcore, but he was, nonetheless, the designated team geek. He'd been an intercept specialist in the Marines, then worked for the NSA for a while. After getting out he picked up a degree in computer science that was almost superfluous to his actual knowledge, which when it came to electronics and electronic intel was enormous. Short, stocky and crew-cut, he was proof positive that you could take the boy out of the Marines but not the Marines out of the boy.

"Got a couple of questions," Mike said, gesturing for Vanner to follow him out of the room. Mike led the way to the war room and grabbed a seat.

"You look like you're getting pretty friendly with some of the Keldara girls," Mike said, raising an eyebrow.

"Is that why you wanted to see me?" Vanner asked, frowning.

"No, but I figure I should ask about it," Mike replied.

"Gildana and I are just friends," Vanner said, shaking his head. "She's really good at picking out freqs. I'm being very proper in all my dealings with her. Speaking of which, I know these girls are being paid for this, but is there some way we can get them rank? They're doing the job of commo and intel techs, which in the military would make them privates or specialists."

"I'll think about it," Mike said. "But watch yourself. I don't want some Keldara Father on my case over a pregnant daughter. Or even one that could be pregnant, if you get my drift."

"Got it," Vanner said.

"On the real reason I wanted to talk to you," Mike continued. "We had a real breakdown in commo on the op. Not a breakdown, exactly, but . . ."

"The team net got filled with chatter," Vanner said,

nodding. "That's partially a matter of training so they don't just jump on the radio."

"I'd like more," Mike said. "Sub freqs for the sub-teams, a general freq for the whole team, then on up. Something where the commander doesn't have to think about it to pass stuff down, though, and can listen in on the chatter. Also, I want to start working on a battle net. Something where call-for-fire, at least by those with the right equipment, is point and click. Probably with a voice backup and confirm, but I want to be able to point to a spot on a map and say: 'Send fire there.' I'd also like to be able to sketch out movements for the teams."

"I can get all that," Vanner said. "Some of it's off-the-shelf and unclass but some of it's classified U.S. and European systems, mostly U.S."

"I think we can swing that," Mike said. "You find the system and I'll get permission for us to get it. Keep an eye on whether it can be integrated into U.S. battlefield systems. If we end up in a situation where we can call for fire from God, I'd like to be able to do it. Look around at some of the firms that do C2 and offer free field trials," he added, grinning. "Try to get a deal; it's not going to be cheap gear."

"Will do," Vanner said. "Anything else?"

"If you and Gildana get to be more than friends, tell me first," Mike said, seriously. "I'll see what I can do with the Keldara. Unless it's a lot more than friendship, in which case you'll be going home with a mother-in-law."

"Wasn't planning on it," Vanner said, frowning. "But it's a thought. She sure as hell is gorgeous."

"And she can cook," Mike said, nodding. "But she'd

have to adapt to an entire new culture. A very, very different one. Think about it carefully."

"I will," Vanner said.

"Now we're done," Mike replied, grinning. "Take care."

"What we're going to do here, is go over the action you just engaged in just like any other test," Nielson said to the gathered Keldara. The hot-wash on the action was being conducted team by team, taking the whole day to go over known faults. They'd started with Team Oleg as the one that had been involved in the most combat. They were using one of the basement rooms in the serai for the review and it was packed with the Keldara sitting on folding chairs and looking nervous. "We will do one of these after every action, so get used to them.

"The first thing to say, and I'll say it again and again, is that you did very well," Nielson continued, looking around at the group. "Especially since you are in the middle of training. But there's no such thing as perfect. This is a method to get closer and closer, though, if you pay attention. Right now, Chief Adams and Sergeants Fletcher, Graff and McKenzie are walking over the skirmish area and working up the full review. What we're doing today is called the hot-wash. We'll be going over individual and unit actions as they are known and determining what we can do better the next time. I'll start with ammunition expenditure."

He pulled up a list with a graph on the computer screen on the wall and pointed to a couple of high points.

"There were over sixty rounds of 7.62 expended per casualty that was found to have been shot," Nielson said, pointing at the two graphs. "Not a total of sixty rounds, but sixty rounds per casualty. The low round count was Oleg, which, given that he shouldn't have been firing at all, was pretty good at only fifteen rounds. Oleg, why did you fire?"

"I . . . wasn't doing anything else, Colonel," the team leader said, uncomfortably.

"You were supposed to be paying attention to everyone else's actions," Nielson said, shaking his head. "Chief Adams is, trust me, much more accurate than you are in a fight like that. But he expended no rounds because he knew he wasn't there to fight. He was there to observe and control. You are given a weapon for one purpose only; self-defense or something that you have to shoot at because you can't get one of the shooters to do it in time. That is it. Period. I can't imagine a reason for you to have expended even one round in this engagement. Did any of the enemy get close to your bunker?"

"No, sir," Oleg admitted, dropping his head.

"Keep your head next time," Nielson said. "You're there to control the flow of the battle. If you have to, lead from the front if you're directly attacked; if you have to engage due to time constraints, you can engage. Otherwise, keep your finger off the trigger! Beso!"

"Sir!" the Keldara said, sitting bolt upright. He'd been bent over talking to the Keldara next to him.

"Three hundred and eighty-six rounds?" Nielson said, clearly amazed. "How in the hell did you expend three hundred and eight-six rounds?"

The day after the hot-wash they took all six teams out

and walked the ground, looking over what they could have done better. Mike determined that Nielson was just better at picking out details on stuff like this than he was. Everything from the timing on when he'd pulled in Vil to when he'd sent Killjoy and Vanim down the hill was reviewed and critiqued.

The third day was a final review held in the main dining room of the serai. Mike had had more tables and chairs brought in and there was just barely room for all the militia and the trainers. They'd even brought in the females from the mortar section who were sitting at a separate table with their trainers. The girls were looking smug as cats at being included in "guy talk."

"Kildar," Nielson said. "Could you stand up?"

"Here it comes," Mike noted to Adams, standing up at the head of the table.

"The recon movement to the observation point was good," Nielson said. "No major flaws there except a lack of putting your point out far enough during the movement. No trash found at your bivouac of the first night although there was debris at the main OP on the hilltop. I won't get into your choice of targets for the sniper operations; that is idiosyncratic and depends upon human factors I won't argue. However, your timing on withdrawal was quite bad. You very nearly got flanked by the pursuit party; you're aware of that?"

"Yes, I am," Mike said, nodding. "I took a few more shots than I should have."

"Arguably, you should not have been shooting," Nielson pointed out. "You should have been spotting and controlling and let Lasko shoot."

"I wasn't sure that would work," Mike said. "The ranges were longer than he'd trained on. I wanted to make sure the sniper fire was good enough to really sting them. But I did pull out too late."

"Your movement, given the closeness of the pursuit, was about par," Nielson said, pointing to the map. "Why did you choose to be the bait and send Praz and Lasko directly up the mountain?"

"I was in better shape to run," Mike said, shrugging. "Praz and Lasko weren't up to my level of condition. As it turned out, they probably could have made it just as well, but it was a tough hump. In the situation, I took the danger point."

"On reaching the ambush point you took one of the security bunkers for your position," Nielson said. "Why? You couldn't maintain view of the battle from there."

"I was following Chief Adams' direction," Mike said. "I assume that the pursuit party was close enough that Adams just wanted me to get to ground and that was the nearest bunker."

"In the planning stage you failed to consider the mortars for support," Nielson said, checking off an item on the list.

"Agreed," Mike said. "I'd thought of them solely in terms of fixed position use. I'm glad you remembered them," he added to chuckles through the room.

"Which brings us to the most critical danger point in this action: command and control," Nielson said. "The true commander of the mission was the Kildar. But he was forward deployed and in action for the majority of the mission. I was managing the battle, but I wasn't in command. The Kildar should have either relinquished command of the battle or moved to a position that he could manage all the pieces. It worked, because the Kildar and I could work together very well. But one or the other of us should have been designated for command and that person should have been in a position to control the flow of the battle."

"I'll comment on that," Mike said, stepping to the front. "I intend to always command from near the front if at all possible. My intention is to make that possible through better technology. But, yes, in this instance I was without effective maps and didn't really know where the pieces were. Colonel Nielson ran this battle and did so quite well."

"Damned straight," Chief Adams said, loudly, starting the applause.

Mike waited for the applause of the grinning Keldara to die and then waved at the group.

"You've completed your first action and your first after action review," Mike said, grinning. "And I'm sure you'd rather be back in combat than having it nitpicked." He waited again for the chuckles to die down, then nodded. "Again, you did well. And if we keep this up, each time you'll do better. But, for tonight, you have met the enemy and survived. There is a custom among the military that from time to time they have a dinner for only their unit, called a dining-in. There are various customs, which we'll work on as time passes. But for tonight, you are the guests of the Kildar. Tomorrow, of course, you're back in training. So . . . watch the beer."

"Kildar," one of the men said, glancing over at the two

tables of women. "What about the women? Are they to be serving?"

"Not if you want fire support next time, Viktor Shaynav!" one of the women yelled back. Which elicited a room full of belly laughs at Viktor's expense.

"No," Mike said, as the doors opened and his various "girls" came in bearing trays. "Tonight you will be served by the women of the Kildar in thanks for being loyal retainers and some of the finest soldiers it has been my pleasure to serve with."

"Christ, I can't believe you got it finished so fast," Mike said, standing on the top of the dam. The outer slope and top had even been seeded and covered in straw to prevent erosion while the inner slope was covered in clay. The weir hadn't been closed, yet, so the stream at the base still flowed freely. But all that took was turning the wheel. It was barely four weeks after the battle and the whole thing was in place.

"I've even got most of the houses wired with some fumble-fingered help from the Keldara," Meller said, proudly. "The big difference was getting the additional equipment."

"What about the channel to bring the other stream over?" Mike said. It was clear the streams hadn't been joined up, yet.

"I used the spare Keldara to put a temporary dam in up there," Meller said. "Then I blasted the channel. It created an embayment so the hydrostatic force wouldn't be so bad. We'll partially fill this with the current stream, then open that up, slowly, to add that stream in. That dam will probably wash away in the spring, but by then you won't need it. You want to do the honors?" the engineer concluded, waving at the wheel that controlled the weir. The controls were propped out over the water on a pier and had an automatic lifting device for when the water rose too high.

"No," Mike said, shaking his head. "You built it. You close it."

"Okay," Meller said happily. He stepped out onto the pier and calmly spun the wheel, dropping the metal plate into its slot and stopping the water from the stream, which immediately started to back up. "We'll open up the other one in a few days when this gets about six feet deep."

"How long to fill it?" Mike asked.

"About two weeks," Meller said. "At which point you and the Keldara will have your power. And we can start running water lines to the houses as soon as we get material."

"Start on that next," Mike said, nodding. "We'll have to figure out something for treatment; this stuff isn't drinkable as is."

"Chlorine's cheap," Meller said, shrugging. "I'll look into it."

# ★ Chapter Two ★

"It's nice to mostly have the house back," Mike said, walking into the dining room. Nielson was drinking tea and looking over some papers while Adams was finishing off a plate of ham and eggs.

"Fewer fights over the girls," Adams said.

The Keldara were well into their patrolling phase of training and that required fewer instructors. With "basic" over, most of the trainers had left. A few were still around for patrolling and advanced training and some, like Adams, Nielson and Vanner, looked to be permanent additions. But the house was definitely less full than it had been. Especially with most of the remaining trainers out running the Keldara around the mountains.

"The girls" were local hookers that Mike had hired for the aid and comfort of poor trainers far from the joys of home. The owner of the local brothel had given Mike a good deal on long-term rental eventually giving up the business entirely, and sending his one remaining girl to join the others.

Four of the five girls were completely standard Third World working girls. Three of them were from the local area farms, girls with no better prospect than being working girls for the rest of their lives, while the other two were Russians. One of those, Katya, was somewhat different. Poisonously mean when she could get away with it, the girl had never adjusted to being "owned" in the way that was common in the area.

Mike, who had nicknamed her "Cottontail," was slowly shifting her out of being a working girl and into pursuits more suited for her high level intelligence and utter sociopathy. He wasn't sure what he was going to do with her long-term—the option of putting her in an unmarked grave was still out there—but he saw lots of potential in the girl if he could just trust her even a bit.

That, however, would not be a smart thing to do.

"Speaking of the girls," Mike said. "I'm going to move Cottontail fully into intel. I wish we had a good Humint trainer around; I think Katya would probably be a good agent."

"If you could trust anything she gave you," Nielson pointed out, looking up from his papers. "Could you?"

"Depends on what was in it for her," Mike said, shrugging. "She really hates Chechens, probably more than she hates the rest of the world. If we use her to develop Humint in the Chechen region it might work."

"She'll need to learn Arabic," Adams said, wiping his plate with a biscuit.

"Berlitz has a course available," Mike said. "Of course, that means letting her out of the house. Hell, I'll give her a handful of cash and tell her she can go if she wants. Win/win proposition."

"What about 'your' girls?" Nielson asked.

In addition to the hookers, Mike had more or less inherited a harem. Sexual slavery was rife in the region and most of it was controlled by the Chechens who used it, along with drugs, as funding for their ongoing war with the Russians. Most of the girls were bought from orphanages or their parent's since the farmers in the region could get nearly a year's income for otherwise "useless" women. But the Chechens weren't above snatching a girl off the street.

One such group had snatched one of the Keldara girls from the local town where she had gone to market. When they took off in their van they passed right by Mike's caravanserai.

He had taken five shots from a Barrett .50 caliber to stop the van, fortunately missing the girls all in the back. Then he and the reaction team of trainers had taken down the two Chechens in the van.

This left Mike with seven girls ranging in age from twelve to seventeen on his hands. Inquiries had indicated that they were no deposit, no return; the various farms that had sold them had no interest in getting them back. After discussing the situation with his local advisers, Mike had accepted that the best course of action was to take them in as concubines. He'd considered various alternatives, but none of them would really work. He'd drawn the line at breaking in the really young ones, but the rest now were his bed warmers.

However, he'd immediately seen the problem with having a house full of teenage girls to manage. So he'd gone to Uzbekistan, where harems were traditional, and hired a professional harem manager. Anastasia had turned out to have far more skills than just harem management. Not only was she great in the sack, she spoke multiple languages and was at home in almost any social environment.

Mike had also hired a female tutor for the girls. His long term plan was to get them trained to a level that they could get into college and get a "real" life. But in the meantime, he couldn't exactly bitch about having five very good looking teenage screw-bunnies at his beck and call.

"None of them are the right mindset to set on something like this," Mike replied. "But Anastasia is fluent in Arabic. Maybe I'll have her teach Cottontail."

"Be careful what she teaches her," Adams said, without looking up. "You might get a very nasty surprise."

"Are you talking about Anastasia teaching Katya or the other way around?" Nielson asked, grinning.

"Yes."

"Genadi," Mike said, as he pulled up in his Expedition next to the farm manager. "I haven't spoken to you in weeks. How goes the farm?"

When Mike had bought the Keldara farm, which essentially meant the entire multithousand acre valley, he had been less than satisfied with the overseer that came with it. In short, Otar Tarasova was a blow-hard and a bully that didn't know his ass from a hole in the ground. The local police chief had turned up Genadi Mahona, who was not only school trained in agronomy but a member of the Keldara. Otar and Genadi had earlier had a run-in and the former manager had forced him off the farm, to the level of having him thrown out of the Keldara.

Mike was impressed by the young man. Genadi knew

the problems of farming in the valley with its very short growing season, but he was also more than willing to bring in modern techniques and equipment to improve conditions. He was also willing to face down the Keldara elders over his changes. The Keldara were open to many new ideas and ways of doing things even while being dead stubborn on others, and many of the elders thought that Genadi was going to starve them all with his new seeds, planting methods, fertilizers and "herbicides." After all, anything that killed the weeds would certainly kill the crops. This year was going to be a test of how well he knew his stuff. Mike was betting that things would go well.

"I could use some hands," Genadi admitted. "When are the younger men going to be free for work again?"

"Not for a few weeks," Mike said, frowning. "What do you need?"

"Small things, but numerous," the farm manager answered. "Some trenching that I can't get a backhoe into, some repairs on the barns that requires strong backs. The old men are doing well, as are the women, but there is only so much they can do."

"We've got a break in the training schedule coming up the end of the week," Mike said, frowning. "I'll see about gettting that break extended from a few days to maybe two weeks. I want them to have a break before we go to patrol phase two. That's going to be a ball buster."

"I'll put it off until then," Genadi said, nodding. "And I'll make sure they have a break towards the end."

"Great," Mike said, grinning. "How's the crop?"

"Even Father Mahona admits that the grains are coming in well," Genadi replied, smiling broadly. "And the peas are nearly ready to harvest. We'll do that with the combine so I won't need the young men. Before it would have taken everyone stripping the plants, but the combine has an attachment that does it for us. Then we'll replant in beets for the fall crop."

"Whatever," Mike said, admitting that he knew nothing about farming.

"It goes well," Genadi said, smiling back. "Very well."

"Good," Mike replied. "That's all I needed to hear anyway."

"The farm goes well," the farm manager said, frowning slightly, "but there is another problem."

"What now?" Mike asked, sighing.

"Father Nona and Father Kulcyanov would like to meet with you, privately," Genadi said. "It is a very private reason, for the Kildar only. Not involving the militia."

"Today?" Mike asked, puzzled.

"Soon," Genadi said, shrugging. "Not right away. Any time this week or next week would do."

"Going to hint about what?" Mike asked, smiling.

"I think they need to discuss it with you," Genadi said, shrugging. "It is for them to say."

"Tomorrow do?" Mike asked. "Afternoon?"

"That is fine," Genadi replied.

Mike entered the caravanserai and looked around the foyer. Two of the harem, Tinata and Azhela, were sitting in the foyer area playing a game involving small colored pebbles. Tinata was a sixteen-year-old with flamboyantly large breasts and flaming red hair that was quite natural. Mike knew for sure and certain that the curtains matched the rug. Azhela was smaller with fine, light brown hair and a smaller chest that, nonetheless, was quite noticeable on her smaller frame.

In a move that made sense to him at the time, he'd had Anastasia obtain uniforms for the girls. They were essentially "school-girl" uniforms, white shirt, blue and green plaid skirts and low-quarter shoes, which had advantages and disadvantages. It cut down on the petty bickering about who got to wear what on what day, and who was prettiest, which was a major point of contention among the girls. However, as with many males, he found the "school-girl" look was a major turn-on. It didn't help that they were, essentially, real school girls. As usual when the girls popped to their feet, skirts swirling, their shirts straining their buttons, smiling, bright-eyed and bushy-tailed and obviously quite willing to satisfy his every desire, whatever important problem had been on his mind went right out the window. The braces that many of them now sported didn't help matters.

Mike dragged his eyes away from Tinata's remarkably fine breasts and shook his head.

"I think I need to dress you girls in chadours," he said, smiling to show it was a joke. "But could one of you ask Anastasia to meet me in my office whenever it's convenient for her?"

"Yes, Kildar," Tinata said, curtseying slightly and bowing her head in a gesture of meekness that Mike knew was an act. The girl was an absolute minx in bed. "I'll go summon her directly."

"Don't bother her if she's doing anything important," Mike said, heading for his office.

"Shall I come back with her, Kildar?" Tinata asked, looking at him out of the corner of one eye.

"No," Mike said, definitely. "But don't go far. I haven't got anything scheduled this afternoon."

"You asked to see me, Kildar?" Anastasia said as she entered his office.

The harem manager had been a member of an Uzbek sheik's harem since she was twelve. She was tall and refined with long, lovely, blonde hair and blue eyes with a slight epicanthic fold. Fine boned with the face of an angel, she could have made big money as a supermodel. Instead she had been immured in a harem for fourteen years with rare opportunities to get out; the flight to Georgia had actually been her first flight on an airplane.

She was trained, and naturally skilled, at managing groups of girls. However, she had few other skills. Since she was getting a bit long in the tooth for the tastes of the sheik, at all of twenty-six, she was looking at being either given away as a bride to some retainer or being sent off with a chunk of money to find a new life. The "new life" would probably be a madame in a whorehouse, given that she didn't know anything else.

The job offer from Mike had been like a gift from heaven. Not only did Mike need a manager, he was far less controlling than the sheik and more than willing to include her in his travels. Then there was the fact that Anastasia was a serious masochistic submissive. The sheik had never had a strong enough hand with the whip in her opinion and was otherwise rather uninteresting in bed, generally going for "wham, bam, thank you ma'am" but not even staying awake for the "thank you" part. Mike was a serious dom and more than willing to satisfy that side of her sexual personality. Then there was the fact that he considered it a duty and a pleasure to make a woman have a good time in the sack. For Anastasia the last months had been heaven. Her only complaint was that Mike still hadn't set up the bondage dungeon in the old cellars that he'd promised her.

"I want you to start working more with Katya," Mike said, waving her to a chair. "I know she's working with Vanner, but I want you to start training her in Arabic."

"I already have been," Anastasia said, smiling. "And German and French. She already speaks Russian and more English than she's willing to admit. I started teaching her other languages to keep her busy. When she's learning, she isn't so much of a problem. And she is very smart. Smarter than I am, I have to admit. She soaks up information and has a remarkable memory."

"Especially for slights," Mike said, sighing. "But that's good. I want you to concentrate on Arabic and Chechen dialects of Russian and Arabic for the time being. Get her able to understand it, clearly, no matter how garbled."

"I understand," Anastasia said, nodding. "Are you sure you can trust her?"

"No," Mike admitted. "But leave that for me to worry about. I'll set it up as a win/win proposition. She can do the mission, or she can run. She won't have enough information to do us serious harm."

"She has been working with Vanner," Anastasia pointed out. "She knows about your intercept capability."

"So do the Chechens," Mike pointed out, sourly. "The Russians leaked it to them."

"But she knows details," Anastasia argued.

"We can change codes after she leaves," Mike said. "And that won't be soon. I'll pull her out of Vanner's section and set her to learning. For that matter, I'll see what I can scrounge up in the way of manuals on infiltration and espionage. I think she'd be good at it. And if she cuts and runs instead, well, then we don't have to worry about her anymore."

"There is that," Anastasia said, smiling. "So, when do I get my bondage dungeon?"

"I'll put it on my construction list," Mike said, grinning. "But this afternoon, I've made another date."

"Tinata," Anastasia said, nodding. "I'd wondered why she was looking so happy."

Mike laid the red-head down on the bed and leaned down to gently kiss her on the neck.

All the girls knew his tastes by this point and Tinata had changed into a pair of five-inch spike sandals. She moaned and twisted aside as he tickled her neck with his tongue, sliding around to reach for his crotch.

"Not so fast, young one." Mike chuckled, sitting down next to her. "We've got all afternoon."

"That is very good," Tinata said, turning her eyes aside in mock shyness. "I can wear you out."

"Good luck." Mike chuckled again, kissing her neck and then digging his tongue into the juncture of her shoulder and neck. There was a muscle there with a nerve running along it that generally got women juicing and

Tinata moaned again as his tongue dug firmly into the nerve juncture.

He slid his hand up her stomach, untucking her shirt and began unbuttoning it. He occasionally just tore one off—he owned the uniforms after all—but this time he was taking his time. Tinata enjoyed being pinned but wasn't into full bondage and still freaked out a bit when he got too rough. She enjoyed a bit of dominance but that didn't mean she was a full BDSM freak. The last two times they'd been together he'd only had time for a quickie. She orgasmed, but barely. He intended to drive her nuts this afternoon. And he had a secret weapon: she was really turned on by giving head.

He slowly unbuttoned her blouse while continuing to suckle at her neck, occasionally putting one hand on her upper arm. The spread of goosebumps was a good indicator of how interested the girl was and this one had bumps to her elbow, good sign.

As the bra came off he slid down her chest, still teasingly, and slowly worked his way around her breasts. They really were quite magnificent, solid and natural DDs but still so young and fresh they were nearly as hard as fakes. They were also quite sensitive and by the time he'd finally worked his way to the nipples, sucking and licking on one while his hand worked the other, she was moaning.

He suddenly reached up and grasped her hair, slithering around so that he was on his back and she was up on her knees.

"Do me," he ordered, pushing her head down towards his crotch.

Tinata let out another moan and slid his pants down,

bringing out his member. She began by slowly licking along the base, working her way up with light flicks of her tongue.

He reached past her arm and cradled one of those magnificent breasts, stroking it lightly with the balls of his fingers as she began to fellate him. The combination of her fetish for head and the sensitivity of her breasts caused her to stop for a moment, just shuddering, as she ran her cheek up and down his dick.

"Keep going," Mike said, grabbing her by the hair and sliding her lips back over his cock. "I didn't say you could stop."

He quit playing with her tits and reached around, grabbing her ass and dragging it closer so he could reach between her legs. He slid his hand under her cotton panties and up onto her clit, stroking her labia and clit lightly.

Tinata started to stop again, shuddering too hard to go on, but he had retained his hold on her hair and he began forcing her up and down on his dick as his finger plunged into her slit.

The girl began to rock and moan while keeping up the suction, as he timed the thrusts at both ends to keep up a constant state of sexual tension. When he judged she just couldn't take any more he pulled her up, ripped her panties off and took her, hard.

Pulling one of her legs up he thrust all the way into her until their pelvis bones met squarely on her clit, elicting a moan of pleasure and a gasp. Tinata had her eyes closed and was already starting to rock into him as he began to pound. He tried very hard not to concentrate on the fact that he was fucking the hell out of a teenage redhead with really great tits. He didn't want to cum until he'd worn her flat out. When he started to feel himself getting close he'd think about multiplication tables. That always got him to back off.

He grabbed her wrists, pinning them above her head with one hand, then started stroking her tits as he thrust. He just used his thumb on the left nipple, brushing it in time with his thrusts.

That really got the girl going. She kept thrusting against him, moaning and crying in pleasure until she came, suddenly and quite vocally, letting out a shriek of pain and pleasure that was surely heard all over the caravanserai.

Mike stopped immediately, letting her get her breath back. He'd been working out ever since he took over the caravanserai and wasn't even winded, yet.

"You okay?" he asked, looking at her as she opened her eyes.

"Oh, yes," Tinata breathed, then laughed. "I am very okay."

"Good," Mike said, sliding back into her. "I'm barely started."

"Oh, God!" Tinata gasped, lying back and quivering as his thrusts caused the aftershocks from her orgasm to crescendo. "Have mercy, Kildar!"

"Not hardly," Mike answered gruffly.

This time he took more time, not just hammering in and out but varying the pace and movement. He would thrust slow and long, all the way in, for five thrusts then pick up the pace over a few more series until he was hitting in a rapid fire he called "bunny fucking." After the bunny fuck he'd back off again.

By this time, Tinata wasn't in any control any more at all. She was just orgasming in rapid sequence, especially as the bunny fucks hit. From time to time he'd back off for a bit to let her gain some equilibrium then go back to it before she could even get a word out. If she could talk, she wasn't fully in the moment from his point of view.

When he got a little tired he slid over to the side, still maintaining penetration, and rearranged their limbs so he could lie on his side. Her right leg was over his left and his right over hers with contact maintained in the middle. He slid her right arm under his body and pinned her other arm behind her head with his left hand. This left his right hand free and he began stroking her nipples again as he continued to slide in and out.

"Kildar . . ." the girl gasped. "Please . . ."

"Please, what?" Mike asked, slowing down but not stopping.

"I . . . please . . . " the girl whimpered. "No more . . ."

"Just a little more," Mike said evilly, sliding his hand down to her crotch.

"Nooo . . ." Tinata whimpered as his finger slid over her clit and started working it.

Mike began hammering her, hard, as his finger continued to work her clit. Suddenly she let out a shriek and began writhing in his grasp, at which point he stopped, withdrawing his hand.

"Oh . . ." the girl said, lying supine on the bed. "Oh . . . God . . ."

"Was that okay?" Mike asked, curiously.

"Okay?" Tinata said, opening her eyes. "I can't see! I can't see anything! I'm blind!"

"Low blood flow to the optic nerve," Mike said, gently. "It passes. You'll get over it."

"That's easy for you to say!" Tinata replied. "Does that mean that this has happened with you before?"

"To women I've been with," Mike admitted.

"You are a danger to all women, Kildar," Tinata said, chuckling throatily.

"So I've been told."

"I think I can see some light, now."

"See, it's passing," Mike said, sliding out.

"Ooooo . . ." the girl gasped. "Warn a woman next time!"

"Why? It's more fun if it's by surprise," Mike said, getting out of bed. "Want something to drink?"

"I should be serving you," Tinata pointed out.

"Be a little hard at the moment," Mike said, opening up the fridge. "Coke?"

"Please," Tinata said, sitting up and fumbling to pull a pillow behind her. "I've never been blind before. It's not nice."

"But it's passing, yes?" Mike asked.

"Yes," Tinata admitted. "I can see shapes."

"Here," Mike said, putting the open Coke bottle in her hand.

She fumbled at it and lifted it to her lips, carefully.

"That's good," she said, smiling. "I'm seeing better."

"Good," Mike said, taking a pull off of his own Coke. "As soon as you can see clearly, we'll start again."

"So you can make me blind again?" Tinata asked, laughing.

"If I can," Mike admitted, smiling. "Are you saying it wasn't fun? Besides, you never finished your blowjob."

Over the next four hours he screwed Tinata through three applications of lubricant and various complaints of swelling, along with more orgasms than the poor girl could count. Only when she was entirely spent and supine did he finally allow himself to cum. And it was a hard one, fully curling his toes.

"Kildar . . ." Tinata said as he slid a towel under her, gently, to catch the outflow.

"Hmmm?" Mike asked, pulling her to cuddle into his shoulder.

"Wonderful . . ."

"Shhh," Mike said. "Sleep."

Mike lay there, thinking about his task list, until her breathing was regular and it was clear she was deeply asleep. Then he slid out of bed, carefully arranging a pillow under her head, and put on his clothes. He had plenty of work he should have been doing, but sometimes you just had to take time to make sure the harem was happy.

# ★ Chapter Three ★

"Okay, buddy, what do you take?" Adams asked when Mike got to his office. The former chief was sitting in one of the chairs with his feet up, apparently awaiting his arrival.

"What do you mean?" Mike asked, sitting down and clearing his screensaver with his password.

"I timed it, this time," Adams said. "Three hours and forty-seven minutes from the first shriek until your door opened. I mean, are you getting black market Viagra or something?"

"I don't need Viagra," Mike said, shrugging and pulling up the spreadsheet on Keldara costs. He'd made a pretty penny from killing wanted terrorists and "securing" a few nukes that otherwise would have left large holes in cities. But the Keldara were costing like crazy and it was just amazing how fast the money bled away.

"Oysters?" Adams asked.

"Christ, you're not going to let this go, are you?" Mike asked, leaning back in his chair.

"How many times did she come, anyway?" Adams asked. "The shrieks were getting pretty muted by the end."

"I don't know," Mike admitted, trying not to grin. "I only counted the times she went blind. That was three."

"Good Lord," the chief said, shaking his head. "So, give. What are you taking?"

"Nothing," Mike said. "I don't take anything. I just don't allow myself to come."

"How?" Adams asked, exasperatedly. "I mean, Tinata is . . ."

"A knockout," Mike finished. "A certified virgin the first time I screwed her, pretty as hell, great tits and a tight pussy. I just think of other things when I think I'm going to come. And keep going. For as long as I want."

"What? Dead puppies?" Adams asked, curiously.

"No, mathematics, generally," Mike admitted. "Multiplication tables. What's eight times seven?"

"Uhm . . ."

"Right, if it's not right there in your head, you have to think about it," Mike said. "Most people do have to think about the sevens and eights in the tables. Anything that requires a bit of concentration. Something you have to think of to recite to yourself. Just . . . distract yourself to get out of the moment but keep them in it. And if you've got a modicum of control you can keep from coming. That way you can make a lady really happy, if you fit even vaguely. If she's not into penile orgasms, there's the fingers and tongue. And once a woman comes once, she generally will keep coming if you keep going. Most of the time they'll say they want you to stop, but unless they're really aggressive about it, keep going. Their orgasams just get larger and larger until they're really over the edge. Simple as that."

"I need to try that out," Adams admitted. "Where the hell did you learn this?"

"I overanalyze," Mike said, grinning. "You've told me so yourself. There's more than one reason that they called me . . . what they called me on the teams. When you're doing a sneak at that level, you have to be able to read a person, to know exactly what they are going to do, to feel everything around you. It's not much different in bed. You're a great entry guy, buddy, but you were never as good as I was at a sneak, right?"

"Admitted," Adams said, shrugging. "And that makes you great in bed?"

"Believe it or not, it's awful close," Mike said, smiling thinly. "They're both about power, trust me. When a woman is that much putty in my hands, it's just like when the knife goes in on a target. There's a reason they call orgasm the 'little death.'"

"That's sick," Adams said, shaking his head.

"I never said I was a well man," Mike replied, still smiling.

"Go ahead and try it on Flopsy, Bambi or Mopsy," Mike continued, listing off three of the hookers by nickname. "Cottontail's impossible; cold as the Antarctic. Don't even try."

"She seems to have fun," Adams said, frowning.

"She's pretty good at faking, but not as good as she thinks," Mike said, shrugging.

"How can you tell?" Adams asked.

"What, you want me to give up all my secrets?" Mike replied, grinning.

★ ★ ★

As soon as it was dark Mike donned combat gear and headed out to his personal Ford Expedition. He'd ordered various vehicles for the Keldara to get the farm on a more modern basis: When he bought the property the Keldara had still been using horse-drawn plows. Besides tractors he'd purchased trucks and SUVs for each of the Six Families. They doubled as transportation for the militia but were mostly used for farm work.

This was his personal Expedition, however, and although it seemed the same as the rest on the exterior, save for a spare antenna here and there, it was significantly modified on the interior. He'd given Vanner a bunch of money, and the electronics wiz had fitted it out with every conceivable bit of gear that he might need to control the militia. In effect, it was a roving command post.

He punched in a code on the dashboard-mounted computer and brought up current locations on all the training groups. Phase One of patrolling was about done and he'd hardly had a chance to go out and check them out. A group from Team Sawn was conveniently near the north road, while being well out of sight behind a ridge, so he put the SUV in gear and headed out.

The caravanserai was perched on a ridgeline overlooking the valley of the Keldara and at a height to be able to barely see into the town of Allerso which was in an upper valley. The driveway from the caravanserai ran down a series of switchbacks to the road that passed along the edge of the valley. The road was slightly elevated so that most of the valley could be viewed as he drove northward. The crops did, indeed, seem to be growing well and there was a new glow of electric light from the houses. When he'd arrived the Keldara didn't have a pot to piss in, much less electricity. If he died tomorrow, or today, which on this road was a possibility, he'd have done that much good at least.

Lasting good, that is. He'd done many things that he defined as "good" over the years, but they mostly involved killing terrorists or finding wayward weapons of mass destruction. But more terrrorists always seemed to arise, hydra-headed, and WMDs were here to stay. There was always some Russian guard willing to sell his soul for a bagful of cash or some muj with a high school knowledge of chemistry whipping up a beaker of Sarin. To put all of them out of business would require changing the world, and that was too big a prospect for any former SEAL.

He cleared the valley and ascended the switchbacks at the north end, heading into the mountains. He was glad the road was clear this time of year. The first time he'd come to the valley of the Keldara he had been lost and the road had been an ice-covered nightmare of a drive. On an early summer night it was simply pleasantly winding.

He reached a good debarkation point where a small parking area overlooked the river foaming through the gorge below and got out, stretching. The night was clear and black as pitch, perfect for a walk in the woods.

He loaded up his assault ruck and picked out an SPR for the trip. The teams were on their last exercise of Patrol Phase One, a two-day hike with various mission objectives. Patrol Phase One was designed to train them in various missions in patrolling in large groups, rotating members of the teams through leadership positions. It was straight out of the Ranger Handbook, which fit the mission of the Keldara better than SEAL training. After they'd gotten used to patrolling in large groups they'd move to Phase Two, which would train them in small units patrolling over large distances, the only way that they would be able to fully interdict Chechen movement in the area.

He deliberately hadn't looked at the particular mission of this patrol. They might be in movement or set up for ambush; it was up to him to find them and determine their mission.

He had to be careful about it, however. The teams were loaded with blanks but carried a full load of combat ammunition; the area was unsecure and their "training" might involve hitting a Chechen group at any point. The Chechens had to know by now that this region wasn't safe. His people had stopped a snatch and wiped out a full battalion attack already in the area. But the Keldara area had been a major path for Chechen groups for some time; the passes in the Keldara AO were the only way through the mountains short of entering the much better protected area around Tbilisi. It was one of the reasons that the Russians, and therefore the American government, were looking for him to shut down Chechen operations in the region.

He first had to cross the rather sizeable stream. While that sort of thing was easy with a group, by himself it required a bit more care. He hunted around for a good ford but there was none in the immediate area. And even getting down to the stream bed from the road was tricky.

Finally, he found a reasonably negotiable spot and slid

down the hill on his butt, ending up with his feet planted on a rock that was actually jutting out of the stream. He secured a climbing rope to the rock and hooked off to it, then slid into the stream.

The current was powerful and bloody damned cold, glacial melt coming straight off the mountains. The rocks were also slippery as hell. He made his way carefully across the current, planting his feet and using the hard point of the rope to stabilize.

He got to the far side and pulled the disconnect he'd tied into the rope, retrieving it and then coiling it and putting it away. He thus was starting off his hunt dead wet, cold and nigh on to miserable. Which was all to the good; he'd been having it too easy lately.

The team had last been placed on the far side of the ridge above him, so he headed up the steep slope. In places he had to push himself up using the trees on the ridgeline but it only took him thirty minutes or so to ascend the ridge and get a good hide.

He pulled out a thermal scope and started scanning the area below him. When he didn't see anything in the spot he'd noted the team in, he scanned around. There didn't seem to be anything in the valley below so he kept scanning around.

The valley the team had been in was a narrow V heading down from the north and more or less paralleling the road at about two hundred meters of elevation. There was a small stream running down the center. It joined with a slightly larger valley that curved in from the east and finally joined the gorge the road wound up, adding the contents of both streams to the river that cut the gorge.

The team was nowhere in sight in the first valley so he kept panning back and forth looking for hot points in either valley. He finally spotted a hot point coming into the larger, perpendicular, valley, but it was coming from the east and nowhere around where the team had been. They'd have had to run like hell to get up to that point and the figures were moving wrong. As he watched, more and more figures came in view and some of them had the distinct outline of horses or mules. It wasn't one of the Keldara teams, that was for damned sure. In fact, unless he was much mistaken, it was a Chechen supply convoy.

He considered for a moment where he'd left the Expedition. Supply trains like this one generally met up with trucks somewhere along the road that he'd parked on. The damned Expedition was directly in view of any-one driving down the road, which was one hell of a note.

He didn't know why this sort of thing always seemed to happen to him. He was like a terrorism fuck-up magnet. All he'd wanted to do was go watch the Keldara doing ops and here he was dealing with a damned Chechen supply convoy. It was such a pain in the ass.

He pulled out a map and slid down the hillside out of direct view. The maps, a new improvement by Vanner, were fluorescent in ultraviolet, so he set the Night Observation Device to UV, slid it down over one eye and opened up the map.

The valley the Chechens were moving down was marked as 415 and, sure enough, there was a narrow trail running along the south side. There was also a ford marked. It was a good thing he hadn't taken a better look at the map or he might have used both and run right smack dab into them coming the other way.

The trail was snaking on the hillside and, based on their movement, they were going to take a good hour to reach the road. Depending on where the Keldara team was, it might be able to get into ambush position. But groups like this usually met up with trucks coming down the road and they'd be coming from the north; even the Chechens weren't stupid enough to run up the valley of the Keldara, and all the sources they used were to the north. That was the whole point of running through here.

Ergo, there was a truck or trucks coming down from the north to meet them. It would rendezvous with them near the ford, transfer cargo and go back north. Guns and ammo coming in, drugs, girls and what have you going out.

This was a mission for more than one of the teams. And he still couldn't find the team he was looking for, so he'd have to call in.

"Keldara Base, this is Kildar," he whispered over the radio. "We have a situation."

Gildana Makanee keyed her headset and waved at Sergeant Vanner as the call came in.

Gildana was seventeen years old, blue-eyed and long-legged with long blonde hair she regularly braided in a thick rope that hung to her lower back. Until a few months before, Gildana had envisioned a life just like her mother and her grandmother and great-great-great grand, dating back to medieval times. She would soon marry, many of her friends had married already, and the man she was to marry, Givi Ferani had already been chosen. Then she would have as many children as she could manage until she was old and gray and worn out from working the farm.

She liked Givi and thought he would make a good husband. He was hardworking and at least had a sense of humor. She really had no dreams beyond having beautiful and healthy children who would live.

Then everything changed. The new Kildar had come and now everything was topsy-turvy. As one of the better readers and writers among the women of the Keldara she had been chosen to assist in the "ops and intel" section and met Sergeant Vanner. He had opened up a whole new world to her and the girls who worked with her. They now controlled the communications for the Keldara militia and some of them worked in the intel section intercepting what they could catch of the limited Chechen radio traffic. The work was long and often boring, but far more interesting than cleaning the house, cooking, hauling water and keeping the fires going. Sergeant Vanner had even gotten her a "correspondence course" on satellite communications and she was working on it assiduously. Along with it had come several other courses on mathematics and she was working her way through those at the same time.

Life was looking up.

"Kildar," she answered in a calm and lilting tone, "this is Keldara Base. Say situation, over."

Calm and unhurried. Sergeant Vanner had drilled that into them over and over. The last thing anyone wanted to hear over the radio was that anyone was stressed out. Keep calm, no matter what was happening.

"I was going out to observe Team Sawn, operating in the vicinity of valley 415. I am at position 918 in view of a convoy of probable tangoes moving down 415 from the east towards a probable rendezvous at 228. Count is thirty tangoes, eighteen pack animals. Weapons not observable at this range. Clear?"

"Tango convoy at valley 415, moving east towards 228. Your position 918. Count is thirty tangoes, eighteen pack animals."

"Roger. Unable to determine position of Team Sawn. Probable vehicle movement from north along Tbilisi Road for link-up. Get Keldara Two, Three and Five in contact. Contact Team Sawn, have them display UV source. Will vector Team Sawn to ambush on convoy if possible. Vector second team to road if possible. Tell teams to go red on ammo."

"Roger, Keldara Six," Gildana said, scribbling notes. She looked over her shoulder at Sergeant Vanner who had slipped on a headset and was nodding at her notes. "Keldara Two is available at this time, Six."

"Roger," the Kildar said. "I'm going to sit tight until I've got an idea where Sawn is. Get cracking."

Vanner had already opened up a window on his screen showing the locations of all the teams and shook his head.

"That's funny," he said. "Sawn's just to the east of him, down in the valley. They're in an ambush position along the side valley, so they're not in position to hit the Chechens. Call them up."

"Sawn Six, this is Keldara Base," Gildana said, switching

frequencies for transmission but leaving open the Kildar's frequency so she could listen if he called.

"Sawn."

"Be aware, there is a Chechen force, thirty tangoes, eighteen pack animals, moving down valley 415, approximately three thousand meters from your position. Kildar is on the ridge behind you, observing from 918. Show UV marker so the Kildar can vector you to them."

"Roger."

Mike blinked as a hot-spot appeared in the valley and then a UV light was laid out, clearly marking the position of the ambush team. They weren't more than five hundred meters below him and they'd been completely invisible to IR. They must have covered themselves up pretty damned good.

He checked his frequency sheet and changed to Sawn's codes. The different connections weren't frequencies, but packet codes for the distributed network that had been laid in over the last few weeks. Besides going out on patrol training, the Keldara had been laying down dozens of "black box" retransmitters. The devices were encrypted and distributed information in frequency-hopping burst packets. Weighing in at a bit less than two pounds, they functioned something like the Internet, picking up the packets and moving them along the best routes. The boxes were now in so many places in the nearby mountains that communications were virtually solid throughout the local area. But only for the Keldara. The system was locked out for anyone else, short of very high-tech and aggressive hacking.

"Goddamn, Sawn, you guys are hidden like a bitch," he said approvingly. "But we're going to have to move. Pick up your team and move south to the trail along 415. And boogie. Go hot at this time."

"Roger, Kildar," Sawn said. The Makanee boy was not by any stretch his top team leader, that would be Oleg Kulcyanov, but he was pretty damned good. And if he could hide that well, it boded well for the mission. Now if the team could just move fast and quiet.

"I'll link up somewhere around the river," Mike said. "Tell your guys if they frag me I will strangle them with my bare hands."

"Understood, Kildar," Sawn said, the humor evident in his voice.

"Kildar, this is Keldara Base."

"Gotta go, Sawn," Mike continued as more hot-spots appeared. It was apparent that the entire twenty-man team had been lightly dug in along the hillside. Too bad they weren't in position to hit the Chechens; it had been a perfect hide. "See you at the stream. Go Keldara Base."

"Kildar, Keldara Three is here," Gildana said, looking over her shoulder at Colonel Nielson. "He recommends vectoring Team Padrek onto the road to the north."

"Have him handle that end," the Kildar answered with a slight grunt of effort. "Be aware that my damned Expedition is in full view on the road. If the Chechens steal my car, tell Padrek to run far and fast."

"Roger, Kildar," Gildana said, smiling slightly.

"I'm going to go link up with Sawn and cover that end," the Kildar continued. "Get the trucks."

"Roger, Kildar."

"Kildar out."

Gildana looked over her shoulder at Colonel Nielson quizzically.

"Vector Padrek to point 583," the colonel said, pointing out a spot on the map near the road to the north. "Interdict all vehicles moving from the north, standard road block. The Chechens will probably be carrying contraband. Rules of Engagement Three. Do not fire until sure of resistance, but stop everything and use full care. Roll out the support team, have them draw RPGs and MGs. They need to be on the road in fifteen minutes."

"Yes, sir," Gildana said. The Kildar had bought a specialized database and she and Vanner had modified it slightly. This was the first test of it in a "real world" mission.

She brought up the database and punched for live-mission. A screen gave her a number of options, each of them marked by large buttons or icons. She chose "roll response team," then "heavy weapon loadout," "road-block," punched in the code for the location when the box came up, chose "rendezvous," then hit the icon for Team Padrek, which was the head of a ram, and last chose ROE 3.

The system automatically generated an operations order including what weapons and ammunition pack each member of the team would carry, which vehicles were available and a map to the position. In addition, there was a frequency list and information about friendly forces in the area.

She hit send and got a pop-up screen that read: "Please detail commander's intention."

She hit the "modify" key and rapidly typed in data on the current situation including the fact that there was probably a truck or trucks headed to rendezvous with the Chechen mule train. Then she reloaded the frag-order.

Nielson considered it for a moment and then nodded. "Send."

# ★ Chapter Four ★

Oleg Kulcyanov's eyes flew open as a buzzer went off beside his bed and the monitor of the computer turned on, flooding the darkened room with light. The printer started spitting out sheets as he rolled to his feet, rubbing his eyes. Another damned drill.

Oleg Kulcyanov was nineteen, a huge bull of a man with a shock of nearly white hair. His great grandfather, Mecheslav Kulcyanov was the head of the Kulcyanov Family. His grandfather had died in a logging accident before Oleg was born. His father was probably going to be the next head of the Kulcyanov Family and in time Oleg would probably succeed him.

While he had been in electric light from time to time in town, until recently he had never considered that he, himself, might live in a house with electricity. He had never seen anyone operate a computer until last February when the Kildar arrived. He had certainly never believed he would use one.

But the Kildar had arrived in the valley like a whirlwind. Before they had assimilated the arrival of a newcomer to the area the Kildar had bought the valley from the bank, and their service with it. More changes started coming with increasing speed: new vehicles, tractors, medical care. Then the trainers had arrived and suddenly the Keldara found their true purpose returning. For the Keldara were warriors at heart.

Oleg went to church every Sunday but the Keldara were not truly Christian. They cloaked themselves in the mantle of that faith, but they had retained their true allegiance through the years, to The All Father One-Eye, to his son Frei the Lord of the Axe, to the Old Gods. They had held true to their faith through generation after generation, working as farmers as the only way to survive but never losing their faith that some day the Way of War would return. And the Kildar had brought it back.

Oleg knew that the Kildar was not a god, but many of the Keldara regarded him as one, an avatar of Frei perhaps. He was certainly a warrior among warriors, as he had proven again and again. And Oleg was willing to follow the Kildar to anywhere in the wide world, for he knew that the Kildar would always lead them on the path of war, where a Keldara could truly be a servant of Frei.

As he read the form on the computer screen he grinned. Finally, it was time to go to war.

He reached out and hit the red button over his bed, then stood up and picked up the papers that had finished spitting out of the printer.

The button activated the lights in the squad bay beyond his room and started a high-toned pinging that was interspersed with a recording by Lydia, Oleg's fiancée.

"Arise, Keldara! Enemies are at the door! Prepare for battle and the day of red war! Bring us scalps!"

Oleg had been sleeping in his uniform pants and a T-shirt. He slid his feet into zipper tac-boots and zipped them up, then threw on his uniform jacket, striding out of the room.

Dmitri Devlich, his team second, was just finished zipping his boots as Oleg stepped into the squad bay. The rest of the team was mostly on its feet, putting on their boots and jackets, as the recording continued.

"Battle this day for honor and the Keldara! Be true to your comrades and warriors born!"

Oleg handed Dmitri the sheets detailing each man's load-out and mission. The sheets were arranged in the same pattern as the squad bay, so all Dmitri had to do was go down the length of the bay handing them out. Each sheet had a picture of the individual squad member, the weapon and ammunition load they were to draw, a list of materials they were to carry and a general mission order including the paragraph Gildana had written about the current enemy conditions.

As soon as Oleg had passed off the sheets he read the section detailing his responsibilities and walked back to his room. He pulled out the correct map-set, checked to make sure it was actually the right one and started buttoning his uniform tunic while rereading the mission orders.

As he was rereading, Givi Kulcyanov came in the room, buckling on his gear and carrying Oleg's in his arms.

"Simple mission," the radio telephone operator said, handing Oleg his body armor and combat vest. Givi was a cousin rather than a brother as the name would imply but they had known each other their whole lives.

"We don't know if this is the only group of Chechens in

the area," Oleg pointed out. "And we don't know what will be waiting for us in the trucks. It might be simple and it might be very hard indeed."

"You're always a pessimist," Givi said, grinning.

"I'm always a realist," Oleg replied, throwing his armor over his head and buckling it on. "That's why I'm the team leader."

When he got to the squad bay most of the team had moved down to the armory to draw their weapons. Their prepacked rucksacks were by the door and as each man drew his weapons for the mission they added them to the load, moving out the door to the waiting vehicles.

Oleg drew an SPR and a .45 caliber silenced pistol, checking each, then slipping in a magazine. Last he put the weapons on safe and picked up his ruck, heading for the door.

Dmitri was by the door as he went out, checking each weapon to see that no one had loaded a live round, yet, and that all weapons were on safe.

"You're the last out," Dmitri said.

"Load it," Oleg replied, heading for his vehicle. "Givi, call in that we're loaded and preparing to roll. Then give them roll time."

"Roger," Givi said.

"I make it as seven minutes, more or less," Dmitri said, climbing in the passenger side of his Expedition. His would be the last vehicle out of the compound. Oleg would be in vehicle three of the five. The lead vehicle traveled well forward of the convoy as a point in case of ambush.

"Agreed," Oleg said, getting in his own vehicle. "Let's roll."

★ ★ ★

Mike crouched by the side of the trail as the team passed. He was both pleased and pissed that not one of them noticed him. He'd intended to close from the rear and call in before contacting the team but had accidentally gotten ahead of them. He was pleased that he hadn't lost the ability to be virtually invisible in the brush and that nobody had reacted to the figure by the side of the trail by fragging him. On the other hand, he was pissed that the Keldara, and even McKenzie, had just walked right past him. If he'd been an enemy they'd be in a world of hurt.

Part of the reason they hadn't noticed him, he had to admit, was his camouflage. From the first he'd determined that the Keldara would have only the best equipment and he'd paid through the nose for it. The camouflage uniform, in particular, had been costly. There was an Italian firm that produced digi-cam, digitally enhanced camouflage, in virtually any pattern. The first uniforms he'd ordered had been standard digi-cam, U.S. military issue. But they hadn't, in his opinion, been perfect for the local terrain. The U.S. digi-cam was designed to blend the wearer in any condition from city to mountain to desert. It wasn't "dialed" for pure mountain/forest conditions.

The Italian firm had sent him several sets of digi-cam in various shades and patterns until he found one that he liked. Then he'd outfitted the Keldara in that. It had been expensive as hell, though. Besides the custom camouflage pattern, the fabric was comfortable, conformable and fire resistant. Each uniform cost about three times that of a standard U.S. digi-cam uniform, but he figured it was worth it. The Keldara were limited in number and were his primary outer defense. Besides, they were friends.

He let the last member of the team, who was correctly checking his back trail, pass by and then stepped out onto the trail. When the Keldara's back was turned, he crouched and let out a slight "psst."

The Keldara spun in place, raising his SPR to his shoulder and crouching to sweep behind him.

Mike, who was within arm's reach, simply grabbed the barrel of the weapon and yanked it out of his hands.

"You've got lousy situational awareness, Yevgenii," he hissed. The name of the Keldara was embroidered in glow-letters on the back of his boonie-cap. "Stand down."

"Kildar!" the boy whispered. "I never saw you!"

"That's why I'm the instructor and you're the trainee, boy," Mike said, quietly.

The Keldara forward of the trail had heard the byplay and slapped the shoulder of the Keldara in front of him, sending the signal up the line of troopers to halt for something to the rear.

Mike handed the weapon back and stepped up along the line of crouched troopers, tapping them on the shoulder as he passed.

"Piatras, how's it going. Ionis, ready to do a man's job tonight? Sergejus, keep your barrel down this time. Stephan, how's the baby?

"McKenzie," Mike said when he got to the command group in the middle of the patrol. "Sawn. Let's get moving; they haven't stopped."

Sawn nodded and tapped forward and back. He waited until he'd gotten responses from either direction, then got the team moving.

They continued down the trail until they got to the stream and then moved off to the right through the woods, weaving in and out among the trees.

As they approached the trail that was being used by the Chechens, Sawn gathered the group into a cigar-shaped perimeter and had them drop their rucksacks. Leaving two personnel behind to keep an eye on the rucks, he brought the team forward to the trail.

He detailed two of the Keldara to move up the trail in the direction the Chechens should approach from, then laid out the rest of the team along the trail, about five meters into the woodline. At the far end he laid in a group across the trail, closing it in an "L" shape.

The ambush was set up on the downhill side from the trail, which wasn't perfect, but it would probably do. They also didn't have any claymores with them, which wasn't great. Nor did they have heavy weapons; this training had been based on recon and light ambushes so the machine guns were back at the base. They did, however, have frag grenades. And the Chechens probably wouldn't have NODs.

With no signal from the observers along the trail the Keldara started working on their positions. There was no time to dig real fighting positions but the Keldara rapidly scraped out shallow trenches, pushing the dirt up in small breastworks in front of them. The leaves they scraped off to the side. When they lay down in the trench they wrapped themselves in a ponchos lined with thermal blankets, then pulled the leaves back over themselves, covering themselves completely.

Sawn's second, Dimant Ferani, followed behind, touching up the positions and ensuring that each position had minimal thermal output. The Chechens rarely used thermal imagery devices but it never hurt to be sure.

Mike had scraped out his own hasty fighting position, wrapped and covered. Under the cover he slipped out a frag grenade and held it in his right hand with his weapon by his right side. Then he settled down to wait.

The Keldara were as perfect as any group he'd ever met. From years of farming and hunting they had enormous patience and the ability to simply sit, or lie down in this case, for hours. They also tended to keep awake, which was a major benefit with ambushes; most ambushers tended to drift off and start snoring. But the Keldara just . . . waited, like expert hunters. He was again amazed by the absolute perfection of the group of rural farmers.

The Chechens, however, were not nearly as good. He could hear them coming long before the signal from the overwatch position that the target was entering the zone. He could also smell them: a tinge of woodsmoke, BO and harsh cigarettes. The latter was so strong he was sure one or more of them was actually smoking.

There was a series of clicks over the radio as Sawn signalled the team to prepare to engage. Mike could hear the sound of the mules' hooves on rocks and couldn't imagine that the normally vigilant animals didn't know the Keldara were there. However, Sawn had obviously chosen the downhill side for more than one reason. There was a current of air coming down the mountainside and it blew from the trail to the ambushers. That was keeping their scent from reaching the mules. As long as everyone was silent, they were golden.

There was another series of faint clicks in his earphones and then a series of beeps. One, two, three . . .

Mike pulled the pin from the grenade and lifted himself to his knees, the leaves and poncho cascading away from him, then threw the grenade uphill into the mass of men and mules in front of him. With that done he ducked down into the hasty fighting position and flattened himself into the ground, as a series of sharp cracks filled the air with a hail of shrapnel.

As soon as the last grenade had detonated he slid his SPR over the side of the small mound in front of him and began picking out targets. The Chechens had gone to ground fast, but they didn't have good cover along this section of the trail and if he couldn't directly target someone, one of the Keldara to the side could. AK rounds cracked overhead but he ignored them, sweeping his weapon back and forth in a search for targets.

The mules complicated things, slightly. Some of them were down, kicking in pain from the riddling shrapnel. Others, however, had broken free and were running loose. One came barreling right over his position, stamping hard on his thigh as it passed.

He'd picked out three targets and downed them when he heard Sawn's whistle for the team to sweep across the objective.

He lifted himself up and kept the weapon at present as he stepped forward. There was a wounded tango on the ground, hit by shrapnel or a round in the leg, he wasn't sure which, with an AK on the ground next to him. Mike swept the UV light from his rifle flash on the tango, made an assessment that he wasn't a leader, and put a round through his head.

He continued across the objective, checking the dead and wounded carefully, until he was well into the woods on the far side. He flipped the sight on the rifle to thermal imagery and swept it up the hillside, looking for hiding tangoes but didn't find any.

Sawn's whistle signalled recall and Mike headed back down the hill to the trail, checking his sector for recovery items. Besides the mules, the surviving ones of which the Keldara were gathering up, he was looking for any intel items such as paperwork. There didn't seem to be much immediately obvious and he left off the search to go find Sawn and McKenzie.

"We've got three prisoners and two somethings," McKenzie said as he approached.

"Somethings?" Mike asked.

"Two bints with the Chechens," the Scottish former SAS sergeant said in his thick brogue. "One with a grenade fragment in her side. Ivan's talking with them at the moment. I get the impression they weren't wives or such like."

"Slaves," Ivan said, stepping up to the trainer's side. "They were picked up on farms over towards the Pankisi Gorge. That and the food on the mules. They weren't bought, the fucking black-asses raided and burned the farms."

"Bloody hell," Mike muttered. "Orphans and damaged goods."

"More lassies for your harem, lad," McKenzie grunted, humorously.

"Raped and abused ladies make difficult harem girls," Mike pointed out, sighing. "What about the other prisoners?"

"One looks like the leader of the convoy," McKenzie said. "The other two were hiding in the woods and put their hands up so fast nobody had the heart to shoot them."

"Probably drivers," Mike said. "Postbattle cleanup time. I'm going to head down to the road and try to intercept the response team on the way up to intercept the trucks."

"They might not be coming tonight, lad," McKenzie pointed out.

"But they will eventually," the Kildar said.

Mike made it to the road just as the first vehicle of the reaction convoy rounded the nearest corner. He stepped out in the road and waved at it as it approached, hoping like hell they wouldn't either run him down or frag him.

"Kildar," Ivar Makanee said as the vehicle rolled to a stop.

"Need a ride to my Expedition if you please," Mike said. The vehicle was a Ford F-350 flare-side and he waved at the point leader to stay in his seat as he climbed in the back.

"Keldara Base, this is Kildar," Mike said, settling into the load of weapons and ammo in the rear.

"Kildar, this is Keldara Base," Gildana said. It was past

her time to be relieved but Vanner had kept her on the radio since she was fully "dialed in" on the situation. The truth was, he couldn't have pried her out of the seat.

"I've linked up with Team Oleg point," the Kildar replied. "I'm going to head up to the roadblock and check out operations up there. Russell's with Team Padrek, correct?"

Gildana looked at her ops screen and nodded to herself.

"Correct, Kildar," she said, looking around the room. She'd put the call in on the announcement system since it was from the Kildar and she caught Colonel Nielson's eye, raising her eyebrows to see if he had anything he wanted to pass on. But the colonel just shook his head.

"I'll head up there and hang around to see if anything happens right off," the Kildar continued. "Make sure that Padrek knows it's us coming up the road, please."

"Roger, Kildar."

"Kildar, out."

She changed frequencies to Padrek by hitting the appropriate icon and took the system off announce.

"Padrek, Keldara Base."

"Padrek Five, go."

"Kildar and Team Oleg are on the way, ETA five to seven minutes. Status?"

"All clear so far," Padrek Five replied. That was Bori Mahona, a distant cousin, like most of the Keldara. He was a serious young man, more studious than most of the Keldara, and she could practically see his furrowed brow over the radio.

"Kildar asks that you not fire on their vehicles," she added, twitting him slightly.

"We're prepared for their arrival, Keldara Base," Bori replied tightly. "Anything else?"

"Negative," she said, secretly happy to have pricked his seriousness. "Keldara Base, out."

"How are you feeling, Gildana?" Vanner asked, sitting down in the station chair by her.

"Good, sir," Gildana replied.

"You need relief?" he asked.

"No, sir," she said as the icon for Team Sawn started to flash. "Go Sawn."

"If you flag out, tell me," Vanner said, sitting back.

"Keldara Base, this is Sawn Five," Gavi Makanee said over the radio. Gavi was a first cousin, about her age and they'd been raised almost as brother and sister. She could see him now, short-cut red hair tousled by his boonie hat, camouflage paint on his face, probably crouched over a scrap of paper carefully doing it all "by the book."

"Go Sawn Five," she said, bringing up the mission report screen.

"Enemy KIA twenty-nine," Gavi said. "Enemy WIA one. Papa Whiskey three. Hotel two. Friendly KIA, zero. Friendly WIA, two, non-critical, say again, non-critical. Ammunition, green. Supplies, green. Large quantity of small arms, food and some contraband. Twelve pack animals functional. Caching or destroying immovable material and moving to road for pickup."

"Roger, Sawn Five," Gildana said, bringing up another screen and dispatching a group of vehicles to go pick up Team Sawn.

★ ★ ★

"Hey, Padrek," Mike said as he rolled off the back of the truck.

"Kildar," the team leader said, ducking his head. "Would you like to take a look at our positions?"

Mike glanced at the team's trainer and then shook his head.

"This is your game, Padrek," Mike said. "The next time you're going to have to do it all on your own, so you might as well start now. I'm just another shooter on this one."

"Yes, Kildar," the leader said, swallowing nervously. "I've laid in positions on both sides of the road and prepared a tree for a roadblock. I'll get with Oleg and get his vehicles in position to reinforce the block."

"Go for it," Mike said, wandering to the roadside with a wave. He hunkered down on a rock, dropped his ruck and stretched his shoulders. To think a few hours ago he was screwing the hell out of a young redhead. What the hell was he doing here?

A couple of the farm trucks were placed to block the road while the two teams began cutting trees to make negotiable S curves that would slow vehicles approaching the position. A forward position was also under construction, the "chicken" pit where a single soldier would be placed to order vehicles into the roadblock.

Meanwhile, the heavy weapons gunners of Team Oleg were building positions along the roadside. If anyone tried to force the block, the Keldara would catch them with raking fire as they tried to negotiate the S cover obstacles.

Last, the drivers of the three remaining Team Oleg vehicles waited in place in case anyone passed them. They could pursue or be used as a secondary blocking point.

Mike's big worry was truck bombs. The defenses were spread out but one truck bomb could cut a swath through the core of the Keldara families. Which would put a pretty large black mark on the record of the Kildar.

Which he wasn't going to fix by worrying about it.

"I've redeployed the group," McKenzie said, coming over to his position in the trees and dropping his ruck. "I'm moving Sawn up forward to close the block if anybody tries to run and putting Oleg's boys on the block itself."

"Works," Mike said. "Get the spare vehicles out of sight and if they get a solid block in place move the ones blocking the road."

"Will do," McKenzie said. "You really expect them soon?"

"No reason the mule train is going to want to wait around, especially this close to us," Mike said, leaning back on his own ruck. "It's been a long day. Wake me up if anything interesting happens."

# ★ Chapter Five ★

"Kildar?"

Mike had awakened when he heard stirring and sat up immediately, checking his weapon.

The vehicles were gone from the block and large timber and boulder blocks were in place on the road. All he could see in view were a few of the Keldara, though.

"There are three trucks coming down the road," Dmitri said, quietly. "Gregor's taxi passed through late last night but we expected him. He ran Captain Tyurin into Tbilisi yesterday." Tyurin was the local police chief. Venal to a fault on minor items, he was a strong supporter of the Keldara militia and its fight against the Chechens. With a regal bearing and uniforms far finer than his official salary could afford he appeared to base his actions in life on Inspector Louis "I am Shocked, Shocked" Renault from *Casablanca*.

Mike checked his watch and saw it was just before dawn.

"Okay, that looks like showtime," he said, getting to his feet and checking the SPR. "Where is everyone?"

"Most are in defensive positions," Dmitri said. "Oleg

left only five in view. All of Sawn's force are in hides or dug in. Sergeant Vanner has sent Lilia up with some technical gear."

"What?" Mike asked, following Dmitri into the woods.

The intel specialist was in an open hole about thirty meters from the road about halfway up the switchbacks. Mike could hear the trucks approaching down the grade as they got to the position.

"Good morning, Kildar," the young woman said, smiling at him in the faint predawn light. She had light red hair that was tied in a bun under her boonie cap and, like all the Keldara women, was almost startlingly beautiful. She looked like an out-of-place fairytale princess dressed in digi-cam.

"What did you bring?" Mike asked curiously.

"Intercept and jamming gear," the girl said, waving at a blinking box at her feet. "And an umbrella mike so we can overhear their conversation."

"Great," Mike said, picking up the directional microphone and waving it towards the waiting Keldara. However, all he could hear from the troops awaiting the trucks was breathing. The Keldara were almost scary. They'd lived together so long that they could communicate at a level that sometimes seemed like telepathy. He saw one of them turn and look at another and make a chin gesture, which was all it took for the other two to redeploy.

The trucks were making too much noise at this range for him to overhear the drivers but he saw them brake as the Keldara in the chicken pit lit off a magnesium flare.

"Five gets you ten they try to run," McKenzie said, peering through a night scope.

"No transmission from the lead truck," Lilia said, looking at her scopes. "No transmissions at all."

"Start jamming on all non-Keldara freqs," Mike said, crouching down and directing the microphone at the trucks, trying to pick up chatter.

"The driver of the lead truck just asked the guy next to him something," McKenzie said.

"Saw that," Mike replied, directing the microphone at them. But there was still too much noise from the truck motor for him to hear anything useful. The passenger in the lead truck took his time answering, though. And when he said something, the truck pulled forward.

"Okay, the passenger in the lead is a leader," the Kildar said. "Get that out to the trooops. I'd like him alive."

"Yes, Kildar," Dmitri said, keying his communications.

"What is this?" the driver of the lead truck demanded as he pulled up next to the small timber and sandbag bunker placed in the middle of the road.

"Inspection for contraband," Juris Makanee said, easily. "Proceed one vehicle at a time around the barriers. If more than one truck enters the barrier area both will be fired upon. Stop halfway down the barriers for preinspection, then you can proceed to the final block for clearance."

"I'm sure that something can be arranged," the driver said, handing over his license with a folded bill behind it.

Juris looked at the license as he absently handed the fifty ruble note back.

"You're cleared to move to the next check point," Juris said, looking the man in the eye. He wasn't Russian or Georgian, probably a black-ass Chechen bastard. But the orders were to stop and inspect, not shoot them out of hand as he'd prefer. "And if you try to bribe the next guard, he'll put a bullet through your head. Move out."

The driver angrily put the truck in gear and jerked forward as Juris waved for the next truck to stop.

"Checkpoint," Mikhail Solovi said, looking across the compartment at Vyatkin.

Vyatkin put his head out the flap of the military truck and looked at the setup.

"This isn't Georgian National Guard, whoever it is," Vyatkin said, sitting back down and looking at the Chechen black-asses in the back of the truck. "Who is it?"

"Keldara," one of them said, frowning. "I told Mashadem we couldn't move through here, but they wouldn't listen."

"Are these the new militia in the area?" Solovi asked, shaking his head. "Bribe them."

"They won't take bribes," one of the Chechens said, fingering his AK. "They are led by an American, the Kildar. They are very loyal. We are totally fucked. They don't take prisoners."

"There were only five I saw," Vyatkin said, looking at Solovi.

"There will be more hidden around the checkpoint," Solovi said. "We need to not be caught in this, Eduard."

"Agreed," Vyatkin said, looking at the Chechens. "You never saw us, understand?"

"Have a good walk back to Russia," the Chechen said as

the two dropped over the back of the truck. "You Russian bastards," he added when they were out of sight.

"Interesting," Mike said. The reception at the back of the trucks was clear as gin. "The last vehicle's filled with troops. Two guys just jumped off the back. Let them get in the woods and then tell Sawn I want them both alive. When the first truck has been checked for explosives, let the second one up to the midpoint check point. Check it while the first one is being cleared, then engage. Blow the shit out of the trail truck, but just kill the drivers of the other two and take down the passengers. I want all that done in one hit."

"Understood, Kildar," Dmitri said, keying his communicator.

"We're clear," Vyatkin said, stopping to pant.

"You are out of shape, Eduard," Solovi said, looking back at the trucks. The lead truck had reached the final checkpoint and he briefly considered whether they should have stayed in the truck. But not even the stupidest guard could miss the armed Chechens in the rear truck. They had supposedly been "guarding" them on the way to the meeting, but they'd spent most of their time being as insulting as they could manage in a hamfisted way.

As Mikhail watched, the militiaman searching the second truck climbed out of the back and walked over to the driver's side. As soon as he reached it, there was a series of pops and the passenger side doors were yanked open by more guards who dragged the occupants out and threw them on the ground. The drivers were clearly dead.

Before the Chechen guards in the trailing truck could react, RPG rounds slammed out from both sides of the road, turning the rear of the trucks into burning shrapnel. The Chechens who made it out of the back were quickly silenced by heavy fire from machine guns, their bodies dancing as the bullets slammed into them from either side.

"*Yob tvoyu mat*," Eduard whispered, looking at the carnage.

"Set up," Mikhail said, angrily. "They knew we were coming. There must be a platoon hidden in those trees."

"Closer to a company, actually," a voice said from behind them.

"Fuck."

"This situation brings out the cliché in me," Mike said, gazing in wonder at the two Russians. "But I'll try to leave it at one. I've got a gun, a backhoe and over a thousand hectares to get rid of the bodies. So why don't you just tell me what you're doing here and I'll be up by a couple of bullets and some diesel on the deal."

"You're American," Mikhail said, sneeringly. "You won't kill us. Just call the damned Georgians and turn us over to them."

"You're so sure of that, tovarisch," Mike said, drawing his .45. "Okay, two clichés. I'll try to keep it down. Last chance."

"You're not going to . . ." Mikhail said, just as the Kildar, without looking, pointed the weapon and shot Vyatkin through the knee.

As the screaming man fell back on the hold of his two Keldara handlers, Mike pointed the weapon at his head.

"This is the deal," Mike said. "I was listening to you in the truck, so I know you're the leader, 'Mikhail.' So why don't you keep your fat friend from having his head blown off, and various unpleasantries to you, by telling me why a couple of Russian hitters are traveling with Chechens."

"*Yob tvoyu mat*" Mikhail said, panting.

"Jeeze, you're stupid," Mike said, pointing the pistol at Vyatkin and dropping him with a round through the teeth that blew out the back of his head, spattering the Keldara and the surviving Russian with brains.

"You son of a bitch!" Mikhail snarled, struggling in the grip of the two Keldara.

"Your turn, comrade," Mike said, pointing the .45 at the Russian's knee. "You've got four major joints. And even after I shoot them, there are various unpleasant things I can do to you. Huh-one, huh-two . . . no? Three."

The Russian screamed as the .45 blew his knee joint to splinters and sagged in the grip of the Keldara, but they held him upright.

"Damn, you're dumb," Mike shook his head. "You're going to die. You've got to know that. And I know you don't have some honor code to stick to. Now, me, I'd take a lot before I'd give up the location of some SEAL buddies. But you? You've got nothing to look to but money. What's the point in suffering for something you're not going to earn, anyway? Tell me what I want to know and I'll put a bullet through your head and put you out of pain. I don't promise more than that, but you can hope."

"Fuck you," the Russian panted.

"Stupid, stupid, stupid," Mike said, kicking him squarely in his wounded knee.

This time the Russian fell to the ground, writhing, despite the best efforts of the Keldara to hold him upright.

"Plug the hole before he bleeds out," Mike said, stepping away. "Don't let his apparent pain give him an opening. But let's try to keep him alive for a bit."

Three Keldara pinned the writhing Russian to the ground while a fourth worked on the knee, plugging it with coagulating-impregnated cotton and then wrapping it in a pressure bandage. It was still bleeding, but not as copiously, when the Keldara was done.

"Feeling better?" Mike asked, stepping up to the Russian and then kicking him, hard, in the bandaged kneecap.

When the screaming died down Mike sqatted near the Russian's head and shook his own.

"Come on, Mikhail," Mike said, sympathetically. "Why were you with the Chechens? What in the hell is going to make them let a couple of Russians ride with them?"

"Weapons . . ." Mikhail grunted.

"Oh, give me a break," Mike said, shaking his head. "Hold out his arm, it's the elbow next . . ."

"No!" Mikhail gasped. "Special weapons. That's all I know. There is a trade. Money for special weapons."

"How much money?" Mike asked.

"I don't know," Mikhail said, desperately. "I was just to meet about security arrangements."

"The Russian mob is selling the Chechens weapons?" Mike asked, musingly. "Vladimir is going to love that."

"Not mob," Mikhail said. "Sergei. Sergei Karensky. He is handling security for someone, I don't know who.

Eduard was to discuss money. He said only that it was very much. Very much."

"Not enough, Mikhail," Mike said, putting the hot barrel of the .45 to the Russian's elbow. "What kind of weapons? How much money?"

"I don't KNOW!" he screamed. "Much money!"

"Where was the meet going to go down?" Mike asked.

"Somewhere near Arensia," Mikhail gasped.

"That's right in the Pankisi, Mikhail," Mike pointed out. "There is no security in that region. How were they getting in, chopper?"

"Cars," Mikhail gasped. "Land Rovers. From the Russian sector. Sergei set it up. Right at the edge of the Pankisi Gorge."

"And why didn't you go in that way?" Mike asked.

"Too risky," Mikhail said. "He can do it once, but only once. Please, I've answered your questions. I ask only that you not kill me."

"I rarely leave enemies alive, Mikhail," Mike said, sympathetically. "You know how it is. You just can't trust a live enemy. You can trust a dead one."

"Kildar," Oleg pointed out from behind him. "He will remember more things. Perhaps if Vanner questioned him more at base, there would be useful information he could extract."

"Hmmm . . ." Mike said, standing up. "Mikhail, here's the deal. Vanner's a very nice guy. Bit of a geek, bit squeamish. If you're very nice to Sergeant Vanner, perhaps I'll let you live and let you retain the use of your dick. Do you think you can be open-minded about that?"

"Yes," Mikhail squeezed out.

"And, who knows, you might even walk without a limp," Mike said, holstering the .45. "They do remarkable reconstructive surgery these days. I had a buddy who was a SEAL instructor who lost his lower leg in Afghanistan and a year later it hardly slowed down his runs. Of course, he lost it to a fucking mine you dip-shit Russians planted. You scattered them all over the fucking country. So you'll understand if I'm less than caring if you do walk with a limp for the rest of your life. Oleg, get this piece of shit out of my sight."

"McKenzie," Mike said when he found the former SAS sergeant.

"Heard the shots," McKenzie said, scooping up a spoonful of beef stew. "And the screams. Anyone live?"

"One," Mike said. "And this is now a sanitization situation. Not because of the bodies, but the Russkies were setting up a meet with the Chechens involving 'special weapons.' We might have queered that by hitting these two."

"Pity," the NCO said, folding the pouch and putting it away. "What do you want to do?"

"I want everything to disappear," Mike said. "Get the Keldara up here. All the bodies go in the ground, the trucks disappear, the mules disappear. The girls go into the caravanserai with the remaining Russian."

"What about the bearers and the Chechen leader types?"

"Take them back to the caravanserai," Mike said. "There are all those cellars and what-not. We'll see what we can get from them."

★ ★ ★

"You're one cold son of a bitch," Adams said, admiringly. "You just tangoed that one bastard and shot up the other?"

"Russians aren't going to work with the Chechens unless they're secret emissaries or there's a hell of a lot of money involved," Mike said, forking up a piece of egg with steak. "If they were from the government they were going to ID themselves right off. We'd protect them like gold and they know it. Ergo, they were with the mob or something along those lines. And that meant big money which meant something special."

"WMDs again?" Adams asked.

"At a guess," Mike replied, shaking his head. "A Russian would sell his own mother for the right money." He looked up as Vanner entered the kitchen, holding sheets of paper. "Get anything good?"

"After they saw what you did to the Russian, all the Chechens opened up. It was a basic supply run with the added mission of getting the Russians to some of the top Chechen guys over in the Pankisi." The former Marine was red-eyed and gratefully accepted a cup of coffee from Mother Savina as he sat down unceremoniously. "The dead Russian wasn't much help but he did have this," Vanner added, sliding a plastic card across the table.

"And this is?" Mike asked, looking at the unmarked card with a series of numbers on it.

"I'm surprised you've never seen one," Vanner said, amused. "They're issued to keep track of Swiss bank account numbers."

"Not from Zurich Mercantile," Mike said.

"Mercantile does it sometimes," Vanner said. "Those are

from Bank Suisse, though. I don't have the codes to open up the accounts, but those are four different accounts in Bank Suisse containing any number of dollars."

"Or none," Mike said. "If they were selling something, there could only be starter cash in them. You can open one with a hundred euros."

"But that is where the money was going, presumably," Vanner said. "The 'big money' this Mikhail guy keeps babbling about. The Chechens confirm that there were 'special weapons' involved, but they don't know what. The rumors range from MANPADs to nukes."

"Find out from our buddy Mikey who else this Sergei guy might use for a contact," Mike said, finishing off his breakfast. "In the meantime, I'm going to go round up one of the girls and screw myself to sleep."

"No rest for the donkeys, huh?" Vanner asked.

"I didn't say you had to do it right now," Mike pointed out. "Let him sweat a while. Without painkillers."

# ★ Chapter Six ★

"Crap!" Mike suddenly muttered, stopping his stroke.

"Kildar?" Jana said, writhing under him. "Kildar, you've stopped."

"I know," Mike said, propping himself up on his elbows. "I told Genadi that I'd meet with some of the elders this afternoon. In about thirty minutes, in fact. Damnit!"

"Surely after last night, they won't mind if you cancel," Jana said, humping into him. "You have time."

"But I didn't tell them I was canceling," Mike said, sourly. "That means they'll be here, come hell or high water. I was so bent on getting it in I forgot."

Firefights always made him horny. He'd been told that was a natural reaction and as a SEAL he'd learned to suppress it, to an extent. But under the current circumstances there was no particular reason to. Which was why as soon as he'd gotten done with Vanner and breakfast, he'd gone to the harem, literally grabbed Jana and dragged her upstairs.

He'd already come once but he could feel at least one more in there and he'd been heading for it happily, with the intent of following it with about twenty hours of sleep, when he remembered the meeting.

"We're going to have to cut this short," Mike said. "Sorry."

"You are the Kildar," Jana said, shrugging. "And it is not as if I have not had mine . . ."

"Father Kulcyanov, Father Mahona, Genadi," Mike said as he entered the parlor, "it is good to see you again. Oleg, long time no see." When he saw Oleg he was especially glad he hadn't canceled; the kid had been out on ops for a week and had a "murthering great" skirmish in the morning. The least the Kildar could do was show up after all that.

The meeting was being held in one of the three small parlors in the caravanserai. One had been set aside more or less permanently as a "recreation room," read bar, for the trainers. The second was commonly used by the harem girls. This one was for when Mike had a small number of guests to entertain. Such as the elders, all of whom could easily fit in the comfortable room.

The room overlooked the gardens by the harem quarters. When Mike had arrived, the gardens had been suffering from decades of neglect. The somewhat inexpert care of the Keldara yardsman hadn't gotten them back to any condition of glory, but they were much better than when he'd arrived. The roses were coming along well and they filled the room with scent.

He'd taken a very fast shower and his hair was still wet. He hoped it wasn't as obvious that he'd just jumped out of bed. However, given the way that the Keldara talked amongst themselves, if not to outsiders, he was pretty sure they knew damned well where he'd been. He hoped they wouldn't take it as an insult. He was only a few minutes late, after all.

"You gentlemen asked for this meeting," Mike said, sitting down on the couch and pouring a cup of tea.

"Kildar," Father Kulcyanov said formally. "We come to speak of the customs of the Keldara."

Father Kulcyanov was not the oldest of the Family leaders, but he was acknowledged as the senior for all matters of protocol and custom. He was, in fact, the high priest of the Keldara's ancient worship. A tall man, he was clearly shrunken from his original growth with clear signs of cardiovascular failure. Once he must have been as large as Oleg, perhaps bigger, and he had been one of the few Keldara to fight in the "Great Patriotic War," WWII, from which he had returned with a chestful of medals.

"I am always observant of the customs of the Keldara," Mike said, carefully. In fact, he had trampled all over a few, but only when it seemed the only way to accomplish what had to be accomplished. In one case, he'd trampled all over their fear of debt by taking a girl with a burst appendix to the hospital in Tbilisi. He wasn't about to let the girl die just because the Keldara couldn't afford the cost. He'd unknowingly trampled all over another by taking her friend, Lydia, Oleg's fiancée, along as a chaperone. It turned out that for an unmarried female he couldn't have picked a worse one.

That had, he thought, been smoothed over. But the presence of Oleg argued against it.

"As you know, Oleg Kulcyanov is fasted to Lydia

Mahona," Father Kulcyanov continued. "There is a problem in that regard. It involves bride price."

Mike looked at Genadi. The farm manager had been a Keldara before being forced off the farm by his predecessor. However, he hadn't just been tossed off the farm but formally cast from the Families. The move had been forced on them by his predecessor, but it put him in a good position from Mike's perspective; he knew the customs but was no longer bound by them. And he could generally talk freely about them without offending the Keldara since he was no longer one of them.

He was also a graduate of the University of Tbilisi and had thought long and hard about the customs so he had an understanding that often eluded both Mike and the Keldara.

"It's a dowry," Genadi said. "It's a long-held and very serious custom, but it has a purpose. It's generally fixed at a year's income for the male. In the first few years of setting up a household, there's a strong loss of income from both sides. The bride generally becomes pregnant quickly and there are household items that are needed. The male also tends to have a fall off of quality of work."

"I'm going to need Oleg at high function this year," Mike said. "But I get your point. How much do you need?"

"This is not a situation where the Kildar can simply gift the bride and groom," Father Mahona said, grimacing. He was one of the younger elders and he and Mike had a very good relationship. So if he was that blunt, Mike probably was in a minefield. "Bride price is a very personal item.

If you gifted Lydia without recompense then it would, effectively, make her your bride. Oleg could never marry her in that condition."

"Not gonna happen," Mike said, looking at Oleg who was looking very unhappy. "Oleg, where do you stand in this?"

"I will let the elders explain, Kildar," Oleg said. The guy looked really unhappy.

"Okay, first things first," Mike said. "Oleg is my top team leader. I'm cognizant of the customs of the Keldara, but anything that reduces Oleg's functionality or loyalty is out the window."

"This will reduce neither, Kildar," Oleg said, definitely, looking Mike in the eye. "This is a long-held custom and one that binds the Keldara. The custom they wish to speak of binds the Keldara to the Kildar. And you are both my commander and my friend. I am in support of it."

"What custom?" Mike asked, cautiously.

"The Kardane," Genadi said, grimacing. "In Western cultures it would be called the '*droit de seigneur*.'"

Mike frowned for a second as he tried to remember where he'd heard the phrase and then blanched.

"You've got to be *joking*," he snapped.

"They're not," Genadi said in rapid English. "It's an old custom. A really old custom, one that hasn't been used since the days of the Tzars. But it's custom and they can live with it."

"Kildar, the Kardane is fully acceptable to all involved," Father Kulcyanov said. "The prospective bride spends one night with the Kildar and the Kildar then gifts her with her bride price. This is a trade for a trade, the opening of the prospective bride for sufficient funds to set up her household. It must be consensual on both sides."

Mike opened his mouth to reply angrily and then shut it. He was the Kildar. He owned the land they lived on and even the houses they lived in. He could simply order them to ignore this stupidity and they might. Or he might find himself in a bitter multiyear war with disaffected troops he had to trust like his own brothers. So . . . don't assault the position, find a way around.

"Okay, Lydia comes up to the caravanserai . . ."

"Don't go there," Genadi said, in rapid English again. "It has to be as it was stated. Don't try to twist it or you'll run into real crap."

Mike sighed. "Explain."

"It has to be value for value," Father Mahona said, seriously. "Full value must be given in both directions or it would be a violation of honor. In both directions."

"Translation," Genadi said, in Georgian. "If you don't open Lydia, she'll be looked upon as too useless to be a woman of the Keldara. She'll be looked upon as unfit since you rejected her in that way. Her honor will be violated by being alone with you and twice violated for being found wanting."

"And she and Oleg don't get married," Mike said, looking over at Oleg. "You're going along with this?"

"I am most worried that you will refuse, Kildar," Oleg said.

"Not that I'm going to . . . be with Lydia?" Mike asked incredulously.

"I would consider it an honor," Oleg said, seriously. "As would Lydia. We have discussed this."

"Crap," Mike muttered. "What is it with women wanting to jump in the bed of the Kildar? Why couldn't this have happened when I was seventeen?"

Both questions were rhetorical since he'd already discussed it to death with everyone from Genadi to Nielson. The Kildar was very high status, not only among the Keldara but among the other groups in the region in contact with them. The girls he'd rescued from the Chechen slavers had practically fought one another for the right to be first in his bed. And plenty of the Keldara girls had made it clear they wouldn't object to even a casual roll in the hay, which was normally *verboten* among the Keldara. The touch of the king was magic and in the region the Kildar was regarded as more of a king than anyone since Louis the XIV.

"How do you stand with this, Kildar?" Father Kulcyanov asked, again formally. "The arrangement is that Lydia will spend one night with you, upon which night you will open her. For this boon you will grant her the boon of her bride price, which is at a mimnimum five hundred rubles."

"Lydia's worth a lot more than that," Mike muttered. She was, arguably, one of the three prettiest of the Keldara women, which put her in the top one percent internationally. Most of the Keldara girls could easily be supermodels.

"Very well, but I have conditions upon this ceremony. For one thing, we will make it a ceremony. If this is to be done, it should be done well."

"What do you mean?" Genadi asked curiously.

Mike hadn't been sure but when the question was

asked the broad outlines dropped in as if he had seen them somewhere. Maybe in a dream, maybe in a book, he wasn't sure. But it was right.

"Genadi, obtain two horses," he said. "A gelding for me, black by preference but most important is that it's rideable and good looking. Obtain a . . . I think they call it a palfrey as well, white by preference. In the meantime, if Lydia doesn't know how to ride sidesaddle, get her instruction, I don't care from where or how much it costs. I will get with Mother Savina on the preparations for Lydia, over and above riding lessons. For one thing, there are . . . call them other riding lessons. She's not going to come to my bed entirely ignorant and terrified. Anastasia will handle part of that, but I'll put Mother Savina in charge. There will be special clothing involved for both of us. And when I come to her house to pick her up, there will be a small ceremony. I'll work on that. This won't take place for at least a couple of weeks. We need to get the horses and riding lessons, first."

"Is this an American custom?" Father Kulcyanov asked, confused.

"No," Mike said. "This is a me custom and you will abide by it."

"More hot, young, virgin pussy?" Adams asked as Mike entered the kitchen the next morning.

"Oh, bite me," Mike muttered, pouring a cup of coffee.

"And I thought that not having to fight over time with Bambi and Flopsy was the good life," Adams continued.

"We're talking about Oleg, here, damnit," Mike

replied. "If I don't handle this just right I'm going to lose the support of my top team leader."

"He's fully on board," Adams said. "I was talking about it with Mother Savina. She thinks it's a great idea."

"Jesus, this culture is sick," Mike muttered quietly, so that Mother Savina, who was pottering around in the kitchen, wouldn't hear him.

"Not really," Adams said, shrugging. "Odd. Quaint. But hardly sick. If it was sick, they would have found a less pleasant way to manage this. What gets me is how well we get along."

"Huh?" Mike said, frowning. "Not that I'm not good for a distraction right now."

"You've spent *some* time in the sandbox," the chief said, shrugging again. "What do you think about your average towel-head versus the Keldara?"

"No comparison," Mike said, puzzled. "The Keldara are can-do. They don't try to stab you in the back. If there's a problem, they fix it or if they can't they get your assistance with it and pitch in as much as possible."

"There's other stuff, yeah," Adams said. "But do they remind you of anyone over there?"

"Not really," Mike said, making a moue of distaste. "If I was comparing them to the towel-heads, it'd be insulting."

"Ever do much with the Kurds?"

"No," Mike admitted, thinking about it. "I was training a group that had a couple in it. But not for long."

"The Kurds are the same way," Adams mused, leaning back. "With the regular Arabs and what have you in Iraq, you're always negotiating. You need something done, you have to scratch a back first, or grease a palm. With the

Kurds it's like . . . BAM! You need something that's in their interest, they're right there in support, be it a firefight or power-plant construction. We just . . . get along better with the Kurds than we do with the Arabs. Gurkhas the same way. You don't get it with most tribal groups, but you do with, oh, say the Massai. And the Kurds. And the Gurkhas. And now with the Keldara. It's like some sort of secret handshake. That's why I agreed with you about the whole commando thing and why I don't let it sweat me when they come up with something like this. The one thing that I never particularly liked about the Kurds is the way they treat their women; the Keldara are at least better at that."

"Well, I'm glad you think it's such a great idea, since you're going to have a part of the whole thing."

"Whoa!" the former chief snapped. "I'm not going to touch Lydia."

"Much as I like her, it's not Lydia that I'm worried about," Mike said. "Mother Savina, come over here. We've got a ceremony to figure out."

Mike had a full schedule for the day. Among other things, he hadn't been keeping up with the progress of the brewery.

When he'd arrived in the valley he'd been surprised by several things. One, of course, was the general good looks of the Keldara. The women were outstanding but even the men were so good looking they could have been actors playing their roles. In most "peasant" cultures, the nature of the work tended to make both men and women hard and ugly. So did the inbreeding characteristic of such cultures. The Keldara were a rare exception that proved the rule.

The second thing he had been astounded by, however, was the quality of the local beer. Georgia was far better known for its wines than its beer and it had been a long time since he'd had really good beer when he arrived. But the beer in the tavern in town had been outstanding, as good as any to be had in an American or German microbrewery. However, when he began interacting with the Keldara he'd discovered that the beer in town was their "bad" stuff; the pure quill was so good it should be illegal.

It wasn't pure beer by German standards, having some additional berries and herbs that were limited to the local area added. But it was truly amazing stuff. Mike had seen the possibilities from the day he took over. The Keldara were depressingly poor by modern standards. His introduction of modern equipment and methods in farming would help alleviate that somewhat, but they really needed a source of capital. They made outstanding beer, people paid good money for good beer. Ergo, they needed a brewery and a distribution program.

The problem was, what Mike knew about either could be written on the inside of a matchbook in crayon. And the Keldara women who brewed the beer did it in small batches.

His answer, as usual, was to delegate. As part of the Keldara spring festival, which was so old it matched pre-Christian festivals found only in ethnology textbooks, a "king" was chosen as well as a "goat," the latter called the "caillean." One of the Keldara militia members, Gurum, an otherwise intelligent and capable fellow, had been chosen as the bannock caillean when he found a bean in his bannock.

The caillean was regarded as an omen of bad luck by the more conservative Keldara and the team Gurum had been assigned to had pinned every problem they encountered on him. So he'd been almost impossible to integrate into the teams.

However, the women were much less attuned to the problem of having a caillean around. So Mike had given him a quick class in Internet research, a reasonable budget and put him to work on the brewery problem. Gurum had asked a couple of questions in the beginning but since the battle with the Chechens Mike hadn't seen hide nor hair of him. And while he'd seen some construction on the brewery site—a bench near the road to town that had once been a toll station—he didn't think it was complete.

When he pulled onto the bench, he was surprised by the almost abandoned air of the place. There was a partial building completed, two stories, more or less, with stone walls and a roof at least, but the doors at the front weren't installed nor were the windows. There were some construction sounds coming from the interior, however, so Mike parked and walked in the front door.

"'Ware, Kildar!" a voice called from above, just as a balk of timber crashed to the floor a few feet from him.

"Thanks for the heads up," Mike said, looking up. One of the older Keldara males was looking through a large hole in the second floor with an abashed expression on his face.

"Vassily, you were nearly out one Kildar," Mike said. "Watch where you're thowing logs next time!"

There was far more work completed than Mike had thought. The upper floors were mostly in and were heavily reinforced with thick crossbeams that were not much more than adzed down tree trunks. The supporting pillars, which were rather close together towards the front, were much the same. Some of the bark was still evident in spots. The right-hand side of the building was open to the ceiling in a loft configuration. Mike wasn't sure what that was for, but he was willing to assume someone did.

"Kildar," a voice called from the back. "We were wondering when you would drop by."

"Hello, Vatrya," Mike said as his eyes adjusted to the gloom. Vatrya was one of the older unmarried Keldara females. He wondered if she was in the same boat as Lydia and hoped that, if so, the brewery would be making enough money soon so the same compromise wouldn't be necessary. On the other hand, he had to admit that the honey-blonde was a fine figure of a young woman. Long legs under that skirt and nice high ones. Not to mention a heart-shaped face and just lovely dark blue eyes.

He realized he was slipping over to his dark side rather quickly. The idea of breaking in several of the Keldara women was more than attractive. But that was the problem; it could quickly become addictive. It would be easy enough to use the excuse to abuse the privilege and he had worked too hard to cultivate the Keldara's respect to lose it that way.

Vatrya was accompanied by a tall, spare, man Mike

didn't recognize. From his clothing, a casual polo shirt and tan slacks, he probably wasn't a Keldara.

"You haven't even met Mr. Brock," Vatrya said, gesturing the man forward. "Kildar, this is Herr Gerhard Brock of the Alten Brewery Company."

"Herr Brock," Mike said, offering his hand.

Brock shook it deliberately in the manner of a European and nodded.

"You are the Kildar," the man said in English with a strong German accent. "A pleasure to meet you."

"And you Herr Brock," Mike replied, trying to keep the confusion off his face.

"The brewery apparatus is in transit at the moment," Mr. Brock said, waving to the rear. "As stated in the contracts, we had the vats and piping in stock. I am assured that locally manufactured materials are available for the barley bins. And, of course, the ovens are being constructed by the Keldara."

"The Keldara are very good at general construction," Mike said, nodding.

"I strongly suggest that you take Gurum's suggestion in regards to the annual convention," Herr Brock continued, stone faced. "It would be the perfect venue for your aims in regards to marketing. Time is, of course, short, but I am being assured that you are capable of managing the requirements."

"We're very adaptable," Mike said, nodding. "And we are used to short decision cycles."

"I am to look on the oven construction," Brock said, nodding in farewell. "I look forward to further conversation with you, Mr. Kildar."

"It's just Kildar," Mike said as the man strode towards the back of the building again. "Vatrya?"

"Yes, Kildar?" the girl asked, her eyes wide and smiling.

"What did I just talk about?"

# ★ Chapter Seven ★

"You want to what?" Mike asked.

Gurum looked uncomfortable sitting in the chair across from the Kildar. But he held his ground.

"The convention for the International Association of Brewers and Brewery Distributors is this year in the city called Las Vegas in the United States. You know of this city, Kildar?"

"Yeah, I know Las Vegas," Mike said, sighing. "Sin City."

"I do not understand, Kildar?" Gurum said. "Sin City?"

"Las Vegas is in a state, like a province, that permits gambling and prostitution," Mike said, sighing again. "Its nickname is Sin City. It alliterates in English. So you want to, what? Have a booth for Keldara Beer at this convention? Do you have any idea what the logistics are for something like that? And where in the hell did this Brock guy come from?"

"Kildar, when you assigned me this task I was challenged by several problems," Gurum said, frowning. "The first being that I knew nothing about brewing. This is a woman's task in the Keldara and they guard their secrets closely.

Mother Lenka was, of course, the person to work with on that. She has agreed to be the . . . the brewmistress for the brewery and has been working with Herr Brock on the design for the initial brews. Herr Brock is with the Alten Brewery in Koblenz, Germany. Alten has its own small brewery going back to the 1800s, but it is also an international supplier of brewery equipment and materials. In addition, they have been most helpful in regards to marketing and shipment methods. At their suggestion, I inquired as to a . . . booth it is called at this convention. The convention had a cancellation, so I was able to secure a small booth. It is in an outlying area, but quite functional for our needs. All of this I have managed to do within the budget you assigned to me, but to actually set up the booth and create marketing materials for it will require a higher budget."

Mike was stone faced through this recital but his lack of expression was hiding deep surprise and respect. Gurum had taken his suggestions and run with them in a way that Mike, even with his experience of the Keldara, found amazing.

"Where'd you scrounge up Alten?" Mike asked, ignoring the question of the convention for the moment. He knew diddly about setting up a booth but he'd been to a couple of conventions where people sold gear that SpecOps groups used. All he really remembered about them was booth babes . . . Now there was a thought.

"Alten was one of the three companies I contacted after an Internet search," Gurum replied. "They were both the most helpful and, when I contacted previous customers, the one that seemed the most well liked and respected. Their prices were slightly higher, but Command Master Chief Adams pointed out that quality is often worth the extra money."

"And they're supplying . . .?" Mike asked curiously.

"Almost all of our equipment," Gurum answered. "As well as marketing and distribution advice. They've built breweries in Europe and the United States but this is the first time they've done one in Georgia or the other Caucasus areas and they seem very enthusiastic."

"You've really taken this bull by the horns, haven't you?" Mike asked, finally smiling.

"I had some questions about it when I started," Gurum replied carefully. "You were . . . busy with many things. I spoke to Chief Adams and he said that SEALs consider intiative to be a good thing. He told me to take as much initiative as I could. I have been careful with my budget, but it will take more to complete the plans and get distribution going."

"I'd figured that the budget really only covered research," Mike said. "Okay, tell me about the convention."

"I have never attended such an event," Gurum admitted. "I have, however, contacted a company that is in the business of setting up for such events. They have supplied suggestions about what we would need. Some of them they can provide; others we need to provide ourselves. They assure me that they can set up a . . . 'turn-key' booth, but we must have certain marketing items prepared in advance."

"Lots of marketing items," Mike said musingly. "Folders, brochures, posters, freebies. I'm not even sure how many of each we'll need."

"In addition, we will need beer," Gurum said, seriously. "Genadi has a lawyer who is handling the farm's legal issues. I have contacted him and gotten permissions to export a batch for marketing purposes and more permissions to import it to the United States. He also obtained permissions for us to import the brewing equipment and a grant from USAID in the amount of $50,000 for the brewing equipment."

"That's a damned big grant," Mike said.

"It was a matching grant," Gurum said uncomfortably. "We agreed to provide $25,000 and they doubled the money."

"And what is seventy-five grand going to buy us?" Mike asked curiously.

"All of the brewing equipment to set up a one hundred hectoliter plant," Gurum replied. "In fact, we're going to have to do some charging internal to the Keldara to expend it all."

"Run that one by me again?" Mike said, confused.

"There is more money in the grant than we actually need for equipment and materials," Gurum said, carefully. "Therefore, we are also using the grant money to pay the Keldara for their work and some is set aside for initial capital before we get a cash flow going."

"You've been talking with Nielson, too, haven't you?" Mike added, grinning.

"Yes, Kildar," Gurum replied with a nod.

"Okay, approved," Mike said. "Top to bottom. And I've got a few ideas about the booth I'd like to bring up . . ."

★ ★ ★

"Hey, Vanner, didn't you buy some whiz-bang photography gear as part of your 'I wanna be a super-spy' package?" Mike asked as he strolled into the intel shop.

"If we have to do HUMINT work, we're going to have to have cameras, Kildar." Vanner sighed. "I bought a pretty good Nikon setup and a few lenses, yes. Your point?"

"I need to borrow it. . . ."

Mike wasn't, by any stretch, a professional photographer. But he'd taken a couple of courses his first time through college and enjoyed them. And there were some subjects that were just purely photogenic.

He'd taken the Expedition down to the valley where the troops that weren't training were hard at work in the fields. The Keldara males, still picking rocks in areas and checking on the progress of the barley, were good for a few dozen shots. But it was when the girls came out with lunch that he really got started.

About a third of the girls from the compound carried baskets with loaves of bread and rounds of cheese poking out from under colorful cloths. The rest, however, were carrying buckets brimming with ice and ceramic beer bottles.

"Lydia," Mike said, walking over to the group, "I need to get some photographs of the girls so we can make up some advertising stuff for the brewery."

"I understood all of that except the last part," Lydia said, smiling.

Mike thought about that for a second and then shrugged helplessly. He hadn't considered that the Keldara had so little access to modern technology and culture that the concept of "modeling" was outside their worldview.

"You know that Gurum is planning on trying to sell the beer at a convention in the United States?" Mike asked.

"Yes," Lydia answered as the girls, and most of the guys, started to gather around.

"Well, we won't be selling it by the glass or bottle," Mike said, frowning in thought. "What we will be looking for is someone who will buy it from us in large quantity and then sell it in the United States. That's called a distributor. What we will be doing is looking for a distributor, a good one that will give us the most money for our beer we can get. With me so far?"

"I can handle even larger words, Kildar," Lydia replied, batting her eyes at him. "Two, even three syllables."

"Very funny," Mike replied. "You asked. Okay, so to find the best distributor, we have to have people notice us. There will be hundreds of small brewers like us at the convention, all trying to get the big distributors to notice them. So, how do we get the distributors to notice us, rather than the other brewers?"

"We have the best beer?" Greznya asked, smiling. Greznya was one of the older unmarried females, a tall redhead with bright blue eyes and pert if small breasts, who normally worked in the intel section. Recently, Vanner had started breaking the intel girls down and assigning them to work with specific teams. Apparently Sawn's team was on field duty. So the girl had gone from running an intercept and analysis section to hauling bread and cheese to the field. On the other hand, she didn't seem to mind.

Mike considered the answer and then caught Katrina's eye. The little minx would have the answer he was looking for he was sure.

"Katrina, how do you get the boys to notice you?" Mike asked, raising an eyebrow.

"Sway your hips?" Katrina replied, grinning. "Look them in the eye? Pout your lips? Drop one shoulder? Put your hand on their arm? Then they'll carry your water and you don't have to."

"Minx," Greznya said with a smile.

"Katrina, however, is right," Mike said, seriously. "We want the distributors to notice us. We will build some displays for the booth that have the 'look' of the valley of the Keldara, we will have bright signs and we will have pictures of pretty girls. Oh, and we will have pretty girls giving out free tastes of our beer. Some of you will go to the convention and serve beer, smiling all the time. But before that we have to make things to give out that have pictures and information about our beer. And for that we'll need pictures," Mike finished, holding up the camera.

"Of pretty girls?" Katrina asked. "Then just take them of me."

"Quiet, you," Mike growled. "I will. But first I want pictures of all the girls. Girls with beer is a good thing for sales. So line up and smile."

It took more than that. The Keldara women were trained almost from birth that they shouldn't use their looks as a weapon. And they were very camera shy at first. But after Mike got a couple of good photos, and was able to show them to the girls using his laptop, they got into the spirit of the shoot.

The best image was towards the end of the shoot, when he had all the girls line up with their buckets in one hand and the other wrapped around the shoulder of the girl next to them. Most of them were holding a bottle in their off-hand and he'd managed to get a decent expression on every face. The boys, thankfully, were more interested in the shoot than they were in food for the time being and didn't so much as grumble about their lunch being held up.

When the food and beer had finally been served Mike discreetly grabbed Katrina and pulled her aside.

"When you get back to the house, have them call me," Mike said. "I'd like to get some shots of you later today. But have your mother call me and set it up."

"Very well, Kildar," Katrina said, batting her eyelashes at him. "But I can go now. There is less to carry back than we carry to the field."

"Okay, but we're going to go by the brewery and pick up a chaperone," Mike said. "I know just the one to use."

"Hello, Mother Lenka," Mike said as he ducked his head in the still-under-construction brewery. "Could I have a moment of your time?"

"There is something you need to know about sex, Kildar?" Mother Lenka cackled. "Or is it brewing?"

"I need a chaperone, actually," Mike said, leading her out into the sunshine. "I'm going to take some photos of Katrina for the brochures for the brewery. But I'm sure as hell not going to go off alone with her."

"And you think that I'm a chaperone?" Mother Lenka said then started laughing so hard she choked. "Oh, Kildar, you tell such good ones!"

"You're just the chaperone I need, old crone," Mike said, grinning and leading her over to the Expedition. "You're an older, married female. Wholly respectable . . . sort of."

"Not even close," Mother Lenka said, still gasping for breath. "They will assume that you just needed coaching with the young one!"

"No, they won't and you know it," Mike said. "But when I ask her to do some of the things I'll need her to do for the shots, you won't so much as bat an eye. Could you imagine if I asked her to suck the foam off the top of an open beer bottle in front of, say, Mother Kulcyanov?"

"She wouldn't even know what you were trying to suggest," Mother Lenka said, giving him a toothless grin. "But I understand. Assuredly I will chaperone you, young man. And if you need any suggestions . . ."

"I'm sure we'll do fine," Mike said. "But I do need to pick up some supplies."

He'd spotted the location while checking out the Keldara doing patrolling ops. It was a quiet little dell, with a small waterfall surrounded by trees. There was a wide grassy area that at the moment was filled with late spring wild flowers and the light was just about right.

He parked the Expedition on a narrow dirt logging road and led the two up to the dell then went back to the SUV for his equipment and the bucket of beer he'd appropriated from the brewery.

"Okay, Katrina," Mike said, handing the girl a bottle of beer and positioning her by the waterfall. "What I want you to do is think of just how wonderful Keldara beer is and when you look at the camera I want you to look at it as if it's the most wonderful thing in the world."

"Make love to the camera," Mother Lenka said, somewhat sadly. "That was what I was told when I would model. Think of the camera as your lover."

"I didn't know you modeled," Mike said, glancing over at her as he considered the light and made some manual adjustments to the Nikon.

"I've done many things you would not think I had, young one," Mother Lenka said, then laughed again. "And many that even you would not believe!"

"Mother Lenka is my role model," Katrina said, holding up the beer bottle and giving the camera a smouldery look. "Like this?"

"That's a start," Mike said. "Work it, babe."

# ★ Chapter Eight ★

Mike hit the answer button on his phone and threw the estimates for the convention booth costs on the desk. He hadn't realized it would be that much. Just getting electric run was a minimum of two hours at $175 per hour. Thank God he didn't need Internet connection! At least the photo shoot had worked out well. He had some killer shots that had been worked into three different brochures and a poster of Katrina that was sure to be a big hit. But the more he looked at the rest of his plans, the more he realized he was going to need some pull in D.C. . . .

"Go."

"Kildar, there is a call from the United States," one of the Keldara women said over the speaker phone. "An officer in the State Department."

"Put it through," Mike replied, picking up the handset. Speak of the devil . . .

"Mr. Jenkins?" a cultured voice said a moment later.

"The same," Mike growled. The only thing worse in the U.S. government than IRS agents, in his opinion, were the Northeastern Liberal brahmins that ran the State Department. And this guy sounded like a classic case.

"Mr. Jenkins, my name is Wilson Hargreave Thornton, I am a desk officer for the Moldava section in the State Department."

"I don't suppose that's located in Minot, North Dakota, is it?" Mike asked. Moldava was the poorest country in Europe, with no major exports except blonde hookers. It was hardly the France desk.

"No, Mr. Jenkins," the man said, laughing dryly and quite falsely. "The Moldava desk is hardly Siberia. It has had some serious action of late. And it's about that that I wish to talk to you. I was asked to do a favor for a senior member of the legislative branch. However, I've exhausted my sources in this matter. When I so informed him he, quite out of the blue, asked if I knew you and if I would contact you for him. I will say you're a hard man to find."

"I like it that way," Mike said.

"So I understand," the man said, chuckling again. He had the dry chuckle of a person who had had their sense of humor surgically removed but tried to act as if it was still intact. "I would like to ask you to come to Washington for a few days and meet with the member I was referring to. He needs someone with your . . . background."

"I don't think so," Mike said. "I don't go around taking orders from 'senior members of the legislative branch.' I don't even take them from senior members of the executive branch."

"Mr. Jenkins," Wilson Hargreave Thornton said seriously, "you have many enemies both internationally and, frankly, within the government. Having a senior senator that owes you a favor is in your best interests. I might add that the senator has already been instrumental in helping you. I believe you recently received a grant from the International Monetary Fund?"

"Yeah," Mike said, grimacing. "I'd thought they were being pretty friendly with the taxpayers' money."

"Nonetheless," Thornton replied, clearly smiling.

"And what the hell does a senator have to do with the IMF?" Mike asked.

"Mr. Jenkins," the State Department officer answered, chuckling, "there are senators and senators. And then there are the ones that can quietly suggest that stalled paperwork be unstalled. Or, for that matter, permanently stalled I might add."

"My . . . background is generally lots of dead bodies," Mike said bluntly, ignoring the implied threat. "Senior senators have a remarkable way of forgetting past favors when bodies turn up."

"Not this time," Thornton said, just as bluntly. "I'll tell you that it involves a young lady who is in trouble. And you are, frankly, the only name that came to mind to fix that problem. Given your . . . background."

"Crap," Mike muttered. They knew his hot buttons, that's for sure. "When?"

"The senator can set aside tomorrow evening for a quiet and discreet discussion," Thornton replied. "Would that work for you?"

"If I can get a plane," Mike said. "And this is not going to be a freebie unless it's dead easy."

"Understood," Thornton replied. "Check in to the Washington Sheraton. The senator will contact you there."

"And you'll disavow any connection to me, right?" Mike said, grinning.

"I'm glad you understand," Thornton said, cutting the connection.

"Anastasia," Mike said, sticking his head in the harem manager's office. "Could you do me a favor and pack me some bags? I have to go to D.C. Enough for a few days. No uniforms. Some casual clothes and a few suits with sundries."

"Very well, Kildar," Anastasia said. "When will you be back?"

"Not sure," Mike admitted. "But that will do for as long as I'll need those clothes. And call that charter company in England and get me a jet. I might as well travel in style."

Mike hated D.C. It wasn't anything personal, just a formless resentment. When he'd been a SEAL, D.C. was synonymous with the "brass," the medal-bedecked bastards, most of whom had never heard a shot fired in anger, who sent the teams out to work miracles and then bitched when they failed. Or performed the miracles but caused a bunch of bad press over dead tangoes.

Now, somehow, he'd ended up being brass. Or close enough as made no never mind. He didn't walk the corridors of power, but if he picked up the phone he could be having a quiet dinner with the President this very evening. Or the secretary of state or defense or the national security adviser. That made him, de facto, a Washington "player," even if he spent his time staying as far away as he could.

And at the moment he was particularly pissed. He was just hanging out waiting for a phone call. He hadn't even brought one of his "ladies" with him to pass the time. All he could do was watch Fox News and kick his heels.

He got up and walked to the minibar, preparatory to just getting stinking drunk and telling the "senior senator" to go stuff his mission, when the phone rang.

"Jenkins," he growled.

"I've set aside a meeting room on the third floor," a faintly familiar baritone replied. "The Sherman Room. Follow the signs."

"I'll be there in a few minutes," Mike said. Might as well find out what the fucking senator wanted.

There were two heavies outside the room. They had the look of Secret Service, which made the "senior senator" very senior indeed. As Mike approached the door a man in coveralls came out carrying a black instrument bag. The "senior senator" had had the room swept before the meeting, which was rather unusual.

"Jenkins," Mike said, stopping at the door and ignoring the technician.

"Cell phone, pager and PDA, please," one of the men said, holding out a canvas bag with a zipper lock.

Mike pulled out his cell phone and dropped it in the bag, then shrugged. The other agent pulled a magnetic wand and ran it over him as the first agent zipped the bag shut and handed Mike the key.

When Mike was swept, the agent knocked on the door and opened it to a faint call from inside.

Mike instantly recognized the "senior senator" when he entered. He couldn't quite place the name, but he'd seen him on TV a few times.

"Mr. Jenkins," the man said, getting up from his seat at the conference table and walking over to the door to shake Mike's hand. He had a a commanding presence and a firm handshake and looked Mike right in the eye. He was a guy you trusted immediately. Just like any good con artist or politician. Speaking of redundancy. "I'm Senator John Traskel."

"New Jersey," Mike said, nodding his head. "You're the guy they're saying's going to be the next minority leader."

"And I'm the senior minority member of the Senate Foreign Relations committee, which is more to the point," the senator said, waving him to the a seat. "But please call me John."

"Mike," Jenkins said, sitting down. "You've got a problem."

"One of my constituents does," the senator said, nodding sagely. He was a tall guy with prematurely gray hair that was perfectly coiffed and his suit hadn't come off the rack. Mike also remembered that there was serious family money behind the senator, something in excess of a hundred mil. Come to think of it, he was also one of the few members of the Democratic party who was a tad right wing on social issues. Which was why he was also being bruited around for a presidential candidate in the next election.

"His daughter has gone missing," the senator continued, opening up one of the folders and sliding a picture of a girl in a bathing suit across the table. She looked about fourteen and filled the suit well. Blonde and very pretty.

"Natalya Fedioushina," the senator continued. "Fourteen."

"Call America's Most Wanted," Mike said, sliding the pic back to the senator.

"She went missing in Moldava," the senator said seriously.

"How the fuck did that happen?" Mike asked, aghast.

"The gentleman is a native Ukrainian." The senator sighed. "His wife was visiting relatives in Moldava when the young lady was kidnapped. Presumably for, well . . ."

"To be sold as a sex-slave," Mike said. "It's Moldava's only real export. And you want me to find her? Do you have any idea what sort of task that is?"

"Yes," the senator said, nodding. "I do. I've seen both the open and the classified data on the sex-slave industry. But we do have one lead."

"Go," Mike said, shrugging.

"This man," the senator continued, sliding another picture across. The pic was taken of a man exiting a small foreign car, a Lada Mike thought from the roofline. Heavyset, dark, he had the look of a Balkans pimp type, one each. "Yuri Smegnoff. He is most probably the man who kidnapped her. Unfortunately, we don't know what he did with her."

"How long?" Mike asked.

"Two weeks ago," the senator replied, slipping the pic back into the file and sliding the whole folder across.

"By now she's in Albania or Serbia being broken in," Mike said, flipping the folder open. There were more pics of the girl and of Smegnoff as well as a list of his common hangouts.

"We just want to know where she is," Traskel said.

"That's not going to be easy, even if this pimp is a good contact," Mike replied.

"You very much want to do this mission, Mr. Jenkins,"

the senator replied tightly. "I need the favor. And you don't want me remembering that you didn't help when I needed it."

"Was that a threat, Senator?" Mike said, smiling but not looking up. "Please. You've got access to some of my files, at least. Any threat from you is hardly going to sway me."

"You're playing with the big boys now, Mr. Jenkins," the senator almost snarled. "This isn't killing a few terrorists on an island in the Bahamas. This is the kindness and consideration, or not, of the United States Senate. You really don't want to piss me off."

"I've been playing with the big boys for a long time, Senator," Mike said bluntly. "Again, water, duck."

"All my constituent wants is his little girl back," the senator said tightly. "Please?"

"Big contributor?" Mike asked, flipping through the file.

"Yes," the senator admitted. "Very large."

"Good," Mike said, closing the file and looking at the senator again. "Because this isn't going to be a freebie. I won't be able to lone-wolf this one. I'll need an intel team and shooters most likely. This is likely to get bloody."

"I believe that you already got a fairly substantial IMF grant . . ." the senator said, frowning.

"Hah!" Mike said, chuckling. "That's barely earnest money. You have any idea how much an op like this is going to cost me?"

"I suppose I should," the senator said, nodding. "A million?"

"More like five," Mike said, frowning. "It's going to be expensive on my end. I'll submit a cost sheet at the end. He'd better pay up."

"That won't be an issue," the senator said.

"You want her extracted?" Mike asked.

"Just found," the senator replied. "When we know where she is, we can use other channels to get her out. Legal channels. I trust that I don't have to suggest that my name not come up if anything . . . untoward occurs."

"I'm very discreet," Mike replied, standing up. "But when I send you the bill, your friend had better pay it. Because if he doesn't, you will."

Mike perused the file as the Gulfstream crossed the Atlantic. Finding the girl wasn't going to be easy but that wasn't what was bothering him. The girl in the photos was certainly pretty enough, but she didn't look like a girl having a great time at the beach. And he was sure the picture wasn't taken in the U.S. The rocks along the beach were limestone or something similar. There simply weren't any major beaches in the U.S. that had limestone around them. Not like the stuff in the pic, anyway. He'd put money on the pic being taken on the Adriatic or Black Sea coast. And the bathing suit she was wearing in the one pic and the dress in the other were European, not American.

On the other hand, the unnamed "constituent" was an immigrant. The pics might have been taken in the Old Country. But the girl's eyes . . . she was not enjoying having her picture taken. It wasn't teenage surliness. She was resigned and unhappy.

Mike frowned and looked close at the bathing suit pic. He wished he had a magnifying glass with him because it looked very much as if the girl had a large bruise on her abdomen. Like from a punch.

The whole op had a bad feel to it. The minor State Department official contacting him, the senator, the pictures. It just didn't add up.

Well, he'd know he'd found out what was really going on when it started to stink.

"Well, it would certainly be nice to have some support from the other side of the aisle," Nielson mused as he looked at the pictures. "And the lady is certainly charming enough in a naifish sort of way."

"Tracking her's going to be a stone bitch, though," Adams pointed out. "Most of the gangs running this racket in that region are Albanians. They're right bastards and mostly come from Albanian clans. They all know each other, so we won't be able to insert anyone."

"Not on the runner's side," Mike said, rubbing his chin.

"What are you thinking?" Nielson asked, looking up.

"I'm thinking that we need Vanner and Cottontail in here," Mike replied.

"That's the op," Mike said looking at Vanner and the Russian hooker. Cottontail was sitting up and apparently paying rapt attention but that could mean anything. Mike had picked her up from the local brothel, very much against his will. The girl was pure poison. Either as a result of her experiences as a sex-slave or from nature she was a vicious sociopath and delighted in making life for everyone around her miserable. Since she'd been living at the caravanserai, Mike had kept her from being too much trouble by keeping her busy, first in studies and then later working with Vanner in the intelligence section. The girl was smart as hell, which was part of the problem; as a whore she'd been underutilized.

But she had the makings of a first class agent. She simply had no soul and was a great actress.

"How are you planning on tracking her?" Vanner asked curiously.

"Well, the first line is that we're going to pay a trip to the pimp and ask him nicely what happened to the girl," Mike said, then looked over at Cottontail. "The other string rests with you."

"You want me to go into that," the girl said, waving at the papers.

"It's not like you don't know the moves," Mike replied flatly.

"What's in it for me?" Cottontail asked, just as flatly.

"Money," Mike said. "Twenty thousand euros for the entire op, assuming you do your job. And you'll get to fuck over the sort of guys that made you a whore. We're going to be having a lot of polite and charming conversation with them."

"Do I get to watch?" Cottontail asked seriously.

"If it fits the mission," Mike said. "And I'll guarantee you that we'll be following. I won't say bad things won't happen to you, but we're going to be on your ass the whole way. I guarantee you won't be stuck back in the system and we'll try damned hard to keep you alive. But mostly it will be up to you. You in?"

Cottontail looked at him coldly for a moment then nodded.

"At the very least, take pictures," she said, suddenly grinning in a way that was truly scary.

"Will do," Adams replied. Of all the men who knew her, Adams was perhaps the only one who liked her. At least in part because he liked right bastards.

"We're going to need to fill out the team," Mike said. "We'll need an intel and operational section and a group of shooters and security. We're going to have to insert across multiple borders, through multiple police jurisdictions and, worse, into multiple gang territories. And after a bit the fact that we're closing on something might become obvious. The intel section . . ."

"Tracking devices," Vanner said, looking at the ceiling. "Bugs. Cameras. Shotgun mikes. Body mikes . . ."

"You're on it," Mike said, looking at Adams. "The shooters . . ."

"Team Sawn is dialed in on entry techniques," Adams said. "Break it down four ways. One team for entry, one for security, attached to each main group. We'll need vehicles . . ."

"The white vans the traffickers use," Nielson said, nodding. "Plenty of room and . . ."

"The Keldara girls that are handling intel and commo will just look like more whores on their way west," Mike said, nodding. "With the shooters as their guards. We got us a plan?"

"Well," Nielson said with a sniff. "It's a start."

# ★ Chapter Nine ★

Mike considered the border crossing as the six vans approached it. It had just flat taken six vans for all the team and their gear.

Set up of the operation had only taken three days. Vanner had many of the items they were going to need on hand and the few that he didn't were more available in the Ukraine than in Georgia. The route had taken them through the Ukraine, and a brief stop at Dnipropetrovsk filled in the gaps. Weapons were easy; the Keldara were very well armed.

However, travelling to Moldava had taken some time. The roads in Georgia and the Ukraine ranged from bad to just awful. And given that the vans were packed with foreign nationals using fake passports and enough weapons for a small coup, discreet travel was the byword. They'd mostly stayed off the major roads, which meant not only circuitous travel but staying mostly on the "just awful" roads.

By the end of the week's trek, Mike felt as if his kidneys had been shaken out through his sinuses.

However, they'd made it to the Moldavan border. The

problem then was that the out-of-the-way border crossing near Ribnita, which according to reports was unguarded, had a couple of Moldavan soldiers running a checkpoint.

"Be of good cheer and tip heavily," Mike said. The headset dangling from his ear was a bit out of the ordinary for white slavers but it wasn't entirely out of character. "Hand me your passports," he continued, looking to the rear of the vehicle.

The seats right behind the driver's were filled by three Keldara in work clothes and jeans. Their heavy-cotton button-down shirts were untucked so the pistols at their waist were concealed. Poorly in a couple of cases, but concealed. The rest of their gear was packed in the cargo area of the van, stuffed into several discreet pullman bags. He just had to hope that the border guards didn't want to search them or they'd find far more than they bargained for.

Behind them were four girls from Vanner's intel section in blouses and jeans. The latter had caused some screaming from the more traditional Keldara but Mike had thrown the weight of the Kildar behind the decision. The girls were potentially vital to the operation and they had to fit in. Most women didn't wear skirts when travelling, even in this part of the world. A couple of the girls had looked askance when told they were going to dress in pants, but most of them had taken to them with glee. Change was coming to the Keldara in the form of Levi's 505s.

In the last set of seats were four more Keldara heavies, the entry team portion of the shooters. They also had pistols holstered at their belts but in addition they had sub-guns under the seat. Mike dearly hoped that they weren't going to start the op by killing a couple of Moldavan soldiers. That would be . . . bad.

"Hello," Yevgenii said to the soldier as he rolled to a stop next to him. "How are you today?"

"I'm out here on this shit road," the soldier grumped as the passports were handed across.

"At least it's not raining," Yevgenii said happily.

Mike looked around carefully. There were only two, the soldier taking the passports and his companion, who was leaning against a tree by the side of the road. If worse came to worse, they could probably take them both down without bloodshed.

The soldier flipped through the passports, pulling out a bill from the top one and pocketing it.

"You are from Georgia?" the soldier asked.

"Yes," Yevgenii said, grinning. "We are a church group going to visit monasteries in your country and Romania."

"And I'm the High Prelate," the soldier replied, handing the passports back. "It is lonely out here, how about some time with one of your girls?"

Mike blinked at the suggestion. It wasn't one he'd run across before, but he'd never been masquerading as a white slaver.

"I think that could be arranged," Mike said, smiling. "I have just the girl for you . . ."

"That one looks good," the soldier said, pointing in the window at one of the Keldara girls. As it turned out it was Vanda, one of Yevgenii's first cousins. He could see the Keldara slowly turning purple at the suggestion.

"No, no," Mike said, trying to keep the desperation out of his voice. If he didn't get this guy to go for Cottontail there was going to be blood on the walls. As he was thinking that, the other soldier started to wander over, wondering what was going on. "I have a very pretty one for you and your friend," Mike continued, hitting his mike. "Adam . . . ovich, tell Cottontail she's got a special duty up front." He only remembered at the last moment to use Russian and he knew he still had an accent. He wasn't supposed to be talking at all! Damn Yevgenii!

"We will want one for each of us," the soldier said, looking in the van at the back. "And I still like that one by the window. She is very pretty and has good tits."

"Kildar . . ." one of the Keldara muttered from the backseat.

"Silence," Mike snapped. "I have a girl coming up for you. She is very good, very pretty and can take you both at once if you wish." He glanced in his rear-view and sighed in thankfulness as he saw Cottontail walking up the line of vehicles. There were a couple of cars stopped behind the line of vans, now. This was going downhill fast.

"Hi, boys," Cottontail purred as she came around the van to the driver's side. "You want some company?"

The Keldara women were justly famous for their beauty but Cottontail had most of them equalled at least. And when she put her mind to it, she could exude a sort of raw sensuality that was riveting. What was most riveting was that she looked like a teen virgin, even if she'd been with more men than a dockside whore and had the soul of Jeffrey Dahmer. Part of the strength of her act was that men rarely really looked at her eyes. Oh, they were stunningly beautiful, but men never got beyond that. They didn't see the little fire of hell burning in the rear of them. Or if they did they thought it was just lust, not pure evil.

"She will be good to you," Mike said, waving them away. "We will pull our vans to the side until you are . . . done."

Mike got out and waved the vans forward and to the side of the small back road, then walked down the line, wishing he smoked. He needed something to steady his nerves. He was fine if it was a matter of killing everyone in the building, hole, ship or even town. But this shit was for somebody who enjoyed it.

He also took the time to wave the two cars that had been waiting through, and then found the chief in the fourth van.

"What was that all about?" Adams asked.

"The soldiers were bored and horny," Mike said, sharply. "They thought it would be a good way to pass the time to 'borrow' Vanda as part of their tip."

"The Moldav bastards," Sedama snarled from the driver's seat as the rest of the Keldara muttered angrily.

"Yevgenii nearly blew his top," Mike snapped. "But this sort of thing is going to come up. Handle it. Talk your way through. I'll tell you when you can kill someone. Don't kill anyone until I tell you. Is that clear?"

"Clear Kildar," Sedama replied, breathing out. "So Cottontail is taking care of it?"

"Yes," Mike said, still angry. As much at himself as at the situation. He should have prepared for it.

"And on another crossing when we don't have her along?" one of the Keldara in the rear of the van asked.

"I'm going to have to think about that one," Mike

admitted. "Giving up the Keldara women is, clearly, out of the question."

"I dunno," another Keldara said. "There's always Anisa . . ."

"Hey!"

Mike was leaning on the front of the lead van, looking at a map, when Cottontail came back out of the woods wiping at the corner of her lip with her thumb.

"Everybody satisfied?" Mike asked, cautiously. He hadn't told her she was going to have to bribe border guards and he felt curiously shamed by the incident. It wasn't as if she hadn't screwed enough men for two more to be no big deal.

"They are," she replied, archly.

"And are they alive?" With Cottontail you always had to ask.

"Yes," she admitted. "I considered it, but it would interfere with the mission, no?"

"Yes, it would," Mike said.

"And the mission is killing many slavers. This is a mission I like. I would not want it to fail."

Her eyes were as clear and innocent blue as a child's.

Chisinau was the capital of the small country of Moldava. Moldava was more an agreed upon border state between Russia and Romania than a real country. Russia had troops on the east side of the Dniester River to support the local Slavic ethnic groups so the central government couldn't really call that "their" territory. The situation was so bleak, they'd even elected a communist as president and more or less regressed to a semi-communist, sort of Stalinist, failed state. Totally landlocked, the poorest country in Europe, its total exports were limestone, hookers and people looking for a real life somewhere else.

The team had been installed at the Hotel Stalin on the outskirts of town. The hotel was near an industrial area and if Chisinau had a better and worse part of town, it was in the worst. In keeping with the general dilapidation of the neighborhood, the hotel looked as if it had been used by every rocker at Woodstock. The carpet, where it wasn't pulled up entirely, was about fifty years old and poorly made then. The rooms were filthy, the corridors were littered and the bathrooms didn't bear description.

It also was doing a booming business. They'd barely been able to get enough rooms for all of them and when Mike checked out their fellow travellers he could see why. They weren't the only people bringing girls through Moldava.

He wandered down to the bar, which gave "dive" a whole new meaning, and looked over the offerings. To his amazement, they had Johnny Walker Red.

"Walker," he said, perching on the rickety stool. The bar was about half filled and the clientele was telling. The men were all beefy and from various bulges mostly armed. The women were all wearing damned near nothing and given the temperatures in the bar they had to be freezing. Most of them also seemed rather . . . subdued. As in "if I make a wrong sound, my pimp is going to beat the shit out of me. In public. And nobody will care."

One of the girls had just had her head pushed under the table when he sensed someone coming up from his off-side.

"Where you in from?" a man said in Russian as he settled in the seat next to Mike.

"Georgia," Mike said, honestly.

"Strange accent," the man said, frowning. "You're not Georgian."

"American," Mike admitted. "This is a way to pay the bills and the fringe benefits are great."

"Now we've got Americans in the game," the man grumped. "I am Ahmed Pasha. I saw some of your girls, though. Very nice. How much?"

"I'm taking them to Montenegro for an auction," Mike said. "They're not for sale. Mike Duncan."

"I saw one, a blonde, very big breasts," the man replied. "I'll give you a thousand euros and you won't have to feed her from here to Montenegro. I don't keep them, myself, you know. I am broker and move them. I know men will give me good price for her."

"I can get better money there," Mike said, laughing. "The buyers are special, pimps with wealthy clients. They want virgins or damned near. Clean and undamaged so they can have them first and hard. That's why I've got so much muscle with me, so the girls don't have to be disciplined. I'll go with the plan. What's the word on the roads west?"

"Ungheni was covered when I came back through," Pasha said. "You have to go all the way up to Balti to get through without a check. But the guards on Balti will usually take only five euros per passenger. They prefer euros. Here in Chinisau so many girls come through, so many men. Some have do this long time, some, like you, just getting started. I know everybody, can find best price for you. Fifteen hundred. She was very lovely. The one wearing the blue blouse. Very nice breasts. Very nice. I, too, have special customers and girls that good are getting hard to find."

"They had guards on Ribnita," Mike replied. "Five euros per passenger and they wanted a freebie. Fortunately I had one that had already been broken in or I'd have been out a lot of money. I've only been doing this for a while, yeah, but I've got a covered racket. Just me and my partner and we cut out the middlemen. When we're done with them we sell them to guys like you; my partner handles that. No dice. Not even in the game. That's Vanda and I'm looking at damned near ten grand for her first. You'd just dump her into the pipeline; if you've got special customers I'm the pope. What was happening in Romania?"

"Not much until you get near Cluj-Napoca," the man said. "There was a checkpoint on the E-60 near Tarnaveni. Real bastards when I went through west. They acted like I was transporting my girls for immoral purposes and against their will. The shame. And it was very expensive in bribes. Ten thousand in dollars or euros? It doesn't matter, that is crazy. I can buy twenty girls for that."

"Don't know how far east you're going, but we hit one like that near Novyi Buh," Mike replied. "I explained to one of the girls that she had to talk us through. Or else. I understand, though, that there was a crackdown in Odessa and some of the guys are looking to move their more noticeable girls. You could probably get some good trades. And she's not really for sale, anyway."

"I operate here," Pasha said. "Although I buy Ukrainian girls. And if you have any more like those, next time through, I'll give you a good deal. I know all the men who buy and sell. I wonder who you know in Montenegro? Ammad? Tufa?"

"Neither," Mike said. "Very small network; I doubt you've run into it. We get high price girls and charge Westerners, mostly American, for the privilege of breaking them in. Charge them through the nose. You have to have the contacts for that. My partner is connected in the States. Then we dump them in the regular channels. We're in the market for those types of girls, though. Bringing these all the way from Georgia is a pain. You know a guy named Smegnoff? I understand he's got some girls that I might want to buy."

"Everyone has got girls," Pasha said, shrugging. "Smegnoff, yes, he has some good ones sometimes. If you really want to see him, he is in the Café Arrendi in the evening. But so do my suppliers. And we don't use them as hard as he does. He had one girl that tried to run away, so he broke her knees. She can walk only with a limp, now. Very sad." He didn't seem terribly broken up about it.

"I need them unused," Mike said, standing up and tossing a twenty euro bill on the bar. "I can do with a couple of very high quality girls, very pretty, virgins, young. I'll give you a good deal on them. I'll be around for a couple of days if you get anything worth talking about."

"Well, we're established," Mike said as he came into the room the team was using as a command post. Vanner was already in place with various electronic gadgets set up and a wire discreetly running out the window. "The agreed cover: we're running high quality girls to Montenegro for a special auction. I put out the word that we're in the market for unspoiled girls."

"I've gotten Smegnoff's cell phone plotted," Vanner said, nodding. He had a set of cup headphones on with one cup dangling. "He's about a half a kilometer southeast of here which plots out as . . ."

"The Café Arrendi," Mike said, grinning as the intel specialist turned to look at him. "Already got the word."

"What's the play?" Adams asked.

"Work him," Mike said. "Then get him someplace quiet and have a nice long chat."

# ★ Chapter Ten ★

The Café Arrendi was a "coffee shop" that fronted for a brothel. It was on a minor street in south Chisinau that was the center of what passed for a red-light district. The traffic movement along the road was slow since business, even in the early morning hours, was brisk. Girls lined both sides of the streets, waving at the passing cars and rapidly boarding those that stopped.

"Pull over, here," Mike said as the van reached the front of the shop. He noticed that none of the girls were waving for them to stop; it was apparent what the van was used for.

What the darkened windows cloaked, however, were five Keldara in full body armor, cradling MP-5s. If anything "untoward" went down in the coffee shop, their job was to extract Mike, and Smegnoff, alive. And since Mike was the Kildar, they were very serious about that mission.

Mike rolled out of the van and stepped between two cars to the curb. He noticed that besides the girls there were men, most of them heavyset and wearing bad suits, scattered along the road. He wasn't sure if they were there to make sure the girls kept working or as external security on the coffee shop. He did spot what was probably the

Lada the picture of Smegnoff was taken by. Of course, there were three other Ladas parked within less than a block of it, but it was nearly opposite the coffee-shop and the right color and trim.

The interior of the shop was run down with rickety tables and chairs and a filthy floor. Mike was almost afraid to try the coffee, but it wasn't all that bad. The girls working the counter were the most rode-hard-and-put-up-wet duo he'd ever seen, a hollow-faced girl with black hair and a bleached blonde. Both were dressed in skin-tight tube dresses and clearly were supposed to be advertising. If they were, they were advertisements for getting every venereal disease ever discovered and probably a few that were barely known.

Mike had spotted Smegnoff when he walked in. The pimp was in a corner with two other males. They had the scent of muscle and helpers at "breaking" girls. They were larger than the pimp but Mike figured if it came down to cases he could take all three of them. And the Keldara fire team was waiting in a van outside.

He sipped the espresso as he drifted over to the table.

"You're Smegnoff," Mike said, sitting down uninvited.

"And you're the new American," Smegnoff said, smirking. "I hear you're in the market for girls."

"Top quality, only," Mike said, nodding and ignoring the muscle. "Pretty, young and untouched."

"What is the fun of selling untouched girls?" Smegnoff sneered.

"Money," Mike said, shrugging. "You can get pussy anywhere. But young, virgin pussy, that's real money if you've got the right customers."

"I have customers like that," Smegnoff said, shrugging. "A few. Everyone does."

"Well, that's my main clientele," Mike said. "I hear you sometimes get pretty top quality girls."

"They're around," Smegnoff said, nodding and eyeing the former SEAL. "Not all the time, you know?"

"Anything at the moment?" Mike asked. "Or, for that matter, anything you can steer me to that hasn't been raped yet?"

"Not right now," Smegnoff said. "But they will be expensive."

"We'll bargain," Mike said. "I'm in town for two days letting the ladies rest. Then we're gone. You've got that long."

"I've got a shotgun mike set up on the Arrendi," Vanner said when he got back. "But his car has a heavy by it. I can't get a tracer on it; the Keldara were too obvious."

Mike looked around the room at the Keldara females and rubbed his chin.

"What are you thinking?" Yevgenii asked, eyeing the Kildar uncomfortably.

"Anisa," Mike said, glancing at the Keldara girl. She was a lovely young brunette with long legs and a classical face.

"Yes, Kildar?" the girl asked, curiously.

"Would you be willing to pose as a hooker?" Mike asked. "We're going to run into this problem again. I could send Cottontail to do it, but what I'd like is to send both of you. One of you to distract the guard, the other to plant the tracer. That way if we have to do it again, or something like it, after Cottontail is inserted you'll have experience. You'll have a Keldara backup team, of course."

"What would I have to do?" the girl asked uncertainly.

"Well, the first thing is getting into character," Mike said.

"I cannot wear this in public!" Anisa wailed.

The tube dress was, okay, pretty darned short. And the girl had clearly never worn high heels in her life. Cottontail, who could walk in them like most girls walked in flats, was smirking as the Keldara female attempted to balance on the top of the stiletto sandals.

Cottontail and Killjoy had been sent out shopping and had come back with everything that Anisa needed to look like a hooker. And the girl did, albeit a rather expensive one.

"I'm having problems with this," Adams said in English, shaking his head.

"So am I," Mike admitted. "But I think it's the best plan to go with."

"Oh, it's not the plan," Adams replied. "I'm wondering how much we could get for her . . ."

"Don't go there," Mike snapped, shifting to Georgian. "Anisa, you look perfect. You'll be fine. All you have to do is walk up to the car with Katya, lean up against it while she talks to the guard, plant the tracer and then walk away with her. You'll be under observation the whole time and the Tigers will be there if anything goes wrong. But nothing will. You'll do fine."

"I cannot walk down the street in this!" Anisa said. "I look like a whore!"

"Uhmm . . ." Vanner said. "That's sort of the point."

Anisa opened her mouth to respond and then shut it when she couldn't think of a reply.

"Well . . ." she said after a moment, half triumphantly. "How am I supposed to carry it dressed like this? Where am I going to hide it?"

"It's not that large," Vanner said, pulling out a gray rectangle that was about the size and general shape of a cigarette lighter. "It's got a contact adhesive on one side. I suppose you should hide it somewhere where it's out of sight and easy . . . to . . . access. . . ." He trailed off.

Anisa looked at him blankly then over at the Kildar.

"On your leg, right up in your crotch is what he doesn't want to say," Mike said bluntly. "For that matter, you might be able to simply palm it. Keep it in your fist. The problem with that is that people will assume it's money or something."

"I don't think this is going to work," Anisa said, holding out her hand for the device.

Vanner helpfully peeled the cover off the contact adhesive and handed it over.

"You can turn your back, now," Anisa said, looking at the men.

"Oh," Mike said, turning around, "right."

Anisa looked at Katya, who was standing with her arms folded, watching, and then shrugged. She took the small rectangle and, spreading her legs slightly, stuck it to the inside of her thigh.

"You can still see it," Anisa said triumphantly.

"Higher," Katya said, sighing angrily.

"If I put it any higher it will be inside of me!" Anisa protested.

"And the problem with that is . . . ?" Katya asked. "Besides, it won't. Just put it higher. There is plenty of room. You just have to actually touch yourself. Don't tell me you've never touched that part before."

"Cottontail . . ." Mike warned.

"Ow! Ow!" Anisa exclaimed as she peeled it back off. "That hurts!"

"It's . . . pretty strong adhesive," Vanner replied, his back still turned.

"Oh, no," Anisa said as she fumbled under the dress.

"What now?" Mike asked in exasperation.

"It's . . . caught," Anisa said, blushing. "On . . . hair. Down there."

"You should have waxed," Cottontail replied, her arms still crossed. "This is silly. Let me carry it."

"I don't think Anisa is up to chatting up a guard," Mike pointed out. "Do you have it in place?"

"Yes," Anisa said, adjusting her dress. "You can look again."

"Now, try walking in the heels," Mike said.

Anisa carefully tottered across the room, stopped at the far side and turned without actually falling down.

"This is insane," Katya said, angrily. "Just let me do it! I can chat up the guard and plant it!"

"She needs to learn," Mike said. "We can't be depending on you to do all the outside work. Anisa, one foot in front of the other, like you're walking on a narrow beam. Move your hips with the motion and your shoulders against it. Undulate. Try it."

Anisa sighed and started back. She did pretty well until she got her hips and shoulders out of sync and Adams had to catch her before she fell.

"Nobody had better ever find out about this," she hissed, pushing herself back up. The chief had been exceedingly careful with his hands, but there wasn't much he could catch that wasn't off-limits. He'd managed by wrapping both hands around her waist. This caused her dress to head north and south, respectively, which very nearly left her unclothed. At least in important areas.

"Try it again," Mike said sternly. "This is training. You are going to be doing a mission every bit as important as the door-kickers. They had to train; you have to train. If I'd thought ahead, I would have brought one of the harem. I didn't. This is my fault. Drop it on me. But we're going to need you to be able to do this. And maybe more than just you. You'll be training at least one other girl in the same things. Get used to it. And everyone is going to know about it. You're going to have a security team watching you."

"Okay, okay," Anisa said, readjusting her dress. "Here goes."

By the end of thirty minutes with Mike coaching her and Katya inserting snarky, but pertinent, remarks, she could walk in the heels and even undulate. A bit. Enough to look like a new hooker on the street.

As the two left, Adams let out a long sigh.

"I'm going to have to either go down on the street and hire a girl or go take a long cold shower," the chief said. "That was just . . ."

"Erotic as hell," Mike replied. "You can understand

why these pimps do what they do. Besides the money, which in this society is nothing to sneeze at."

"It almost makes me rethink my choice of career," Adams admitted. "And they get to do this all the time."

"And beat the girls around when they screw up," Mike added.

"I'm not particularly into beating on women," Adams said, shrugging.

"Well, most of the girls they get don't exactly want to be hookers," Mike pointed out. "And even the ones that do don't want to give up most of their hard-earned money to the pimps. So they beat on them until they learn better. It's a sucky situation. And you know the fun part?"

"What?" Adams asked, frowning curiously.

"How many whores have you fucked in some third world shit-hole?" Mike asked, turning to look at him. "We're the reason this goes on. You can't just say 'it's males' when you're one of the males that benefited by it."

"Tell me something I don't know." Adams shrugged. "I don't notice you losing sleep over it."

"I do, sometimes," Mike admitted. "And I'm the one that enjoys beating on women. I wish I had the money to buy up every whore and potential whore on the planet and put them somewhere safe."

"But if you did, you'd just have more kidnappings."

"There's that," Mike admitted, sighing.

"You ever think about this whole system as a good thing?" Adams asked.

"What in the hell do you mean by that?" Mike snarled.

"Think about it," Adams replied calmly. "In the States, the predators snatch some girl off the street, rape her and kill her. Here they snatch them off the street, rape them and then sell them. Alive."

"Now there's a hell of a thought and no lie," Mike said quietly. "But you think that some of them don't die in the process?"

"No, a bunch of them do," Adams admitted. "But a bunch of them live, too. For a given value of life. Which means still breathing. Concentrate on bringing home a live one and leave the fucking existentialism for after the mission, SEAL."

"Will do, Chief," Mike said, grinning.

"Now I'm gonna go find some abused, raped, forced-to-be-a-whore whore and fuck her silly ass off. For cash. Without beating on her. End of angst."

# ★ Chapter Eleven ★

"I don't know where to look," Anisa said, nervously trying to adjust her dress so she wasn't showing so much skin.

"Anywhere but at the cars," Cottontail said easily. She clearly didn't care if her dress was riding up. Or down. She looked as if she was terribly bored and more than willing to just have the damned thing fall off. "If you look at the drivers they might stop. That would be good on one level; we'd look like we were actual working girls. But we'd have to turn down the offer. Unless you're planning on doing a trick while you're doing this and I don't suggest it."

"I'm not," Anisa snapped.

"Well, that's one problem off my mind," Cottontail said, smirking. "You might want to try it, though. You don't have a pimp to take all the money and cash is cash. Well, the Kildar might want a cut."

"I'm not going to . . . do that with a man other than my husband," Anisa said.

"And probably the Kildar, right?" Cottontail said, snidely. "For your 'bride price,' right? What do you think that is but turning a trick? Maybe you could work up the bride price while you're here . . ."

"Stop it," Anisa said angrily. "Just . . . stop, okay? We're here to work."

"Well, it's work . . ." Cottontail said, trailing off. "There's the car."

"I see it," Anisa said, nodding.

"Don't look directly at it." Cottontail looked around. "Look at the other girls, instead."

Anisa looked around and sighed.

"They are all dressed so . . ."

"Sluttily," Cottontail said, laughing nastily. "Men like that. They like to have women that are fast, cheap and easy. They don't have to worry about whether we like it or not. Most of them like that we don't. They like to hurt us, to use us, to make us feel less than they are."

"Not the Kildar," Anisa pointed out.

"Even the Kildar," Katya replied sharply. "He likes that he owns us, that he can use us."

"He treats you well," Anisa protested.

"But he still owns us," Cottontail snapped, turning to look at the girl and waving at the whores along the street. "We're no better than these! We're owned by the Kildar and he uses us at his pleasure! The only difference is we don't walk the street! We just live in his brothel for the use of him and his friends."

"He said he offered to let you all go," Anisa argued unhappily.

"To where?" Katya snapped back. "What can we do but make our way on our backs? There are plenty of girls here who chose to be here, because even this is better than wherever they're running from! Because they don't have any other choice but to sell their bodies. They don't have a family to go back to . . ." She stopped and turned away, her face hard.

"Is that what happened to you?" Anisa asked quietly as they continued walking.

"I don't talk about it," Cottontail said bitterly.

"Do you have a family?" Anisa asked, still quietly.

"Just shut the fuck up, okay?" Katya replied. "We're nearly there and we need to get our game face on."

"Okay," Anisa said nervously. She very carefully did not adjust the lower part of her dress.

The guard was a beefy guy in a sweat-stained shirt and trousers. He was leaning on the hood of the car, casually watching the girls on the street. In Anisa's opinion, if he was supposed to be guarding the car, he was looking at the wrong people. Or, maybe not, given what she was planning on doing.

"Hi, big guy," Katya said in Russian. "My friend and I were having an argument."

"I saw," the man said stolidly.

"I say that you can tell the length of a guy's parts by his hands," Katya said, slinking up to him. "And I notice you've got really big hands . . ."

Anisa smiled in what she hoped was a winning way and leaned up against the hood, turning away slightly. Patrick had told her the easiest way to place the device would be in the wheel well. The device had a magnet and the adhesive so it should stay.

"What do you say?" Katya asked, leaning up against the guard. "How are you . . . hung?"

"Well enough for you," the man said, less stolidly. "Care to find out?"

"Maybe," Katya said, coyly. "I've just had an hour session with a guy whose dick was smaller than my finger. And I could do more with my finger than he could with his dick. Do you think you could do better?"

Anisa reached up under her skirt and ripped off the tracer, trying not to whimper as she pulled out a fingerful of pubic hair. Katya was right; she should have shaved. She never had but she'd heard about it. It seemed terribly . . . whorish. Okay, so she should have shaved.

She turned back towards the guard, slipping her hand under the wheel well and pressing the tracer into place.

"I'm busy now," the guard said, sliding his hand up Katya's dress and fingering her. "I'll be off in about an hour."

"And I'll get you off in much less," Katya said, pouting. "But I'll see you then. You're going to be around here?"

"For sure," the guard said, running his hand over her breasts. "I'll look forward to it. Bring your friend."

"Sure will," Katya said, walking off. "She needs the attention of a real man, too."

"He stinks," Anisa said as they walked away.

"So do most of the Keldara," Katya replied. "So do most tricks, at least around here. It's like they've never heard of soap. Now let's get back to the hotel and maybe I can get some hot water to wash his stink off."

"He's moving," Tolenka said.

"Got it," Jov replied, putting the car in gear. The four-year-old gray Lada had been purchased earlier in the day in a very informal transaction involving cash and a promise to get the tags transferred. It was less conspicuous for a stakeout than one of the vans. But a van was right around the corner, loaded with shooters. For that matter, there was an MP-5 at Tolenka's feet.

"The tracer's working fine," Endar said, looking at the screen on his lap.

"Don't pull out, yet," Killjoy said from the backseat. He was one of the American trainers who had accompanied the mission. The Keldara were getting pretty damned good as shooters, but they still didn't know diddly about moving around in the world. Killjoy wasn't exactly a world traveller but he had more experience than the Keldara and could think on his feet. He also was somewhat smaller than Russell, which was why he was crammed in the back of the small car.

"He had a couple of girls with him," Tolenka added.

"Could mean anything," Killjoy noted.

"Speaking of girls," Jov replied. "I couldn't believe it when I saw Anisa!"

"Watch your mouth," Endar snapped. Not only was Anisa his cousin, he'd worked with her in the intel section and respected her.

"I'm not saying anything wrong," Jov said, smiling. "But . . . All Father! I never realized what legs she had!"

"Jov . . ." Endar said, angrily.

"Can it," Killjoy said. "Jov, pull out. Endar, where'd he go?"

"He turned. Right. I think about three blocks away."

"Turn right at the next street," Killjoy said, looking at the map. "He's headed across the river. We'll parallel, then fall in behind at the Soseua or whatever that damned road is called."

★ ★ ★

"He's gone to a townhouse across the river," Vanner said, looking at his screens. "Confirm it's him by intercept. He called someone named Vass and asked him if he had any girls meeting your requirements. Also if he'd ever heard of you. No indication that he's worried about Americans coming down on him."

"Odd, that," Mike said musingly. He was ensconsed on the bed with his fingers interlaced behind his head, looking at the ceiling. "She had to have told them that she was an American, right? She's at the very least a legal resident. And she would have told them her father would pay money to get her back. I mean, getting back a kidnap victim over here is no big deal. You pay off the police, they don't try to arrest the kidnappers."

"So what's really going on?" Vanner asked.

"That's what I'm going to find out," Mike said, sitting up. "Somewhere along the way. But right now, I need to know more about this guy. I'm heading for bed and so should you. By morning I want full intel on him."

"Got it," Vanner said.

"But put one of the girls on duty and you rack out," Mike added. "I'll be right next door."

"He went back to the townhouse last night at eleven," Vanner said, rubbing his eyes and sipping coffee. "He took two girls with him and no guards. Over the next six hours, girls came trickling in in ones and twos. Looks like about a dozen. There was at least one male present when he arrived and when he left he brought a different girl with him. The townhouse is two story, but it appears it may have a basement. I've got Sawn down at the building records office looking for blueprints. He returned to the coffee shop and has not left. Neither has the male at the townhouse and there appear to be at least three females still in the house. The surveillance team was relieved at seven AM. Overnight they put up three surveillance cameras and laid in two window microphones on the townhouse, one of them by his apparent office and another by his bedroom. You want the take?"

"Is it what I'd expect?" Mike asked, biting on an already stale roll.

"Pretty much," Vanner said. "The girls in the house are apparently not fully trained. They're in the process of being prepared, so to speak. This is the analysis from my section and I've audited enough of the take to agree. I'm a little reluctant to have the Keldara girls doing point on this. It's pretty brutal."

"They'll find out what it's all about when they get married," Mike said, shrugging. "Have a talk with them as a guy, though. I don't want them getting so emotionally scarred they're put off of sex for life. And who else is going to do it? The shooters?"

"Point," Vanner admitted. "We also placed two mikes in the coffee shop, near his usual table, and I've, of course, got his cell phone wired."

"If Adams ever shakes a leg, get him up to speed," Mike said. "I'm going to go shopping."

"Mr. Duncan," Ahmed Pasha said, sitting down next to him. "A little early for Johnny Walker is it not?"

"The sun's over the yardarm somewhere," Mike said, swirling his drink. "Do you live here?"

"No," Pasha said, lifting his chin and clicking in negation. "But it is a good place to conduct business. Many traders come in here. How are your girls?"

"Almost recovered from the rigors of the trip thus far," Mike said. "We're definitely leaving tomorrow morning."

"I have found one girl that would possibly meet your requirements," Pasha said, leaning over conspiratorily. "A young Ukrainian girl. Very nice, very pretty. Blonde. Not much in the breast department but unspoiled and very pretty. And they may yet grow; she is quite young."

"Works," Mike said, nodding. "Yours?"

"A friend's," Pasha said. "I can introduce you, if you wish."

"Pasha, you don't have any friends," Mike said. "What's your cut?"

"Ten percent," Pasha said. "Minimum of one hundred euros, cash."

"You really think this girl's worth a thousand euros?" Mike said with a laugh. "Right. Pull the other one."

"Pull the other what?" Pasha asked, confused.

"Sorry, doesn't translate," Mike replied. "I was saying that you were not being truthful with me. Girls here go for less than five hundred euros, even the best."

"This one is unspoiled," Pasha said, sternly. "She will get you much money where you are going. Enough that you will pay."

"We'll see," Mike said. "Here?"

"I have a room here," Pasha said. "Two eleven. That is neutral ground, yes?"

"Okay," Mike said with a sigh. "When?"

"I will call my friend," Pasha replied. "Perhaps soon after noon."

"Okay," Mike said. "I'll give you my cell number."

# ★ Chapter Twelve ★

Pasha's room, as befitted a more or less permanent resident, was much cleaner than the ones Mike had secured. That seemed to be mostly his doing. Whatever his failings as a slave trader, he was apparently quite neat in his housekeeping.

Mike was in an easy chair nursing another Johnny Walker when there was a knock at the door. When Pasha opened it, a man pushed a young girl into the room and then followed it up with a slap to the back of her head to make her step farther in.

"Here's the stupid slut I was talking about," the man said harshly. He was at least in his sixties with a red face and nose half hidden by a white beard. He'd make a nice Santa Claus and Mike wondered if he used that to pick up his victims.

The girl was clearly frightened, even terrified. And, yes, very pretty. About five one, long blonde hair and blue eyes. And no more than twelve. She was just starting to get the gangling growth spurt that kids hit at that age and might, indeed, grow some more tit. He wasn't sure she was even menstruating yet.

"Very nice," was what he said.

"Strip," Santa Claus ordered the girl.

"Please," she whimpered. "I just want to go home . . ."

"Strip, stupid whore . . ." Santa Claus snarled, drawing his hand back.

"No marks!" Mike snapped, standing up and walking over. "Girl, I must see what I'm buying. Take off your clothes."

"Please, no . . ." the girl begged, looking up at him with tears in her eyes.

"This is how you do it without marks," Mike said, sighing and gripping the back of the girl's head with his thumb and forefinger. He applied pressure, hard, and received a gasp as the girl's knees buckled at the pain. "Take off your clothes, you stupid slut."

The girl looked at the three hard-faced men and then closed her eyes and began removing her clothing.

When she was fully stripped, Mike walked around her, shaking his head. She had welts on her back, ass and budding breasts.

"You hit her on the breasts?" Mike asked angrily. "With what?"

"My belt, of course," Santa Claus snarled. "What do you expect me to do? She needs to be trained but I'm hardly up to it anymore!"

"Christ on a crutch," Mike muttered in English then continued in Russian. "These damned bruises will take weeks to fade! I'm planning on being in Montenegro the end of next week; she won't be presentable by then!"

"She's untouched," Santa Claus snapped. "She's a virgin. That is worth something."

"She's bruised," Mike snarled. "Two hundred."

"Forget it!" the slaver replied. "Put your clothes on, bitch."

"Wait, wait," Pasha said. "We are friends here. Let us sit and drink tea and talk."

The girl had quickly scooped up her dress and underthings in her hands but Pasha shook his head.

"No," he said to her, pulling the clothes out of unresisting hands. "Stand by the chairs; there is much to discuss."

Pasha poured green tea and laid out a service on the table as the girl stood by, shivering in the cold of the room. Mike ignored her, as did the others.

"You have at least a week of travel, if you are staying off the major roads," Pasha said, sipping his tea. "This will give most of the bruises time to fade."

"Not all of them," Mike said, poking the girl on the ass. "This one cut the skin for that matter. She'll scar."

"A virgin," Pasha noted.

"No proof of that," Mike pointed out. "She was probably raped by her uncle who sold her to this guy."

"I took her from an arcade," Santa Claus replied with a shrug. "These young girls, they trust me because I look like Saint Niklaus. And I did not rape her. Even with the Viagra, sticking it in young pussy like this is too hard. I use the older hookers who are looser."

The girl had put her face in her hands and was quietly crying when Mike stood up.

"Lie on the bed," Mike said, pushing her to the bed.

"If you take her here you must pay for . . ." Pasha said.

"I'm checking," Mike snapped. "Lie on the bed, on your back, with your knees up in the air."

"Please," the girl whimpered through the tears.

"Shut up and do what I said, slut, or you'll be hurt again," Mike said sternly.

When the girl was on the bed he stuck his fingers in her pussy and spread it as wide as he could. Even with the dim light in the room he could see the hymen and it was unbreached.

"Virgin all right," he admitted grumpily. "Get up and put your clothes on, bitch."

"There, a virgin," Pasha said, happily. "For that, two hundred is much too little. Fifteen hundred euros."

"You're crazy," Mike said, shaking his head. "No more than three. So, Santa, you ever go over to Romania?"

"No, only the Ukraine," Santa Claus replied as the girl finished dressing. "Little slut, sit on my new friend's lap and show him how biddable you can be."

Mike let the girl sit in his lap and ran his hands over her stomach as she quivered in fear. He was careful to try to skip the bruised areas but she still was quaking, which didn't help much. He had a very real problem with being the sort of son of a bitch he was playing and the entire scene was turning him on more than he liked. He knew the girl could feel a very solid erection under her pert little ass and he knew that made him not only a Class A son of a bitch but a pervert. Unfortunately, short of castration he wasn't sure what to do about his little problem. Other than killing bastards who actually let their demons out. Such as the two other males in the room.

They chatted about the bad roads, the problems with weather and the unreliability of finding virgins as they sipped green tea. From time to time one or another would make an offer. Mike almost walked when they balked at thirteen hundred euros until he realized that would be leaving this poor kid in their hands. He finally dickered them down to nine hundred euros but not a penny less. He only got the hundred euros off because of the bruises and by actually getting up and walking halfway to the door.

He pulled out the cash and forked it over with a grim face, then slapped the girl on the back of the head.

"If you think that you have had it bad so far, try to run away from me," Mike growled in her ear. "I will do terrible things to you. Terrible terrible things. Are you going to try to run?"

"No," the girl said, resignation in her voice.

"You could run from the old man, maybe," Mike pointed out. "But I can outrun you. And if I have to even hurry, not only will you not be a virgin by tomorrow, I will sell you to the worst whorehouse in Istanbul for seamen to fuck all day long. And the reason I will sell you there is because you will be too messed up for anyone else to buy you. Do you understand me?"

"Yes," the girl replied, her head down.

"Let us go," Mike said, nodding at Pasha and the still unnamed Santa Claus. "If you can get more like this, we can do business in the long term. But no marks!"

"I'll see what I can do," Santa Claus said, smiling and standing up. "It was good doing business with you."

"The same," Mike said graciously, taking the girl by the wrist and leading her to the door.

His rooms were a flight up and down the hallway. When he got to the command center room he paused.

"I'm glad you didn't run," he said, quietly. "The reason

is, I'm not a slaver and I would not want to have to hurt you. But you must not talk about what you see in here, do you understand?"

"No," the girl said fearfully.

"You will," Mike replied, knocking on the door.

One of the Keldara girls answered the knock and looked in surprise at the girl Mike still had by the wrist.

"Greznya," Mike said, thankfully. "Just the lady I needed. Come on, girl. What's your name, anyway?"

"Oksana," the girl said, quietly, her eyes widening as she saw the computers and electronics set up around the room.

"This is Greznya, Oksana," Mike said, gently pushing her farther into the room. "She's not a slave, not a whore. She works for me. We're doing something here and it's necessary that I act like a slaver. I'm sorry that you were put through that, but you are safe, now."

"Really?" Oksana asked, panting.

"Really, really," Greznya said, smiling. "This is the Kildar. He is a renowned fighter and he does not harm women."

"Unless I have to," Mike pointed out. "Sorry about what happened in there. But that fat bastard was about to smack you one across the face. Again."

"Come in," Greznya said, sighing. "We know something of what you have been going through and we are very sorry. Where are you from?"

"The Ukraine," Oksana said. "Near Kremenchug."

"Well, we have much to do," Greznya said, pulling her further into the room and settling her in a chair. "But we will see if there is a way to get you back there. You have family?"

"No," Oksana replied quietly. "I was raised in orphanage. They had sent me out only the day before. I was at a fair when the man, Hadeon, approached me. He offered to buy me lunch and I was very hungry. Then he said he could get me a good job in Italy."

"Which is one of the places you might have ended up," Mike said, sighing. "I won't speak as to the quality of the job, since that's rather obvious. I'm sorry, Oksana, but that story is very common. This is how many girls end up in places like this." He paused and looked around the room at the monitors. "Well, not like this."

"What is this?" Oksana asked, finally settling down. "What are you doing?"

"We're tracking a girl who was kidnapped, as you were," Greznya replied. "We know she came as far as here. We are trying to find out where she went."

"Why?" Oksana asked, suddenly tearing up again. "Why do you look for her when nobody cared about me!"

"Because her father is rich and has powerful friends," Mike said bluntly. "You have neither a rich father nor powerful friends. Well, you didn't." He looked at her and cocked his head on the side. "I'm not sure what we're going to do with you. I needed to buy you because it made our cover stronger, but I'm not sure what to do with you, now. I'd hoped you'd have a family to go home to."

"So you could get more money?" the girl asked unhappily.

"No, I have plenty of that," Mike said, waving his hand around the room. "This isn't cheap. No, you were going to be returned gratis. But with nobody to go home to . . . Well, that presents me with a problem. I'll think about it."

★ ★ ★

When Mike left the room, Oksana looked at Greznya with wide eyes.

"He is very strange," the girl whispered. "He frightens me."

"Well, you don't have to be frightened of him any more," Greznya replied. "And as for the being strange . . . you get used to it."

"We got anything different?" Mike asked as he wandered next door. Vanner had moved the data analysis section to the adjoining room since the other one was both crowded and busy.

"Very straightforward," Vanner said. "We haven't really had a lot of time to pin down his movements, but it looks like he mostly is a repeater."

"So we have a choice of taking him down at the café or at his house or in movement. And he's got, effectively, hostages, at each point."

"He didn't bring a girl back with him in the morning," Vanner pointed out. "If he doesn't tomorrow . . ."

"Works. I'll send Adams out to find a quiet spot."

# ★ Chapter Thirteen ★

"Bravo team in position."

Mike looked back at the van full of Keldara and nodded to Yevgenii.

"Alpha in position."

"Target is moving. Target is unaccompanied, repeat unaccompanied."

"Roll the op up," Mike said quietly.

"Roll up," Yevgenii repeated.

"Roll up confirmed," Vanner replied. "We are out of here in one five minutes. Team Charlie is in place to recover telltales."

"Don't forget to pay the bill," Mike muttered. "Don't send that."

"Roger," Yevgenii replied. They were both in civilian clothes with body armor underneath. The team in the back was in full battle rig. Smegnoff was a hard worker and it was just after dawn. He'd been heading back to the café to get some paperwork done. He also apparently counted down his cash in the back room. That was where the majority of his "associates" and his main base for farming his girls and doing deals were located.

"Target is repeating, repeating. Kramor Prospect so far."

"Get ready," Mike said, turning his head. "It looks like us. Close up."

"Close up," Yevgenii said as he started the van. "Close up."

Santos Street was two lane with cars parked along both sides. The van for Alpha team was parked in an alley halfway down the block.

"Closed up," the following team called. "Target is turning on Santos. One, two . . . Go! Go! Go!"

Yevgenii threw the van into drive while hammering the accelerator. The lightly loaded van jerked out into the road in a cloud of blue smoke and immediately began disgorging fighters in full battle dress, with MP-5s and silenced SPRs pointed at the oncoming Lada.

Smegnoff was a survivor of numerous street battles and he had quick reactions. He didn't bother to come to a full stop before throwing the Lada into reverse and hitting the accelerator. His problem was that the four year old Lada following him slammed into him from the rear and then went to full power, turning his car sideways across the street.

It was less than ten meters to the car and before he could try to drive out of the ambush the lead Keldara had smashed in his driver-side window. The second in line dropped his MP-5, drew a taser from his holster and fired it into the slaver.

In no more than seven seconds the slaver was in the back of the van, wrapped in rigger's tape, leaving only two smoking Ladas for the police to try to explain.

★ ★ ★

"Good morning, Yuri," Mike said pleasantly as the man's eyes flew open from the ammonia capsule. "Did you have a good rest? I'm sure you recognize the after-effects of chloroform; you've used it a time or two."

"Muh-wugfuh?" the man said through the rigger's tape on his mouth.

"Oh, sorry," Mike said, reaching up and ripping the tape off the man's face.

Yuri Smegnoff was taped to a chair that was firmly bolted into the middle of the floor of an abandoned factory. It had probably been a supervisor's chair when the factory had been in operation. Now it served Mike's uses perfectly. He had to give Adams a bonus for scrounging up the facility on such short notice. Another note to make; they needed to do more ground work at each stop. This wasn't the last such interrogation that they'd have to do.

"Ow! What the fuck is this? I don't know who you are but—"

"Yuri, Yuri," Mike said kindly. "All I am is an honest businessman trying to do a job. Now that job is for people who view you and me as no more than insects. In your case, one to be stepped upon. You've made some very powerful people very angry, Yuri. Now, this can go easy, or it can go hard. Let's make it easy, shall we?" He drew out a folder and pulled out a picture, flipping it in front of the man's face.

"Now, I know you see a lot of young women," Mike said nicely. "But I'm really hoping, for your sake, that you recognize this one. Because if you don't, I'm going to have to improve your memory."

"I . . . I do," Yuri said, licking his lips. "Yes, I remember her."

"Ah, good," Mike said. "Now, Yuri, there's a thing about my friends here," Mike said, gesturing at the Keldara standing behind the chair. Yuri hadn't even noticed them and when he turned around his eyes flew open. Mike had chosen two of the larger shooters and they were both holding MP-5s at port arms and wearing full battle armor. "They're really simple farmers from the back hills. And they're simple people. They have a very strong code of honor. So they really don't like lies. Not a bit. And since I'm their leader, I need to uphold that tradition. So, please, Yuri, let's not be lying as we go on. You do remember her, yes?"

"Yes," Yuri said, licking his lips again. "One of my catchers picked her up near the town square. She said she was Ukrainian, that she was looking for work."

"Go on," Mike said.

"Can I have some water?" Yuri asked, carefully. "I am very parched."

"It's an effect of fear," Mike pointed out. "It comes from the adrenaline. I'm sure that many of your little girls had very dry mouths. Did you give them water, Yuri? No, I thought not. So, you picked her up near the town square. And you brought her to your townhouse?"

"Yes," Yuri said, starting to breathe hard.

"And you settled her, there, I'd think," Mike said, raising an eyebrow. "We're men of the world; we know what that means. You dipped your wick and that of a couple of your guards. You beat her around and told her she belonged to you, now. All the rest of that sort of thing. Yes, Yuri?"

"Yes," the slaver said quietly. "But this is who you look for? She had no friends!"

"We'll get to that later," Mike said, smiling. "So, you settled her down and then what, Yuri? She's not walking the street for you. We've checked rather carefully. So, where'd she go, Yuri?"

"I did what I always do," the slaver said with false bravado. "I sold her. I don't remember to who."

"Ah, Yuri, Yuri," Mike said, reaching back and accepting a large sledgehammer from the Keldara. "Bad answer."

"No, look, I can try . . ." the man said as Mike moved the hammer back and then forward into his left knee.

When the screams died down, Mike leaned forward to the man's ear.

"Yuri, Yuri, my friend. We are friends, right? Yuri, that was a bad answer. Do you know why that was a bad answer, Yuri?"

"I need to remember . . ." Yuri whispered.

"It's because we've had your house and coffee shop bugged for the last day and a half," Mike replied. "You talked about how you keep careful records. You sold two girls yesterday, Ionna and Sofiya, to a man named Markov. We've got rather good pictures of all three of them. Sofiya is a lovely lady, isn't she? And you got seven hundred euros for her, as I recall. And you told Markov that you kept all of your information to hand, in your PDA. So, Yuri, why didn't you mention your PDA to me, please?"

"No names," Yuri gasped. "No names."

"Why, Yuri?" Mike asked, straightening up. "Because the men you sold her to are very dangerous? Yuri, I eat people like you, and the bad men you work with, for lunch. And is there something they can do to you that I'm not going to, Yuri, my friend, my buddy? So, who did you sell her to? Actually, what's the password for your PDA? My little geek friend would very much like to know. He says he's having trouble hacking it."

"Hey!" Vanner said from the back of the room. "These things aren't easy. He's used at least a ten point encryption and you can't just hammer them on the ground and pull out the info!"

"No, but I suppose that's possible with you, isn't it, Yuri?" Mike asked, smiling in his most friendly manner. "So, Yuri, password, please?"

"No names," the man gasped again then shrieked when Mike lightly kicked his knee.

"Yuri, Yuri, I grow tired of this," Mike said, picking up the sledge again.

"Please," Yuri said, eyeing the heavy hammer. "Please. I can't give you names."

"Oh, Yuri, and you were doing so well," Mike said, tossing the hammer onto his shoulder. "How many women have begged you, Yuri? Did the one that tried to run away beg you, Yuri? And why should I listen to your pleas when you didn't listen to theirs? So, Yuri, count of five," Mike continued, lifting the sledge. "And after we've worked through the major joints, there are always the intermediate bones . . ."

"Capital A, zero, One . . ." Yuri gasped.

"I'm in," Vanner said a moment later. "What name did you use for her?"

"Her name was Natalya," Yuri said. "Natalya Y I think."

"Natalya," Vanner muttered. "Damn there are a lot of

Natalyas in here. Try Natalya S, Yuri. That was two weeks ago."

"No, she was two or three months ago," Yuri said. "There are pictures."

"Sure are," Vanner said, wonderingly. "Kildar, you need to see this."

Mike set the hammer down and walked over to where the intel specialist was holding the PDA up.

"I've hotsynched it," Vanner said, unplugging the cord. "We've got the whole thing. Including his list of clients and who bought what girl, etcetera. But you've got to see this."

Mike picked up the PDA and looked at the picture. Then he walked back over and opened up the folder, pulling out the pic of the girl on the beach.

They were identical. And there was more than one. Most of the rest were of the same girl, without the bathing suit.

"Nice tits," Mike said. "We've got what we want. Close it down and call in the clean-up team."

"Penny for your thoughts, Mike?" Adams said.

They'd made it from Chisinau to Vatra Dornei in one day by hard travelling. The crossing at Gotesti had been guarded but they'd gotten through that by slipping the appropriate amount of Klei to the guards.

Once in Romania they'd gotten on National Route 17, which would have just about been an adequate to a poorly maintained county road in a poor county in the States, and made the best time they could, ignoring the potholes to the extent they could. By just after dusk they'd made it to

Saratel, short of Cluj-Napoca but not by much. However, that was the area that Pasha had reported had roadblocks so Mike decided to settle in at a small hotel that generally catered to Transylvanian tourists and move on the next day.

He set the bottle of beer on his stomach and considered the chief's question.

"Well, I'm wondering if we weighted the body enough," Mike admitted. "I think a couple more concrete blocks would have been a good idea."

"He'll stay down long enough," Adams said, shrugging. "And it's not like they're going to be looking at us. He had a lot of enemies. We were barely on his radar horizon."

"And I'm wondering what the hell I'm going to do with whatsername," Mike admitted.

"You mean Oksana?" Adams asked. "Nice girl. She can ride on my lap the rest of the way."

"I mean long term," Mike replied. "The same problems apply to her that apply to all the other waifs I've been picking up. I need to find a boarding school in Argentina or something that will start taking them in."

"Worry about that after the mission's over," Adams suggested.

"Good point," Mike said, frowning and taking a pull off the beer. "And I'm wondering just what the fuck we're really chasing."

"Ah, now we get to the source of your angstiness, Great Leader," Adams said. "You got another one of those?"

"Cooler," Mike said. "There are three bits of information to sort. What we were told. What we know is true. And what we know about the overall situation. We were told that the girl was a dependent of a rich constituent. That is, almost certainly, a lie. If she was, when she got into that crap she would have screamed bloody murder about how they could make more money off of her from her father. And Yuri was pretty damned sure that she wasn't an American. When he was begging for his life, he added that she didn't even speak English, only Russian. So . . ."

"So, she's not what the fine senator told you," Adams said, belching. "We're still going to find her, right?"

"Oh, yeah," Mike said. "For one thing, there's a rich senator who owes me one huge fucking favor for sending me on a wild goose chase when I could be fucking my harem. And for another, this has already cost like crazy. He's in for the five mil or we'll be committing crimes against the peace in the Continental United States. I'm wondering why we're really here."

"Well, we know the senator really wants to find her," Adams pointed out.

"Do we?" Mike said. "Or are we just being diverted from something else? Is the senator, for example, running a scam with the Chechens to get us out of the valley so we can get hit while the team is gone?"

"Pretty unlikely," Adams said, frowning. "I don't know what they could use as payment to the senator and so we're gone? The other five teams are still there. And Nielson's running the store. That one doesn't wash."

"I'm brainstorming," Mike pointed out. "First you come up with the ideas. Later you knock them down. Okay, that one wasn't so great. But why? And if he does want her found, why? And why me?"

"You can find her and are imminently deniable,"

Adams pointed out. "How many people could testify that they saw you and the senator together? And nobody but the two of you know what was said in the room."

"The secret service guys saw us meet," Mike said. "On the other hand, I don't know they're service. And that guy on the Moldava desk."

"And you know he exists?" Adams asked.

"Ouch," Mike said, grimacing. "Nope."

"Something for Vanner to research," the chief said. "And one more thing."

"Go," Mike said.

"Who besides Nielson is briefed in and not on the op?" Adams asked.

"Nobody," Mike said, frowning. "Why? You think somebody's going to try to clean us up? Good luck."

"There's always poison, but no," Adams said. "I was wondering who could be broken free to go have a chat with your friends in Washington."

"No one," Mike admitted. "But good point. At this point we're in fuck-up zone. I'll put Sawn on it. I can spare him. We're really running the team and he can think on his feet. Time to cover our ass."

"Or somebody's anyway," Adams said. "I'm pretty sure we're going to end up getting fucked somehow."

"Or somebody will," Mike said.

# ★ Chapter Fourteen ★

Timisoara turned out to be a fairly interesting place, for a Romanian city.

Much more Western in design and feel than the other towns they'd passed through, Timisoara had a rich history. The fertile bottomland around the river Timis had attracted settlement as early as 200 BC. Subsequently, the area had been held successively by the Dacians, the first known settlers, the Romans, the Magyar, the Ottomans, the Hapsburgs and every other notable group in Eastern Europe's history. Burned to the ground by the Mongols, burned again when retaken from the Ottomans, who had made it a central military repository and armory, it was rebuilt for the last time by the Hapsburgs and still retained their baroque influence. It was that influence, to a large degree, that set it off from other Romanian towns.

The reasons it had been fought over so often were apparent. The Timis River gave it easy navigation and it had close ties to the various mines in the Transylvanian region. With a strong road and rail network, it was one of the vital strategic points in the area called the Banat with links to Hungary, and thus the West, and Serbia to the Balkans.

The same reasons that every major conqueror had captured or destroyed it now made it a central way-point for the transport of nubile flesh.

Smegnoff's helpful PDA had listed the buyer of Natalya as one Nicu Gogasa, a man with whom he'd done extensive business. There was even a pic of Gogasa sitting in the Café Arrenica with the late and unlamented Yuri, both of them with young, lightly dressed females sitting on their laps. They were clearly good buddies. Nicu was much slighter than Yuri and better, even flashily, dressed. He looked more like a mildly successful American pimp than a mafia thug. There were contact numbers including cell, a PO box for mail, and a physical address: the Club Dracul. They even had a Web site that included a map.

Many Romanian official records turned out to be on the internet. From these, with the sometimes problematic assistance of an online translator, Vanner had been able to determine that Nicu Gogasa was listed as the sole owner of the Club Dracul. Mike found it unlikely that he was really the sole owner. He looked far too flashy. Clubs were a great place to wash money, so the mob was probably a silent backer. But it meant he was probably going to be around the club.

So it was in this happy state of mind of having all the initial intel he needed that Mike pulled up in front of the Club Dracul in the company of Russell. The former Marine barely fit in the rented Fiat, which just made Mike all warm inside.

The first thing to make him pause was the security. Two guys in battle dress, both damned near Russell's size, were guarding the door, while a third bouncer in a T-shirt that revealed bulging muscles was sweeping for weapons.

The second thing was the line, which stretched down the block.

"Mr. Gogasa is apparently making money," Mike said as they cruised past the entrance looking for parking. "Law Level Nine protocols."

"Crap, I hate those," Russell muttered, reaching under his jacket and beginning to divest himself of weapons. It took a while.

"Alpha Team," Mike said, keying his mike with his voice. "Law Level Nine zone. Battle armor. Probable heavy weapons."

"Great," Adams growled back. "Try not to start a free-fire."

Mike finally found a parking space in a for-pay lot and headed down towards the line for the club.

"Your motivation is I'm important and you're my muscle," Mike said over his shoulder as he walked past the line, reaching in his pocket.

"Your motivation is to get us out of this fucker alive," Russell replied.

The bouncers in armor eyed both of them as they approached the front of the line but it was the sweeper that waved them to a stop.

"I understand there's a cover," Mike said, flicking a folded hundred euro note up where it could be seen over his thumb.

"That covers it," the bouncer growled in accented English. He took the bill, but still insisted on sweeping them. Mike wasn't as sorry about leaving the weapons behind as he was about the radios and cameras.

The line skipped, the two of them walked in, paid their real cover of seven hundred and twenty-five thousand lei, or about ten euros, got their hands stamped and walked through the doors.

Romanians considered the popular Western image of "Count Dracula" as an insult. "Dracul" translated as "Dragon" and was the name of an ancient order of Romanian knights, the equivalent of being named to the Order of the Garter. Vlad Tepes was, in fact, a defender of Romania against incursions by the Ottoman Empire and was celebrated in Romania not as a blood-drinking monster but as a strong and willful leader of the anti-Ottoman forces, a sort of fifteenth century George Washington.

The fact that he occasionally ate his dinner while surrounded by hanged bodies was politely overlooked.

The Club Dracul, however, bowed to the Western tradition. It was more Gothic than most Goth clubs in the States, with coffins on the walls and ankhs being the primary symbol. The waitresses were dressed in long flowing gowns, slit down to their navels in the front and up to their waists on the side, and wore heavy black eye shadow and lipstick. The pointed teeth on many of them came as something of a shock, though, even to Mike who had spent plenty of time in Goth clubs in the States.

Unsurprisingly, the club was dark as hell. There were three elevated dance floors, each with a girl or girls up on them wearing from very little to nothing at all, and two floor-level dancing areas. These were crowded with both males and females. The Romanians clearly believed in combining regular dancing with strip. For that matter, as he was checking out the environment Mike saw one of the girls he'd pegged as a patron get up on the platform and start making out with the dancer while slowly stripping.

"Okay," Mike said. "I think this is my kind of place."

"What?" Russell shouted over the heavy European industrial-dance music booming from speakers set all around the periphery.

"Let's get a drink and pace!" Mike replied.

"Special dance, sir?" a nearly naked brunette asked, rubbing up against Russell.

"Maybe later," Russell replied, looking around.

"Grab her while you can," Mike said over his shoulder.

"Here," Russell said, handing her some cash. "Walk with us."

"We want someplace out of the way," Mike shouted at the girl as they walked to the bar. "But where we can watch!"

"I no speak English," the girl replied. "You wanna good time? I not expensive."

"She speaks enough English," Russell shouted.

"Is it just me, or would a firefight be quieter?" Mike screamed back. He was definitely going to be hoarse by the end of this evening

"Much!" Russell yelled back.

They got their drinks, and a "pay-me" drink for the brunette, then circulated as the girl continued to try to scam Russell out of all his spare change.

"Eleven o'clock," Russell yelled.

Mike looked left and got a glimpse of the tango. Nicu was near the back of the club at a semicircular banquette.

He had a girl on either side, then a couple of guys that Mike pegged as friends or business acquaintances. There were a few more girls scattered around but most of the people in the immediate vicinity were muscle.

There had been more muscle scattered around the room but it was definitely concentrated in the vicinity of Nicu. And the muscle around him was as heavily armored as the bouncers out front. And more heavily armed. One of them was toting a Czech Skorpion 9mm SMG on friction straps.

Mike got all that in one quick glance then spotted a table where they could keep an eye on the tango and the floor.

When they were in posession of the table, Mike leaned over to Russell.

"Go lay the bitch and check out the security in the rooms," Mike said as quietly as he could under the circumstances.

"Will do," Russell said, taking one of her upper arms in a hamlike fist.

"He be very good to you!" Mike yelled to the hooker as they walked away.

"You be good to me?" a female voice near by his ear.

Mike turned to look into an exquisite pair of nearly black eyes. Very shapely. So was the rest of the body when he got his eyes off of hers. And he could see that plainly because every stitch she had on was see-through.

"Maybe," Mike yelled back. "You sit and talk. I pay."

"Okay," the girl yelled back. "I speak English."

"So what the fuck are you doing in a place like this?" Mike asked, looking around for a waitress.

"Making money," the girl replied with a laugh. "You want drink? I get."

"Only one for you," Mike said, pulling out a twenty euro note and handing it to her. "Get something real for yourself and come back! There's more where that came from."

"I will," the girl said, eeling away through the crowd.

When she got back, with a real honest-to-God energy drink, she handed him the change.

"Yours," Mike yelled. "And here," he continued, handing over another twenty. "That means you stay with me for an hour."

"Twenty minutes," the girl replied, tucking the the money into her G-string. "Twenty minutes, twenty euros. You want blow? You want fuck?"

"How much?" Mike asked.

"Twenty minutes, twenty euros," the girl yelled back, laughing.

"What's your name, girl who laughs?" Mike asked.

"Nikki."

"Sure it is," Mike replied, shaking her hand. "I'm Mike."

"Sure it is!"

"Nice club," Mike yelled back, looking around.

"Is only good dance club in Timisoara," Nikki yelled back. "All others closed. Government shut them down. Said they were illegal brothels!"

"So is this," Mike pointed out.

"You noticed!" Nikki said, laughing again. Very merry eyes. "See man in corner?"

"There's a bunch of them," Mike pointed out.

"Silk suit, silk shirt, open at collar, gold chain, Tanya and Svetlana feeling him under table?"

"Got it," Mike yelled.

"Nicu Gogasa. Owns club. Says he owns club, anyway. Twenty euros, twenty minutes. Fifteen to him, five to me. And all of the five goes to pay off my 'debt' for when he bought me from the man who raped me. Or to food or my clothes that I don't even want."

"That sucks," Mike said, distantly. It was clear he wasn't really listening.

"Very," Nikki said, her face suddenly hard. "But all other clubs, close by government."

"Somebody's got the ear of the government," Mike said, looking around.

"Club is owned by Albanians," Nikki said, turning sideways and spitting on the ground in a most unladylike fashion. "Run whores through here. Bring them in from all over. Then they go away."

"When are you going to go away?" Mike asked, looking at her darkly.

"Soon," Nikki said, no longer laughing. "Club always have new girls. That what makes it best in town. Would leave if I could. Can't."

"No papers," Mike said. "Where are you from?"

"Belarus," Nikki said. "You know story, right? You been in clubs like this, yes?"

"Many times," Mike said with a nod. "Was it a waitressing job in Italy?"

"Taking care of kids in Belgium," Nikki said sadly. "I was looking forward to it."

"Things suck all over," Mike replied.

"Seem like nice guy," Nikki said. "Like boyfriend I had in Belarus. Why you go to clubs like this?"

"To meet pretty girls like you," Mike said.

"No," Nikki said. "Eyes are wrong. Not watching girls, watching men. Not gay ones. The breakers."

"Bouncers," Mike corrected automatically.

"That too," Nikki said, reaching out and turning his face to her. "And breakers."

"Gotcha," Mike replied. "Good work if you can get it."

"You think?" Nikki asked angrily.

"What would you say if I told you I was shopping?" Mike asked, turning to look out at the floor again.

There was a pause and he looked over at the girl.

"I'd say maybe," Nikki admitted. "Is that what you do?"

"Maybe," Mike said. "How much for you?"

"To buy?" Nikki asked angrily. "You think you can just buy like so much vodka?"

"If I walked over to whatsisname and offered him five grand euros, what do you think he'd say?" Mike asked, turning to look at her again.

"I think your twenty minutes are up, that's what I think," Nikki said, turning away.

"I don't," Mike said, grabbing her arm. "Sit and talk. You've got five more minutes. Don't make me take it up with the management."

"You would," Nikki said, sitting down and crossing her arms in front of her chest.

"Let me put it this way, would you rather stay and take your chances with the Albanians or with me?" Mike asked, turning at movement and realizing it was Russell coming back through the crowd.

"I think the Albanians," Nikki spat.

"Bad bet," Mike said as Russell sat down. "Well?"

"Wired to the max," Russell replied. "Camera and probably sound."

"Live on Candid Camera?" Mike asked. "Must be off-putting to the customers."

"They were concealed," Russell said. "I had her get on top so I could get a good look around."

"You're not shopping," Nikki said.

"Shit!" Russell snapped. "She speaks English?"

"Quite well," Mike replied. "Go on."

"Security door at both ends," Russell said, looking at the girl. "Booths along the sides, curtains. She was very professional but still sort of stumbled through the motions. She hardly cried at all, though. These are intermediate whores. They're still getting settled in."

"You're looking for better trained?" Nikki asked nastily.

"We're doing research," Mike said. "On the sex trade in Eastern Europe."

"Sure you are," Nikki snorted.

"Parts of it," Mike said. "And you talk a lot. Don't you get in trouble for that?"

"All the time," Nikki said.

"They're good about not leaving scars," Mike noted.

"You should look under my hair," Nikki said. "And the needle marks don't show up much."

"Gotcha," Mike said, standing up. "Come on."

"Don't go over there," Nikki said, pulling back. "Please."

"Time to find out what you're worth," Mike replied, dragging her towards Nicu's table.

She straightened up and tried to appear as if she liked the idea as soon as a bouncer looked her way and had almost managed a smile by the time they got to the table. One of the muscle stood up and held his hand out to stop the twosome but Nicu waved them forward with interest in his eyes.

"Mind if I sit?" Mike said, waving at the chairs filled by women.

"No," Nicu said, glancing at Nikki darkly.

"Nice club," Mike said. "Very classy."

"Thanks," Nicu said, looking sideways at one of the men at the booth and then back. "What can I do for you?"

"How much for this one?" Mike asked, waving at Nikki.

"For the night?" the pimp asked, grinning. "Five hundred euros. She could have told you that. Should have told you that," he added, looking at Nikki again, this time with a smile that promised pain later.

"No, to buy," Mike said. "I'm in the market."

"That, of course, would be out of the question," Nicu said, smiling faintly. "That would constitute sexual slavery. This young lady is free to come and go at any time."

"Sure she is," Mike said. "Half the cops in town would pick her up for you if she could even get out of the club. We've danced through all the proper forms. How much? Time is money, Mr. Gogasa."

"And you are?" Nicu asked, suddenly curious.

"A drunk American who wants to buy a sex-slave," Mike said blankly. "Of course. What else?"

"Many things," Nicu said, glancing sideways again. Mike ignored the look but he'd now pegged the "associate" as something on the order of a control.

"Well, what I actually am is a guy passing through with a group of girls intended for sale in Macedonia," Mike said. "A special sale. Very special. I think she would do well at it."

"And I can believe that or not," Nicu replied.

"Would you believe five thousand euros?" Mike asked.

"Hah!" Nicu said, grinning. "You make me laugh. I will make more than that off of her before I sell her."

"You don't sell her," Mike pointed out. "You move her to your boss's network." He glanced over at the "associate" and nodded. "Right?"

"And we will make more," the man replied, coldly. "Far more."

"Maybe, maybe not," Mike said. "Sure, you move her through the network, maybe to Albania then over to Italy. Then up to the rest of Europe, maybe the U.S. or U.K. But what's going to happen along the way? You lose how many girls that start from here? What's your actual profit per girl? I know I will. And you don't have to deal with her support anymore. Or the possible loss. Raise, fold or call."

"Fourteen thousand," Nicu said, glancing over at the Albanian with a raised eyebrow to which he received a nod.

"Out of the question," Mike snapped. "Half that, maybe. I can walk out onto the street and buy any four free women for that much."

"But she is trained," Nicu pointed out. "She has been taught not to try to escape, what that gets her. And she has been trained to give sex well. Would you like her to show you how well she sucks? Nikki is a very good sucker. Thirteen is a very reasonable price."

"All of that is assumed," Mike pointed out. "And your

training is sunk costs," he added, gesturing at the muscle. "You pay them from the profit from the bar, not even counting the money you're laundering through here."

"What money?" the Albanian asked angrily.

"Oh, get off it," Mike snapped. "Clubs are perfect laundering spots. Did you take in a thousand in cover charges or ten thousand? How are the police to know? Water the alcohol and charge it at full price, then figure on the margin. Then there's the girls. Are they turning ten tricks a night or twenty? The difference between the two all goes in your pocket. Do me a favor and don't take me for an idiot, okay?"

"Okay," the Albanian said. "But you must take us for idiots. You come in here with a bullshit story about selling girls in Macedonia. To who? I know all the buyers in Macedonia."

"I don't know who they go to after our special customers are done," Mike said. "I just get them to the house in Macedonia."

"There was a crackdown on those," Nicu said, frowning. "Most got shut down."

"Jesus," Mike said, looking at the Albanian. "You don't keep him around for his brains, do you? Who forced the crackdown?"

"IFOR," the Albanian said, looking at him carefully. "And KFOR. And you're American military. The haircut, the build. Their fucking Special Force, yes?"

"So you think they really cracked down on our house?" Mike asked.

"You buy for the military?" Nicu asked, really confused now.

"Of course not," Mike said, sighing. "Soldiers can't afford what we sell."

"You make black funds," the Albanian said, nodding as he sat back. "You run house that raises money so your military can do the things your government doesn't pay for. The things your parliament cannot know about, yes? Twelve thousand. Because the American military has been very good to my people."

Mike had to admit that the Albanian would make a great writer for the Democratic Underground. Of course, there was more than a gram of truth to it. He did do black work and he was doing some fundraising. He'd have to give it some thought. But he knew he didn't sell girls. End of existential angst as the chief would say.

"And for the Israelis, yes?" Nicu said, the light finally dawning.

"There are things you don't talk about," Mike said with another sigh. "But let's just say that Mossad got its funding cut way back this year, just when we really needed them to keep funding their Damascus office. Okay? And thirteen is out of the question. I need to make a damned profit, okay?"

Over a couple of drinks and more than one copped feel they got an eventual price of ten five worked out.

"And you think you will make a profit from her in Macedonia?" the Albanian asked.

"For what we offer rich bastards from the States and Japan?" Mike asked. "You betcha."

"We have such visitors," the Albanian said, still clearly puzzled. As well he should be; Mike was spinning bullshit so fast it was practically brown silk.

"Look," Mike said, shaking his head. "What is the U.S. Military known for?"

"Destroying countries?" one of the other men asked.

"Very good bombs?" Nicu said.

"Invading any country that has oil?" the Albanian asked, shrugging. "Being very good at killing people and less good at finding them?"

*You just wait, motherfucker*, Mike thought.

"Okay, all of that," was what he said. "But the main thing that matters here is we don't talk. What happens at the house, stays at the house. Period fucking dot. That's something that our customers can depend upon. We don't have fucking cameras in the booths. Hell, we don't even have booths. You have your choice of anything from silk bedrooms to the dungeons. And anything goes if you've got the cash. Understand?"

"I have never heard of this house," the Albanian said, frowning.

"See? Now go get your clothes, honey," Mike said, looking at Nikki. "You're mine, now."

Once they were out on the street, with Mike and Russell flanking the whore, Mike leaned over to her ear.

"Nikki, you really don't want to run," he whispered. "Not just because of the bad things that Nicu will end up doing to you if you do. Just go along with us and you won't be sorry."

"So I can be raped in a dungeon by rich old men?" Nikki asked, breathing hard and fast as they approached the car. All she had was a tube dress and a small bag that couldn't hold much more than cosmetics. He had to wonder where the clothes she'd "bought" had gone.

"Well, it's that or the Albanians, honey," Mike said. "And just don't ask stupid questions until we can get someplace to talk, okay?"

"What are you?" the whore asked.

"Like I said," Mike repeated. "Shut up. Russell, sit in back with her."

"Miss," Russell said as he opened the door for her. "Please don't try to run. If you did I'd have to restrain you. I'd try not to hurt you, but you're a lot smaller than me and you'd probably get hurt anyway."

"Where would I run to?" she asked bitterly.

# ★ Chapter Fifteen ★

It was a silent twenty-minute ride to the hotel and then another silent three minutes to the set of rooms Mike had found.

"Russell, go debrief with Vanner," Mike said as he knocked on the command room door. He knew there'd be at least some Keldara women there. "He'll need your input on the club layout."

"Oh, Kildar," Anisa said, blushing. She was wearing the tube dress and high heels, very much the same uniform as Nikki, if in different colors.

"You really are a whoremaster," Nikki said bitterly.

"Not quite," Mike said, trying not to smile at Anisa's discomfiture. "Doing some training, Anisa?"

"Uhmmm, yes, Kildar," the girl said, still furiously blushing and pulling her dress down. The maneuver just about got Mike a view of nipple, which caused her to blush and back up so fast she nearly went ass over teakettle.

Katya was in the room, dressed in jeans, and for the first time Mike saw what looked like a real, honest, smile on her face. In fact, all of the Keldara girls were in the room along with Oksana and there were three more dressed in tube dresses and trying to stand on high heels.

"Been doing a lot of training, Cottontail?" Mike asked, breaking into a grin. "I gotta say, if I really was selling hookers, I'd make a mint off of you girls."

"Don't even joke about it, Kildar," Greznya said, gasping. "We've been listening to far too much of what happens to them."

"Sorry," Mike said, contritely. "Speaking of which, various gals, this is Nikki from Belarus who up until recently was a whore in Nicu's club. I want you to suck her brains dry. Do we have maps, yet?"

"Blueprints of the club as well as his apartment building," Greznya said, getting up and going over to a table to flip through some sheets. "We're not sure where he breaks the girls in, or where he keeps his records."

"You're *not* a whoremaster," Nikki said, looking around at the girls. The Keldara girls were all fiddling with their dresses, nervously. She clearly wasn't sure what to think. They were dressed as whores and as nervous as new ones but they certainly didn't look as if they were in fear of him.

"I am not a whoremaster," Mike said. "I know you have a tendency to chatter, Nikki. Even if you get a chance, do not chatter about what is happening here. Lives depend upon it. Okay?"

"Okay," she said, puzzled.

"Ladies," Mike said, looking around and trying not to grin again. "I leave it to you. And . . . this looks like good training!"

"As in unpleasant and uncomfortable?" one of the girls trying to balance on stilettos asked. "These shoes hurt."

"Exactly," Mike said, walking to the door. "Good Training!"

"You worked in Nicu's club?" Greznya asked, settling Nikki on the edge of the bed with a Coke.

"Yes," Nikki said, looking around. "What is this?" she asked, staring at Katya and Oksana. There was something different about them, she could tell.

"We were hired to find a girl who is in the sex-slavery industry," Greznya said. "Sometimes we have to pose as hookers, which is why the girls are practicing. It was sort of a joke; only Anisa has had to do it."

"And me," Katya said, sipping at her drink which was clearly alcoholic. "But I'm a real whore, just like you."

"And what about you?" Nikki asked, looking at Oksana.

"She was going to be made into one," Greznya answered. "The Kildar bought her, instead."

"He was a little late for me," Nikki said bitterly.

"He will be late for almost all the women around here," Katya said with a slight slur in her voice. "He was late for me. Hell, he used me as one. Still might. And worse. I'm a whore, why not? Once a whore, always a whore."

"You are more than that," Anisa said sharply. "Much more."

"Whatever," Katya replied.

"Hail, hail, the gang's all here," Vanner said, walking through the adjoining door.

"Nikki," Russell said, nodding at her.

"Hi," Nikki said, smiling to see a familiar face, even if it was Russell's.

"We need to look at the blueprints," Vanner said, walking

over to the table. "What Russell is sketching out doesn't sound like the design on the paper."

"It's not," Russell said, glancing at the blueprints. "The sex booths are through here, which shows a solid wall. It looks as if they knocked a door into this section, here," he added, pointing. "This place used to be a couple of warehouses; they've redesigned it."

"Nikki, right?" Vanner said, gesturing at the girl. "Have you been in much of the club?"

"Some," Nikki said, walking over and looking at the schematic in incomprehension. "What is this?"

"It's like a map of the building the club is in," Vanner replied. "I know it's confusing, but don't worry. We'll walk you through it. . . ."

"I hope you have something for me, Vanner," Mike said the next morning when he strode into intel. "I had a crappy night's sleep and the smoke from that damned club is killing my lungs."

"Well, at least some of us got some sleep," Vanner replied. "No rest for the staff pukes, huh? Yeah, we got some stuff but it's basically crap."

"Go," Mike said, flopping into an armchair.

"Okay," Vanner said, flipping up the blueprints for the club on an easel. They'd been heavily marked over and some of the areas were either entirely unmarked or marked with dotted lines making approximations. "First part of the crap."

"I can see," Mike said. "They've really worked that building over. And I don't see where they've got the guys watching the security cameras."

"We've positively established it as being right here," Vanner said, waving his hand over one quarter of the more-or-less-square building that wasn't mapped. There were some doors around it, but nothing inside the box.

"That's bad," Mike said.

"It gets worse," Vanner said. "There are cameras on all entrances. Nikki has seen the security in full rig and they're heavy. Up to RPG."

"How very good," Mike said dryly.

"They stay in the club, in a barracks," Vanner said, glancing at his notes. "But it's in the security area. The girls don't go in there to service them. Nicu moves in a three vehicle convoy. Leaves late, comes back late, around noon. Sometimes goes out of town."

"Shopping," Mike said.

"Shopping," Vanner confirmed. "His convoy uses multiple routes. The only confluence is his apartment and the club. Sometimes he takes girls, especially new ones, to the apartment. Apartment has security all over it, too."

"All over?" Mike asked.

"All over the ground floors," Vanner said. "We've got cameras on the club and the apartment."

"Does he keep records of the girls?" Mike asked.

"Presumably," Vanner said. "Or someone does. But that would be in the offices." He pointed to a spot on the blueprint near the back of the main club area. "To get to the offices you have a couple of choices. Go through the club, go through the girls' dormitory, which has very tight security, or go through the security area itself."

"No," Mike said. "You're thinking two dimensionally."

"The roof?" Vanner asked incredulously.

"It's worth looking at," Mike said. "Brainstorming. Okay, convoy, multiple routes. Lots of bystanders around in the club and heavy security. Lots of security on the apartment. Records in a practical vault. Nikki tell you about the Albanian?"

"The guy who actually sold her?" Vanner asked. "Brami Dejti. Former officer in the NLA. Got made fighting the Serbs, worked his way into fundraising by sex, slavery and drugs. Arrested for war crimes, rape and murder of females, mostly, associated with the NLA, never prosecuted. He got released by the Belgian contingent of KFOR and nobody ever brought it up again. Arrested in Greece for pimping, released. Arrested in Belgium for suspicion of transportation of women for immoral purposes and kidnapping. The two witnesses, the whores, disappeared. Case dropped. That guy?"

"Where'd you get it?" Mike asked, nodding.

"I pulled up a list of known players and ran the mug shots past Nikki," Vanner said. "For damned near two hours. After that it was easy. Interpol has a rap sheet the length of Albania on the guy. Somehow he always slips out of the net."

"Interpol is the epitome of European policing," Mike said. "All the information in the world and no real success at stopping crime. We need to work on him. Maybe more than Nicu."

"He left last night in a convoy of three Mercedes that from the looks of them were armored," Vanner replied. "We might be able to get something more tomorrow night. If he shows."

"We need them both," Mike said. "Together. And we need their records."

"That means taking down the whole club, Kildar," Vanner said, frowning. "You're not talking about that, are you?"

"I dunno," Mike said. "I'm going to think on it. Find me a way in that doesn't require shooting. Anything. Find it. If we can get somebody inside, we're going places. Short of that, I'm out of ideas. We'll have a meeting this afternoon to toss ideas around. You, me, Adams, Sawn, Russell, Nikki and a couple of the Keldara women."

"Will do," Vanner said, sighing.

Mike looked around the room and then at the unhelpful blueprint on the easel.

"Nobody?" he asked. "I mean, I knew I was stumped, but you're all smart people. Somebody's got to have an idea!"

"Well, I'm stumped too," Adams admitted. "But I know the way I think. If you can't get in easy, get more firepower."

"I'm not calling in the Families to deal with one damned link in the chain," Mike said.

"Well, I'm just not the Mission Impossible type," Adams replied. "Vanner?"

"I could try to remote access their computers," the former Marine said, musingly. "I've got the systems to do that. The walls on the warehouse are old Russian concrete. It's pretty lousy stuff; it falls apart pretty quick normally. But the problem with it is it's ferroconcrete. Instead of using rebar, it's laced through with wire mesh. That acts as a Faraday cage; no signals get out. I'm pretty sure there's hardly any cell phone connection in there. I know I haven't picked up cell calls from Nicu or Bramji."

"What about the roof?" Greznya asked. "The walls stop signals, but does the roof?"

"Checked," Vanner sighed. "It's metal. Stops 'em dead."

"I am still not so sure about reading this map of the building," Nikki said diffidently. "But there is something on it I don't understand." She got up and walked over to the blueprint, tracing a section. "What is this?"

"The warehouse had in-ground drains," Vanner said. "It's the sewage connection for them. I looked at that; it's marked as being only three inches wide. Really fucking thin for the purpose, but I suppose that's Soviet architecture all over."

"It looks larger," Nikki said. "This is the marker?" she added, pointing to a number.

"Yeah," Vanner said, curiously. "Why?"

"This is in decimeters," Nikki pointed out. "Three decimeters. That is about this big," she pointed out, holding her hands apart.

"Damn," Vanner said, standing up and walking over to the map.

"Fifteen inches," Adams said. "Still very damned small. I wouldn't want to try to get shooters in there."

"No," Mike said softly. "But you can get someone or even something up it."

"It runs under the club," Vanner said, tracing the line. "And under the offices and through the girls' rooms into security. The entrance is over on that side. There are drains marked."

Mike walked over for a closer look and shook his head.

"There wasn't a drain opening there," Mike pointed out. "Nikki, this is between the bar and stage two. There's not an opening there, is there?"

"No," the girl said definitely.

"They'll have laid the floor in over them," Vanner said positively. "Nicu wasn't the first owner of the club and from the looks of the paperwork the previous owners were forced to sell. He might not even know about it. And one of the drains is right under the offices."

"What can we do with that?" Mike asked.

"Let me do some shopping," Vanner said distantly. "At the very least I can get a recon probe up it. Maybe by the end of the day."

"Get some of the Keldara into the club," Adams said. "Rotate them through, picking up intel. They'll need to keep their mouths shut and their eyes open."

"Just the men or women as well?" Greznya asked. "The girls are trained for intel gathering. Not this type, but they understand the concept."

"There were plenty of customers going there just to dance," Mike pointed out. "Send in a shooter and one of the intel girls as a pair. How many of the girls would be willing to do it?"

"Most," Greznya said, smiling. "Totter in on high heels, yes?"

"They'll need more practice," Mike said, seriously. "They'll need to be able to dance on them."

"I'll get with Katya to show us," Greznya said with a nod.

"Okay, let's break this up," Mike said. "Vanner, go

shopping. Take a couple of the Keldara shooters and a girl if she wants to go. They need to get used to city life."

"Will do," Vanner said. He had pulled out a scratch pad and was writing on it.

"Take Killjoy with you," Adams added. "That way he can answer questions while you shop."

"Got it," the Marine replied.

"Greznya, talk to the girls," Mike said.

"I will, Kildar," the girl replied.

"It's not a plan, but it's a start."

# ★ Chapter Sixteen ★

Patrick Vanner was running on too little sleep and he knew it. However, he'd found everything he needed shopping, and putting the pieces together had been relatively easy. Once he'd gotten the pieces and put together a plan, he'd turned it over to Greznya. The girls had gotten used to tinkering with electronics and the design changes were relatively simple. The device was mostly hollow, anyway, and had a built-in spot for a camera. All they'd needed to do was install the bits he'd picked up, a few black boxes he always kept around just in case, and do the systems integration. He'd gotten in a power nap.

All that being said, he knew that he'd come up with the idea while in a sleep-deprived haze. In other words, it might be genius and it might be utter stupidity. Since he wasn't sure which, he'd carefully avoided discussing it with the Kildar or Adams and had sworn Killjoy to secrecy.

Which was why the former Ranger was with him in the sewer tunnel.

"I think you're bent," Killjoy said, lifting the device into the tunnel overhead.

"It's designed to avoid walls," Vanner pointed out as he

checked the take from the device. "All we have to do is put it in the tunnel and let it go. It's perfect, really."

"It's nuts," Killjoy said. "Even if it works."

"If it's stupid and it works it ain't stupid," Vanner replied.

"Don't go quoting Murphy's Law of Combat to me," Killjoy said. "Not while I'm doing this. It makes me wonder if the smell from the sewer is making me as bent as you are."

"Just turn on the motor," Vanner said dazedly. "I'm getting a good feed from the camera and the intercept systems are nominal."

"Okay," Killjoy said, flicking the switch on the base of the thing.

"Right, here goes," Vanner said, touching a control.

There was a series of beepings that emitted from the tunnel.

"Don't tell me you didn't pull the sound box," Killjoy said.

"I'm pretty sure they won't hear it," Vanner said. "And, no, I forgot to tell the girls."

"Like they wouldn't know about it?" the former Ranger asked.

"Hey, they're the Keldara," Vanner said, shrugging. "It's not like they go to a lot of movies. They've never even seen *Star Wars*!"

He hit another button and there was another series of beeps.

"You go, R2," Killjoy said, chuckling.

And the miniature R2D2 toy began making its way up the tunnel and into the darkness.

★ ★ ★

"Where's Vanner?" Mike asked as he walked into the command post. "I looked in intel and he wasn't around."

"Getting some sleep," Greznya said, peering at her laptop computer screen. "He's planted an intercept system under their offices and we're getting the take from their computers. Getting in through the sewer worked, by the way."

"Can you hack their girl database?" Mike asked.

"Not yet," Greznya admitted. "They're using the computer at the moment and that takes too fine of a touch; we'll have to wait until Patrick wakes up. What we're doing is getting the information that they're seeing. Which is mostly financial at the moment. And we got their passwords when they punched them in. And Nicu uses a laptop with a WiFi link. He accessed it and updated it when he got into the club and we got the take from that. And he left it on but wasn't using it so we sucked it out. But it doesn't have a back-list of girls on it, just 'current projects.'"

"Anything we can really use, yet?" Mike asked.

"Nope," Greznya admitted. "Wait for Patrick to wake up. He didn't get any sleep all last night or today."

"Okay," Mike said. "I'll go bother somebody else for a while. Send somebody to get me when he's up and functional."

It was nearly midnight when Mike got called to the intel room.

"You got something?" Mike asked, looking at the group gathered around the computers.

"Sort of," Vanner said with a grimace. "They've got, they think, pretty good security. It's not as good as they think, but it's pretty good." He spun around in his chair and stood up, stretching his back.

"There are three different computer systems running in the room," Vanner said. "Nicu's laptop, an internet connected computer and a remote computer without any external connections. Their internet communications systems are encrypted with PGP and the computer's got three firewalls, one hardware and two software. The hardware and one of the software firewalls have known holes in them. The third doesn't. It's Romanian and if anybody's found holes in it I haven't been able to track the information down."

"So we're still not in their computers?" Mike asked.

"Not really," Vanner said with a sigh. "I tried slipping in a trojan and got whacked. Hard. They damned near traced me. Well, actually, they did trace me. To a university computer in the U.S. that I've got a trojan on. From there the trace went cold. I don't think it was someone in the room; it was an automated response. But I've already determined that the information we need isn't even on that computer. It's on the computer without outside access. There's no way to get information off of it except to connect. If I can get a connection on it I can suck it out in about ten minutes. But I'll need at least ten minutes with the computer to do that. And the office is manned around the clock. Oh, and one huge problem we keep running into."

"What?" Mike asked, sighing.

"Everything is in fricking Romanian," Vanner said,

shrugging. "You read Romanian? I don't. We're using automatic translators. You know how good those are."

"What about Nikki?" Mike asked.

"She speaks English and Russian," Vanner replied.

"Go roust out Russell, a Keldara girl and one of the Keldara shooters," Mike said after a bit of thought. "Have them go find a street hooker that speaks Romanian and English. Reads it, too. One that won't be missed. Bring her back here. We'll just take her with us when we leave."

"That's pretty damned cold, isn't it?" Vanner asked, incredulously.

"We'll pay her," Mike said, shrugging. "And figure out something better she can do than being a hooker when we're done." Mike folded his arms and looked at the blueprint again. "Can you sleep, again?"

"In a while," Vanner said.

"Good, get some more sleep. We'll brainstorm this again in the morning. I've got an inkling of a plan; we'll see if it holds up to scrutiny."

When Mike entered the command center the next morning, there was a new face.

The girl was in her twenties, thin, dark and attractive but with a very hard face.

"Kildar, this is Ruxandra," Vanner said by way of introduction.

"Hello, Ruxandra," Mike said, sitting down. "Is she briefed in?"

"Yes," Russell said.

"And are you willing to help us, Ruxandra?" Mike asked, raising an eyebrow. "I mean, of your own free will?"

"I'm still wondering about that," Ruxandra admitted, staring at him darkly. She had really good eyes for it. "I'd gladly see Nicu in hell, though. One of my friends was picked up by his men and I never heard from her again. Then her body turned up off the coast of Italy. It had been in the water for a long time, probably dumped off the coast of Albania. Another girl, she didn't want to give the blowjob, yes? She tried to bite. Nicu had her front teeth hammered out. Now she does not bite, yes? I'd be more happy to help you if I was sure he was going to die."

"I think that's going to be how it has to go," Mike said. "I've worked this over half a dozen ways. I'll run through a few of them.

"Way one. We find one of the guys that works in the office in the evening that we can dope up someone to impersonate. Grab him, slip our guy in, suck the computer and our guy goes out."

"Welcome to Mission Impossible," Adams said, shaking his head. "They speak Romanian, Mike."

"Yeah, that's only one of about a thousand problems," Mike pointed out. "Way two, we just go with a frontal assault. We'd have surprise. We can get some weapons in the room in advance. I suspect that Nikki knows a couple of the girls who would bring stuff in for us. Right?"

"Possibly," Nikki said. "They are not swept when they come in the back entrance. And there's nothing keeping them from going into the club."

"Set up assignations with the girls off-site, discuss it with them, let them do it if they wish, hold on to the ones that balk. Then hit the front and rear, hard. Go for Nicu and the Albanian from the front while the back team goes for the computers."

"We'd take a lot of casualties," Adams said, frowning. "That was my thought. And I don't want to think about the mess. Lots of dead civilians. Even if the Keldara picked their shots, Nicu wouldn't. For that matter, we don't know that some of the girls wouldn't burn us. We could be running right into an ambush."

"Right," Mike said. "Now, the question is, if things go down, what do Nicu and the Albanian do?"

"I'd say, head for either the office or the security barracks," Vanner replied. "There are more cars out back. I'd say if they have to, they escape that way rather than out the front. There's a door near his booth that goes to a hallway that leads to the office. Turn left on it and you're headed for the girl's area and the security barracks. He'd hit that door if anything went down. Then either sit it out in the office or head out the back to escape. There are three rear entrances."

"We need a person to go up the tunnel," Mike said, shutting his eyes.

"It's too damned small for the Keldara," Adams said. "Even the girls."

"Yeah," Mike said. "But Oksana would fit. Greznya, go get her, would you, please?"

When the girl was led into the room she was clearly frightened.

"It's okay, Oksana," Mike said, gently. "I asked you to come in here because I need you to do something for us. It's going to be hard and it's going to require that you be brave. Do you think you can do it?"

"I'm not really brave," Oksana said, honestly. "I'd like to be, but I am always fear."

"Being brave doesn't mean not having fear," Mike said, shrugging. "If you don't have fear, you can't be brave. You have to overcome fear to count as brave. Do you think you can overcome fear?"

"I don't know," the girl said. "What do you need? Do you want me to be with man? I do not want to be with man."

"No," Mike said, shaking his head. "This is going to require physical bravery in a different way. Have you ever been in a small place?"

"Yes," the girl said. "I like it in a small place. I feel safer."

"That's good," Mike said, nodding. "Oksana, we need someone to crawl into a very small, very dirty and nasty place, and put some things in there. Up a tunnel."

"That . . ." the girl said then paused. "I do not know if I would like that."

"If you do it, we can capture and kill slavers," Mike said, leaning forward. "I don't know if we can free more girls like you, but we will give them more of a chance. Some of us are probably going to die doing this. If you don't do it, more will die. I am really hoping that you will do this. We need you. Very much."

The girl regarded him for a moment and then tilted her head to the side, looking him in the eye.

"When you bought me, you treated me very bad," the girl said. "Why did you do that? The Keldara women, they say that you are a very nice man."

"I am a very bad man who tries to be nice," Mike said,

not turning away. "This is the truth. I did what I did because if I did not, the men in the room would have suspected I was not who I said I was. They would have thought me soft, a weak man who could not be a slaver because I was too nice."

"Did you enjoy it?" Oksana asked.

Mike looked at her for a long moment, then shrugged.

"Yes," he answered, simply, still staring her in the eyes. It was as if there were only two people in the room. "I would not have done it if I didn't have to. But, yes. I am not a nice man. I am a very, very bad man who has chosen to be nice most of the time. I do many things that are for the side of what I call 'good.' But many of them are very bad things, like what I did to you. I do them for good reasons. But my bad side enjoyed it very much."

"You tell me this even though you want me to do something for you," the girl said wonderingly.

"If you do this, you are like a soldier that works for me," Mike said, shrugging. "I must be honest with my soldiers, with my troops. I must be honest and loyal with them as they are honest and loyal with me. If I don't, it doesn't work. I have shown them my bad side and my good. They choose to believe I am, at heart, a good man. I don't argue it with them. Maybe they are right and I'm wrong. But the things that I do are as much to make up for my bad side as they are for any other reason. Perhaps that makes me good. I don't know. All I know is that I must be honest."

The girl stared at him for a moment more and then looked away, breathing out.

"Yes, I will do this," she answered. "But you pay your soldiers, yes?"

"Oh, don't worry," Mike said, grinning. "You'll get paid."

"Good," the girl said. "And I get to keep it?"

"You'll get to keep it," Greznya said, looking over at Mike with a strange expression.

"Two thousand euros for this mission and as of today you go on base Keldara intel operative pay," Mike said. "Greznya, she's now in your section."

"Good," Greznya replied. "I can use another girl who actually knows how to use high heels."

"Good indeed," Mike said, distantly. "Okay, Vanner, I'm going to need most of the shooters taken off of intel duty. Figure that out. Adams, you and I are going to work out the entry plan. We're also going to need a place to rehearse."

"I'll get some of the girls looking for that," Vanner said. "They were the ones that found the warehouse in Chisinau."

"How much Semtek do we have with us?" Mike asked.

"About sixty kilos," Adams said.

"We're going to need most of it," Mike replied. "And we'll need some field expedient CS."

"I'll add that to my list," Vanner said.

"Chief, my room in fifteen, bring all the maps and updated intel data," Mike said, nodding. "And Oksana?"

"Yes . . . Kildar?" the girl asked.

"Thank you."

# ★ Chapter Seventeen ★

Mike looked over at the chief a couple of hours later and shrugged.

"Think it's going to work?"

They'd been over and over the design of the club, but in the end a modified brute force method was all that they could come up with. And even that meant putting some "principles" on the line. If they screwed up, the Keldara were likely to be in a very deep crack. On the other hand, Mike, personally, probably wouldn't be around to care.

"Oh, it'll work," Adams said. "What I'm wondering is if it's worth it. We're going to lose people. At least one, probably three."

"So are we doing this for money?" Mike asked. "Or are we doing this for the mission, whatever that means?"

"Or are we doing it because we're just curious where the trail leads?"

"That too," Mike admitted.

"You're risking a lot for curiosity," Adams said.

"If it was just curiosity, I don't think I would," Mike admitted. "I'd just pull back and tell the senator the trail was too cold. But I'm not doing this for pure curiosity or for the 'mission.' And certainly I wouldn't pay two or three Keldara for five mil. I've got the funny feeling that this little Ukrainian whore is way more important than the senator was willing to admit."

He looked up as there was a knock on the door and slid a cover sheet over the plans.

"Come."

Greznya stepped into the room and looked around.

"I hope I'm not disturbing," she said.

"We're about done," Mike replied.

"I was wondering something," the woman said, looking over at the chief.

"I've got to go start getting the troops dialed in," Adams said, standing up with a file in his hand. "You two talk."

When the chief had left Greznya sat down and regarded the Kildar thoughtfully, then frowned when he smiled.

"What?"

"I was just thinking of the changes in the Keldara since I've taken over," Mike said, still smiling. "They wanted to kick Lydia and Irina out of the Families for being alone with a man, even though there were four people in the car and it was a medical emergency. And look at you, now. Not to mention being willing to, effectively, throw the chief out for a private chat."

"I see the humor," Greznya said, finally smiling.

"So what's wrong with how I handled Oksana?" Mike asked.

"You're sure that's it?" the girl asked.

"Yep," Mike said. "I saw your look."

"I was just wondering . . ."

"What I did to her?" Mike asked, his face hard.

"Oh, no, she told me that," Greznya said. "And I said much the same things you said to her. Except the part about you being evil. And I wasn't sure how you actually felt about it. But . . . the way you spoke to her. How . . ."

"How did I know to treat her that way?" Mike asked, leaning back. "I asked myself the same thing. I wasn't sure if I was manipulating her or not. But I felt like I had to treat her as if she mattered. Because she does. As a human being and as a member of the team."

"I think that's it," Greznya said, smiling. "You treat people as human beings, no matter who they are. This is why we love you."

"That's a bit strong," Mike said. "And I've treated people as things, plenty of times. I'm doing it right now, looking at the plans, knowing that some of the Keldara are going to die in this raid. And I've done it to women plenty of times before."

"But you speak to a young girl as if she is the most important person in the world," Greznya said. "Nobody has ever treated her as if she was important. You treat us, the women of the Keldara, as if we are important. In the Families we are only as important as our wombs and the 'women's work' we do."

"And is it manipulation?" Mike asked. "Don't ask me back. I don't know. All I know is that there are people who are important to my mission. And I treat them that way. Whatever the mission might be. However, once they are members of the team, they are always members of the team. If I treated you, tomorrow, as if you had no importance, then the next time I needed you, the next time the mission needed you, I wouldn't be able to depend on you. I guess it is manipulation. But it also includes loyalty in the mix." He paused and shrugged, grinning. "Call it military leadership."

"Now I know that Oksana is smarter than I am," Greznya said, staring at him thoughtfully.

"Why?" Mike asked.

"Because I have to agree with her. You are both crazy and very scary. But I will still follow you wherever you lead, Kildar."

"Yeah, but am I right?" Mike said, shrugging. "I have to wonder about this entire mission; there is no way we're going to get the data we need from the club without some casualties."

"We are the Keldara," Greznya said, shrugging and looking away. "You are the Kildar. We will follow wherever you lead."

"But . . ." Mike said, noting the body language.

"There is really no 'but,'" Greznya said, getting up. "For the rest . . . I think you should talk to Sawn."

"Why?" Mike asked.

"Because I'm a lady and I can't use those words," Greznya said, nodding as she walked out.

"Kildar," Sawn said, not looking up from the MP-5 he had broken down on the bed.

"Greznya said I should talk to you," Mike replied, settling into a chair. "About the mission."

"She mentioned that," Sawn said, still not looking up. "I sort of expected this to be tomorrow, though."

"Unfortunately, tomorrow is when I'll need to give the mission a full go," Mike said, stretching out his feet as the

Keldara began reassembling the sub-gun. "So, what do you think? I won't promise to take your recommendation, but I want some thoughts."

"Go," Sawn said, shrugging and closing the gun. He jacked the breach and stared into it, ensuring that there wasn't a round in the chamber.

"Why?" Mike asked. "I mean, curiosity, sure. And I've got the feeling that there's something very sniffy in Washington but I can't be sure unless I follow the trail to the rot. But we *are* going to take casualties, Sawn. They're probably going to be shooters. But there's always the possibility that they'll be one of the ladies. Or me or Adams."

"Go," Sawn said, finally looking up. The stare forced Mike to pause. Each of the teams had a . . . call it a personality, one that they got from their team leaders. Oleg's team was blunt and implacable as a tank going through a wall. Vil's team depended on speed and finesse, grace over power. Sawn's team, though, was the thoughtful one. Not that they couldn't go hard against the bad guys, but they tended to think their shots, to take just a tad of time contemplating before doing unto others. That might be only a fraction of a second, but the result was usually smarter and tighter than the other teams. Sawn's team had been up on the rotation for this mission, but Mike was glad. This mission had required a lot more think and a lot less "implacable" than Oleg could have handled. Team Sawn was a good choice.

All of that thought, all that contemplation, came from Sawn. Farmers didn't tend to produce philosophers but Sawn was a close as the Keldara came. He had a depth that Oleg, Vil, Padrek and the others didn't possess. And that depth turned out to be filled with quite a bit of anger.

"There are a number of reasons," Sawn continued, looking back down at the weapon in his hand. "This is the first true mission which the Keldara have attempted. If you withdraw, even for the reason of sheltering us, it will affect our confidence. Oh, not entirely, but we will be forced to question whether you would have taken a team of Americans in, if you would have trusted them . . ."

"But . . ." Mike said, stopping when Sawn raised a hand.

"I said a number of reasons, Kildar," the team leader said, looking up and smiling tightly. "That is but one, and the least. The second reason is what you have said. America, Washington, affects the entire world. We had not realized to what a degree, hidden away in our valley. But now that we are looking out of our hole, looking again at the world, America affects *everything*. If there is this . . . evil somewhere near the core of your government, finding it is important. To you, to America and to the Keldara. Without digging out the rot, we cannot know if it will harm us. But knowing that the rot is there, without digging it out . . . that is like a tooth that you let fester. It will kill you in time."

"Okay, I'll buy that one," Mike said, frowning. "My fault for dragging you into it."

"You are the *Kildar*," Sawn said, suddenly letting his anger show. "It is not our horror, not our shame, that we are your fighters, your guards, it is our *honor*, Kildar. We *share* your danger, willingly and even with joy. You have given us, again, our honor. And as you gain more dangerous, more powerful, enemies, *our* status raises thereby."

"Okay, that one's sort of . . . twisted," Mike said, chuckling. "But I sort of get it. If you're going to believe in the way of the warrior, you have to believe *all* the way."

"And there is a last thing," Sawn said, seating a magazine in the weapon. "This . . . trade. It is dishonor upon us all." He turned and looked out the window at the city and shook his head. "Our women have been stolen, Kildar. When we were weak, when we had nothing and certainly no weapons, people who *think* they are warriors came upon us and treated us like *peasants*. We are not peasants, Kildar. We have had to do what we have done over the years, so many years even we did not realize until you came to us. But we are *not* peasants, Kildar, and these men, in this trade, have dishonored our lands, our homes."

He turned back to Mike and his eyes were bright with his anger as he jacked a round into the chamber.

"Do not even *think* of turning back, Kildar," Sawn said, gritting his teeth. "I would that we could kill them all. Kill them until the All Father cried out in horror and the sun bled."

"This is very scary, indeed," Oksana said, looking at the hole.

"You can do it," Russell replied, fitting the package in the tube. "I know I can't," the massive NCO added with a grin. "You just push the package up the tunnel until I tell you to stop and then back out. If you get stuck, I'll pull you out with the rope."

"Okay," Oksana said, trying not to breathe.

"You'll be on the radio the whole way," Vanda said. The female Keldara was fiddling with the receiver box for the telephone headset Oksana was wearing. "Count to five, slowly."

"One, two, three, four, five," Oksana said.

"Can you hear me?" Vanda asked. "I mean, in your earphone?"

"Yes," Oksana replied.

"We're good."

"Okay, Oksana," Russell said, putting one hand under her shoulder and wrapping the other around her lower thigh. "Up you go."

Whether she wanted to or not, Oksana was lifted up to the tube.

"Stick your arms in," Russell said. "Push on the package. I'll push you in for the first bit."

As Oksana placed her hands on the inside of the tube she felt herself gently but firmly rammed into the hole. The package was right inside the opening but by holding her hands out she was easily able to push it ahead of her.

Someone had found a suit of a strange, slick, material called "Tyvek" that covered her from head to foot. That was nice of them since the interior of the tunnel was very dirty. And some of the Keldara soldiers had given her pads for her elbows and knees and leather gloves with rough palms so they would help her crawl. She supposed the least she should do was keep going.

"You there, Oksana?" Vanda asked.

"I'm here," Oksana said. "I am crawling forward."

The tunnel was very tight; she could barely move her arms, but she could push with her legs and pull a little. Bit by bit, pushing the package ahead of her, she moved down the tunnel.

"There is not much air in here," Oksana said, panting.

"Slow down a bit," Vanda said. "We've got hours to do this. Don't push yourself and you won't need as much air. So, you're from the Ukraine? Where?"

"I was raised in an orphanage in Kremenchug," Oksana said. "It was not very nice."

"I'm sorry," Vanda said. "Wasn't there anything that you liked growing up?"

"There was a garden that we got taken to, sometimes," Oksana said, pushing forward again, slowly. "It was very beautiful in the spring and summer. But in the orphanage there was not much. Even the place where we played didn't have grass, only some weeds."

"Do you know what you want to do when you grow up?" Vanda asked.

"I think I want to be a fashion model," Oksana said. "I see their pictures in magazines and they are all so beautiful."

"I suppose that is a goal," Vanda said dubiously. "Have you ever considered being a gardener . . . ?"

Sawn looked around the lobby of the embassy. The guard on the front, a Romanian security guard, had directed him to the visa section. But that was not, really, what he was here for. However, as he'd been briefed, there were two Marines in dress uniform in the lobby, standing at parade rest. He walked over to one of them that had more stripes.

"I am told the guard on the gate I am here for visa . . ." Sawn said.

"The visa section is down the hall, sir," the corporal said, pointing. "Good day."

"I am not here for visa," Sawn said. "I am courier for station chief. Please direct me to secure point to wait for clearance. Code is Kildar Seven Three One Two."

"Interesting clearance," the man behind the desk said, looking at his security screen.

"Yes, sir," Sawn said. "I am not know. I am only courier."

"You're a team head for the Kildar," the man said, looking over at him. "Sawn Makanee, head of Team Sawn. There's even a not-very-good picture of you."

"I would not know anything about that, sir," Sawn replied.

"I'm sure you wouldn't," the CIA station chief said, smiling. "What are your orders?"

"I am to be directed to secure console," Sawn said. "I am to enter password and put in file from disk. I am to run destruction program on file and then take file to burn point for burning. I have had all steps described to me."

"I'm sure," the station chief said, rolling his tongue in his cheek. "There was a disappearance in Chisinau last week. A slaver."

"I am not sure what you say, sir," Sawn said, looking honestly puzzled.

"And a report that a group of Georgians were passing through the town," the station chief pointed out. "Men transporting women to Macedonia, if I recall correctly, for purposes of prostitution. I don't suppose there is any connection?"

"I would not be able to say, sir," Sawn replied.

"So where is the Kildar?"

"I am not sure what you ask, sir?" Sawn said. "Can I just do upload, now?"

"The guy who gave you the packet. And your instructions."

"I am given to them by man on the street and paid money," Sawn replied. "May I do upload, now?"

"Are we going to have a disappearance, here?"

"I should be going, now," Sawn said, standing up.

"Sit down," the station chief snapped. "You're in an embassy in a secure section. You walk out when I tell you to walk out!"

"Yes, sir," Sawn said, sitting down. "Permission to speak freely, sir?" His accent had apparently disappeared.

"Yes."

"You really don't want to ask questions, sir," Sawn replied. "You really don't want to have ever seen me, to have ever heard the name Kildar, to have ever thought about any connections. Not if you value your career, sir. Because, sir, the Kildar is here for very senior American, sir. That he is here, you need to forget. If anything happens, you need to not make the connections, sir. Or very senior American will be very upset, sir. I was told to pass this to you, sir, by the Kildar, who, yes, gave me the package, sir. And to note that all he needs to do is get on the telephone and you will find that Romania is a much nicer place than Ghana or Benin, sir. I don't even know, frankly, where Ghana or Benin are, sir, but I think you'd rather be in Romania, yes?"

The station chief's face had gone from the red of anger to white and then back to red.

"You little shit, you can't just walk in here . . ."

"Sir, is telephone number," Sawn said, pulling out a number. "Would you call, sir?"

"What is this?" the station chief asked, looking at the slip of paper. It was a number in D.C. and by the exchange it was in the Pentagon. There was even a scrambler code. Fucking Defense Department getting in on intel, of course.

"Please to call, sir, or let me leave," Sawn said, tilting his head to the side. "Your choice."

The station chief looked at him haughtily for a moment and then picked up his secure phone.

"Pierson."

"And you are?"

Colonel Bob Pierson looked at his phone. The call was coming from the CIA station chief's office in Bucharest, Romania. He hadn't even known there was such.

"This is Colonel Robert Pierson, Special Operations Liaison Office. And to whom am I speaking, sir?"

"This is Jasper Weatherby, I'm the CIA Station Chief in Bucharest. I've got a young man in my office who wants to use our secure room to send a message from someone called the Kildar."

"Has he got codes?" Pierson asked.

"Yes, I've checked the database and he's one of this Jenkins' character's team leaders."

"Then let him send the message," the colonel said, his brow furrowing. "What's the problem?"

"The problem, Colonel, is that I've got what looks like a rogue DIA black op going on in my patch! I've seen the data on Jenkins and I don't want to be the one to clean up the mess!"

"Oh," Pierson replied, smiling as he leaned back in his chair. "So you're saying you're not going to let him use your secure facilities because you don't want Mike in your patch. I can see that. Tell you what, just have the Keldara toddle back to Mike and tell him that. Not a problem, I'll guarantee it. Mike won't bother you any more."

"Let me be clear, Colonel," Weatherby said, tightly. "I want him out of Romania. Now."

"I'll pass that on," Pierson replied. "Look, I'm sure you're busy and I know I am. Just send the Keldara back and forget it."

"Very well, Colonel," Weatherby said. "Thanks."

"Not a problem," Pierson said. "Good-bye."

"I won't ask what you're doing in Romania," Pierson said over the secure link.

"You didn't get the message?" Mike asked incredulously.

"The station chief blew his lid and I had him send your unnamed Keldara back," the colonel said. "He should be on his way. Tell him no big deal. I'll send a courier over. Where are you?"

"You don't want this going by anyone who's not one hundred percent, Bob," Mike replied tightly. "You really, really don't. I think . . . no, I know I got scammed. The message laid it out to date and more or less asked if you-know-who wanted me to go home with my tail between my legs and discuss it with the person that sent me or to keep going."

"You're being so discreet it's scary," Pierson said.

"I don't want to end up on C-Span, Bob," Mike replied.

"That's scary all right," the colonel said, breathing out. "I need that data."

"Damned straight," Mike said.

"If Sawn's not gotten too far, have him go cool his heels in the embassy," Pierson said, thoughtfully. "I need to make some calls."

"Mr. Makanee?" the Marine said politely. "Could you come with me, please?"

"May I ask where we are going?" Sawn said, just as politely.

"The military liaison office," the Marine replied.

As they were walking down to the office Sawn saw the station chief walking in the opposite direction. There were two Marines with him. One was carrying a box that appeared to contain personal effects while the other was discreetly if unmistakably escorting him.

"This is an outrage!" the station chief snapped as he approached Sawn.

"Sir, your orders are to remain silent," the Marine trailing him said definitely. "Further attempt to speak will require that we restrain you, sir, with respect."

The station chief opened his mouth to respond and then clamped it shut.

Sawn ignored the byplay, with the exception of stepping politely out of the way, until they were passed.

"Thanks," the Marine escorting him said. "Turn right at the next corridor."

"I did not think it best to argue in the hallway," Sawn replied, turning the corner.

"Oh, thanks for that, too," the Marine said. "But I

meant getting rid of that guy. He was a real shithead. I'd love to ask what this is all about, but I know better."

"The reason I'm here is that we are not sure," Sawn admitted as he entered the Office of Military Liaison.

# ★ Chapter Eighteen ★

It was well past his official quitting time, but Bob Pierson wasn't even sure what that meant anymore. Generally, this job had involved sixteen-hour days running up to sixty in the bad times. The military had long before learned to count "days" as the period between one solid sleep and the next and ignore such things as the rising and falling of the sun. And he was afraid this was one of those "bad" times. When Mike got that cagey on the phone he was onto something hot. And the mention of C-Span meant he was afraid it was going to explode.

So he sat and tapped the balls of his fingers together, wondering what was about to come in on the secure server.

SIPARNET was the military's internet. Set up like the civilian internet it was entirely separate and transmitted only over secure lines. Theoretically, it was uncrackable. Lord knew the military tried to keep it that way, tried very hard. And, thus far, there had been no leaks. But there was always a first time. Pierson had half considered that they might want to hand carry the data back to the States. But Mike must have thought it was time-critical.

His inbox dinged and he hit the message with a sigh.

A moment later, after the second "Holy Fuck!" he picked up the secure line to the Office of the Secretary of Defense. This was going to be a long one.

"This is Pierson in OSOL," he said. "I need to talk to the secretary. Now."

"We're over time for our cover," Adams pointed out as the Keldara fast-roped off the balcony, again.

"Well, I'd say we're dialed in," Mike replied. "I'm hoping for some word from Pierson, though."

"Thus Nadzia following you around with the sat phone," the chief said, looking over at the Keldara girl. She was wearing a short dress and more makeup than he'd ever seen on a Keldara female.

"And she builds the cover," Mike said.

"Speaking of which, I haven't gotten my ashes hauled in a few days," Adams pointed out.

"Be discreet and smart," Mike replied as the sat phone started to beep.

"Kildar," Nadzia said, walking over.

"Jenkins," Mike said once he got the headphone in.

"Approved," Pierson said. "Find the girl and gather all possible intel. You can probably guess how high that went."

"I take it that it only went up one chain," Mike said.

"Absolutely," Pierson replied. "And nobody actually had the conversations. Nobody had lots of conversations late into the night. And nobody is going to say anything about it, ever again."

"Gotcha," Mike said.

"Except one thing," Pierson replied, then paused. "I need to send that by courier, though. Damnit. I don't want any more conversation on this than necessary. It's incredibly inflammatory. Mike, you might want to just back out."

"Forget the other unless it's truly pertinent intel," Mike said. "And, no, I'm going to follow the trail. I said I'd know what was going on when it started to smell. I think I'm getting a whiff. And it stinks like hell."

"Be careful."

"There's careful and then there's careful," Mike said. "Out here."

He watched the Keldara slide down the rope again and fan out as one of the Keldara intel specialists followed them down. Anisa, who was no more than seventeen and until six months before had never seen a computer, never driven a car, never been on a date, was wearing the same black uniforms and body armor as the fighters. She ran immediately to a computer on a desk, threw the monitor on it to the side and began removing the cover. In no less than thirty seconds she had it disassembled and the hard drives stashed in a pouch. Despite the gas mask she was wearing.

Thirty seconds later, all the Keldara were back on the balcony.

"I think we're ready."

"It's a profitable night," Dejti said, looking around the club.

"They are all good nights," Nicu replied.

"I said 'profitable' not 'good'," the Albanian replied.

"This is much better than running around in the mountains being chased by the Serbs, yes?"

"Sometimes," Dejti said, stoically. "But the tension is the same, yes? Or don't you feel it? I have felt this before. There is something moving. The American is back in the house, with some of his girls. You see?"

"I saw," Nicu said. "They're buying drinks and whores. What about it?"

"I don't trust him. He doesn't have the right feel."

"You worry too much," Nicu said, shrugging.

"And you don't worry enough," the Albanian said darkly. "You think that because we have done well, that it will always continue. You think that because we have the government, that there are no other forces against us. That is what Kadul thought, too. And now who owns the club? Perhaps the Americans are looking to take over, eh?"

"Calm down," Nicu said. "I will get you a girl, a young one. Have your fun with her, you will feel better."

"No, not tonight," Dejti replied, looking out at the dance floor. Too many of the fucking guards that were supposed to be looking for threats were looking at the women. Most were not his people. He could trust his tribe, but too many had to be in positions like his, handling the money and the girls. Muscle you could hire, but could you depend on it? If not, when things went wrong, could you depend upon them to die, to keep you alive, to fight for you like members of your family? No. That was why it was Albanians who were on his cars. It was Albanians in the office, counting the money and bundling it. Nicu thought he ran the club. Let him handle the women; Dejti's people handled the money.

"Tonight I want to be clear," Dejti continued. "There is a feel in the air, yes? Like before a storm when you are walking in the mountains; you can feel the prickling on your skin? Like before an ambush."

"There will be no ambushes here," Nicu said, yawning. "And I wouldn't know about storms in the mountains. I'm a city boy."

"So you are," Dejti replied. *You useless shit,* he thought. As soon as he could get a decent Albanian to replace him, Nicu was going to be a graveyard boy.

"You need a girl," Nicu said, waving at one of the guards. "Dragos, go and get Bohuslava. You'll like her," he added to Dejti. "Very young, very new, from Slovakia. Beautiful. Don't mark her too badly, please."

"I said I didn't want a girl you stupid—" Dejti started to reply, then stopped as screams and coughing erupted on the dance floor.

"What is happening?" Nicu yelled as the music kept throbbing.

"Someone dropped a stink bomb!" the nearest guard said, just as Nicu caught a whiff of the stench. Already people were crowding to the exits.

"Fucking jokers," Nicu growled, standing up just as the ground thumped hard, twice.

"This is no joke," Dejti shouted. "Out! Now!"

"What?" Nicu yelled. "Why?"

"Because, this is an attack," the Albanian yelled as he ran for the back door to the offices.

Mike leaned back in the booth and tried to ignore the stench.

"I'm really wondering about this," he said.

"Timing," Adams said. "And . . . now."

The three Keldara girls got up and started screaming and coughing, running for the nearby door that had just been opened. Nicu had finally gotten up and was hurrying for the same door, his bodyguards closing in around him.

Mike, Adams and Russell got up and followed the girls, shouting at them to calm down. Mike caught one just before they reached the line of bodyguards.

"You little bitch!" Mike yelled, slapping the girl so hard she fell over. "You don't try to run on me!"

He turned to grab at another, who had literally bounced off one of the guards, and continued through with a stab into the guard's gut. The polymer blade sank up to the small hilt and he yanked sideways, but left it in the wound, as the guard started to crumple.

Adams and Russell had each accounted for two more and that left just one between the door and Mike. The guard had drawn a gun but had no fucking clue how to use it at that range.

Mike ducked down and sideways, wrapping a hand around the barrel and left the guard with a broken finger that had nearly been ripped off.

Nicu was through the door but Mike took up a stance and put a round right through his leg as Russell turned and shot the nearest guard that hadn't been covering the retreat.

"Sixteen seconds," Greznya yelled, ripping off her shoes and rolling to the side. She somehow had acquired a pistol as well and used the body of one of the dead guards as a resting spot to fire across the room, taking out another guard. "GO!"

Russell was already through the door, dipping down to lift Nicu by his collar as the assault team came through the door to the offices. There were two guards between them and Dejti and one got off a burst from his Skoda Skorpion. It was his last action as the following Keldara put two rounds in him, center of mass. The other guard had already flown forward, his face blasting open as a 9mm round from Chief Adams blew through the back of his head and out the front.

Dejti had drawn a pistol but he was surrounded and slowly laid it on the ground, his hands in the air.

"Twelve seconds!" Greznya yelled, backing through the door and closing and bolting it.

"Tag and bag 'im," Russell said, thrusting Nicu at the Keldara now filling the hall. Two were covering the far end, one was working on the downed Keldara and the other two caught Nicu, rapidly wrapping his hands and mouth with rigger's tape.

"You're going to die for this," Dejti said as Russell caught a tossed roll of tape and pulled off a strip.

"I've heard that one before," Mike said.

"Seven, six . . ."

"How's Endar?" Mike asked as the van pulled away.

"Bad," Yevgenii answered, pulling off his black balaclava. "I think even if we could take him to the hospital he would not make it."

"Vanner, status on the casualty?" Mike asked as soon as he had his headset in.

"Gone, sir," Vanner answered. "I get terminal reactions. He took one through the aorta, I think. They must have been using hot rounds."

"That Skorpion was a 5.54 variant," Adams said. "It went right through the plate. I checked. Three rounds, one of them dead through the target point."

"Understood," Mike said. "Continue plan."

"What do we have?" Mike asked as he walked into the new command post.

It was another abandoned warehouse. The former Eastern Bloc was littered with them. Mostly they had held military equipment that was designed to fight the evil Americans and their hordes of puppet-state armies. Once the world woke up and shook off the miasma of communism, they'd been filled with nothing of much use. The military equipment was sold off at ten cents on the dollar, if that, the factories mostly shut down, and the warehouses now awaited someone to fill them with . . . something.

At the moment this one was filled with white vans, computers, cots and Keldara racking out on the floor and talking in low tones about the op. It had been successful, but the loss of Endar was clearly weighing on them.

And towards the back it was filled by two guys trussed up in station chairs and the group regarding them with interest.

"We got anything useful to ask them yet, Vanner?" Mike asked.

"Not really," Patrick replied. "We're still looking for Natalya. Do you know that they've moved over two hundred girls named Natalya alone in the last year. Twenty in the period we're looking for."

"You should be through twenty already," Mike said.

"Their database is for shit," Patrick sighed. "They're using Excel if you can believe it. Finding a grouping of Natalyas is easy. I think it's only twenty in the date range; some of the dates aren't input right. And I've looked at those; she's not any of them. So I'm expanding the search."

"Hurry," Mike said, turning to look at Nicu and Dejti. "I'm looking forward to asking these guys the right questions."

"Ah, here she is," Vanner said, happily. "She was received on the fifteenth of May and shipped out on the third of July. The guy transporting her was called Mehmet Hubchev and she was going to the Belgrade facility . . ."

"So we're going to Belgrade?" Mike said.

"But!" Vanner added. "There's a note that she was to be transshipped to Rozaje. Where in the hell is Rozaje?"

"Montenegro," Adams said. "Near the Albanian border."

"That got a rise out of Dejti, here," Mike said, stepping forward and yanking the tape off the Albanian's mouth. "So, Dejti, what's so important about Rozi or whatever?"

"I tell you nothing!" the Albanian said, spitting at him.

"Hey, a live one," Mike said. "Chief, the screams really hurt my ears, stuff something in his mouth."

"Okay," Adams said, stepping forward while he drew his knife. He took Nicu's ear in a thumb and forefinger and then cut it off, neatly. Then in one swift motion he stuffed it in Dejti's mouth and followed it with a wad of cloth. "That do?"

"Works," Mike said, stepping around the back of the chair to pick up the sledgehammer. "Now, it only took a couple of wacks from this to get Nicu's friend . . . what was his name?"

"Yuri," Vanner said helpfully. "Hey, boss, there are only a couple of girls in each shipment sent to this Rozaje place. Most of them get sent to other brothels or straight to Albania with notes to check them for breaking and then send them through the pipeline to Italy. I only count . . . twenty females in the last six months that went to Rozaje. I've got it on a map; there can't be much of a brothel there; it's tiny."

"So, Dejti," Mike said, pulling the hammer back. "We're going to talk about Rozaje."

Once the screams had died down, Adams reached for the ear. Then he picked up a smaller sledge, held the Albanian's mouth shut by pushing up on his chin and smashed out his teeth.

"Sorry about that addition, boss," he said, fishing in the whimpering man's mouth. "I didn't want him biting me while I got Nicu's ear out. Guess where I got that idea?"

"Not a problem," Mike said. "As long as he can talk. So, Dejti, what's the deal with Rozaje."

"You look for girl," Dejti said. "One girl."

"That's right, one insignificant little Ukrainian hooker," Mike said. "So what's so important about Rozaje?"

"If she went to Rozaje, she is dead."

"We will find who did this and kill them," Luan Dejti said, looking around the shattered office. Not much was visible; it was clear that whoever had hit the club had left explosives behind. Those had started a fire and even the police said there was not much evidence. Witnesses had seen some people enter the back rooms, but nobody could identify who they were. Except the dead guards, possibly.

"They were professionals," Yarok Bezhmel said. Bezhmel was one of the few "made" men in the Albanian mafia who was not an Albanian. The former Spetznaz officer was highly regarded by them, however, for his professional training and total ruthlessness. "The shooting was short and precise, the bombs were precisely placed and whoever took down the guards at the door killed four guards armed with pistols and machine guns with nothing but plastic knives."

"So, who are they?" Luan asked. "I want their balls. He was my cousin. We cannot just walk away from this."

"Oh, no," the Russian said, squatting down and picking up a spent cartridge. "Hmm . . . American 5.56 for their M-16s and variants. I'd say that, somehow, you have angered the American military my friend. That would explain the precision, at least. I would say that this is the work of American special operations. Their SEALs or even Delta Force. Perhaps one of their quieter groups that works with the CIA or the Defense Department intelligence. Yes, that would be it most likely. Their 'black ops' groups. So, who did you anger in America?"

"This should not be," Luan said breathlessly. "What have I done?"

"Perhaps you got the wrong girl," Yarok answered, standing up. "I heard that Yuri in Chisinau has disappeared. A very clean operation, very professional. He did much work with Nicu, no?"

"Yes, but I have no idea how much," Luan said, waving around the room. "Everything is destroyed!"

"And if anything is gone, it is not evident to the fine Romanian police," Yarok said, dusting off his knees. "I think I need to go to Chisinau and ask questions. Also of your employees here. But I will have better questions when I return. Will you reopen the club?"

"Perhaps," Luan said, frowning. "It was a very good business for us. But I will need a new front man. I don't suppose you want to run a club?"

"Not at all," Yarok replied. "But I do need you to get some people together for me, some people that are good with weapons. Very good. We will need them."

# ★ Chapter Nineteen ★

"Well, I'd say that our cover is going to be pretty thin after that one, Mike," Adams pointed out.

Mike looked out the window of the small hotel south of Belgrade and shrugged.

"I suppose we know the next main objective," Mike said. "Bastards."

It was raining in Serbia and the hills to the south were cloaked in clouds. A shitty day for a shitty discussion.

"It was, more or less, what we said they were doing with the girls," Adams pointed out.

"Yeah, but I really hoped that it didn't exist in reality," Mike said.

"The world's a fucked up place," Adams opined. "So, do you think the senator was a client?"

"But why's he looking for a girl that's dead?" Mike asked. "That just doesn't make sense."

"We don't know she's dead," Adams pointed out. "We only have what Dejti said."

"They snuff all the girls that go to Rozaje," Mike said, still looking out at the rain.

"Most," Adams said.

"He only said that after we'd broken his other leg," Mike said. "I'm not sure it was good intel. Besides, he was hard to understand after you broke out his teeth."

"So we go to Rozaje, discuss it with this Bulgarian that runs the place," Adams said. "We discuss it with him really personally."

"I'm thinking about that," Mike said. "But there's a bunch of problems."

"It's in the KFOR sector," the chief said. "I think the Fijians have got that area at the moment."

"I really don't want to get in a fight with KFOR." The Kosovo Force was an international peacekeeping enforcement group placed in the Kosovo region of Serbia after the brief Kosovo war. Effectively, they policed the region. If the Keldara went in and wiped out another Albanian brothel they wouldn't be dealing with just the local police. And KFOR had access to modern forensic techniques. They might not choose to use them under the circumstances, but it was something to think about.

The worst bit, however, was what was unsaid.

"And KFOR knows about it," Adams pointed out.

Up until then. Damn.

"He's sure?" the President asked.

"As sure as he can be, Mr. President," Pierson replied. "I sent him a code disc so we could send and receive highly encrypted transmissions. His last transmissions indicate that the compound in Kosovo is used for terminal sexual purposes . . ."

"They bring in hookers from around Eastern Europe so

rich and very sadistic bastards can kill them during sex," the defense secretary said, bluntly.

"Yes, sir," the colonel said. At this point, he'd gotten used to briefing the President; it went with the job. Office of Liaison was founded to keep the current president up-to-date on what was going on with very black, very special operations organizations around the world. Pierson had gotten Mike dumped in his lap on his first operation, back when Mike had a real life and a real name. Since then he'd been Mike's "control," to the extent that the former SEAL had any such thing.

If anyone, he should have been the point of contact on this mission. It was obvious, now, why the senator had not used him.

"What in the hell was Traskel thinking?" the President snapped. "Did he think that Mike wouldn't find out where the girl had gone?"

"It's possible, Mr. President, that he was unaware," Pierson pointed out. "We don't know that the senator was a client."

"He traveled to Eastern Europe during the same time frame," the national security advisor pointed out. Her normally dark face was gray with anger.

"So did three other senators from his party," the secretary of defense pointed out. "And two from yours, Mr. President. So did their families. And it was a very open trip."

"At the taxpayers' expense," the President said angrily.

"Actually, Mr. President, it was paid for by a special interest group," the secretary of defense replied. "The International Association for Women's Rights. Apparently they hadn't anticipated how . . . interested the congressmen and senators would be in the subject; there are quite a few confidential reports on the trip. Much went on that would be rather—"

"That if the American public got wind of it would cause a firestorm," the national security advisor said with a sigh.

"I'm thinking less of the senator than of his son," the secretary said musingly. "He had an entire report all of his own."

"If we even hint about this . . ." the President said.

"We can't do a thing," his chief of staff said. "We need those reports to stay absolutely confidential. If there's even a hint that anything about that trip came from our party, it would blast back on us, hard."

"And in the meantime, we continue to just let it happen," the national security advisor said, coldly.

"You know the problems with stopping it," the President pointed out. "The pressures are too high for us to do more than spit in the wind. And we've got other fish to fry, like stopping terrorists from attacking the United States. In the meantime, it goes on. And, no, I don't like that. Do you think I wouldn't stop it if I could?"

"No, sir," the NSA said, sighing. "It just, sorry, pisses me off."

"Well, I suspect that this one operation is going to get stopped," the secretary of defense said, smiling. "And stopped hard."

"What are we going to do with Endar?" Adams asked.

The question of what to do with three bodies was the current topic of discussion. Two of them were easy. There are a million ways to get rid of a body, some of which even worked if you didn't want it discovered. However, all of them were a bit cold for one of your own troops. And repatriating the body was out of the question.

"We're going to take a little side trip," Mike said. "There are some nice beaches down on the Adriatic coast and I think the girls are due for a break."

"We're just going to cart a body around for the next few days?" Adams asked, aghast.

"Look," Mike said. "We're carrying eight girls who look as if they're intended for immoral purposes, over sixty weapons, body armor, night vision goggles, entry tools, bugging tools, hacking tools and at least six remaining kilos of explosive. What's a couple of bodies to add to that?"

"Smell?" Adams asked.

"Get some dry ice."

Yarok scanned through the computer records, looking for he knew not what.

He'd told Dejti that the group was American special operations, but he still wasn't sure. The methods were the same; if he had to guess he'd say SEAL by the entry patterns and the way the groups moved, based on the few remaining eyewitnesses. But there was no reason he could find that an American special operations unit would attack the Albanians. Quite the opposite, in fact, given some of the videos in Dejti's hands.

He'd nosed around Chisinau, a bastard city in his opinion, and some of Yuri's associates had mentioned a group of Americans that had also been nosing around.

They supposedly had Georgian girls they were taking to a "special auction" in Montenegro. The also had more muscle than was normal, at least fifteen or twenty Georgians.

The database he was looking at was from Interpol, a listing of potential security threats in and around the EU zone. The problem was, there were so many he wasn't sure what he was looking for. The group might not have even been Georgian, but he was concentrating there. But between the Ossetian separatist movements and the Chechnyans . . .

He stopped in his perusal and backed up a page. There was a note in the database about a new Georgian militia with American training. A mountain infantry group called the Keldara.

"An American using the name of Michael Jenkins has begun to form a new militia in the Georgian mountains. Said militia has engaged with Chechnyan terrorist groups twice. Equipped with light small arms, the group has undergone training with five or more Western special operations trainers. Results of training unknown."

There was a picture of "Jenkins" and he matched the description of the American in Chisinau. Of course, so did half the men in the world. But Yarok copied it off the database and mailed it to his men in Timisoara to show to the witnesses from the club.

He briefly considered simply turning the information over to the Romanian authorities. They'd put the word out through Interpol and that would certainly inconvenience this "Jenkins" character. But it wouldn't fulfill his mission, which was to put the man in an unmarked grave.

However, Interpol also kept a database of people using

hotels. It was slow to update, but it might give him an idea where Jenkins was going . . .

The girls liked the hotel.

The Hotel Caesaria was on the Adriatic coast of Montenegro, a narrow strip of land that included the cities of Kotor and Perast. The town of Zelenika, which was where the hotel was located, could barely count as a town, much less a city. There was a straggle of old houses, a small market and a wharf to support the primary local industry: small boat fishing. The majority of the boats looked as if they'd been constructed in the time of the Argonauts. They were open "caiques," lightly built wooden dories originally designed for one or two men to row them or to use small sails. Their only concession to the twenty-first century was the addition of small diesel motors. The fishermen would generally leave in the afternoon, go out in to the reefs that choked the area, lay down gill nets with gourd floats, then pick them up the next morning, starting usually at dawn.

Zelenika was near the opening of a large bay that serviced the boat traffic of both Kotor and Perast. There wasn't much for either; local trade was highly limited and there wasn't even a regular ferry service to Dubrovnik, the nearest major city, much less to Italy which was just across the Adriatic. Zelenika was the definition of "backwater." The hotel was just down the road from the main "town," near the very tip of the cape that protected the bay.

There were a few beaches but mostly the coastline was too rocky for good swimming. There was, however, enough room for some sunbathing and a small beach by the hotel. Mike had explained to the girls that, as part of their cover, it was important that they looked as if they were just on a trip and getting a little sun. After some pro-forma protests, most of the Keldara had suited up and headed for the beach along with the three "liberated" hookers.

Which left Mike out in a small Lada, looking for a boat. Two, actually.

Zelenika mostly fronted on its excuse for a wharf. The small bay that the city faced was curved in a semi-circle with ancient jetties protecting it from northerly gales. The wharf itself was a seawall that looked as if the original stonework was Roman and had rickety wooden piers jutting out from it. It was backed by a narrow street made of flag-stones patched with everything from bricks to concrete to sand. There were a couple of sailboats anchored in the middle of the bay and a few ancient speedboats tied up at the piers. Nets were hung up along the seawall to dry but no fishermen were around when Mike parked his car, removed the distributor to hopefully prevent its theft, and began looking for a bar.

The first storefront was a general store. Just checking around, Mike went inside.

There was a woman who looked to be a hundred, and was probably forty, sitting behind the counter watching some show in Serbian. It mostly involved women crying, which was about par for this region. The shelves were filled with some of the worst snack foods Mike had ever seen, and he'd been in plenty of third world stores. For that matter, most of them looked as if their sell-by date was before his birthday and they were covered in dust. He peeked in the two refrigerators and backed away hastily. The contents were mostly local erzatz Coke knock-offs. He'd had one of those during his previous trip through the area and regretted it for days.

As he went out he had to shake his head. There was a postcard rack celebrating the wonders of visiting scenic Zelenika. Most of the postcards were faded to the point of illegibility. He wondered who ever figured this place for a major tourist destination.

The second store was a fish market. From the smell, he was more than willing to pass right by.

The third, however, was what he was looking for. The small restaurant and bar—the distinction was small in places like this—had a few rickety tables out front and a big sign in Serbian that had seen better days. Under it another weathered sign proclaimed that he had found "The Head of the Albanian."

His kind of place.

Mike sat down at one of the tables, which rocked ferociously on the flagstones of the street, and wondered if he'd get any service.

After staring out at the not-particularly-scenic scene in front of him for about a half an hour, and noting the lack of boat traffic, he saw a man come out from the back wiping his hands on a rather dirty cloth.

"You want drink?" the man said in passable English.

"Wine," Mike replied. "In the bottle."

"Carafe," the man said, slapping the back of his right hand into his left palm in the local signal for "all gone."

"Carafe, then," Mike sighed. The alcohol would probably

fix whatever was growing in the carafe. "Some bread and fish. As long as it's not from the place next door."

"No problem," the man said, grinning a gap-toothed smile. "Is fresh."

"Fresh last week, probably," Mike said.

"Today," the man replied. "Fishermen come here. I buy their fish. You want prawns?"

"Steamed, if you can," Mike said, nodding.

The prawns—local shrimp and about half the size of a small lobster—were actually pretty good. They'd be better with drawn butter, but that had never caught on in the Adriatic region. Hell, in the Mediterranean, for that matter. The wine, on the other hand, was paint thinner. Mike ordered tea, hot, which wasn't exactly awful, and sipped at that.

It was about three PM when the fishermen started to show up. Mostly they headed for their boats and started to load the dried nets into large baskets, then stowed them in the covered forecastles. However, a few stopped into the tavern for a belt before heading out.

When most of the boats were gone, one of the men who was clearly a fisherman remained, morosely sipping at the paint thinner wine.

"No boat?" Mike asked in Russian.

"Is in yard," the man replied in something that was half Serbian, half Russian. Both were Slavic root languages and hadn't actually drifted that much. They were about as similar as two types of German. "You fish?"

"I want boat," Mike replied. "Two. One to buy, one to rent. Where's yard?"

"Down around corner," the man said, pointing to the south east. "I show you?"

"And get a cut?" Mike asked, smiling.

"Is good day not to fish," the man said. "Especially if I get some money anyway."

On the east side of the town was another small bay Mike hadn't suspected was there. There weren't any piers but there was a narrow strip of sand and rocks where a small boatyard existed.

There were about three caiques in various stages of completion, two more drawn up and being worked on, supposedly, and a few small speedboats. Most of the latter were clearly the worse for wear but two were in decent condition at first glance and one even had an outboard motor mounted.

"This is Drulovic," the fisherman said, walking up to a man who was bent over a torn-apart diesel. "Drulovic, this is man who wants boats."

"I need one of those," Mike said, pointing to the caiques drawn up on the shore. "To buy. And a speedboat to use for a day or so. Both have to work."

"Those I'm making for people," Drulovic said, wiping his hands on a cloth. "One of the others, it was Vasa's. He's gone. Never paid me. It needs work."

"Two days," Mike said. "That's when I need it. How much?"

"Two thousand euros," Drulovic said, shrugging.

"Three hundred," Mike said, automatically.

"You want it working in two days, you give me two thousand euros," Drulovic said, grinning. "And you give me another three thousand as deposit on other boat. What you going to do with it?"

"Bury somebody," Mike snapped. "Five hundred for the caique; it only has to work for a couple of hours. And a thousand deposit."

"A thousand for the caique," Dulovic said thoughtfully. "A thousand deposit and a hundred to use the other."

"Done," Mike replied, dipping in his pocket and pulling out a wad of cash. "Half now, half when I pick it up."

"You carry a lot of money around," Drulovic mused as he counted out half the money.

"Very few people are stupid enough to try to steal from me," Mike replied, handing over the wad of cash. "Otherwise I'll need to buy another boat."

# ★ Chapter Twenty ★

"Okay, you are officially nuts," Adams said as Mike pulled the caique up on the rock-strewn shore of the cove.

Finding the right place for the ceremony had turned out to be the toughest job; coves along the Adriatic that were landable at all tended to have villas. As did this one, the difference being that the owners weren't home.

Most of the Keldara were gathered on the shore. Endar had been loaded on a bier made of four different woods while the two slavers still rested in the plastic bags that, along with liberal addition of dry ice, had kept the smell down for the last week.

"First the wood," Mike said. "You got the kerosene?"

"Of course I have the kerosene," Adams snapped. "And this is going to be visible for miles!"

"By the time anybody gets to the boat, they're going to be toast," Mike replied. "Everybody checked out."

"I even paid the bill."

"Sawn."

"Yes, Kildar," the Keldara team leader said, stepping forward.

"The wood is to be loaded by Tenghiz and Padrec,"

Mike said, stepping back. "Then the bodies by Slavic and his team. His weapons are to be laid by Rusudani. You will take the position of Priest of the All Father and sing him to sea."

"Yes, Kildar," Sawn said, nodding.

"Before we begin, I will explain," Mike said, stepping onto the moonlit beach. All lights had been left behind in the vans along with a small security detachment composed mostly of the trainers. "The translation of the song of the wanderers shows that your tribe came, long ago, from among the ranks of seafaring warriors. It was their tradition to send their great warriors who had died in battle to sea. They would shove a specially made boat into the sea and set it afire. We're going to drive this one out to sea and then set it on fire with Endar, his weapons and his dead foes. I cannot bring Endar back to the valley. This is the best choice I can think of."

"We understand, Kildar," Sawn replied, nodding. "It is said that even in the days of the Tsar a few of the dead each year, especially the Family seniors, would be burned on the pyre. This is a rite we accept. Thank you."

"Like I said, best I can do," Mike answered shrugging. "Lets get started."

Sawn wasn't the best singer among the Keldara, but he was pretty good. And he'd heard the words of the funeral rite, the Keldara funeral rite, enough times to be able to repeat them. Mike wasn't sure what language they were in; it certainly wasn't Georgian and he suspected it wasn't Celtic like the song of the wanderers. The latter was sung each spring by the best voice in the tribe. At the last ceremony McKenzie, the former SAS NCO, had been able to partially translate it as an epic about a wandering group of fighters that had come from the far north and been captured and enslaved, then forced to defend an inhospitable fortress on the edges of the empire. The clues in the song were clear to Mike, who had wondered about some of the oddities of the Keldara and the caravanserai.

The original Keldara had been a group of Norse, and apparently Scot, warriors that had made their way down through the Mediterranean until they encountered the Byzantine Empire. Since they were clearly related to the guards of the Byzantine Emperors, the Varangian guard, they were grouped with a small team of actual Varangians and sent to guard the caravanserai, which at the time was a lucrative income generator on the Silk Road.

Since that time, with influxes of succeeding waves of invaders, their fortunes had fallen even further, leaving them as mere farmers in a lost mountain valley. But the warrior core remained and had been brought out by the training of the American and British soldiers Mike had brought in.

Now, the circle closed. The latest Keldara dead, like their forebearers of old, would be sent out to sea on a wooden boat with the bodies of his foes at his feet and his weapons piled at his head.

It was a hell of a lot better than being dumped in an unmarked grave. And since Mike intended to take the boat to damned near the horizon before lighting it off, there was little chance anyone would notice. Or, given the area, care.

Of course, they'd pulled the ammo. They were going to need it.

# ★ Chapter Twenty-One★

The villa was actually southwest of Rozaje, right up in the mountains near the Albanian border. The road from Rozaje, according to the map and satellite photos, stopped not far beyond the villa, but a collection of trails was evident as well, some of them passable to all-terrain vehicles. It was likely that the villa was on a smuggling route from Serbia into Albania. The same routes had supplied the KLA during the war against the Serbians.

Mike had expected that getting into the area would be harder than normal. The region was under the sporadic control of the Kosovo Force and Mike had expected more efficient checks than had been characteristic up to this point. The first check, the "border" crossing from the Serbian controlled area, had really had him worried. The troops were French and thus, he'd assumed, unbribable.

However, while there were French troops in the area, the actual border crossing had been under the control of Serbians. Mike had spoken to them in Russian and put in the usual tip. The Serbs had looked in the vans, seen that the cargo was mostly women, and waved them through.

From there the trip had been smooth. There were

two internal checkpoints that had caught them but at the first the same tip had worked and at the second Katya and Nikki had sealed the deal. Mike was still unsure about bargaining his way through on the backs of the girls, but if it worked he wasn't going to knock it.

Montenegro was an anomaly. Depending upon who you asked, it was either a province of Serbia, according to Serbia, an independent state, according to most of the residents, or something in between, according to most of the rest of the world and certainly to the U.S. government. In 1992, in the wake of the Dayton Accords, the then legislature and president had agreed to not separate from Serbia, as Croatia and Bosnia had done. The decision was so controversial that even the U.S. government didn't recognize it. Furthermore, the Serbians were unsure how to deal with it since Montenegro had its own freely elected government and, notably, its own burgeoning army. So for the time being, nobody rocked the boat. Technically, it was a province, but in reality it was an independent state.

The name "Montenegro" translated as "Black Mountain" and in keeping with the name, Montenegro, whether it was a province or a country, was definitely mountainous. The mountains weren't alpine in their heights, not even up to Georgian standards, but they were pretty serious hills. The country stretched from the plains of, definitely, Serbia to the Adriatic and the very limited flatland was either cultivated or covered by cities.

Their objective was in keeping with the terrain and, therefore, wasn't a pretty sight from the perspective of assault.

"Right on the hilltop," he noted, looking through the binoculars and taking pictures.

"The outer perimeter security is KFOR," Adams noted. "Fijians."

"We're going to have to figure something out about them," Mike said. "We don't want to go around killing KFOR troops."

"Tasers?" Adams asked.

"Maybe."

The high hill had a wall terraced into its sides as well. Anyone approaching was going to be in view. And Mike had gotten a count on at least six guards inside the compound. That meant, at a guess, something on the order of twenty total in three shifts. They'd have to lay this one out carefully. A frontal assault had all the makings of a disaster.

"We'll leave a couple of the Keldara up here to get the guard schedule," Mike said, sliding back down the ridge overlooking the compound. "Two days to prep. Let's get working on a plan."

"Guards change three times per day," Vanner said, pointing to the sand table of the compound that was set up in the small conference room the hotel hosted. If the owners had questions about why a group of slave traders wanted a conference room, a hefty tip had answered them. "Girls normally arrive during the day and not later than midnight, according to our sources." By which he meant the now deceased Dejti.

"This is going to be hairy," Vanner continued, looking at his console. "We don't even have a good internal schematic.

What if they dump their records when we hit? I mean, even if they've made backup DVDs, you throw those in a microwave and set it on high and they're toast."

"I think we might be overmuscling this one," Mike said, looking at the window design again. Over the years, Western special operations and their intelligence support units had developed an encyclopedic database of windows and doors throughout the world. Even older, by definition custom-made, windows such as those on the villa fit basic parameters which were in the database. And Vanner just happened to have acquired a copy.

Mike sometimes had to wonder if Vanner was his actual control.

"Define," Adams said, looking up from the rough floor plan that had been worked out from external observation. The outer rooms were sketched in, lightly, with vast areas of gray area. They knew there was a basement, there was a visible door, but they had no idea of the layout.

"Well, overmuscling is when you're using too much force for a mission," Vanner said, looking up from his computer with a smile.

"Wise ass," the chief growled. "So what are you thinking?"

"I'm thinking we're going to need Lasko and Praz," Mike replied musingly. "And some special equipment."

"Make up a list," Vanner said, sighing.

"And we need more interior data," Mike said, rubbing his chin in thought. "We can try to find one of the Albanians that work there and bribe him for a layout . . ."

"They're all from one clan," Vanner said, flipping through a chart of the known guards. "At least it looks that way."

"Which would be risky," Mike continued. "We can try to insert a girl into the place, such as Katya . . ."

"I was wondering why you'd been carting her around," Adams said. "Besides for looks."

"Might I remind everyone that this is a snuff house?" Vanner pointed out. "Whoever goes in there probably isn't going to come out!"

"It's Katya," Mike said, offhand, then smiled. "Just joking."

"Thank God," Vanner said, breathing out.

"Besides," Mike continued, still looking at the windows, "what I really meant was that I'd be damned surprised if Katya got snuffed. Even if we weren't banking on her getting intel out to us. I mean, think about it: Fat middle-aged European or American or Japanese rich jackass, poor-little-practically-virginal-crying-thing . . ."

"And you've been teaching Katya hand-to-hand, haven't you?" Adams said, nodding. "You think . . .?"

"No," Mike replied. "Because I don't think she could get the intel out. Kill her perp, sure. If it was an assassination mission I'd send her in a heartbeat, pardon the pun. But for this, I don't think she's right."

"So . . . what?" Adams said, throwing up his hands.

"Pleased to meet you . . ." Mike whispered, finally looking up, "won't you guess my name?"

"The group that hit the Club Dracul is called the Keldara," Yarok said, bringing up the first slide. "They are a Georgian militia group, using the women smuggling routes and a cover of being sex smugglers. There are about fifteen to twenty shooters in the group as well as some women from their tribe. I'm not sure of the function of the women. In addition, they've picked up one or more women from normal sources on the way."

"Where are they now?" Boris Dejti asked, angrily. "We will rape their women before their eyes then gouge them out."

Boris Dejti was the senior Dejti clan member in charge of all the scattered "operations" in the Balkans. There were members of the clan more senior than he, but they were all semiretired in the backcountry of Albania. However, Boris realized he was going to have to have a talk with the Senior Fathers about the events of Club Dracul. And he wanted to be able to give them a timeline on how long it was going to take to avenge the attack.

"You will be lucky to kill them at all," Yarok said. "Remember what they did to the club. Its defenses were formidable but they took it down with, at most, one casualty. I think you had better leave them to me. As to where they are, they were supposed to be going to Montenegro. They certainly haven't used a major hotel there, but that might have been disinformation. The last report I had on their movements was in Serbia. They may be heading for Kosovo."

"Then they are heading into the lion's den," Boris replied happily. "We will find them and kill them. There are many fighters available in Kosovo and Montenegro."

"You're certainly permitted to try," Yarok said with a sigh. "But don't say I didn't warn you. I'd recommend increasing security at facilities in the south. They have taken at least three people and probably tortured them for information. They are looking for something. When we figure out what, we'll know where they are going . . ."

Mike loved the night. Of course, that was fundamental to his one great gift, but he still loved it.

The night had never held any terrors for him, even as a child. He remembered walking through darkened woods when he was no more than eight and simply being enthralled by the difference between the night and day. At night, every sound was clearer and sharper, all his senses alive to the slightest hint of wrongness.

Like the waves of smell wafting off the Fijian sentry.

There was a thirty meter open area to cross to the first terrace and the sentry was on a regular beat. One hundred paces south, turn, one hundred paces north. On the other hand, he wasn't Teutonic in his pace. Quite often he'd simply stop and lean against the wall. If that happened while Mike was crossing, it would be a bitch.

The choices were simple, fast or slow. If Mike waited until the sentry was near the end of his beat and then darted across, he could be up on the second terrace before the guy reached the end. On the other hand, if he stopped and turned, Mike's movement was sure to give him away.

However, if Mike went slow there was a good chance he'd be caught in the open area by the sentry. He was good enough that the sentry might simply walk past. Might.

There was a small niche in the wall of the terrace where some stones had fallen and lay scattered in the grass. As a hiding place it would normally be discounted, but between Mike's ghillie suit and luck, he could probably hole up there to let the sentry pass.

As the sentry continued on his southward journey, Mike opted for a middle ground. He lifted himself up on fingers and toes, a leopard stance, and slithered out onto the close-cropped grass.

There was a half-moon tonight, but the clouds were fairly solid. The mottled light actually made seeing harder. If the clouds broke up he might have problems. For now, though, they were still solid. There was also a slight breeze from the southwest, blowing any sound he might make, slight at best, away from the sentry.

Mike kept his head down, looking mostly at the grass with occasional glances at the sentry, and envisioned himself as darkness and silence. He wasn't sure if the mental state was really helpful or not, it seemed like mumbo-jumbo to him, but he'd used it most of his career and even if it was only self-hypnosis he wasn't going to change things now.

He made it to the niche and paused as the sentry turned to head back. All the cover he had was the broken wall and his ghillie suit. He had a silenced .45 if it came down to cases, but he really didn't want to kill this Fijian guy. For one thing, he didn't deserve it. All he was was a poor guy far from home told to guard a facility. There was a 99.999 to infinity percent chance that the guy had no idea what was going on in the villa. But even if he did, Mike would eventually have to fess up to having offed him. Which would drop him in the clacky. Killing Albanian pimps was one thing, killing a soldier on a UN sponsored peace-enforcement mission was another. Words would be had. And then there was the fact that it would probably blow the mission.

The sentry made it to within five meters of Mike's spot and stopped, turning to look out at the darkness and stretching his back. He propped his weapon on the wall, about three feet from Mike's niche, leaned back against it and fumbled in his pocket for a cigarette and light.

Mike closed his eyes as the lighter flared and the smell of cheap, strong tobacco wafted over him and tried not to sigh. Lord only knew how long the guy was going to rest there. Mike was just settling in to wait when he heard a hail from the north and cringed; the sergeant of the guard was wandering around. He'd only done that one other night. Why tonight?

Mike didn't speak a word of Fijian, but he'd spent enough time around grunts and doing guard duty himself to fill in the blanks.

*"What a night, huh?"*

*"Just like last night. Nothing to fucking do but look at the woods. Why the fuck are we here?"*

*"Because we're too poor to be sitting on the beach in Fiji."*

*"I should have gone to work for my cousin Emil at the dive shop."*

*"I didn't know your cousin Emil had a dive shop."*

*"Sure, down in Toraborabawankununka. You know it."*

*"Sure, Toraborabawankununka Dive and Sport. Hey, I used to go there when I was on vacation . . ."*

Mike suddenly realized he was muttering the lines of dialogue and stopped as the sergeant said something he translated as "Well, I've got to get back and check my paperwork . . ."

. . . and wandered back to the north.

He was definitely getting too old, and too introspective, for this work.

With the sergeant headed north, the guard headed south. Mike waited until they were both separated by at least thirty meters from his position, stood up, stretched his aching joints and oozed up onto the wall.

Thirty yards from the woodline to the first terrace. Three terraces, each between twenty and thirty meters wide. Then the final wall up onto the balconies. From the terraces, except when he scrambled to the next higher, he wasn't visible to the sentry below. And the terraces weren't patrolled. But there were Albanian guards up on the patios around the villa. This far down, he wasn't going to be particularly visible to the guards, who did not use night-vision systems. But as he got closer he'd be more and more likely to get spotted. From here on out, slow and cautious movements were the order of the evening. In and back.

The Albanian guard was visible up on the patio. He was looking out towards the woods, not down at the terraces, as far as Mike could tell. But movement drew the eye. Mike eased over the wall onto the first terrace and then oozed, slowly, across the terrace until he was in the shadow of the second wall. So far, no alarm.

If the shit totally hit the fan, a Keldara reaction team was in the woods to cover his withdrawal. Of course, that would blow the mission, permanently. If that happened they might never find out what happened to the girl. And then the President would get all pissy and the senator would go on doing what he, presumably, did. That wasn't on.

Mike lifted up and checked on the sentry who was apparently, from the smoke and slight IR signature, taking another smoke break. Lifting up further he saw that the Albanian was talking to another guy, their heads turned away from the view. He slithered up the rocks of the wall, then began sliding across the open area just as the moon broke out of the clouds.

He froze, immediately, not looking up. His face was covered in camouflage makeup and the ghillie suit had a light mesh mask in addition. But a face always seemed to be the easiest thing to pick out. He simply waited on the sward, sweating a little despite the cool of the night, until the moon went back behind the clouds. Then he started his sneak again.

Three terraces, each of them bringing him closer to the Albanian who was hanging out at the top. Within an hour, Mike was crouched at the base of the wall of the last terrace, smelling the thick, acrid stench of the Albanian's cigarette. This one was, if anything, more vile than the Fijian's. Mike had never seen the point in using tobacco; all it did was blunt the senses and ruin your night vision. On the other hand, he loved it when enemies used it.

There were eight guards on duty in the house. Five were on exterior duty, one on each side with an additional one by the gate on the east side and two were, apparently, on various internal points. The eighth acted as something like a sergeant of the guard, roaming from point to point to make sure the others stayed awake and alert.

During the day and into the evening there were, in addition, about five Albanians and a handful of local workers. The locals were probably ethnic Albanians for that matter.

Getting past the Albanian was going to be harder than getting past the Fijian. The open area at the bottom was larger than the one at the top for one thing. And the Albanian didn't seem to be wandering. He was just hanging out in place with a full view of the final stretch of ground and of the patio to either side.

Mike stripped off his night-vision goggles and lifted up a mirror, angling it over the top of the wall. As he'd climbed he had shifted to the north and he was about twenty meters from where the Albanian was standing, leaning with his arms on the low railing or wall that surrounded the patio. It was, apparently, concrete or similar materials formed in a lacy, open pattern. First there was the open area of the terrace, then the six-foot-high wall, then a slight ledge, then the railing.

Getting over that railing was going to be impossible if the guard was standing in plain view. Which was why Mike planned on distracting him.

He reached into his utility pocket and pulled out a small flashlight. When he flicked it on, nothing appeared to happen, but that was just if you had the wrong vision.

"There's the signal," Sawn said, picking up the UV light from the flash through his night-vision goggles and nodding at Vanner.

"Roll the party," Vanner whispered into the mike.

★ ★ ★

"It's nice to finally get to have some fun," Greznya said, flicking a lighter into life and applying it to the string of firecrackers.

"I've never actually set fireworks off," Katya replied, holding up a long tube. "What is this?"

"Roman candle," Listra said, smiling. "We'll save that until we have their attention. . . ."

At the first sounds of gunfire, Kreshnik Daci's head snapped up. It had been a long and tiring night and he was spoiling for action. When he'd been sent out to help the far flung reaches of the gang run by his family clan, he'd expected much more fighting and more of a view of the world. Thus far, he'd beat up a few uppity bitches in Lunari, guarded a group of girls in transit in Serbia, loaded some on a boat to Italy and ended up guarding this place. None of it was contributing to his real dream, which was to get a student visa to America.

Short of that, he wanted to shoot someone.

So he actually hoped someone was attacking the villa. Anyone who did so, though, had to be insane. They'd have to assault up the slope in full view of the guards who had more than just the Czech Skorpion he was toting. They'd get slaughtered if they tried. Which was all right by him.

However, the gunfire was not close. It was on a hill about five hundred meters away to the southeast. He wandered in that direction, just as a ball of fire drifted up and then swore. It wasn't gunfire at all, just some kids playing with fireworks. Okay, so from the tracers, they were also shooting off a gun, but they weren't shooting at the villa.

"Kreshnik!" Imer called over the radio. "What is happening?"

"Some fireworks," Daci replied, walking down to the southeast corner of the patio. "Some kids probably. Somebody shooting off an AK, too. But it's not coming this way."

"Oooo," Gustini Huksa wooed as a bottle rocket ascended and then erupted in a shower of sparks. The southern guard had drifted over to the corner and now lit up another cigarette. The flash bastard smoked American Marlboros. Gustini had been assigned to Herzjac, the main town that supplied IFOR with its girls. There he'd struck up a deal with one of the UN vendors: two cartons of Marlboros for one hour with a girl. It was a win/win situation for the two since the vendor could "loss" the Marlboros and Gustini didn't even have to do that much paperwork with the girls. When he left he turned the source over to another guard for a share of the action. He still got a couple of cartons of Marlboros every week. "Nice. I wish I was out there rather than stuck in this rathole."

"Sooner or later we'll get to go somewhere else," Kreshnik opined with no real hope. He had been told that assignment to this villa was a sign of the trust and respect that the clan had for him. So far, it seemed like a dead end.

The fireworks didn't last long and as the last faded, Imer appeared.

"Nice, you're both watching the fireworks instead of your posts," the older man snapped. "Get back in place and make sure no one has gotten past you."

"How could they?" Gustini argued, waving at the hilltop. "It would take a ghost to get up the hill without us seeing him!"

# ★ Chapter Twenty-Two ★

Mike stepped through the door and closed it softly on oiled hinges. The alarm had been tricky but the lock was totally vanilla.

The room he was in was a rather pleasant dining area with the look of a breakfast room. The floor was hardwood with thrown carpets that had the feel, from their depth and softness, of being costly. Clearly no expense had been spared in hosting the exclusive clientele. He had a hard time putting that together with the nature of the establishment, but he supposed that after a hard night torturing the whores the customers were probably ready for a good breakfast before they began their day.

It wasn't, however, useful from his point of view. The single interior door didn't show any light so, after carefully oiling the hinges and checking for alarms, he opened it soundlessly.

The hallway beyond was, indeed, unlit. It was hardwood again, and he stepped carefully but still elicited a squeak. Moving down the edge limited the noise. To the right, near the end, there was a door with light coming from it and the hallway intersected a lit corridor there.

He slid up his vision system and he inched silently down the hallway to the lit doorway. Squatting down and keeping an ear out for approaching guards he slid a fiber-optic camera under the door. Paydirt.

The interior was an office and security room. One of the guards was napping in front of a computer console that was playing back either a scene from in the building or a similar rape video. There were three computers in the room, including the one the guard was napping in front of, along with file cases and paper scattered over a desk.

Mike snapped a couple of pics of the room, then slid the camera out. Stepping to the corner he moved the camera out at ground level and looked around. There was one more guard, as well as the rover, to find. He saw nobody in the cross corridor but there was another lit room. The far end opened out into a large room. From the exterior map they had developed, that would be the main entrance. The doors along that hallway were more or less mapped from exterior observation. The one with the lit doorway was the guard room, then there were two parlors for "meet and greet." The last was always curtained, so its purpose was unknown. There were two external rooms along the hallway, also purpose unknown. The end of this corridor would terminate in the ground floor kitchen. Somewhere, there were going to be stairs to the upper floors and to the basement.

Mike eased back down the unlit corridor, sliding the camera under the unlit doorways. The exterior "gray" rooms were bedrooms. From the accoutrements, they were designed as low-impact bondage rooms. The beds had shackles on them but there was no sign of suspension gear and cleaning them up would be a pain.

The inner rooms, however, were apparently for rougher play. One had a bed in it, but it was covered only with a matress cover, and stains on the side indicated that blood had been spilled. The other was a straight torture room. Getting the camera in that room was tough since the door was solid to the floor. But there was a rubber lintle and Mike pushed it in.

No girls, though. And the rooms still didn't have the look of serious killing rooms.

Mike paused as he heard a door open and close followed by footsteps coming down the lit corridor.

He opened the door to the room adjacent to the office and oozed over to the partitioning wall. Slipping out a contact mike, he placed it on the wall and slid in an earbud.

The door to the room opened and there was a barked exclamation followed by the sound of a chair, along with a body, hitting the floor. The following conversation was in Albanian, which Mike couldn't even begin to make out. But the chewing out was clear enough. The rest, as things settled down, was unclear. Finally, it finished and the supervisor left the room.

Mike waited until the footsteps had died down and the guard in the room started snoring. Then he stepped back out into the corridor.

Mike continued down the corridor to the door at the end and checked that. Kitchen. Okay, that was an exterior, but they hadn't been able to get a full view. There didn't appear to be anyone in it at the moment. He oiled the hinges and opened the door carefully.

The room was big and well scrubbed with a large range, industrial refrigerator and a center prep island. Stepping into the room he could see five doors besides the one to the exterior. One of them, from the look, was a walk-in fridge or freezer. He'd check that last. One checked out as a large pantry, a second opened onto another interior corridor, the third opened onto a small room that appeared to be another office, the fourth, though, led to stairs both up and down. Basement entry and a way to the top floor.

He stepped over to the freezer and took a look inside, then backed away hastily. There were a couple of large sides of meat towards the back but two bodies of young women dangled from hooks towards the front. Both had the marks of having been savagely tortured. One had a cut throat and the other looked as if she had been strangled.

Mike slid out a low-light camera and took pics of both girls, then quietly closed the door. Neither was the target and getting pissed about the find would simply degrade his performance. He put the sight aside and checked the door to the stairs.

The stairs down were simple wood; those going up were covered in carpet. He chose up first, stepping along the side to reduce squeaks.

The landing at the top had another door, this one bolted on the inside. He quietly slipped the fiber-optic camera under the door.

The hallway was brightly lit and it took his eyes a moment to adjust. When they did, the first thing he noticed was a guard sitting in a chair and napping at the far end of the hall to the left. That would be to the north.

He stepped back down the stairs, going all the way to the bottom floor. There was another bolted door and he checked under it.

The basement was a pure torture dungeon. There were a couple of cages along one side, various pieces of furniture including a St. Andrew's Cross and a saddle as well as suspension devices. There were also a couple of metal tables and a bed with rubber sheets on it. The tables had been cleaned, but from the looks of the floor bad things had happened.

He slipped into the room and looked around carefully. He had to step up on one of the tables to find what he was looking for, but he finally found the first one hidden in the suspension rig: the room was wired for full audio and video. He doubted the monitors were live at the moment, but it would be a bad thing if they were.

Okay, the layout was solid. Time to egress.

He moved quietly back up the stairs to the kitchen then down the hallway to the breakfast room. He half-wished he'd brought some poison along. Serve the bastards right. He'd done as much, or worse, to men in the past. The recent past come to think of it. But that was a target and the purpose now was obtaining information. Not just to get his rocks off.

The worst part was that he knew that the whole setup held an attraction for him. Inside he was, face it, the sort of person who patronized this establishment. He had thought more than once about not only rape but torturing a woman just to get his kicks. Killing her even. Brutally and with the greatest possible fear and pain inflicted.

That didn't mean he did it. He had the . . . discipline to control that particular demon. Admittedly, he channeled it into things that were damned near as horrible. But this was . . . vile.

And he was going to end it.

"Any trouble getting through customs?" Mike asked.

"Not really," Praz said, shrugging. The retired member of the Army Marksmanship Training Unit was the Keldara sniper instructor. Short and muscular, he had come in second twice in a row on the "long shot" at Camp Perry, being beaten out by the same Marine sniper. Mike had his eye on the Marine as soon as he quit the Corps. "They thought we were crazy, but they didn't give us any hassle."

"What is the mission?" Lasko asked, setting the long cases down on the bed. The former hunter was one of the oldest Keldara in the force, but he'd hardened like teak. Thin and wiry, he looked like nothing so much as the mountain goats he normally hunted. The goats were wary and had very keen vision; in general the only shot even a very good hunter got was at over five hundred meters. Lasko was a firm believer in coming back with as many goats as expended cartridges and he usually did.

"Right up your alley, Las," Mike said, his face hard. "Choosers of the slain."

"Sniper teams in position," Praz said over the radio.

"Dart team one in position," Sawn whispered. "All targets present."

"Dart two in position," Parak whispered. "Ready."

"Bravo entry, ready," Adams said.

"Alpha entry . . ." Mike whispered back, looking around, "ready. Initiate."

Sawn peeped through the scope and calculated the wind, again. The darts were very low velocity and tended to drift with the slightest wind. And the range was long for the shot. He wished that it was Praz or Lasko doing the shooting, but he would have to do.

There were four of the Fijian guards gathered by the lower gate to the villa. One was the sergeant, which was what they had been waiting for.

Sawn took a deep breath and then paused and looked at Parak.

"Two right," Sawn said, wiggling the dart held between the fingers of his left hand.

"Got it," Parak replied laconically. The team sniper was far more sure of his shots.

"If I miss . . ." Sawn said.

"Follow over," Parak said. "Copy. Same for you."

"You won't miss," Sawn said, taking a breath and letting it out.

He took his first shot, followed quickly by Parak's first. The sergeant stopped gesticulating and reached for the dart that had sprung up on his chest, looking at it in a puzzled manner.

By the time he'd started toppling Sawn had rotated the bolt of the air gun and slid in the next dart. He hadn't even lined up his next shot, however, before Parak fired. Sawn took his time, though, making sure of his target and trigger control before firing. That dart sunk in as well and the Fijian guards on the gate were all down.

"Target one down," Sawn whispered, sliding back through the concealing underbrush.

"Target two down."

"Snipers."

Praz looked through the scope and calculated the shot one more time. The east target was easy, the south target harder. And there was no telling when the rover would show up.

He took a slight breath, waited for his heart to pump to diastolic and then gently squeezed the trigger of the customized sniper rifle.

"South target down," Tariel said. "Not moving."

Praz had felt the round was right and was already tracking to the second target. The question was whether he would hear the first fall and, sure enough, he was moving, reaching for a radio. Praz led him a touch and fired.

"Miss," Tariel said as the man paused and looked around wildly, crouching behind the ornamental railing. He had his radio up, now, and was talking into it excitedly.

Praz rotated the bolt one more time and lined up the target's head. At this range it was not exactly an easy shot, but it was the only portion in view. Wait, wait, squeeze.

"Target," Tariel said. "He's all over the patio."

"I can see that," Praz said, sliding back and wiping at the sweat on his forehead. "Keep looking for targets."

"Wake up you idiot!" Imer Emini said, running into the computer room. "Kreznik said we were under attack!"

"I heard," Oltion Dzaferi said, sitting up and wiping his eyes. "Where are they?"

"That is what all this is there to tell us!" Imer snarled, waving at the computers. "Turn on the monitors! Kreznik, report!" Imer paused and looked at the radio, shaking it for a moment in frustration. "Gustini? Pejerin? Victor? Anyone?"

"Shkumbin, here," the upstairs guard replied. "What is happening?"

"I don't know," Imer replied, breathing hard. "Go to one of the girls' windows and look out. See if you can see anything. Oltion, get those black-asses on the phone and ask them what is happening!"

"I go," Shkumbin said grouchily.

"Stay on the radio," Imer continued. "Keep talking. Oltion?"

"There is no reply from the black-asses," the technician said, shrugging. "I need to turn on the lights to see with the monitors."

"Not yet," Imer said, cautiously. "Shkumbin?"

"I'm in the girls' room," Shkumbin replied. "I see nothing out the—"

"Target, upper window three," Tariel said, quietly.

"Got it," Lasko replied, stroking his trigger.

Imer looked up at a crash from above and then snarled. "Get on the phone to town! Tell them we're under attack!"

"Phones are out," Oltion said, shaking his head. "And internet."

"Begin dumping," Imer said, shaking and drawing his pistol. "I will go buy you time to dump all the data . . ."

The last thing he consciously recognized was the sound of the door blowing in.

"Computer room secure," Mike said, lifting his balaclava. "Clear. Vanner, get to work."

"On it, boss," the intel specialist said, sitting down at the first computer and waving Greznya to the second.

"I count eight tangoes down," Adams replied. "Preparing to sweep upper floors."

Mike stepped out into the corridor as more Keldara women flooded into the room. Keldara were moving from room to room in a coordinated sweep, searching for additional targets.

"Bravo Six," Adams said. "Sweep complete. One down tango in an upper room, courtesy of Lasko, at a guess. Six girls."

"Grab 'em and get down here," Mike said. "Vanner?"

"We've got the hard drives," Vanner said, standing up. "What about the files?"

"Savo! Packs!"

"Ignition system in place," Adams called. "The place is rigged."

"Five minutes, people," Mike called as the Keldara women started ripping files out of the drawers and filling the bags the militiamen held out to them. "Greznya, start the count."

Yarok looked at the devastated villa and shook his head.

"They took down the Fijian guards with tranquilizer guns," he said, sighing. "They clearly did not want to anger KFOR excessively. Then they, apparently, took down the villa's defenses, took the girls and probably other information and torched it, rather expertly, on the way out. There was one Fijian guard who said that from the time he heard the first shots to when the vehicles left was no more than five minutes."

"I will kill them all," Boris roared. "This cannot be permitted!"

"Oh, agreed," Yarok replied, sighing again. "But you'll recall that I recommended increasing security at all facilities in this area. There were only the normal eight guards here."

"That should have been enough," Boris snapped. "Especially with the Fijians. These Americans are wizards!"

"Hardly," Yarok said, musingly. "They took down the outer guards with snipers. Good ones, too. I have found one sniper point, I believe, and it was a seven hundred meter shot with a crosswind. That is a world-class sniper. However, with the outer guards down, that left only four. What I'm wondering is how they found the plan to the house."

"What do you mean?"

"To do something like this, this cleanly, you have to know where you are going," Yarok said, rubbing his lips in thought. "You need a layout to the house. Otherwise you're running around trying to find your targets. I would say, from the time that was given by the remaining guard, that they had to have the layout to the house. And given the defenses, I don't see how they could have entered it beforehand. So . . ."

"You're saying we have a leak?" Boris asked coldly.

"I'm saying it's a possibility," Yarok admitted.

"I will look into this," the Albanian promised.

"Do," Yarok replied. *That will get you off my back while I take care of the real business.* "In the meantime, I'm going to try to find where they ran to to hide. I doubt that Rozaje is going to be their last target. It will be interesting to see where their final destination lies."

# ★ Chapter Twenty-Three ★

Mike leaned back in the beach chair and readjusted his sunglasses as a really stunning woman wearing barely a G-string walked by.

"What did we get, Patrick?" he asked. The beaches of the Adriatic had their good points. At the moment, he was fixated on two of them.

Getting across the border into Croatia had been relatively easy. There were dozens of small border crossings near Vinica and Citluk that had lax security. Smuggling was endemic in the area and the few crossings that had guards were entirely revenue generators. They had been more than willing to take their usual cut for smuggling girls.

The coast of Croatia had numerous islands and beaches and was a destination spot for summer tourists from throughout Eastern Europe. A quick change of demeanor and the group were tourists, schoolkids taking in the sun along the Adriatic. They'd even been able to check into a decent hotel for once.

And all the Keldara girls had broken down and gotten swimsuits. For the cover of course. Most of them were far less daring than the lovely blonde, Czech or Slovak at a guess, who had just wandered by, but they were still an eyeful.

"They apparently did get full audio and video on their clients," Vanner said, tightly. "I only . . . audited it. But it's pretty rough. The problem being, there are only five DVDs from the haul. And our girl isn't on any of them."

"That's good I suppose," Mike said.

"Yeah, but they're only recent DVDs," Vanner pointed out. "The rest were transported out to a town called Lunari."

"Crap," Mike said, picking up his sunscreen and wiping some on his chest. He'd picked up a hell of a farmer's tan over the winter and spring.

"But . . ." Vanner said, "I'm not sure it matters. We got the rest of their records. They didn't keep electronic records, but the files were solid. And there's interesting news."

"Don't keep me waiting," Mike said, watching a couple of the Keldara girls splashing each other. He briefly considered joining them and then suppressed the idea.

"The thing is, all the girls that went to Rozaje didn't die," Vanner said. "We're having a hard time translating all the files since they're in fucking Albanian. I'm having to scan them in and OCR them then run them through a translator. You know how funky that can come out. But we're sure that some girls leave. Sometimes they had too many there. A client or clients wouldn't show up, whatever. They'd end up with too many girls from time to time and they'd ship out the excess."

"Don't tell me Natalya slipped through the cracks," Mike said, incredulously.

"That's the way it looks," the intel specialist replied, grinning. "She got transported to Lunari along with a bundle of DVDs."

"Shit," Mike said, sighing. "What do we have on Lunari?"

"It's not going to be fun," Vanner admitted. "It's the center for girl running, and drug running and gun running in Albania. Totally lawless. It's controlled by about six different clans or gangs; there's not much distinction. The government doesn't even try to control it. Landlocked but not far from the sea. From the intel I've managed to get, not much, it's also pretty carefully controlled. There are notes about elaborate security systems. And the gangs are heavily armed. There's some stuff in the files on it, too, but . . . getting through all of them is going to take time. I could use some help on translation."

"Any idea where, exactly, the booty is?" Mike asked.

"Yep," Vanner said. "Natalya, and the DVDs, were sent to a particular brothel run by the Dejti gang."

"That's a familiar name," Mike mused.

"He was, apparently, one of the guys in tight with the clan," Vanner said. "That's going to be an issue. Long term, at least."

"Oh, I don't think so," Mike said, standing up. "I'm going swimming. Want to come?"

"In a minute," Vanner said, swallowing. "There's something else. We didn't get the DVDs, but we did get their client list and payment rendered for services, so to speak."

"And?" Mike asked, pausing.

"I ran a bunch of names through the internet," Vanner said, shaking his head. "It's not exactly a Who's Who, but there are a lot of . . . well, rich people at least. And a few that are just powerful. Jesus, Kildar, this data is political dynamite!"

"I'd figured as much," Mike said, sighing.

"The former French commander of KFOR, for God's sake!" Vanner said.

"That explains the security," Mike said, dryly. "What about our friend the senator?"

"Senator Traskel isn't on it," Vanner said, tightly. "Neither is his son. But . . . there is someone you've heard of. . . ."

"Oh . . . blast," the President said, looking at the message.

"There was just the one word, sir," Pierson replied. "But I think the meaning is clear."

"Senator Grantham!" the secretary of defense snarled. "Impossible! I've known him for . . . decades!"

Senator Pat Grantham was the senior senator from South Carolina, a staunch supporter of the President, noted for his religious views and outspoken religious conservatism. A determined but honorable in-fighter in the Senate, losing him would be a nasty political blow to the President's agenda.

"Who knows what evil lurks in the hearts of men," the national security advisor replied. "He was on the junket, too. I don't see how it changes things."

"Well, it's going to make our jobs harder," the chief of staff pointed out. "I'd be more than happy to see Traskel gone. Grantham, on the other hand . . ."

"There is no 'other hand'?" the President said, definitely.

"None. As with Senator Traskel, I'm going to wait on solid confirmation. But if we get it, Grantham will no longer be a senator. Period."

"The senator's from another party . . ." the chief of staff pointed out.

"I don't care," the President snarled. "Not One Damned Bit. I doubt I can give him the justice that he so richly deserves. But he will no longer be a senator of the United States."

Mike was surprised at the extent to which the Keldara girls were willing to play a little grab-ass. He'd put it down to the "Kildar" effect, but they were playing with the militiamen as well. Hell, even Oksana was out there, playing in the very small waves. Mike hadn't tried any grab-ass with her, only to find the girl, along with some of the Keldara girls trying to tackle him. He'd let them dunk him and then swam through their legs, pulling them under and then pushing them back to the surface; very few of them were strong swimmers. They'd been amazed and alarmed at how long he could hold his breath.

The problem with the grab-ass was that it was getting him horny. And the Keldara girls were off-limits. So, for different reasons, were the girls they'd "picked up." He still wasn't sure what to do with them. Transferring them from sexual slavery to the harem, a different form of sexual slavery for all extents and purposes, didn't seem like a decent use of his time. Something would have to be done, but that was for another day.

With a certain amount of reluctance he finally climbed

out of the water and wandered back to his beach chair. Which was occupied.

"You're . . ." Mike said and then paused.

"Daria," the girl replied, getting up. She was about nineteen at a guess, one of the girls they'd recovered from Rozaje. Tall and statuesque, she had a great set of knockers and an air of naivete that had to be an act. "Sorry, was I in your chair . . . Kildar?"

"Call me Mike," Mike said, waving for her to get back in the chair as he squatted down by it. "How are you doing?"

"The nightmares are less," the girl said quietly. "We knew what we were there for; the guards made sure to tell us. And we could hear some of it. Girls would leave and not come back. I was sick when I arrived and I wasn't presented."

"Good thing," Mike said. "I'm sure you would have been a first pick."

"Thank you so much," Daria replied, her face tight. "I thought the same. The doctor had just given me a clean bill of health. They told me I was going to be presented to the next . . . customer."

"And now you're not," Mike said. "Be happy. Enjoy the sunshine knowing you're going to get to keep enjoying it."

"Am I?" Daria asked, pointedly.

"Uhmmm, yes," Mike responded. "Right now, I can't afford to let you leave. You're still, effectively, a prisoner. But you won't be raped or beaten and when this mission is done I'll drop you anywhere you care. Back home if that's what you want."

"Home," Daria said, quietly. "I don't know if I recognize the word. If you're talking about the Ukraine, there is nothing there for me."

"We'll figure something out," Mike said, picking up his sunglasses.

"Where do you live?" Daria asked. "In Georgia? But you are American."

"I've got reasons to live there," Mike said, shrugging.

"And you have a house there," the girl said, tilting her head to the side.

"And a harem." Mike shrugged. "I'm sure you've been talking to the Keldara girls."

"Is that where we will go?" she asked carefully.

"For a time," Mike said, shrugging again. "Until we figure out what else to do with you. I've got to figure something out; the caravanserai's going to fill up with women otherwise and then it'll be nag, nag, nag all day and night. 'Kildar, when will I have my turn? Kildar, can I have a new dress? Kildar, am I the prettiest?'" He grinned at the girl and was surprised to get a grin in return.

"I can tell you live with women," Daria said. "You have that look."

"Domesticated, that's me," Mike sighed. "Just a hopeless love slave to women's desire . . ."

"And you get nothing?" Daria asked lightly.

"Oh, I suppose so," Mike said, grinning again. "But I try to give as good as I get."

"I get nothing," Daria said, shrugging. "I was virgin until . . ."

"Get a good job in Western Europe?" Mike asked.

"Yes, but, I knew about the problems with that," Daria

said, frowning. "The thing was, the person who . . . sold me was my boyfriend!"

"Ouch," Mike said, shaking his head. "That's cold."

"He said that he knew someone who could get me a job in Belgium," Daria continued, looking out at the sea. "I am trained as secretary, yes? I can read and write in English, French and German. My boyfriend . . . well, he is not great man. Has no job but . . . I like him."

"I had a girlfriend one time. She said that she was a bum magnet," Mike said, nodding. "She wasn't, by the way, referring to me. But . . . there are women who attract those sorts of guys like flies."

"That is me," Daria continued, her nose thinning in remembrance. "He is introduce me to another man who said he had contacts with business in Belgium . . ."

"I'm sure he did," Mike said dryly.

"We meet . . . three times before I agree to take job," Daria said, sighing. "He is having letterhead and letters of employment. But I have not the exit visa or entry visa, so Pasha . . ."

"Pasha?" Mike said, crinkling his brow. "Ahmed Pasha?"

"That was his name, yes," Daria said. "And there was another man with him, Peter . . ."

"Looked like Santa Claus?" Mike asked.

"Yes!" Daria said, turning to look at him.

"You need to talk to Oksana," Mike said, his jaw working. "So, you certainly didn't make it to Belgium."

"They took me over the border to Moldava," Daria said. "There . . ."

"They raped you, beat you and took away your

passport," Mike said. "So you couldn't leave without their aid. And sold you to the Albanians."

"Yes," Daria said, turning back to look at the ocean.

"Run into a guy named Dejti?" Mike asked.

"Yes," Daria replied, quietly.

"Well, he sleeps with the fishes."

Daria paused and frowned, then shrugged.

"That means nothing to me," she admitted.

"American slang," Mike replied. "It means I broke both his knees and then shot him through the head and dumped his body in a lake."

"Oh," Daria said, breathing out. "Oh."

"I doubt you ran into a man named Nicu . . ."

"In Romania," Daria said, her face hard. "It was he who sent me to Rozaje." She paused and quirked an eyebrow. "Fishes?"

"Fishes."

"I am not sure how I feel about that," she admitted.

"That's because you're a nice girl," Mike replied. "And I am not a nice man."

"That I don't believe," Daria said, laughing breathlessly. "If you were not a nice man, we would have been left in the villa, still chained up, waiting for the next men to take us."

"Believe it," Mike said flatly. "Because I do nice things, does not mean I'm a nice man. The men who raped you, the men who beat you, simply do the things I would like to do. And occasionally do when a young lady likes that sort of thing. I'm not a nice man. A nice man would not beat another human being to death with a sledgehammer."

"Dejti?" Daria asked.

"Nicu's boss," Mike replied.

"Dejti poked my breast with needles," Daria said, softly. "And shocked me with electric cables. He hit me in the belly so hard I was peeing blood. He didn't leave any scars on the outside . . ."

"But he left them on the inside," Mike said.

"Many." She paused again and then shrugged. "You know women who like this sort of thing?"

"My harem manager for one," Mike said, smiling faintly. "Anastasia used to . . . belong to a shiek in Uzbekistan. She told me she was happy to come work for me, because he would not hit her hard enough. She likes to be whipped and hurt. Giving her what she wants, without causing scars, is hard."

"She is your harem manager?" Daria said, shaking her head. "I have a hard time thinking about that."

"They are girls that I picked up for various reasons," Mike replied. "I didn't know what to do with them, so I kept them as girlfriends, concubines really. They can leave any time, I even offer them a stake to get started. None of them took me up on it. When they get old enough to make it in the world, and educated enough, I'll kick them out the door. In the meantime I'm giving them an education and a chance for a real life."

"And they give you sex?" Daria said tightly.

"I don't force them," Mike said, shrugging. "Most of them were from small farms in the mountains. They considered it an honor, which surprised me. The thing they call me, Kildar, is a sort of nobleman in the area. But . . . yes, they give me sex. You can say they pay their way that way, but I prefer to think of it as consensual. We all live with the lies we tell ourselves."

"Yes," Daria said, sitting back and sighing. "That we do."

"So what do you think I should do with these girls?" Mike asked. "I've got everything from Oksana, registered virgin and orphan with nowhere to go to . . . you, I suppose. I assume you have somewhere to go back to?"

"If I could face it," Daria said. "My parents told me not to leave. They did not like my boyfriend."

"Looking them in the eye will be tough," Mike admitted. "But . . . 'home is where, when you have to go there, they have to take you in.'"

"And where is your home?" Daria asked.

Mike stopped and blinked. Home still meant the U.S. to him. His parents were dead; he hadn't talked to his sister in . . . years.

"Thanks for asking," Mike said, frowning. "The answer is, I don't have one."

"You should have a home," Daria said, frowning in turn. "You are a good man, you should have a good home."

"I suppose it's with the Keldara," Mike replied, still frowning. "They are the closest thing to family I have. For years, home was the Navy, the Teams and BUD/S. I was married, but that came apart after I got out. Now . . . I don't know."

"You should marry again," Daria said definitely.

"When I find the right girl, maybe," Mike replied. The sun was slowly descending to the west and the temperature was dropping steadily. He wasn't bothered by it, he'd gotten used to far worse on beaches all over the world, but the girls were getting out of the water and shivering. “Looks like time for dinner,” he added, standing up.

Daria followed him as he headed back to the hotel and he turned to look at her, quirking an eyebrow.

“I was wondering . . .” the girl said, then shrugged. “It is nothing.”

“Tell you what,” Mike said, quirking one cheek up. “Let’s talk about it upstairs.”

When they got to his room, Mike waved her to a chair and flopped on the bed, propping up some pillows behind him.

“One of the things we haven’t done on this op is introduce a consistent rape counseling program,” Mike said. “Or an abuse counseling program. Why? Because we’re on a combat op and it’s not important to the operation. And, frankly, we don’t have any counsellors. Maybe we should bring in some touchy-feely types to cover the bases, but we haven’t. I haven’t. Comments?”

“Why should you care?” Daria asked, shrugging one shoulder.

“If it’s affecting the mission,” Mike said. “We’re stuck with you girls for the time being. If you’re not functional, it affects the mission.”

“We’re functional,” Daria said, angrily. “And you’re not stuck with us.”

“Yes, I am,” Mike replied. “You’re aware of who we are and what we’re doing. If we just dropped you off on the street, the news would get around. Besides, as part of my not being a nice guy, but trying to act like one, I can’t just drop you on a street corner. So I’m stuck with you. And if you're getting huffy about that and decide you're going to storm out, you'll discover we've got plenty of rigger tape."

"Rigger tape?" Daria asked, confused.

"Duct tape, then," Mike said, rolling over and pulling a roll out of his jump bag.

"We're still prisoners, then," Daria said.

"Yep," Mike replied. "Just like before. But we're not planning on killing you as part of sexual funs and games. Only real difference. Oh, and you're not going to get raped. And we'll try really hard not to raise a hand to you. But, yeah, you're still prisoners. It's just a more comfortable jail."

"Then why don't you rape me?" Daria said, breathing hard.

"Don't tempt me," Mike said. "Seriously. Don't. You're a real looker. And the reason is, I try to act like a nice guy."

"What if I told you I wanted you to?" Daria said, looking down at the floor and blushing. "What if I told you that as much as I hated what happened to me . . . I liked it as well?"

"Then I'd tell you that I'm not a rape counselor," Mike replied with a dismissive shrug. "I'd also tell you that you're not alone. Bum magnets tend to end up in abusive relationships. I would guess that your bum boyfriend occasionally slapped you around, right?"

"Yes," Daria said, looking up. "I should have stopped him, but . . ."

"You loved him and he loved you," Mike finished for her, shrugging. "It ain't love, honey, it's abuse syndrome. Hell, it's being a submissive. Not necessarily sexually, but in general. You probably felt like you deserved it, that it was all your fault."

"Are you in my head?" Daria asked angrily. "Is this some sort of mind thing?"

"No, it's being old enough and experienced enough to have had the conversation before," Mike said, shrugging again. "You're hardly alone. Abuse like that happens all over, honey, even in the United States. You never had sex with your boyfriend?"

"No," Daria said, blushing again. "I drew the line there, even when he became angry. And he only hit me when he was drunk. One time he tried to . . ."

"Rape you," Mike said.

"I was going to say force me," Daria replied. "It was not really rape—"

"Yeah, it is," Mike snapped. "Date rape is rape. Period fucking dot. So you drew the line there, now what?"

"Now . . ." Daria said and stopped.

"You said that some of the abuse you enjoyed?" Mike asked calmly.

"I should not," Daria said, dropping her face in her hands. "I think I am a very bad person."

"Item number sixty-two of the checklist," Mike said, chuckling.

"What is so funny?" Daria snapped, glaring at him.

"You were brought up to be a very good girl," Mike said, still smiling. "To not have sex until you are married. But you feel the want of it?"

"Yes," Daria admitted. "Very much."

"I won't ask if that's an 'especially now' answer," Mike said. "But the point is, if you're forced, then it's not your fault. If a man makes you do it, you are not so bad a person. It is one of the reasons that you want to be forced, to be made to have sex. Yes?"

"I . . . hadn't thought of it that way," Daria admitted.

"If you are tied, how can it be your fault?" Mike asked. "But if you still like it, that still makes you a bad person inside. So you want to be hurt for being a bad girl. Am I close?"

"Yes," Daria answered quietly.

"All right," Mike said, shrugging. "Let's talk about that. Part of it might be because of the rape. But . . . did you ever think that way before the rape? I mean, did you fantasize about things like that when you masturbated?"

"That's a very personal question!" Daria snapped.

"This is a personal conversation," Mike replied. "The question is, did these feelings come about as a result of the rape, or did you have them before?"

"Some of them . . ." Daria said, softly. "Some of them before."

"There are books and books written about what you're feeling," Mike said. "The term is sexual submission. Lucky for me, I tend to run into them a lot since I'm a sexual dominant. Opposites attract and all that. The point is, you're not bad for feeling that way. It's a normal, hell, probably a majority, feeling in women. It's even a desire in some men. So the first thing to get into your noggin is that you're not evil for feeling that way."

"It feels . . . wrong," Daria said. "Bad."

"And some women enjoy being told how bad they are," Mike said. "That's all fine and dandy, as long as it's really a consensual thing between two rational adults. Or more, sometimes. The point is, it's okay to feel that way, okay to play out those fantasies. As long as you know where to draw the line. The term is 'the bedroom door.' As long as your fantasies are play, whether it's in a bedroom or a living room or the kitchen, the whole house or on a mountainside, as long as the play ends at an agreed upon point, it's just fun."

"Fun," Daria snorted. "I want . . . I want to be told I'm bad."

"And as long as that's in the bedroom, metaphorically, that's all fine and good," Mike replied. "Daria, look at me."

He waited until the girl looked up and met his eyes.

"You're a good girl, a fine woman," Mike said, holding her eyes with his. "You just have the need to be told otherwise. Do you want to be spanked? To be abused?"

"Yes," she admitted, still looking him in the eye.

"But you don't want that to be your life, right?" Mike said. "Tied up and hit, carefully, and told you're a bad girl in bed, sure. But not hit in the face because supper's late."

"No," Daria said, shocked. "I mean, yes, the first but not the second."

"You're a sexual sub," Mike said, shrugging and leaning back. "My favorite kind of girl. But the point is, at the end of the play you go back to being your own person. Owning yourself. Loving yourself and knowing that you are not a bad person. If you can't do that, you're never going to be the person you can be."

"But now I feel as if I really need it," Daria practically wailed. "I want it all the time—"

"Item twenty something on the post-rape checklist," Mike said. "Nymphomania. The female in the situation shifts to desiring sex. If it's going to happen, anyway, they might as well learn to enjoy it. A lot. And do it. A lot. Even when they aren't forced to."

"You're saying I'm sick?" Daria asked carefully. "Nymphomania is being sick."

"Not really," Mike replied, shrugging. "You're just having a standard reaction to your form of trauma. Sorry if it makes you feel less special. Not sorry if it makes you feel less bad. Because you're not. You're a fine young lady. You've just been through a traumatic experience and you're reacting to it in fairly well recognized ways."

"So what do I do about it?" Daria asked, sitting up.

"That's where my knowledge sort of breaks down," Mike admitted. "The thing about rape, especially when it happens to a person with little or no experience of sex, is that it changes the wiring for what is positive and negative sexual experiences. You can't really know what your sexual interests, your needs, are. Look, my ex-wife did some rape counseling. Most of the stuff I know comes from her and girlfriends who have been abused. I'm not an expert. Okay?"

"Okay," Daria said, carefully. "But you're as close as I can get right now."

"Right," Mike admitted. "Especially since you're still, effectively, a prisoner. Even if I went out and found a counselor, he or she would be sucked into the same void. So I'll just tell you what I know. The thing about rape is that it sort of changes the wiring. There was a boy that my wife counseled. He'd been homosexually raped when he was thirteen or so. And he'd been homosexually oriented ever since. So he was in his mid-twenties or so and all of a sudden he starts getting interested in girls. He's not sure what's happening, so he goes back into counseling. Turned out, he wasn't really homosexual at all. His orientation was as a result of the rape, period. So right now, it would be hard to tell what your real orientation is."

"So what do I do?" Daria asked. "What do I do about the . . . the nightmares? About the feelings?"

"Well, one thing is you talk about them," Mike said. "This is a good start. And if you're fixated on certain kinds of sex, try them. You're not a virgin anymore. If you want to have sex, have sex. Over time, your real orientation will probably, I dunno, realign? Talk to some of the other girls about the feelings they have, the nightmares they're having. Talking about it hurts when you do it, but it will help."

"I'll tell you one nightmare," Daria said. "It's that this is all an elaborate joke to break us down again. That we're going to go right back into being whores. That's not even a nightmare; it's something I worry about all the time."

Mike opened his mouth to reply and then paused.

"You know, there's an aspect of this I hadn't considered," he admitted. "If we bungle one of the upcoming ops, you might just end up that way. Back in slavery, that is. Hell, the Keldara women would. Although I think the rest of the militia would turn up pretty quick with Nielson leading them. I probably ought to figure out a way to get you all back to Georgia. You'd be safer there. Not safe, exactly, but safer."

"To be part of your harem?" Daria asked bitterly.

"Like I said, I'm not sure what to do with you," Mike replied.

"Can I just go home?" the girl asked softly.

"Not until the op is over," Mike said. "You understand why."

"Understand, yes," Daria said. "Happy about, no."

"Not much I can do about your happiness," Mike replied with a shrug.

"You can do one thing," Daria said.

"And that is?"

"I need . . ." She paused and looked at the floor. "I want . . ."

"You know that this is probably just your reaction to what you went through, right?" Mike asked.

"Yes," she admitted. "That doesn't relieve the need."

Mike cocked his head to the side and really looked at her for a moment.

"Daria?"

"Yes?" she asked, looking up.

"Take your clothes off."

"What?" the girl asked.

"I'm going to relieve both our needs," Mike replied, standing up and walking over to her. "I'm not sure if it's a good idea, but it's the best one I can come up with right now. The bedroom door is, metaphorically and really, shut. You can choose to not play the game if you wish."

"I choose . . ." Daria said then paused. "I think I choose to play."

"Fine," Mike said, walking over to one of the other chairs and sitting down. "Then stand up and take off all of your clothes."

The girl looked at him for a moment and then stood up and started to slowly undress. She started off looking at him but when she started to slip her dress off she had to look away.

When she started to sit down and remove her shoes, Mike waved at her to stop.

"Keep the shoes on," Mike said gruffly. "I like high heels. Here is the deal. You've been an actual sex-slave. Some of the play is based around that sort of situation. Are you going to be able to take that?"

"Yes," Daria said, softly, still looking at the floor. "As long as I'm sure it's play."

"Are you?" Mike asked.

"Yes," Daria admitted. "I trust you. I don't know why I do, but I do."

"It might have something to do with my rescuing you from durance vile," Mike told the naked girl. "Or my winning smile. But we're going to have to establish the parameters. That is, we're going to have to find out what I can and cannot do. And you're going to have to know how to end the play. Are you listening?"

"Yes," Daria replied. "Can I put my clothes back on?"

"Not unless you want the play to end," Mike said. "Do you?"

"Not yet," Daria admitted. "I am very confused. I want to do this, but I am frightened. I was stripped like this to be sold to Ahmed Pasha. It was very humiliating. This is very humiliating. But . . ."

"You like it," Mike said.

"Yes."

"Go over to the bed and get a pillow," Mike ordered. "Put it on the floor and kneel on it. There," he added, pointing to a spot a few feet away from his chair. "Keep your head down when you are kneeling. You will only look at me when I order you to do so. The response to that is 'Yes, master.'"

"Yes . . ." Daria said, pausing with a catch in her voice. "Yes, master."

When the girl was kneeling, Mike leaned forward.

"From now until the end of play, you are my slave," Mike said. "I will order you to do things, I will force you to do things. You will obey my orders. Do you agree to this?"

"Yes, master," Daria said, her head bent in submission.

"Before we begin, we have to know what you will accept and what is not acceptable," Mike said. "Is there anything that you will not accept? Answer truthfully."

"I don't want to be hit in the face," Daria replied, shivering. "And I don't want to be burned."

"I will not hit you in the face," Mike replied. "What about anal sex?"

"I don't like it," Daria admitted. "But . . ."

"It's humiliating?" Mike asked.

"Yes," the girl answered, softly.

"And you like to be humiliated," Mike said. "You like to be shown what a bad girl you are."

"Yes," Daria said, her face working against the tears.

"Time out," Mike said, sitting up. "When I say that, we're out of play and it's time to talk. How are you feeling?"

"Strange," Daria admitted. "Very weird. Like I'm not really here."

"Detached?" Mike asked. "Floating? Almost like you're not in your body?"

"Yes."

"A normal reaction," Mike said. "Do you like it?"

"Yes," Daria admitted.

"Am I causing bad flashbacks?"

"No," she said, blinking. "Strippping sort of did. But this . . . no."

"Okay, we'll continue," Mike said. "If at any time, you have to stop, you can say 'time out' or 'yellow' or any odd word. But if you say 'no,' or 'stop,' or 'please' or anything else along the lines, it means 'You're doing great, do it harder and meaner.' Understood?"

"Yes," Daria said, half laughing.

It was the first time Mike had heard her so much as chuckle and he took it as a good sign.

"What are you laughing about, slave?" Mike snapped. "Drop your eyes to the floor where they belong!" He stood up and walked over to her, circling her predatorially.

"You have been a very bad girl, Daria. You defied your parents, had sex out of wedlock and admitted that you enjoyed it. You are a bad girl and you must be punished."

"Yes, master," Daria said softly.

Mike dipped into a bag and came out with a couple of lengths of soft rope and a cloth. He tied her hands and ankles and looped the two ropes together to hogtie her on her knees then blindfolded her with the cloth. He carefully pulled most of her long, blonde hair out from under the blindfold and then grabbed it, hard, pulling her head back and making her gasp in pain.

"You've been a bad girl, little bitch," Mike rasped. "And you're going to be punished for it." He slipped his bathing suit off and slapped her on the face with his cock. "Say 'I'm a bad girl.'"

"I'm a bad girl," the girl sobbed.

"Whatever punishment my master gives me, I deserve," he said, slapping her on the face again.

"Whatever punishment my master gives me, I deserve."

"Take it in your mouth, bitch," Mike said, shoving his dick in her mouth. "Suck it like I know you do. Suck it hard or you'll be punished."

He wasn't sure if it was natural talent or the training she'd gotten since being kidnapped, but Daria truly knew how to give a blowjob. She could have sucked a golf ball through forty feet of steel hose. He felt like his dick was being hickeyed. She might be the best blower he'd ever had, which was saying something. He hadn't planned on blowing a load in her mouth, but the blowjob was too good to pass up. When he felt himself starting to orgasm, he blew most of it in her mouth, then pulled out and pumped the rest onto her face and gorgeous tits. And she swallowed automatically after barely a choke. Damn she was good.

"Slutty little bitch," he growled into her ear, rubbing the cum onto her face and breasts. "You're nothing but a slut, a little bad girl. Say you're a slut."

"I'm a slut," Daria whispered, shaking her head as if to try to throw off the cum.

"I'm going to show you what sort of slut you are, bitch," Mike whispered. He grabbed her by the hair with one hand and wrapped an arm around her body, lifting her bodily and throwing her onto the bed. "Bad girls get beaten."

"Please don't beat me, master," the girl whined. "I'll be good."

"I'll teach you to be good," Mike said, pulling his belt off his trousers. He untied her wrists, then retied them to the front, stretched them over her head and rolled her onto her stomach. "You're a bad girl and you need to be spanked."

"Please . . ." Daria whined. "Please don't . . ."

Mike pinned her hands over her head, wrapped a leg onto her body to hold her in place and began whipping her on her gorgeous ass. He wasn't using full strength by any stretch of the imagination, since he wasn't sure what she could actually stand.

Daria bit into the cloth of the bedcover, whining and trying not to scream.

After a while Mike stopped and lifted her head up by her hair.

"Have you had enough, bitch?" he growled.

"Master," Daria gasped. "Please, I've been very bad . . ."

Mike twitched an eyebrow up and forced her head back down into the bedcovers. This time, he parked higher, pinning her arms with his leg and began whipping not only her ass but her back as well, carefully keeping clear of the kidney region. He also hit harder.

She began shuddering and sweating from the pain, moaning into the bed and occasionally screaming. But if she really wanted him to stop, all she had to do was spit out the bedcover so Mike kept at it.

It was at times like this that he considered the fact that in a "scene," the sub was actually in charge. Here he was doing all the work and she was getting exactly what she wanted without having to do anything but take the pain, which she actively enjoyed. It was an odd dichotomy and he found that he suddenly wasn't as into it as he usually would be. Part of that was keeping one eye on the fact that the girl had been recently traumatized. He wasn't sure if what he was doing was helping or reinforcing the trauma. But Daria, like Anastasia, seemed to be one of those girls who just soaked up pain and turned it into pure pleasure. It was almost disheartening. He really enjoyed inflicting pain and suffering; having someone absolutely and totally enjoy it was a letdown.

He suddenly realized that he'd completely lost his erection. That's what came of philosophizing in the middle of a scene.

Mike shifted again and grabbed her hair, turning her face towards his crotch.

"Lick it, bitch," he growled. "Lick it and suck it like the little slut you are."

She took it in her mouth and began expertly sucking it again, which got him back to a world-class erection in no time.

"You're a little fucking slut," Mike snarled, dipping into a bag and pulling out a condom. "You're worth less than the price of dog turds. You're worth nothing." He pinned her down and spread her ass, shoving his dick into it, hard, as she moaned in pain.

"You're a useless little slut," Mike growled in her ear, clamping one hand over her mouth and wrapping the other around her throat. "You think I'm a nice guy, I'm not. I'm an evil, raping, bastard, just like the evil raping bastards that kidnapped you. And I like to rape my little bitches and then kill them. And that's what I'm going to do to you, bitch. I'm going to rape you in the ass and strangle you at the same time. Nobody will care about a little bitch like you, anyway."

He knew he had her now, since she was struggling against the bonds. But he had her pinned flat with his weight and she wasn't getting away from either hand. He kept talking to her, threatening her and abusing her as he kept one hand clamped over her mouth and the other applying light pressure to her windpipe. He pumped hard on her gorgeous ass for a few minutes and finally came.

"Are you all right?" he asked, withdrawing both hands and easing out of her ass.

"You really scared me," she said, breathing hard. "I wasn't sure . . ."

"It's called edge play," Mike replied. "Creating a condition of doubt in the mind of the sub. You weren't sure if I was serious or not."

"Yes!"

"I wasn't," Mike said, rolling over and undoing her hands. "Seriously."

"It was scary," Daria admitted, sitting up and untying her ankles. "But I liked it. I was sure enough that you weren't going to do it that I wasn't panicking, but . . ."

"Well, let's try something else," Mike said, standing up and walking to the bathroom.

"You mean you're not done?" Daria asked, surprised.

"Oh, hell no," Mike said. "Be right back."

He came back with a hot wash cloth and gently wiped the cum from her face and breasts.

"You're gentle," she said, lying back and sighing, then gasping a bit as he hit a sore spot.

"How's the back?" Mike asked, caressing her breasts a bit more than was strictly necessary.

"Sore," she admitted. "But not as sore as my ass. You hit me very well."

"Thanks," Mike replied, sliding the washcloth down her stomach and taking one of her nipples in his mouth.

"Oh, that feels good," Daria said sighing.

"Should," he replied, blowing on it lightly to get it to stand up. "You have a gorgeous body, did you know that?"

"It is okay," Daria said, shrugging.

"It's absolutely exquisite," Mike replied, lowering himself on the nipple again. He'd eased the washcloth down her stomach and now slid it between her legs, giving the area a thorough cleaning. He wiped the outside, then slid his finger, encased in the rough cloth, into her vagina.

"Oh," Daria sighed. "Oh . . . god . . ."

"You like it rough, huh?" Mike chuckled, biting on her nipple lightly. "I'll give you rough . . ."

He rolled onto her and pinned her legs open, biting on her shoulder and thrusting his fingers into her vagina repeatedly. She began panting and sighing so Mike kept at it, thrusting with his fingers and biting her on her neck, shoulder and chest, appearing to lose control as she bucked under him and moaned. Finally, as she appeared to be nearing climax, he slid another condom onto his dick and thrust into her.

She settled a bit at first but the continuous hard thrusts warmed her back up as he growled in her ear and continued to pinch, bite and twist her nipples roughly. He pulled her legs up and grabbed her sore ass, eliciting a half scream of pain. Finally, she panted and moaned her way into a screaming climax that had him clamping his hand over her mouth to save his ears as much as for decorum. Hell, Sawn was in the next room and it was going to be obvious that the Kildar was up to his old tricks.

The girl didn't seem to be a multiclimax type, so he slowed just enough to let her get her wind back and then drove in, hard, getting his third orgasm of the encounter. It had to be the tits.

"That was . . ." she whispered, then moaned as he carefully withdrew.

"Decent?" Mike asked, cleaning up and then pulling her in to cuddle on his shoulder.

"Very nice," Daria whispered. "I did not think it could be that way."

"Welcome to the real world," Mike said, yawning. "I'm for a nap, how 'bout you?"

"I think I could use a nap as well," Daria admitted. "Can I sleep here?"

"Just try to leave," Mike said, curling into her.

# ★ Chapter Twenty-Four ★

"None of them have left," Ctibor said, as Yarok walked into the apartment. "They usually stay at least two days in one place, by the look of the previous data."

The Albanian hit team had taken up four apartments in the building. It was owned by the Albanian mob, so getting the apartments had been simple enough, if rough on the previous tenants. But the tenants had left behind some nice furniture. Unfortunately, it was not going to be in very good condition when the team left; the "shooters" Boris had turned up were mostly gutter scum. What was it that British general had said? *"The scum of the earth enlisted for drink."* That was what Boris had found for him when he asked for professionals. Yarok wondered, briefly, which general it had been. Montgomery, probably.

"I'm not happy with taking them down in the hotel," Yarok said, rubbing his lips with his fingers. "Is the team all here?"

"The ones that are sober," Ctibor said, spitting on the floor. "You'd think the Albanians could round up better men than this."

"It would have been better if we'd caught them in that

hotel in Kosovo," Yarok admitted. "But around here all you can get is gutter thugs. Even the veterans of the war mostly have real jobs. Or they work for rival gangs."

"So what do you want to do?" Ctibor asked, shrugging.

"We will hit them tonight," Yarok said, decisively. "Before dawn."

Mike blinked and opened his eyes at the ring from the cell phone and started to roll over only to find that he was totally tangled in sheets and covers. He managed to untangle without disturbing Daria and snagged the phone.

"Jenkins," he growled.

"Kildar, it is Gurum."

"Gurum?" Mike asked, rubbing his eyes and wondering why the brewery manager would be calling him while he was on an op.

"I am in the city of Las Vegas, Kildar," Gurum said. "The booth for the convention is well prepared and the company is in the process of installing. But you said that you wanted some of the Keldara here for the booth. I had left the choice up to you, Kildar, but when I called home they told me you were . . . on business."

"Shit," Mike snapped, sitting up. "I completely and totally forgot."

"I can hire local models, Kildar," Gurum said. "They are not cheap and I will have to hurry to find Keldara dress . . ."

"No," Mike said, thinking rapidly. "I've got a better idea."

★ ★ ★

"You want what?" Pierson snapped.

"We need to meet," Mike said. "About the other thing. And I need to get some people into the U.S. Now. We have what is called a win-win situation here."

"You're joking," Pierson said, sighing. "You want visas for thirty something complete unknowns?"

"And I'm going to need some passports, too," Mike said. "I can get the photos, but I'm going to need them by the time the plane lands in the U.S. And the visas on file."

"Why don't you just fly back yourself?" Pierson asked exasperatedly.

"Because we're in Indian Country," Mike pointed out. "I'm not going to just drop my team in Indian Country, Bob."

"Shit," Pierson replied tightly. "Okay, okay. But you'll need to go to the embassy. What kind of passports?"

"Georgian, I guess," Mike said. "No, scrap that. I know a better way to get them. But we're going to need somebody in the States to receive us that knows not to ask too many questions. The thing is, we're going to Vegas. That's right next to Nellis, which has some really good secure rooms. Oh, and we're carrying about seven hundred pounds of print intel on the op that's going to need some Albanian translators. Very closedmouth ones. I'll drop the original electronic EEI with you as well. That's in half a dozen languages, including Romanian."

"I'll get you a secure fax number to send the information on the girls to the embassy," Pierson said, relenting. "I need to start making some phone calls, though, right now."

"That's fine," Mike said, sitting up and slapping the still sleeping Daria on the rump and eliciting a yelp.

"We're going to have to move like lightning to make the convention."

"The stakeout just called," Ctibor said. "They're packing up."

"Shit," Yarok muttered over the phone. "Any idea where to?"

"No," Ctibor admitted. "We couldn't get a mike into the rooms. The stakeout has a shotgun mike, but the men who are loading the vans don't seem to know. The stakeout said that one of them said something about a convention."

"That tells us a lot," Yarok snapped. "Find out where they are going."

"Perhaps we can hit them en route?" Ctibor suggested.

"Maybe. Tell the stakeout to follow them. We'll need more than one car to follow."

"I'm on it."

"Vanner," Mike said, slipping the intel specialist a note. "Call this number. It's a chartering company I've dealt with before. Tell them I need a large plane as fast as possible. My usual pilot if he can fly it."

"Yes, sir," Vanner replied, grinning. "How are we going to get the girls into the States, sir?"

"I'm on it."

"This is highly irregular, Kildar."

"I know, Minister," Mike said, rolling his eyes. "And I am sorry to place this burden upon you, knowing that your time is extremely valuable. But it is most urgent and very important. I know that aspects have the attention of the President of the United States. While the situation does not directly affect Georgia, it has very wide-ranging implications. And it is imperative that I take the full team to the United States as soon as possible. Tonight if we can."

"I will call the embassy in Croatia immediately," the Georgian minister for external affairs said with a sigh. "But I will want to know that this is for an important purpose."

"I will convey that to the President, Minister," Mike said, rolling his eyes and wondering how many favors he was going to owe by the time the night was over.

"Mike," Adams growled over the radio.

"Go," Mike said.

"I think we have a problem. I've spotted the same white Lada four times since we got out of town. Either the guy's going to Zagreb just like us or we're being followed."

"Crap," Mike said, shaking his head. "We knew it had to happen sooner or later. Okay, evasion plan Alpha. Sawn, you monitoring?"

"Yes, Kildar."

"Follow the agreed routes and meet at the agreed rally point. Adams, you have pick-up. Everyone go to scrambled cell at this time." Mike pulled out his map and studied the roads. "Yevgenii, take the next left . . ." So much for making good time.

"Yarok," the security specialist growled. He'd had a hard time getting all the vehicles for the assault team, most of whom were half or all the way drunk. While the

American had taken less than fifteen minutes to get on the road, it had taken him over an hour.

"Ctibor. They're splitting up. I think the trail car was made."

"I told you to use more than one car!" Yarok fumed.

"I had a hard time getting more," Ctibor complained. "And we never caught up. The stakeout car is still following one group that is on the main highway to Zagreb, but the other vans all have pulled off."

"Follow the group on the main highway," Yarok said. "They have to rendezvous somewhere."

"Okay, Garold, they're still on us," Adams said over the radio. "Break it down. I'll stay on the highway."

He watched as the other vans pulled off the main road to Zagreb and then shook his head.

"That's right, little lamb," he crooned. "Stay right on my tail."

# ★ Chapter Twenty-Five ★

"Hello, Mr. Jenkins," Hardesty said as Mike reached the top of the rolling ramp. "Larger crowd than normal?"

John Hardesty was a tall, slender and distinguished looking former RAF fighter pilot who had gotten out with the fixed intention of becoming a pilot for British Airways. The problem with that being that, like the RAF, BA had been having cutbacks for years. Unable to get the job of his dreams, he'd settled for flying rich bastards around in private jets.

One day he'd gotten a charter that looked to be the usual, flying a rich American bastard around Europe. However, it had turned out somewhat differently than he'd imagined. The first odd note was that the rich American had turned up with just one suitcase and a small backpack instead of the loads of business suits the pilot had expected. And the destinations had been . . . odd. Small towns in Russia, rather notoriously dangerous towns in Serbia. And instead of the usual "I've got a business meeting tomorrow morning, we'll be taking off at noon," the passenger had required that he and his copilot to be on-call twenty-four hours a day. And had usually turned up in the middle of the night, reaking of cordite, his clothes spotted with bloodstains. At one point he turned up with what was clearly a low-class Russian hooker and carted her around for the rest of the trip. Hardesty tastefully ignored the fact that she had recent bruises from a beating.

The passenger also turned out to be travelling under at least three false names, and clearances for entry to countries had been remarkably smooth. He might be a hitman, but if so he was a hitman for a government, which made him almost respectable.

The various flights had culminated in Paris where the passenger had advised him to get to an airport well away from the City of Light and choose a hotel room that didn't look in that direction. The news the next day that a nuclear weapon had been found in Paris, and been disarmed, came as no real surprise.

Since then he had carted "Mike Jenkins," AKA Mike Duncan, AKA John Stewart, AKA whoknowswhat around to various spots in Europe, the United States and Southeast Asia. Since that first wild charter there hadn't been a hint of gunpowder. Until tonight. Tonight he had the feeling things were going to get wild and wooly. Again.

"A bit," Mike said. "And documentation is following. We've also got a bit of luggage."

"Plenty of room in the compartments," Hardesty said, leaning down to glance under the fuselage as the Keldara began unloading. Some of the bags looked suspiciously long. "I take it none of it's going to explode?"

"We're leaving the Semtek, if that's what you mean," Mike replied, standing by the females as the girls walked by.

"Nice joke," Hardesty said, smiling. Then he looked at Mike's face. "You were joking, right?"

"Customs is going to be handled on the far end," Mike replied. "But we'll be leaving a good bit of the material on the bird. So figure on a five-day layover in Vegas."

"You weren't joking," the pilot said, shaking his head as one of the Keldara men went by with his arm in a sling.

"We've gotten drivers to take all the vans to the embassy," Mike replied. "But while I'm willing to leave my Semtek, I'm not willing to leave all the gear. Or the ammo," he added as the Keldara men started filing up the stairs with various rather heavy bags that might or might not contain such things as guns and ammunition.

"There are times that I really wish you'd picked another charter company as your flyers of choice." Hardesty sighed. "On the other hand, the young ladies are quite charming, are they not?"

"About half of them are intel specialists," Mike said. "The others are hookers that have been freed from Albanian gangs. One of which is, apparently, hot on our tail. As soon as the last of our party turns up, you might want to be ready to take off. Fast."

"Really, really wish . . ."

"If wishes were horses, beggars would ride."

"This is most irregular," the second assistant to the ambassador from Georgia to Croatia moaned as he looked at the pile of blank passports. "Most irregular."

"You want irregular?" Chief Adams sighed. "There's an Albanian hit team on my tail. There's a plane waiting to fly to the U.S. at the airport. And I've got to get from here to there, with these passports, and without getting killed. So just do me a favor and stamp the appropriate spots so I can get the hell out of here before we have a firefight in the embassy, okay?"

"You are joking, yes?" the official moaned.

"I am joking, no," Adams said, picking up the official stamp. "So you want to stamp them or not? Your call. But I'm not leaving without them."

"Mike, got the documents," Adams said, leaning over to look out the window of the van. He was currently parked on Georgian territory, but the minute he pulled out he was going to be in Indian Territory. With no backup.

"Hold one," Mike said. "Any sign of shooters?"

"Not so far," Adams replied.

"Well, we'll just have to go for the trailer."

"IFOR duty desk, Sergeant Simmons speaking, how may I help you, sir or ma'am?"

Simmons was a reservist from Tennessee with the Fifth Regiment. All in all he'd much rather be back in Murfreesboro watching NASCAR, but duty in Bosnia these days was pretty tame. And the girls were plentiful and downright fine. Cheap too. There was worse duty. He'd already done one tour in the sandbox and that classifed as "much worse."

"Sergeant," a man said in a hoarse whisper. "Thank God I finally got to an American. I've got a real problem."

"Sir, IFOR is not available to help distressed citizens . . ." the sergeant replied, sighing. Every time somebody lost a passport or got mugged or rolled or something, they fucking called IFOR. He flipped open his Rolodex looking for the number for the local police.

"It's not that," the man whispered. "I'm running from a group of Albanian terrorists. I'm an Albanian American, okay? My name's Hamed Dejti. I grew up in San Diego, okay? I was down in Kosovo, I was visiting relatives, okay? I was in a café and I heard some of the men talking about bombing one of the IFOR camps. They had a car and the explosives but they were arguing about who was going to drive it, okay? I guess I left too fast, they must have suspected I heard them. I mean, they were talking about the stupid American that didn't understand them, okay? I've been running from them ever since. I tried to get the border guards to help me . . ."

"Sir, are you sure about your information?" Simmons said, hitting the alert button and rolling out the duty guard platoon. This wasn't a mugging. The voice had a definite American accent and the caller was clearly scared. He just wished he had a tracer circuit.

"They said they were going to strike one of the American camps," the man said, more definitely. "They didn't say which one. But that's you guys, right?"

"Where are you right now, sir?"

"I'm at a payphone on Gajdekova Street," the man said. "The only ones I know about are in a white Lada, parked a half a block from the Georgian embassy. I'm right across the street. I think they want to kill me, but there are too many guards around. I'll wait here until somebody gets to me. I can't even get to the American embassy, they cut me off! Please . . ."

"Sir, I'm scrambling the duty platoon right now," the

sergeant said, looking up as the duty officer walked in, scratching at his stomach under his uniform. "We're on it."

"Adams."

"Cavalry is on the way. As soon as our friends are occupado, boogie. We're only waiting on you."

"They're in the Georgian embassy," Ctibor said, pointing with his chin.

Yarov leaned down to mask his face and looked towards the gates of the embassy. It was an old mansion with an iron spike fence around the courtyard and a baroque exterior. The guards didn't seem to be paying any attention to the white Lada, but he could see the van parked by the side entrance.

"Well, we're in place, but that's only one of them," Yarov replied. "We need them all."

"Why did they go to the embassy?" Ctibor mused.

"Because they knew we couldn't get at them, there," Yarov said. "The rest might have already rendezvoused and this is a throw-away group. We'll wait one night and if they don't move . . ."

He looked up and shook his head as a group of Humvees, with the one in the lead sporting the blue light of an MP vehicle, raced down the road at high speed. The side of the Humvees were painted with the American flag and a large yellow blazon he didn't recognize.

"Fucking IFOR," Ctibor growled. "Fucking Americans. Why can't they just go back to their own damned . . ."

He paused as the vehicles screeched to a stop and began disgorging troops in full body armor.

Yarov started to back away from the Lada and stopped as an M-16 was thrust in his face.

"Up against the wall, dirt bag!" the American private from the Fifth Cavalry screamed, grabbing his arm and turning him around. "Hands above your head."

He twisted his head sideways and growled as the white van sedately drove out of the main entrance to the embassy. As it passed the street scene of American troops rounding up "dangerous terrorists," whoever was driving tooted their horn in farewell.

Fucking Americans.

# ★ Chapter Twenty-Six ★

"Jenkins," Mike said, picking up the phone.

The 757 was configured with a large passenger area in the rear and a small office compartment up front. Mike was currently in the office, discussing the recent mission with Vanner and Adams.

"This is Captain Hardesty," the pilot said dryly. "You might want to know that we are now 'feet wet' over the Adriatic."

"Thanks," Mike said, chuckling. "Feet wet" was a military term for leaving an area of operations over the water. Dating back to the Vietnam War, it was the traditional call that the unit and aircraft were safe from interference by hostiles. "I'll be even more happy when we're feet wet over the Atlantic."

"I'll give you a call," Hardesty replied. "We will, however, be refueling in England. One hopes that this charter will not cause inconvenient questions to be raised upon landing."

"Unlikely," Mike said, smiling. "I think that even if any questions are being raised, the British government is going to be more than willing to avoid them given some of the information we've probably acquired."

"I've got at least one name from the British Foreign Office," Vanner said, looking at his notes. "I haven't translated the file, yet."

"*More* than willing," Mike repeated.

"I see," Hardesty replied. "Very well. Flight time to Las Vegas with stops to refuel will be about twenty hours. You might want to get some rest. We'll also be picking up a change of pilots in England. They're . . . briefed."

"Good to hear," Mike said. "Talk later."

"So far, we're not getting real far on the data we picked up in Rozaje," Vanner said. "The translation is going really slow. But there's one bright spot. We don't have their DVDs, but the video was stored on the computer and then the DVDs were burned from it. I'm going to run a file reconstructor on the data and see if we can find any bits from the previous videos. It doesn't look like they cleaned the computer but the bits are going to be partial."

"Tell me what you get," Mike said, yawning. "Can any of the girls run the program?"

"Yeah," Vanner replied. "I'm going to let them work it while I get some shut-eye. But I want to scan the files. The girls have seen just enough of this stuff to know they don't want to see any more."

"Agreed," Mike said tightly. "Get started on it and then get some rest. We're going to need you fresh in Vegas."

"Will do," Vanner said, picking up the laptop and leaving the office.

"If we have to go to Lunari it's going to be tough," Adams said after the intel specialist had left. "We don't have much on it, but what I've been able to glean indicates that the town's a fucking fortress. More than one, since all the gangs have houses there and they don't trust each other."

"We might be able to do something with that," Mike said, yawning again. "What goes for Vanner, goes for you, too. Get some rest. I'm going to need you alert whenever we get there."

"I was planning on it," Adams said, getting up. "You too."

"I will," Mike replied. "I'm going to watch some news and then rack out." The couch in the compartment converted to a bed and he was planning on taking the unusual step of using "rank has it's privileges."

"See you in the morning," Adams said. "Or whenever it's going to be."

Mike flipped open his own laptop and scanned the news. The top news story on the Fox site was the search for a missing girl in Kansas. Which meant dick all to him. Next down was the battle over the current Supreme Court nominee. The nominee was stuck in committee, naturally. The liberals were screaming about the nominee's "non-mainstream" religious views, by which they meant he was a practicing Catholic and had firm views on abortion and other "life" issues. And Grantham was the chairman of the committee, he noted.

It was assumed he would be voting with the President but he'd hardly been supporting the nominee in the last few days, which was worth fifteen minutes of comment from political and legal experts. The senator, it seemed, had twice missed opportunities to move the nominee out of committee and on to a floor vote.

France was trying to crack down on Islamic jihadists and having a rough time. The French security forces had been on high alert ever since the previous year when a nuke was set to blow in Paris. However, the French judiciary and various liberal groups were creating roadblock after roadblock against deportation of even the most extremist members of the Islamics.

The majority of the Islamics were found in southern France and around Paris. And the majority of those were housed in "government housing" neighborhoods composed of block after block of massive apartment buildings. The neighborhoods had become "no-go" zones for the police and in places there had been pitched battles that were nearly the equal of the "insurgency" period in Iraq. It hadn't, quite, reached the level of civil war, but if it were anywhere but France the news media would be all over it. As it was, the only term that came to mind was "downplayed." There was one shot in the background of what had to be an RPG being fired at French police, who appeared to be in retreat. It sure as hell didn't look good and he was glad he was out of it. He might drop a line to the Chateauneuf and see how bad it was.

And in the tail end of the news was a poll showing that the lead in the presidential polls was Barbara Watson, former first lady, junior senator from Massachusetts and a card carrying bitch from hell. If there was anything she hated more than conservative political positions it was the military. Still deployed all over the world trying to fight the good fight, the military was sure to be gutted, War on Terror or no, if she took office. And the intel groups would be hamstrung.

Mike wasn't sure if the news was just particularly bad or if it was just fatigue. But it seemed like everything he had worked for most of his life was going down the tubes. The only good news was that the Georgian government seemed to be stabilizing and even the Ossetians were coming to the table. The way things were going, Georgia was going to be a better place for him to live, all around, than the States.

Thoroughly depressed, he killed the TV and the lights and lay back, watching the stars through the narrow windows of the plane.

Mike rolled to his feet, disoriented, as the plane began its descent. He rubbed his eyes and looked out the window, still disoriented. According to his watch it was eight AM, but the sun still wasn't up. Oh, yeah, they were flying with the sun. This was going to get annoying. Jet lag was a bitch.

"Ladies and gentlemen, we're beginning our descent to Gatwick Airport in England," Captain Hardesty intoned. "Please reconfigure your seats and such like for landing. We'll be refueling and picking up breakfast. I'd appreciate it if the English speakers could translate, since my knowledge of Georgian is sadly lacking. Mr. Jenkins, if you could pick up the phone, please?"

"Jenkins."

"We've received an inflight advisory that members of the British government will be visiting with us while we're in England," Hardesty said, neutrally.

"Oh, really?" Mike asked. "I'm going to need to make some phone calls."

"Please do," Hardesty said. "As long as they don't get my plane impounded and my pilot's license pulled. I am officially disavowing any suspicion of illicit activities, I might add."

"Nice to know," Mike said, chuckling as he hung up the phone. He dialed a number from memory before checking his watch. It was still the middle of the night in the U.S.

"Office of Special Operations Liaison, Navy Captain Parker speaking. How may I help you, sir or ma'am?"

"That's a mouthful, Captain," Mike said. "Mike Jenkins. I'm checking in. We're landing in England and we're apparently getting a deputation from the Brits. Comments?"

"Unknown at this time, Mr. Jenkins," Parker said after a moment. "I'll need to make some calls."

"Please do," Mike said. He picked up the phone and connected to the rear cabin.

"Yes, Kildar?"

"Greznya? I hope you got some sleep."

"I got quite a good sleep, thank you, Kildar," Greznya replied.

"Are Adams and Vanner functional?"

"They will be after another cup of coffee," Greznya said. "And Vanner has something he's looking at. Would you like them to step up front?"

"No, I'm going to head back," Mike said. "See you in a bit."

The rear of the plane was configured for about twice as many people as there were Keldara so Keldara were sprawled everywhere. Adams was getting them up and the seats reconfigured as Mike stepped through the door.

"Be with you in a second, Mike," Adams called.

There were two flight attendants on the plane and Mike waved one of them over.

"Is there a way to access the intercom back here?" Mike asked.

"Right here, sir," the woman said, picking up a phone and hitting the appropriate button.

"Rise and shine, Keldara," Mike said in the Keldara dialect of Georgian, which he was fairly sure the crew wouldn't be able to understand. "We're about to land in England. When we do we're going to be getting a visit from some representatives of the British government. I'm not sure what they're going to be asking about, but I suspect it has to do with our visit to Romania and points south. In that case, nobody speaks English at all well and understands it even less. If it comes down to lawyers, guns and money we've got all three on our side as well as some very interesting video footage. Enough about that, though.

"As you all know, we're headed for the U.S. to attend a convention and try to sell our beer. In addition, I'll be meeting with members of the U.S. government and will be discussing our recent trip. Hopefully, we'll be able to trade for some intelligence on our next objective. But that's for me to worry about. What you are going to be doing is selling beer. Gurum will be running that side of things. I don't want any caillean stuff to interfere. Gurum has done a good job this far and it's time for us to backstop him. The girls will be wearing traditional dress, handing out beer and smiling at the customers. The boys will be making sure the customers keep their hands to themselves. Pictures may be taken. In that case, smile for the camera. I don't know how much of it Adams, Vanner and I will be available for, so you're mostly going to be on your own.

"Las Vegas is called Sin City. There are various vices available to the visitor. But I know that the Keldara are far too meek and gentle to engage in such things as fornicating with prostitutes, gambling and drinking."

He waited for the expected chuckles to die down and then shook his head.

"Okay, so maybe you're not. But there are lots of ways to get in trouble that you're not aware of. So most of the trip I'd like you to stay around your rooms or down at the booth on your schedule, which we'll come up with and publish. I'll try to squeeze out some free time so you can see the town with local guides. After the convention, though, I suspect it will be back into the belly of the beast. So have as much fun as you can."

"Kildar," one of the Keldara women said as he hung up. "Phone."

"Jenkins," Mike said, picking up the handset.

"Parker," the caller said, briefly. "Answer to your question: Your activities came to the attention of MI-6. They put the Georgians together with the Americans and came up with you as being the likely person. When we were questioned on it, routinely, we were noncommittal. They apparently have specific concerns, unspecified according to the report. My guess is that they want to talk about their unspecified concerns."

"We're carrying our gear," Mike pointed out. "A search

of the plane will lead to embarrassing questions. For that matter, we're going to need some interference run in the States."

"You're not debarking or unloading until Las Vegas, right?" Parker asked.

"Correct."

"It's handled," Parker said. "When you land in Vegas, get your troops settled in at whatever they're doing. You'll be contacted at your hotel and flown out to Nellis for debrief and data comparison."

"Got it," Mike said. "Anything else?"

"Not here."

"Out, then," Mike said, hanging up the phone.

"Kildar," Vanner said as he finished. "We've got something."

"Something useful?" Mike asked. "Finally?"

"Very."

"There were over two hundred file snippets on the hard drive," Vanner said, leaving his trayback down with the laptop on it as the plane descended. "I haven't had time to look at all of them, much less get a feel for who all the people on them are, but I found this . . ."

He hit play and the screen showed a masked but naked man in bed with two women, girls really. One of them Mike recognized immediately as their target, the other was unknown.

"The other female is Ludmilla Seventy-Eight," Vanner said, continuing to let the video stream without sound. The scene was pretty clear. Neither of the women were having fun as the man worked "Ludmilla" over with what looked like a soldering iron and a pair of pliers. The target, Natalya, was simply chained to the bed in a position where she had to watch.

"The video is broken, but the end is there," Vanner continued in a strained voice.

The next snippet showed the same scene, but in that portion Ludmilla was on her face with the masked man apparently taking her anally. From what was visible of her back, she had apparently been whipped in one of the missing segments. As Mike watched, the masked man wrapped a thin cord around the girl's neck and strangled her while he was taking her. When her struggles had ended, permanently, the man got off of her and the video abruptly ended.

"There's no way to tell that that's Grantham," Mike commented.

"Well, there's one corroborating item," Vanner said, backing the video up and turning on the sound while handing Mike a pair of earphones.

Mike didn't really want to watch the video again but he put on the earphones anyway.

*"Fucking bitch,"* the masked man snarled. *"Little fucking whore. I'm going to do you in every hole and then fucking kill you. You're playing with the big boys, now! Beg me for your life and you might live, bitch . . ."*

The video continued in the same vein for some time and Mike finally hit the pause button.

"And?" he asked.

"Here's a video of Grantham talking to the cameras," Vanner said.

Mike watched that video as well and listened to the

voice with his eyes closed, then played the snuff film as well with his eyes closed.

"Same voice," Mike said, shaking his head.

"I thought so, too," Vanner said. "But something was bugging me about it. So I took a good look at the video."

He brought up a screen capture in PhotoShop. The capture was of the masked man, stretched out next to the murdered girl and working her over. He'd apparently stretched his back and he was at full height.

"The bed is a standard European double," Vanner said, bringing up a ruler tool. "The height of the bed is seventy-eight inches." He laid the ruler down and got a length off of it. "Senator Grantham is six foot one or seventy-three inches." He laid the ruler down and got the height off of the figure in the video.

"Doing the math," he continued, pulling out a cocktail napkin and sketching the numbers on it, "I get that the guy in the video is only five feet ten inches tall. More like five nine. Max of five eleven."

"So what's with the voice?" Mike asked. Something was nagging at him about the video but he couldn't put his finger on it.

"Various ways it could be cloaked," Vanner said, shrugging as the wheels chirped on touchdown. "There's a device that goes on the vocal cords that can change a voice. Not perfectly, but close enough for this. Not my area of expertise and I don't have the equipment to do a really tight voice compare. But what this looks like is a deliberate frame of the senator by person or persons unknown."

"And you can bet that Traskel is in it up to his patrician eyeballs."

# ★ Chapter Twenty-Seven ★

"Mr. Jenkins," the first man through the door said, holding out a limp hand to be shaken. "Horace Wythe-Harcourt of the Foreign Office. A pleasure to meet you."

"And you, sir," Mike said, nodding as two more men came through the door of the plane.

"Jasper Drake, MI-5," the second man said, nodding. "And my counterpart from MI-6, John Carlson-Smith." Drake was tall and slender with an air of respectability about him that would have done for a banker.

"Pleasure," Carlson-Smith said, shaking Mike's hand firmly. Carlson-Smith was a short-coupled, broadly muscled blond man with a nose twisted from a fight.

"What can I do for you, gentlemen?" Mike asked, waving them to seats in the office compartment.

"To be clear about our intentions," Wythe Harcourt said, smiling, "we're not going to ask you about the special operations group you have on the plane or your cargo."

"About forty automatic weapons, RPG launchers, ammunition for both and sundry other devices of destruction," Carlson-Smith said, also smiling. "Why'd you leave the Semtek? Certainly not space considerations. We have people in the Zagreb airport, you see."

"So what are you going to ask about?" Mike said, ignoring the question.

"We believe that you have recovered intelligence from a villa outside of the town of Rozaje," Drake replied smoothly. "It has come to our attention that a member of the British government has recently been making decisions that are . . . somewhat out of character. Actually, three members. All of whom recently served in the Balkans and all of whom have known proclivities that might have been . . . assuaged in that villa."

"Crap," Mike muttered. "You've got yourself a real problem, then."

"You don't have intel?" Carlson asked. "I'm surprised. From the after action report it was a very clean op."

"Cards on the table and no repercussions, then?" Mike said, smiling also.

"None," Carlson-Smith replied, directly. "We just want the take."

"That's going to be a problem," Mike said. "There's three 'takes.' They kept paper records and made videos. But the vids were then burned to DVD and sent elsewhere. There are some remaining snippets on a hard drive. We've got the hard drive and the paper records, which are in Albanian, but not the DVDs. And I'm taking all of it to the U.S. We've got a higher priority problem than a couple of diplomats."

"I'm not sure that will work," Wythe-Harcourt said smoothly. "The problem is that there may or may not be other records that are a higher priority problem, as you put it, for Her Majesty's government as well as allied governments. We would very much prefer that the information remain close, if you will."

"So what you're saying is that we're not leaving with our intel?" Mike asked bluntly.

"We assure you that all the information that is germane will be handed over to the American government," Wythe-Harcourt said calmly. "It's simply that we actively prefer that those items of interest to Her Majesty's government not go astray as it were."

"Well, then we've got ourselves a problem," Mike said, still smiling. "You see, there is information that is of very great importance to the people and government of the United States in that intel. So you'll see where I've got an issue with turning it over to you. At least as much of an issue, if not a greater one, than you have with turning it over to the U.S. government. I see a very ugly stalemate."

"We need that hard drive," Carlson-Smith said tightly.

"Calmly, John," Wythe-Harcourt said, smoothly. "This is why we are negotiating."

"I'm not sure what the basis of negotiations would be," Mike said, shrugging. "You're not going to let me take off with the intel and I'm not going to turn it over. I didn't get rid of all my Semtek, by the way, and you're going to have a very hard time capturing the data before it's destroyed, given that I've got twenty top-flight troops on the plane. SAS isn't going to do you much good except to get the data destroyed and make one hell of a mess. And an international incident between two countries that have a very special relationship."

"So you're not going to give it up?" Drake asked musingly.

"Over my dead body," Mike said. "Literally. That is how you're going to have to get it. And the bodies of my troopers."

"Calmly, Mr. Jenkins," Wythe-Harcourt said, sighing. "Calmly. As I said, negotiations. Your concern is understandable. Is ours?"

"It's a matter of relative concern," Mike said. "There is data in there, that we have found, that is uncontrovertible proof of crimes committed by a senior member of the U.S. government. That's not going anywhere but a very secure facility in the U.S. And we're not sure we have all of it. Further, there may be other data as dangerous. This data is extremely sensitive but right now all you have is the Sword of Damocles hanging over a few of your minor diplomats. That's a world of difference from what the U.S. is looking at. Relative concern."

"We have information that there may be a higher degree of concern for Her Majesty's government," Wythe-Harcourt said, deadpan.

"How high?" Mike asked carefully.

"Very high," Carlson-Smith practically snarled. "Very damned high."

"Stalemate again," Mike said, shrugging. "Anybody? Because I'm not planning on going home empty-handed. And Gatwick Airport is a lousy place for a firefight, I'll also admit. People would ask questions and there'd be all sorts of media and . . ." He shrugged and smiled. "For that matter, they'd ask questions if the plane simply sat here for a few days." He paused for a moment and then shrugged.

"Let me bring someone else into the discussion," Mike said, musingly. "If I may?"

"Someone . . . discreet?" Wythe-Harcourt asked.

"My intel specialist," Mike said. "Former Marine intercept specialist. Did time with the NSA. Good enough?"

"I suppose," Drake said.

Mike picked up the phone and hit the connection to the rear. "Send Vanner up. Tell him to bring his computer and notes," he said then turned back to the threesome. "Care for some coffee while we wait? Or, pardon, tea?"

"Yeah, boss?" Vanner said when he came through the door.

"These gentlemen are from the British government," Mike said, waving him to a seat. "They think there are some Rozaje files that are important to them. Important enough that we're not taking off until we turn over all our intel. I told them over my dead body. And yours, by the way."

"Oh," Vanner said in thought. "Yeah, I guess it would be over mine, too. Hell, even the girls'. Even if they didn't know why."

"So let's discuss the take with these gentlemen and try to come to some sort of arrangement," Mike said.

"So you're saying we don't trust the Brits with this stuff and they don't trust us?" Vanner asked.

"That would sum it up nicely," Drake said dryly.

"I think that's it," Mike said, frowning at the Brits. "I, frankly, don't know any of you from Adam. And strange things happen with intel in bureaucracies. I know the people I'm going to be turning this over to. I trust them not to abuse it."

"And for our part, I must add that we most especially do not trust you," Wythe-Harcourt admitted. "You're a free agent, an international security contractor with a very shady reputation holding the blackmail equivalent of a nuclear weapon."

"There is that," Mike said with a grin. "And I've got copies, moreover. Horrible thing. Vanner, how many video clips did you get?"

"There were a bit over two hundred listed 'scenes' in the files," Vanner said, temporizing. "I haven't translated all of them, but there are about the same number of video clips, most of them incomplete. Natalya was listed on three scenes before being translated. I cross-referenced those scene files and found the one we were looking for in the hard copy. But finding the video was more luck than anything. I had to scan through clips of the scenes one by one but I found her on the seventh clip. That was the one I showed you. But I don't know what is on the other scenes and there's no file directory to cross-reference to the hard copy files."

"There were two hundred women killed in that place?" Wythe-Harcourt asked, his eyes wide.

"Approximately," Vanner replied. "Women were not killed in all of the scenes but in a few of them more than one was apparently killed. The highest I found was three. I think that guy needs to be tracked down and taken out; he apparently hardly engaged in rape, just torture and murder."

"Later for that," Mike said. "Gentlemen, what are you looking for? Maybe we can just extract the hard copy files and try to find the video clips and turn them over. Understand, the Albanians still have the DVDs."

"I'm not sure that will be sufficient." Wythe-Harcourt sighed. "And we'd very much like to avoid naming names at this juncture."

"Screw this," Mike said, picking up a phone. "Greznya, get me OSOL on the line."

"Mr. Jenkins," Wythe-Harcourt said, firmly, "I really believe that the fewer people brought in on this . . ."

"And I believe that this decision is at the wrong level," Mike replied bluntly. "Like I said, I don't know you guys from Adam and as you said I've got no cred in your eyes. So let's get people with cred involved. This is too high level for us to be dicking around with."

"I'm here at the personal orders of the Foreign Minister," Wythe-Harcourt said, just as bluntly.

"Head of MI-6 for me," Carlson-Smith said.

"Head of MI-5 in my case," Drake added.

"And I've got marching orders from the President," Mike snapped. "I think I trump."

"Parker."

"You're sounding tired," Mike said.

"End of shift," Parker said. "Pierson's supposed to be in in about an hour. What do you got?"

"The Brits are refusing to let us take off with the take," Mike said tightly. "They're afraid that someone senior is on camera. Someone senior in the British government."

"Oh, joy," Parker said with a sigh. "And we have . . ."

"We have something very interesting," Mike said. "Among other things, we've got data that tends to disprove our previous intel. The person named previously does not appear to be really present. But there is enough there for a slighly lame frame of said person."

"Interesting," Parker replied. "We need that data."

"That's what the Brits are saying," Mike said. "And they've got the guns to prove it."

"I hope it doesn't come to that," Parker said.

"Yeah, especially since without this take the previous information is out there," Mike said. "We need bigger guns in on this."

"I'll make some calls," Parker said with another sigh. "I'm going to have to wake people up."

"Great," Mike said. "Especially since right now my body has no idea what time it's supposed to be."

Mike ended the connection. "Parker is waking up some of our more senior people," he said, picking up his coffee. "You can hang out here, or you can call your people and tell them to start expecting very important phone calls."

"If you don't mind, we'll stay here," Drake said, pulling out his cell phone. "But we would like to make some calls also."

"Kildar," Greznya said, sticking her head in the door. "Colonel Pierson for you on line two."

"Got it," Mike said, picking up the phone and hitting the connection. "Jenkins."

"Do you just enjoy kicking hornet nests?" Pierson asked. "There I was, minding my own business, eating my breakfast like a real human being . . ."

"Tell it to the Brits," Mike said, glancing over at where Carlson-Smith was scanning the video footage and taking notes.

"I understand that you're going to get clearance soon,"

Pierson replied. "But we're going to have the Brits 'assisting us in our investigations.'"

"Works for me," Mike said. "As long as I can take off . . ."

"Kildar," Greznya said, breathlessly, glancing around the room. "A very important call on Line Three."

"I'm talking to Colonel Pierson," Mike said, covering the receiver.

"More important!" Greznya said, her eyes wide.

"Hang on, Bob," Mike said, putting him on hold and switching lines.

"Do you just enjoy kicking hornet nests?" the President asked, tiredly.

"Jesus, did they get you up for this, sir?" Mike asked.

"Yes, they did," the President replied. "Actually, they got me up to field the call from the prime minister. You're getting clearance to take off if you don't already have it. When you get here, all the data, every snip and dribble, gets carted to a base along with your intel people. The Brits are sending over some people to keep an eye on it at the same time. Since we were on a very secure line, the prime minister told me who was suspected of being in their video and I agree that not letting it become public knowledge is a good idea."

"Bloody hell—" Carlson-Smith snapped, hitting a computer key.

"Was that who I think it is?" Vanner asked, his eyes wide.

"I think they just found what they were looking for, Mr. President," Mike said, at which four heads snapped up, even the two glued to the computer screen. "Is it who you thought it was? The Pres already talked to your prime minister and he'd like to know."

"Yes," Carlson-Smith snarled. "It is."

"They confirm, Mr. President," Mike said.

"Get that intel to the U.S., now," the President ordered.

"Yes, sir," Mike said.

"And don't lose it!"

"Will do, sir," Mike replied.

"Carlson-Smith will remain with the materials for the rest of the flight," Drake said, hanging up his phone. "You're cleared to take off. You're to fly direct to Washington, Dulles Airport, refuel and then direct to Nellis Air Force Base. You will offload your materials there, as well as your intel specialists, and then fly to Las Vegas. The landing in Nellis will not be recorded. We'll brief your pilot on the new itinerary. Mr. Wythe-Harcourt and I will debark and brief our respective bosses."

"Well, I just debriefed the only guy I consider in the category," Mike said, waving the phone. "Who was it, by the way?"

"That's none of your business," Carlson-Smith snapped.

"The British Home Secretary," Vanner replied. "And Jesus does that guy have a tiny dick."

# ★ Chapter Twenty-Eight ★

"Daria," Mike said, sitting down next to the girl. "I'm sorry, I haven't been ignoring you. There's just a lot going on."

A lot was an understatement. Despite the President's assurances, various hoops had to be jumped through. Among other things, it turned out that Carlson-Smith didn't have his passport with him. Mike had offered one of the blank ones from the Georgian embassy, but that had been politely declined. The delay, however, even with *no* problems in the U.S., was going to make their arrival in Las Vegas tricky at best. Mike had, along the way, managed to convince people that he had a real need to go to Vegas first, so the landing in Nellis had been put off until the Keldara, and Mike, were dropped in Vegas. Which left just a few little details to clean up.

"I understand, Kildar," Daria replied, smiling. "How is it going?"

"Well, we're on our way at last," Mike said. "But I was wondering if you could do me a few favors."

"Of course," Daria said, smiling. "Here?" she added with a wink.

"Now, now," Mike said, shaking his head. "I need you to call ahead and talk to Gurum. Find hotel rooms for everyone. Some of us might not actually make it to Vegas but I want everyone to have a room. We probably can't . . ."

"This is done," Daria said, pulling out a notebook. "The group that canceled at the convention had a block of rooms reserved. I found out about it and contacted them. They still had the rooms held, but had finally decided that they were not attending. I secured that block of rooms for us at a very reasonable rate. Since we needed some more space, and the hotel was mostly booked, I also secured the penthouse suite for your use, anticipating that Chief Adams and Mr. Vanner would be using it as well. I asked about information security on the room and the hotel has assured me that since the usual users of the room are major American businessmen who often discuss proprietary business in the penthouse that it is quite secure. I spoke with Gurum, who is a very nice man, and ensured that there was access to food for the Keldara. I also talked to the intel girls and they have sufficient 'traditional native costumes' for the convention."

"Oh," Mike replied.

"I spoke with Chief Adams as well," Daria continued. "We're at about sixty percent on small arms ammunition, one hundred percent on RPGs and have a sufficiency of grenades. He wanted me to remind you that we need more Semtek and that if we have to go into Lunari that we're probably going to need more troops. We also need resupply on first aid equipment. And we only have sufficient rations for one day for the entire group." She paused, looked at his expression and shrugged. "I'm trained as a secretary and manager. And my father was a colonel in the Ukrainian Army."

Mike opened his mouth to reply, then shut it.

"Is there anything for me to do?" he asked, somewhat plaintively.

"Just sign the appropriate checks," Daria said, smiling prettily. "Oh, and I need your passport."

"Why?" Mike asked, pulling it out.

"We're hoping you have all the right entry and exit stamps," Daria replied, flipping through the passport. "And you do."

"What's that going to get us?" Mike asked curiously.

"Mr. Vanner thinks that he can create stamps for the rest of the passports from this," Daria said, tucking the passport away and making a note. "We're going to need Croatian entry and exit stamps, at the very least. And I think that's it."

"Are we paying you?" Mike asked incredulously.

"No, as a matter of fact. But I'm trying to help."

"In that case, take a note to double your pay," Mike said, smiling. "Seriously, Anastasia does some of this for me in Georgia but I could use a real assistant. And you seem to have things remarkably under control. Are you open to a job offer?"

"Does it involve shooting people?" Daria asked carefully.

"No," Mike said, then shrugged. "I'd suggest that you take some training, purely for defense. But what I'm thinking of is what you're doing, a personnel and logistics person for missions, assuming there are other missions, and being my personal assistant. I suspect that in Georgia you're going to be bored, but when we're doing things like this you sure won't be."

"What would something like that pay?" Daria asked carefully.

"Well, it would include room and board at the caravanserai," Mike pointed out. "On the other hand, there's not much to do there. As to the pay, we can work that out and find something equitable."

"And what about . . . the other?" Daria asked, just as cautiously.

"What other . . . oh," Mike said, then shrugged. "Up to you. If you consider it a duty, don't worry about it. I've got more women problems than I'd prefer. On the other hand, if you consider it a fringe benefit, we can work something out," he added with a grin.

"For now, I think I'd put it in the category of 'fringe benefit,'" Daria said, smiling back. "I accept the job offer. We'll work out the pay."

"Thanks," Mike said, standing up. "Get used to finding out-of-the-way buildings to beat people to death in."

"I'm sure they'll deserve it," Daria said, smiling darkly.

"So how are you going to use my passport to fix everybody else's?" Mike asked Vanner. "Copy the pages?"

The intel specialist was seated at a table at the rear of the plane, working on his computer.

"Won't work," Vanner said. "The Georgian passports have different watermarks. I scanned in all the entry and exit stamps on your passport including most especially the Croatian one. Now I'm creating a three-D model of what the stamp looks like," he continued, spinning the computer around so Mike could see.

"Very nice," Mike said dryly. "It looks like a stamp. And that gives us . . . what?"

"Well," Vanner said, hitting a key and looking at a large item that looked vaguely like a printer on the floor, "in about fifteen minutes it should give us a Croatian entry stamp."

"How?" Mike asked.

"That," Vanner said, pointing at the box, "is a desktop manufacturing device. Give it any sufficiently small three dimensional design and it can make it. Right there."

"You're kidding," Mike said, furrowing his brow. "Right?"

"Nope," Vanner said, grinning. "It's no good for multi-part machinery but it can make any solid object that's smaller than its collection area. The technique is called sintering. The machine takes the CAD diagram and splits it into thin layers. The way it used to work is that each layer would be laid down and then welded to the lower layer, sintered actually. This one is a rapid system that lays the whole model down, layer by layer, then heats the item up and forms it in one go."

"I almost hate to ask how much that thing cost," Mike said, shaking his head.

"It was the first run of a new generation of them," Vanner replied. "And a lot. But I thought it might be useful to have along. And I got a deal on it as a beta tester."

"We're going to need more than one," Mike said, thinking about the future.

"Well, I've got an in with the manufacturer," Vanner said, grinning.

"You do have ink, right?" Mike asked as Vanner slid the still hot stamp into a holder. It sure looked like an entry stamp.

"Fourteen different colors and shades," Vanner admitted. "I mean, I'm not a professional forger, but I can hum a few bars." He picked up a piece of paper and opened up a stamp pad with Mike's passport open on the table in front of him. Humming, he inked the stamp and then stamped it on the piece of paper.

"Looks . . . pretty much the same," Mike admitted.

"It should, it was made from this model," Vanner said. "I had to work out the background watermark and I think that might have led to some thin spots . . ." He pulled out a loupe and considered the stamped paper under the light. "Yeah, there are some rough spots. But if it's not a close inspection it should work. And if any of these passports get a close inspection we're going to have problems."

"Well, we should be okay on the U.S. end," Mike said. "Where's the MI-6 guy?"

"Going over the hard copy files," Vanner said. "Turns out he speaks and reads Albanian."

"I hope he's not developing more intel than we'd like," Mike said. "Where?"

"Front of the compartment," Vanner replied. "I'm going to get started on the exit stamp. . . ."

"This is horrible stuff," Carlson-Smith said, skipping to the next video.

"See anyone you recognize?" Mike asked.

"Unfortunately, yes," Carlson-Smith said tightly. "I was assigned to the Kosovo sector for some time and I recognize several gentlemen who are or were similarly assigned."

"Interesting that they were able to get them there," Mike said. "I suppose you've also seen the video that we're interested in."

"Vanner pointed out the file," Carlson-Smith said. "I've avoided it. That's for you Yanks to fix up. The rest of this is going to be more . . . difficult. They've compromised the bloody head of the French force in Kosovo. And he's been promoted. He's in charge of the military-civilian liaison office in France that's supposedly been backstopping Interior Ministry Forces on rounding up France's Islamics. Which has been notably unsuccessful, I might add."

"I'm missing something," Mike admitted.

"The Albanians have been working with the muj for some time," Carlson-Smith said dryly. "Nothing that the bloody media is willing to bring up, but they trade information among other things. I'd give odds that our friend General Robisseau has been feeding information to the targets in France. Probably because he was 'encouraged' to do so by his Albanian friends."

"Crap," Mike muttered. "Any Georgians in there?"

"Not as far as I can tell," Carlson-Smith said with a chuckle. "But there's more than one American and quite a few Japanese. Check this one out," he added, hunting in the files for a moment.

Mike watched the resulting playback for a moment and then turned away.

"So?" he asked. "I've seen a couple."

"Didn't recognize the gentleman?" the MI-6 agent asked, smiling thinly. "One of your bloody liberal strategists, mate. Been on TV any number of time. Big money collector."

"Cleaning this up is going to be a nightmare," Mike admitted. "Multiple countries, multiple jurisdictions. And all people that could afford the squeeze, which means either rich or powerful or, generally, both. Who bells the cat?"

"Who indeed, mate," Carlson-Smith said, jumping to another file. "Bloody hell, another one. Junior member of the Foreign Service. Works with the UN in Kosovo. Refugee relief. Rich liberal poofter. I'd have guessed him for being under the whip, not holding it."

"I'd think he'd be getting his pussy from refugees," Mike noted.

"He probably was," the MI-6 agent admitted. "But getting rid of the bodies is tough. And when you abuse them beyond a certain point, they go talking to the press. That gets your career sidetracked. You have to leave the Foreign Service and go work for an NGO, which doesn't have benefits nearly as good, does it?"

"Point," Mike said. "What are the benefits of working for MI-6?"

"You get to look at really nasty porn," Carlson-Smith said darkly. "And you get to deal with lowlifes and drug dealers. Then there's the terrorist informers, most of whom don't actually know anything, but are more than willing to take cash for nothing. On the other hand, it's got great dental."

"Sounds great," Mike opined. "James Bond and all that."

"People think that," Carlson-Smith said with a sigh. "But it's more like your CIA, isn't it? I mean, yes, we get weapons training in class and all that, but we never bloody use the things. I haven't drawn my weapon in my whole career and very rarely carry anything for that matter. Very few of us do. Neither do your CIA intel fellows, believe me. The paramilitary types like NVA are a different story, of course. They're the wet-work fellows."

"So what *do* you do?" Mike asked, curiously.

"As I said, run around dealing with lowlifes and trying to get someone to tell us something true," the MI-6 agent said, shrugging. "You build up a group of contacts and get information in any way that you can. It's more glad-handing than running around with beautiful women and killing supervillains. Most of it's quite boring, really."

"Sounds that way," Mike said with a snort. "I'll take James Bond any day."

"I'd rather be doing that than this, mate," Carlson-Smith said. "Among other things, there are things that man is not wot to know or something like that. And this is one of them. Something you'd best keep in mind."

"What do you mean?" Mike asked, frowning.

"There are going to be quite a few very powerful and very unhappy people when this particular ant-pile gets kicked over," the Brit said, shutting down the video program. "I'm covered since I'm just a dumb bureaucrat doing my job. Except for those IRA bastards, nobody personally cares about one agent or another. Sure, the odd muj will have a whack at us, but that's just business.

You they're going to hold personally responsible. The people on these files, they're going to lose and lose big. But so are their supporters and sponsors. And they're still, mostly, going to be in power, either directly or indirectly. Even if parties fall as the result, which they just might. Just by finding these files, you've made some powerful enemies."

Mike thought about that and shrugged.

"Let 'em come."

# ★ Chapter Twenty-Nine ★

"Everybody has their customs and immigration form filled out," Adams said as Mike waited nervously for the inspectors from BCIS to board the plane. They'd stopped at Dulles to take on fuel and for clearance and Pierson had assured him that clearances were taken care of. But after the stop in Britain, Mike was half anticipating being taken into custody along with the whole team.

The plane had docked to a tubeway. Mike wasn't in a position to see down the hallway but he could hear the footsteps approaching and was surprised by the degree of reaction. He'd gotten shot to ribbons on more than one occasion, but for some reason this meeting was filling him with dread. Probably as a result of the conversation with Carlson-Smith. The MI-6 agent was calm as toast, however. As he'd said, nobody was going to hold him personally responsible for the files. Hell, the data on the computers was illegal, forget the guns and ammo in the cargo hold!

The customs inspector stepped through the door and shook Hardesty's hand and it took Mike longer than it should have to process the face.

"My name's Pierson," Colonel Pierson said, smiling at

Hardesty disarmingly. "I'll be processing your crew and passenger's manifest while my associate does a quick check of your cargo hold."

"A pleasure to meet you," Captain Hardesty said, swallowing nervously.

"Pierson?" Mike asked, his eyes widening at the sight of the Army colonel in the uniform of a custom's agent.

"Ah, Mr. Jenkins, I presume?" Pierson said, smiling. "Let me just check on the crew's documentation and I'll be with you and your . . . group in a moment."

"Yes, BCIS is shitting a brick," Pierson said when he'd sat Mike down with a stiff bourbon. "And State is shitting a brick. And the National Security Council is shitting a brick. Which is why I'm here instead of a regular inspector and why a Navy commander from OSOL is carefully ignoring the contents of the hold. Satisfied?"

"I should have trusted you when you said it'd be taken care of," Mike admitted, smiling finally. "But that's not the only reason you're here."

"No," Pierson admitted, looking over at the MI-6 agent who was watching him carefully. "And, as agreed, all the original files are going to Nellis for your review, Agent Carlson-Smith. But you said Grantham wasn't the culprit and the President wants that data as soon as possible."

"Let me get Vanner," Mike said, picking up the phone.

It took Vanner a few minutes to run through his song and dance again but when he did Pierson leaned back and nodded in satisfaction.

"Grantham's been acting weird, lately," Pierson said. "I mean, yes, he's his own man and he works the Senate as he needs to, cutting deals, concentrating on what he thinks is important. But the decisions, the votes and actions he's been taking, are completely out of his normal line."

"The Supreme Court nominee?" Mike asked.

"That's just the most noticeable," Pierson replied, nodding again. "But that's the big one. He's stalling the guy in the Senate. It's the first changed vote that the President has had a chance to place on the bench, a conservative for a liberal. The news media is screaming, the liberals are screaming and Grantham should be acting decisively. Instead, it's like he's trying to run out the clock or something."

"So somebody is blackmailing him with the video?" Mike asked. "Traskel?"

"That would be the prime suspect," Pierson admitted. "But that doesn't mean it's him. It could be any enemy of Grantham's normal positions. And it would be a stupidly long-ball shot for somebody like Traskel. He's been in the Senate for years; is likely to stay there for years, there's no reason for him to have set this up."

"Well, it's connected to Traskel somehow," Mike said, frowning. "I mean, he knew to send me after this particular girl. And why her, I wonder?"

"Natalya's in the video *but* she survived the scene," Carlson-Smith said. "She's more likely than most to be able to identify the perp."

"There's another way to do it," Vanner said. "Voice print. The person has had his voice modified, but you're still going to be able to pull out some data and get a voice recognition on them."

"We'd have to have a matching voice print," Pierson pointed out.

"Echelon could run it in a couple of hours," Vanner said, shrugging.

Echelon was a "black" operation of the NSA that monitored world-wide voice and internet communications searching for keywords.

"Okay, assuming that Echelon really exists . . ." Pierson said dryly.

"I used to work at No-Such-Agency," Vanner said, just as dryly, using the nickname for the NSA. "It wasn't an off-the-cuff estimate, Colonel."

"Okay, assuming we could get the NSA to admit it exists, for this project, which has major political overtones," Pierson said, raising his hands. "Even admitting that, the voice is disguised and NSA won't use it, period, for investigation of American citizens. Even under the Patriot Act. And I'm pretty sure we don't want to open that can of worms for this. This is horrible, but it's *definitively* not terrorism related. In fact, except for being something like a constitutional crisis, it's not even national security related!"

Pierson paused and shrugged unhappily.

"What should be done, by the book, is that the data would be turned over to the FBI," the colonel continued. "There's a process for that, now. Information gathered during an intelligence operation that points to a crime committed can be forwarded to the FBI for investigation. The problem is, the FBI doesn't have jurisdiction. What we have here is a rape and a murder. Those are civil crimes. They occurred in Montenegro, which is the only jurisdiction that could try them."

"So we either turn the data over to the Montenegrins,"

Carlson-Smith said musingly, "which would give them blackmail material on half the governments in the Western World or . . . we let them walk?"

"No," Pierson said, shaking his head. "What the President wants to do is very quietly show the data to the appropriate people. Quiet meetings that result in the perp simply no longer being in anything that resembles a position of power. And it won't matter which side of the aisle they are on, or what country they're from. He's discussed this with the prime minister and the prime minister is on board. But . . ."

"But we have to have all the data," Mike sighed. "We've got to get the DVDs."

"And anyone associated with the Albanian operation," Pierson agreed. "And then there's the other side. Who bells the cat?"

"The State Department," Mike said with a shrug.

"Nope," Pierson replied. "Currently, what you're carrying is very closely held. And it's going to stay that way. No leaks. God-help-us-please, no leaks."

"Agreed," Mike said, frowning. "But you're not suggesting . . ."

"Either we or the Brits will handle the introductions," Pierson said, his face hard. "But you're going to be the messenger."

"Like hell," Mike said, shaking his head. "No fucking way."

"You're not an operative of the American government," Pierson continued, tightly. "You're just . . . you. You'll handle the data presentation and get the appropriate assurances from the people you deal with on what is to be done. But the bottomline is that every single person has to exit the government, and anything government affiliated. No nongovernmental organizations, no military contracts, no lobbying. They become common citizens and disappear. Hopefully, most of them will commit suicide."

"Then we might as well scrap most of the data," Mike said, frowning. "All we'll need is the hard copy of who was involved, and the DVDs."

"Agreed," Pierson said, nodding. "We'll lock down the data in a vault and it won't ever go anywhere."

"No," Mike said, looking distant. "If I'm the guy carrying the message, then I'm the guy holding the data. They won't trust anyone with that data, including the United States government. I've got a hole that's plenty big enough for it. We'll bury it under the caravanserai. I'll tell them where it is. And tell them to leave well enough alone. They won't believe it if I tell them it's been destroyed, which would be my first choice. We'll just . . . hold it. Someday, it will just be history."

"I'm not sure the prime minister would agree with that," Carlson-Smith said.

"And I'm pretty sure the President wanted to keep them in Nellis," Pierson said, frowning. "That's a big damned responsibility to just delegate."

"Who are you talking to?" Mike asked tightly. "Think about how we met, Bob."

"That's different."

"How?" Mike replied. "The President and the prime minister will geek. Trust me. Because this way, these things don't hang like a Sword of Damocles at every high level meeting. They'll go from Nellis to the caravanserai and be buried. You'll pull the data about American and British members for America and Britain to deal with. The rest are up to me. After we find the DVDs. Hopefully they haven't made copies."

"You'll have to make sure of that," Pierson said darkly.

"I'm not even sure I can get the DVDs," Mike said, breaking his stare and sighing.

"We've got improved intel," Pierson said. "Not much of it, but some. That, too, will be available at Nellis. There's one oustanding issue: information control. Who knows what in your teams?"

"The Keldara know pretty much everything about Rozaje," Mike said, frowning. "But the Keldara don't talk . . ."

"Can we trust that, though?" Carlson-Smith asked.

"Could you trust the Gurkhas?" Mike asked. "This is the business of the Kildar. The Keldara don't talk. Even then the information on who and what is pretty tightly restricted. I had Vanner keep it away from the girls just because of what it was. They've looked at the files and made some lists. But even then it's very close. I'm not even sure that Adams knows any names except your foreign service guy and the not-Senator-Grantham. We'll keep it close. Vanner will lock it down as of now. Scrap the Albanian translators; we won't need them for the rest of this."

"So it's tight," Pierson said, sighing hopefully.

"It's tight," Mike said. "And with the Keldara, and me, it will stay that way."

"And you'll take the messenger duties," Pierson said.

"And the guard duties," Mike replied. "After we have the DVDs. I'm going to need support for that. A lot."

"You'll get whatever we have," Pierson said. "Anything you ask for, trust me."

"And then I get to be the Chooser of the Slain," Mike said, grimacing. "Great. Oh, there's one more thing."

"Which is?" Carlson-Smith asked.

"When we find out what the link is to Traskel, I get to break it too."

# ★ Chapter Thirty ★

"Gurum, it's good to see you again," Mike said, looking around the gate area.

Las Vegas McCarran International Airport was, for most visitors, their first introduction to the state of Nevada. For good or ill, that first impression was of slot machines. Lots and lots of slot machines. They seemed to be stuck into every nook and cranny and most of them were in use by arriving, departing and even transferring passengers trying their luck.

Other than that, and the ads for casinos, it was much like any other airport and the Keldara had seen a few at this point. The group still gawked as they exited the walk-way from the airplane.

"Vanner, sorry, you're going to have to forego the pleasures of Sin City," Mike said, shaking the sergeant's hand.

"I'll pass," Vanner said, smiling. "Been here, done that, lost my shirt."

"I'm not planning on gambling," Mike said, looking around. "I'm doing enough of that as it is. I'll be out to visit in a day or two."

"Got it," Vanner said, stepping back into the tubeway. "Good luck."

"Same," Mike said, turning back to the Keldara brewery manager. "What do you have laid on, Gurum?"

"There is a bus waiting, Kildar," Gurum said, leading the way into the airport. "I was not sure about luggage. . . ."

"The Keldara have everything that we're bringing here," Mike said, gesturing to the Keldara troopers loaded down with black luggage.

"We have the rooms laid on and the booth is set up," Gurum burbled. "There was a pre-day but we were not prepared for that; I hope it doesn't hurt sales—"

"Couldn't be helped," Mike said, feeling the effects of both jet lag and culture shock. Not so many hours ago, he was running from an Albanian hit team.

"The convention begins tomorrow," Gurum continued. "It is only three o'clock, here. The Keldara could take the evening off and look around—"

"The Keldara are going to the hotel and going to bed," Mike said. "With pills, if necessary. It will help reset their body clock."

"Very well, Kildar," Gurum said, his brow furrowing. "But I need a few for set up. There is more work than I had expected. And . . . I think I overestimated the trouble of setting up the booth I designed."

"How much trouble could it be?" Mike asked.

"Much," Gurum admitted. "I truly do need some Keldara, Kildar. Please."

"Okay, okay," Mike said, shaking his head. "We'll need four of them functional tomorrow, but you can have at least ten."

"Thank you, Kildar," Gurum said, breathing a sigh of relief. "Thank you. That way we should be able to get fully set up."

"I'm almost afraid to ask what you did to the booth design," Mike said, shaking his head.

"It is . . . a very noticeable booth, Kildar," the brewery manager admitted.

"What's laid on for tomorrow?" Mike asked, trying to shake off fatigue. He needed to be sharp. As much as the current mission mattered to the world, getting a distributor for the Keldara would affect them for a long time. For good or ill. It was important and he had to simply compartmentalize the other mission. Among other things, they couldn't even talk about it, here.

"We will have the booth open all day," Gurum said. "Daria sent me a roster of the female Keldara to set up a schedule. But there is a problem."

"And that is?" Mike asked, yawning.

"There is a local law that anyone serving alcohol must be of eighteen years or older," Gurum pointed out.

Mike blinked for a moment and then frowned. The Keldara girls were professionals doing a tough job so it was hard for him to remember, most of the time, that they were teenagers. Most of them. Greznya was over eighteen and so were a couple of others. But most of them were sixteen or seventeen. Beyond that age, most of the Keldara women were mothers and they weren't attached to the operational teams. He had a sudden mental image of Anisa sliding down the fast rope into the office in Club Dracul and stripping out the computer in mere seconds. The girl had just turned seventeen a month ago.

"There are only five of the girls who are eighteen or over," Gurum pointed out. "That is enough for one or two to cover the booth all day but the convention runs for five days . . ."

"This is what I get for putting their real ages on their passports," Mike said with a sigh. "And I'm not going to call DIA and ask them for a bunch of false IDs, just to sell beer. We'll put everyone that's of an age to work. We've got two more women that can fill in for that matter. If the guys have do some of the serving, fine. The rest can just be booth babes and charm the customers."

"Very well, Kildar," Gurum said, sighing. "I had hoped you would agree with that."

"I'm nothing if not reasonable." Mike smiled at the Keldara. "Now, where's the bus?"

Mike had forgotten how much he hated trade shows.

The convention was in one of those massive, echoey convention centers that seemed to be designed as a stable for sperm whales. It was certainly big enough; just walking from one to the other was a workout. One that Mike, after the stresses of the last few days, wasn't going to bother with. He had no interest in picking up a bag full of pens, coasters and T-shirts from beers he was never going to drink.

The International Brewery Wholesaler's Convention had its good points, he had to admit. The Keldara "booth" was in the Beer Garden where over forty breweries, ranging from Anheuser-Busch to . . . well, the Keldara with their patented "Mountain Tiger Brew," offered free samples. Mike had tried a couple of the other brews and then given up. There just wasn't anything on earth that compared to Keldara beer.

And others seemed to agree. Since a few hours after their opening, as the word got around, there had been a continuous line for the Keldara beer. And most of the drinkers had just sort of . . . hung around. Part of that was the beer, but a big part of it was the Keldara girls.

The girls staffing the booth, both those serving and those just being friendly, were soaking up the attention and flirting for all they were worth. They'd never been in a situation where men were vying for their attention and they were clearly enjoying themselves. And the distributor reps, almost entirely male, were enjoying themselves as well. The Keldara girls were spectacular and so . . . naif that the distributors found them too charming to resist. He wondered what most of them would think if they knew what the girls had been doing for the last few weeks. Or that the "bar backs" hefting the barrels like they were made of air could probably kill everyone in the convention in less than thirty minutes.

Gurum had done a good job on the booth as well. And he was right, it was noticeable.

It turned out that after checking shipping costs, the amount of beer they were taking would cost far less as a container shipment than it did sending it by air. The problem being that even with that amount of beer, it would only take up part of the container. There was a way to do that, called Less Than Truckload, but the cost difference wasn't all that great.

So Gurum had looked at the problem and, with the

usual Keldara ability to look outside the box, had decided to use most of the container for other "stuff."

What the rest of the container held was mostly stone. Specifically the granite the Keldara picked from the fields every spring and used for everything from fences to house walls. It was the same granite that the brewery was being constructed from.

With the help of the ten Keldara that Mike had loaned him, Gurum had built a miniature Keldara "brew house," complete with a display of original Keldara brewing methods, a small "fence" that channeled the convention goers into the area and a "bar" constructed of undressed granite with a wooden countertop. It was, by far and away, the most spectacular booth in the convention and Mike wondered whether others would try to top it the next year.

"Are you Mr. Jenkins?" a heavyset man asked, plopping down on the stone bench the Keldara had installed along the wall.

"Yes?" Mike said. "And you are?"

"Bob Thomas," the man said, holding up an electronic device that looked something like a PDA.

"I'm not sure what that is," Mike admitted. Gurum had handed him one early that morning, but Mike had parked it behind the booth.

"It's my card," the man said, smiling. "I guess you lost yours?"

"No, it's in the booth," Mike said. "So we trade cards with that thing?"

"That's how it's supposed to work, yeah," Thomas said, grinning and putting it away. "Your information is on your badge, too. But you're the brewery owner?"

"Co-owner, sort of," Mike said, shrugging. "I set it up as a way for the Keldara to build capital. I supplied the funds and the land, they're supplying the labor and knowledge. I think we're splitting the barley and hops. It's pretty complicated."

"How?" Thomas asked. "And why's an American backing a Georgian start-up brewery?"

"The Keldara are sort of my retainers," Mike said, frowning. "I know that's a weird way to put it, but it's the closest to reality that I can find. I own the land they live on, their homes and most of their tools. And I can't sell it back to them, either, legally. They also like it that way; it's custom for them. Anyway, I bought this farm and it came with . . . retainers. So I built the brewery mostly to give the women some income. They don't have any the way that things are set up now."

"What about the men?" Thomas asked, frowning. "If you're talking about tenant farmers, the men aren't going to have much income either."

"Ah, well," Mike said, quirking up one cheek. "There's a brochure about the Mountain Tiger Militia in there, too."

"I read it," Thomas said, his brow furrowing. "I thought it was a joke, all that about defending the valley from Chechens and stuff."

"Not at all," Mike replied. "The men get paid as part of the militia. Some of the women, too. Actually, what you're looking at is mostly a militia team. The girls that are chatting up the customers are intelligence specialists. Most of them speak two to three languages and are experts in electronic intercept or intelligence analysis.

The men are militia members, at least as well trained as American Rangers and all of them with combat experience. They lost a member just a few days ago."

"And they're selling beer?" Thomas asked, tilting his head to the side.

"And they're selling beer," Mike agreed. "So that they can get some income into the valley that's not dependent upon the Kildar. That being me."

"And if they get so successful they're independent of the Kildar?" Thomas asked.

"Then I'll still have a very nice house in a very nice valley," Mike said, grinning. "And part ownership in a very nice brewery."

"So what do you do, Mr. Jenkins?" Thomas asked. "Where'd your money come from? And how'd you end up in Georgia?"

"Well, if I told you that I'd have to kill you," Mike said, then laughed. "Seriously, I was a SEAL, then I started a company that made classified communications widgets. That was before 9/11 and I made money but not world class. Then, after 9/11, the widgets got very important and I got bought out by a major defense contractor. After that I didn't have much to do. I didn't want to start another company so I travelled. While I was travelling I literally got lost and ended up in Brigadoon, so to speak. And here we are."

"Starting up a brewery isn't cheap," Thomas said. "You made that much money selling to the defense contractor?"

"Close enough," Mike said, shrugging. "Most of the stuff I've done, including the widgets, has been classified. I was sort of serious that I couldn't explain where all the money came from. But the brewery had some help from the IMF as a matching grant. And the barley is, more or less, free. Ditto the hops and the other ingredients. We'll have to buy some extra stuff but not much. And the labor is cheap to set up. If we can get a fair price for the beer, we'll make money. The Keldara will make money. It will take me a while to recoup my investment, maybe more time than a lot of investors would like. But I'm in it for the long haul and it's mostly for the Keldara."

"You like them," Thomas said, gesturing with his chin at one of the girls who was chatting with two guys, both of whom had the expression of pole-axed oxen.

"They're damned good people," Mike said, thoughtfully. "Damned good."

"And the girls are pretty, too," Thomas said, grinning. "Where'd you get the model on the poster?" he asked, gesturing into the brewery. In pride of place over the bar was a poster-sized pic of Katrina. She had a bottle of beer that was foaming over and her lips were pursed to sip off the excess. The caption was "Are You Tiger Enough?" Mike was pretty sure that when that got back to the elders, and got explained to a few of them, he was in for a very tough conversation.

"Katrina Makanee," Mike said, grinning. "She's Vanda's . . . cousin or something. I took the picture."

"You're kidding," Thomas said, his eyes wide. "I figured you had it shopped out."

"Nope," Mike said, still smiling. "I took all the pics in the brochures and the posters." The pic of the girls lined up with their bottles had been made into a banner that fronted the entire display.

"You're a man of many talents, Mr. Jenkins," Thomas said. "My partners and I would like to meet with you and your manager this evening."

"Up to Gurum," Mike said, wondering what was happening out at Nellis and when he'd be called out there. "He'll set up the schedule. I may not be available; I have some other business going on here in town."

"Well, I hope we're able to meet," Thomas said, heaving himself to his feet. "It was a pleasure to meet you." Thomas paused and looked at the booth, shaking his head. "They really have to fight terrorists?"

"We had an attack by a short battalion, about two hundred, a month ago," Mike said, gesturing with his chin. "The guy heaving a barrel was one of the snipers. The girl chatting with that guy in the blue shirt was on a mortar. The redhead serving beer was handling the communications. So . . . yes."

"I hope you don't mind if I say we can use that," Thomas said, thoughtfully. "Beer drinkers tend to be patriotic. 'Buy Keldara beer and you're helping kill terrorists.' "

"And various other bastards," Mike said, thinking of the most recent mission.

"Kildar," Daria said, walking over. "There is a call from the suite. You have a call there."

Which was where the secure phone had been installed. Game time.

"You'll have to excuse me," Mike said, nodding at Thomas. "I hope to meet you later."

"Good luck in your other business," Thomas said, nodding in farewell then turning to Daria with a smile.

★ ★ ★

"Jenkins," Mike said, leaning back in the seat.

"Mike, there's a jet waiting for you at the airport," Pierson said. "We need you out there by three."

"Can do," Mike said, sighing. "Why three?"

"You'll see," Pierson said, cutting the connection.

# ★ Chapter Thirty-One ★

Nellis Air Force Base was one of the most secure bases in the United States. Plunked in the middle of thousands of miles of just about nothing, the base was called "Dreamland" since it was the center for testing the most advanced concept aircraft in the world. It was from Dreamland that the entire stealth series of aircraft had been envisioned, designed and produced.

So when Mike landed, he wasn't expecting a tour and he didn't get one.

The G-V jet, with window shades covered, rolled to a stop inside a hangar before the door opened and a polite but definite Air Force SP led him across the hangar, down a windowless corridor and up to a security station by an elevator.

"Mr. Jenkins, your badge," the SP sergeant manning the desk said, nodding. "Please place your hand on the scanner and your eye up to the cup."

Mike hadn't used a retinal scanner before but it was pretty straightforward.

"You don't have a retinal scan," Mike pointed out as a badge with his picture on it was handed across the desk.

"We do now," the SP sergeant said. "And your fingerprints. We normally match them, but we didn't have a comparison set."

"Don't let them get out," Mike said, frowning. "Where?"

"The elevator," the SP said, waving. "Wait for it, swipe your badge through the reader. It will take you to your floor. Have a nice day, sir."

Mike got on the elevator unaccompanied and swiped his card. There wasn't even a readout so he had no idea how many floors he was descending but it was pretty far.

"Deep here," Pierson said, greeting him with a smile when the elevator door opened.

"And cold, too," Mike added; the air conditioning had to be set to about sixty.

"It's for the computers," Pierson said, waving him into the government-green corridor directly in front of the elevator, which was at junction. There were doors down all the corridors, but they all had electronic locks on them. It looked like something from a nightmare and Mike wondered how many of the workers down here had cracked over the years. "I'm told there are more Crays in this facility than any single facility in the world."

"I thought NSA had a lock on them," Mike said, frowning.

"And do you really think they're in *D.C.*?"

"You guys look like you've been working hard," Mike said when he entered the conference room. Vanner, Carlson-Smith and Greznya were sitting at the table just about surrounded by paper.

"We have," Vanner said, crossly. "I thought thirty-six hour days had ended when I got out of the Corps."

"If you've actually been going that long, you need to crap out," Mike said seriously. "Judgement really starts slipping after thirty or so."

"We're about done here," Vanner said, shrugging. "There are seven Brits in the files, twenty-three Americans of various political grades and the rest are other lads. We've broken them down by country and created a special DVD for each country indexed to the files along with a . . . prospectus of their actions in Rozaje."

"The big winner numerically appears to be the Nips," Carlson-Smith said. "No real surprise. But the prime minister is going to be very surprised what his under minister for external security has been getting up to."

"That's the guy who more or less runs the JDF, right?" Mike asked, shaking his head. "Okay, if our people are willing to cut you loose, we'll borrow a secure vault and fly you out to Vegas for a short R and R. Pierson?"

"They need to wait a bit," the colonel said, frowning. "And I'd suggest a shower and a shave. We're having some VIP visitors in about a half an hour."

"Christ," Vanner said, standing up and stretching his back. "We don't exactly have a brief set up."

"Just get cleaned up, Patrick," Mike said. "And you too, Grenzya. Your clothes are here, right?"

"And your plane," Pierson pointed out. "And its pilots."

"I'll need to keep it here until this stuff is ready to go," Mike said, shrugging. "Can do?"

"Can do," Pierson said. "Where's the index?"

"Here," Vanner said, sliding it across the table to him. "Tabulated by country, then by name. Each of them has a short synopsis of who they are in the real world and what they did at Rozaje. There's a pack of DVDs, too . . ."

"I've got it," Mike said, sitting down. "Colonel, could you find someone to scrounge up the showers and what-not for these three?"

"There's a security issue with the Brit data," Carlson-Smith said, uneasily.

"I'll keep that in mind," Mike said, opening up the thick file folder. "Ah, England, let's start there . . ."

"Mr. Carlson-Smith, if you'll come with me," Pierson said, smiling. "He does that to get on your nerves, you know," he added as they entered the corridor.

"And it works," the MI-6 agent admitted. "I could wish we'd never let that stuff leave jolly old England."

"The DVDs are in Albania," Vanner pointed out.

"So you've said," Carlson-Smith replied. "Repeatedly. And how are we going to get our hands on those I'd like to know. Lunari's a place angels fear to tread."

"We won't send angels," Pierson said, opening up one of the doors with his passcard. "Gentlemen, showers and clean clothes await. Miss, if you'll accompany me. By the way, the door locks when I close it. Just hit the buzzer when you're ready to head back. You have about twenty-three minutes."

Mike looked up as a man in a suit stepped through the door unannounced.

"Who the hell are you?" Mike asked, then stopped and nodded as the President followed the secret service agent into the room. "I must be getting tired, Mr. President."

"I can understand that, Mike," the President said, walking

over to shake his hand. "I was told some of your intel people, and a Brit, were going to be here."

"They've been on straight ops for the last couple of days, Mr. President," Mike replied as the President was followed in the room by the national security advisor, the secretary of Defense and a man Mike didn't recognize.

"Step outside," the President said to the three secret service agents that had come in the room. "You're not in on this one."

"Yes, sir, Mr. President," the lead agent said, nodding to the other two.

"I thought they were supposed to argue about that sort of thing," Mike said, smiling and standing up. "And I'm at the head of the table."

"Sit, Mike," the President said, collapsing in one of the seats. "We have an hour to do this. I'm on my way to California for a meeting with the governor and to look over the latest damage from an earthquake. Which was fortuitous since it meant I could clear my schedule for this meeting." He looked up as Colonel Pierson came in trailed by Vanner, Carlson-Smith and Greznya.

"Mr. President," Mike said, waving at the three. "MI-6 Agent John Carlson-Smith, Patrick Vanner, formerly of the U.S. Marines and NSA, and Greznya Kulcyanov of the Keldara."

"A pleasure to meet you all," the President said, standing up to shake their hands. "Mr. Carlson-Smith, I want to assure you that I've spoken with the Prime Minister and he and I are in agreement on the way to implementize this situation."

"Yes, sir, Mr. President," the MI-6 agent said uneasily.

"I'm John Parais," the unnamed man said, extending a hand. "undersecretary of defense for intelligence gathering and analysis. As soon as we're done here, we'll get you on a secure line to Lord Arnold so he can clear up any questions."

"Yes, sir," the MI-6 agent said, apparently relieved that there was another professional in the room.

"I'm also going to remain here with a small team," Parais continued. "Not to look at the data, though. We've got some additional intel on Lunari."

"And it's Lunari that we need to talk about," the secretary of defense said.

"Indeed," the President agreed. "Don, you take it."

"We need those DVDs," the secretary of defense said, leaning forward. "And it's been agreed that, yes, Mike, you'll be the one to secure them. That does remove various problems while effectively dumping them on your shoulders. But the President has managed to convince the prime minister that you have broad enough shoulders."

"Thanks," Mike said dryly.

"But we do need the DVDs or . . . how we would prefer to handle this simply won't work," the NSA said.

"Agreed," Mike said. "And I suppose sending in Delta . . ."

"Has been discussed and ruled out," the President said. "We need someone who is highly deniable. Admittedly, there has been—"

"Enough contact that I'm sliding out of that realm," Mike said with a chuckle. "But I'm the best thing you've got."

"That's it in a nutshell," the secretary said. "The same

goes for the various other black ops groups. When you hit Lunari, there are probably going to be too many traces left behind to totally deny which group did it. Bodies among other things. I'm sure you'd prefer to pull out all of your dead—"

"We try," Mike said, remembering the Viking funeral.

"But you might not be able to," the secretary continued. "Ditto on Delta or ANV or ILS. Yes, they'll go in sterile, but."

"But," Mike said. "The problem being that I'm sure I can't take the bordello with one team and I'm not sure I could do it with the whole Keldara. And if I call in the Families, it leaves us uncovered at home. Bad things can happen when that happens."

"Which is why a Special Forces team will arrive in Georgia the day after tomorrow to train in-country militias," the national security advisor said, smiling. "Three teams, actually, with a company of Rangers in augmentation. Do you think that will be enough?"

"Yes," Mike said. "But they'd better be carefully briefed on Keldara culture."

"Your Colonel Nielson will remain in place as a liaison," the secretary said. "He's being temporarily reactivated so he'll outrank the team commander. Effectively, he'll be in command."

"Oh," Mike said. "So much for deniability."

"It's still there," the NSA said. "Thin but there. We do this sort of thing all the time with various groups. The Keldara are well liked by the Georgian government."

"How much do they know about this?" Mike asked.

"Not much," the NSA said. "And the less the better."

"Yeah, I wouldn't want them trying to get their hands on the booty," Mike said, shrugging. "Not that they would. Trust me, the room that this is going in will be wired to destroy everything. And the Keldara will trigger it even if I'm dead."

"Works for me," the President said. "But you're going to have to get the DVDs from Lunari. And we're going to need the American data."

"Vanner?" Mike asked.

"I have it here," Vanner said. "Once we had the basic database set up, it was easy enough to pull out the Americans. Greznya?"

"Here, sir," the Keldara girl said, pulling a folder out and carrying it over to the President.

"What about Grantham?" the President asked. "We got a brief description from Colonel Pierson, but . . ."

"Here, sir," Vanner said, turning to his computer and then stopping. "This is . . ."

"Just run it, Marine," the President said. "I understand what we are dealing with."

"Yes, Mr. President," Vanner said, bringing up the image on the plasma screen over Mike's head and explaining why it couldn't be Senator Grantham murdering the girl.

"John?" the President asked, turning to Parais.

"I'd like confirmation from my own analysts," Parais said, frowning. "But I'm not going to ask for it. But with the original, I will do my own confirmation. Pending that, I have to agree with Mr. Vanner. That is not Senator Grantham."

"Who is it?" the President asked rhetorically.

"Doing a voice comparison will be hard," Parais said.

"The quality of the data has been damaged by the voice modifier. I'm not sure we could be certain of the identity based upon that data. Even if we ran it against Echelon, we'd probably come up with hundreds, possibly thousands, of hits. The reason being, we'd have to spread the net for the hits. We couldn't say 'Give me the person this is' because it would bring back either 'no one' or someone that sounds just like that, which probably wouldn't mean Grantham because just because it sounds like him to the human ear, doesn't mean it matches signal . . ."

"It doesn't," Vanner interjected. "We checked. The signal spread is all wrong."

"So that's a confirmation that it's not Grantham," Parais said, nodding.

"Explain," the President said.

"The human voice is more than just what we hear," Greznya said, softly. "There are not only undertones and overtones, things beyond our range of hearing, but frequencies within the sounds we can hear that are canceled out. When you take all of that and break it down, it creates a very distinct signature, the 'voice print' of a person. I actually ran the comparison of this man's voice against Senator Grantham's. You can see where the voice has been modified and where it has not. And there has been no modification of the under- and overtones. It has only seventy points of congruence to Senator Grantham and three hundred noncongruent points. And additional fifty three were ambiguous and fell outside standard probability."

"I brought Greznya rather than one of the other girls because she's my best person at voice recognition," Vanner said. "She can pick out which Chechen or Russian commanders we're picking up on the basis of less than a full word."

"Sort of like when a radio station plays just one bit of a song?" the President asked.

"Yes, sir," Vanner replied. "And she's very good at voice analysis as well."

"This is not Senator Grantham, whoever he is," Greznya said, softly but firmly. "I have listened to six of his speeches and compared them to this person's voice, tone and word choice. Admittedly, the subject matter is highly different, but this person uses certain word strings that are not consistent with the senator. And that is ignoring the fact that the voice analysis is not a match."

"Any idea who he is?" the President asked, just as softly, looking with interest at the girl.

"He is an American," Greznya said. "He naturally has an accent consistent with the northeastern United States. He has some habitual phrases that he may use in common company, notably 'playing with the big boys' and 'gaming the future.' He is between twenty-five and thirty at a guess based upon his natural tones. He is a nonsmoker. There is no sign of smoking degradation in his voice, however there is slight age degradation. I would say that he is college educated or at least uses large words frequently. More than that I cannot tell."

"That's a bit," Parais said, nodding. "We'll look at it as well."

"Carefully," the secretary of defense said. "Very carefully. And you're going to need to bring the FBI in on it."

"That, unfortunately, is an absolute," the President

sighed. "Okay, Mike, you don't do this for free. What's the cost on Lunari?"

"I'm also not a mercenary, Mr. President," Mike said after a moment's thought. "I do what I do and if there's a reward I collect it. The question I've been asking all along is 'why go to Lunari?' I know why I did the other things I did; Lunari is a bit more nebulous. Clear a senator? Not sure I care enough to lose a single Keldara. Make sure that a Brit Foreign Office brahmin isn't being blackmailed? Ditto. Money has never been the reason I do what I do and you know it."

"It's important," the NSA said, frowning. "Very important. If it weren't, would we be here?"

"I know it's important," Mike said. "I'm just wondering if it's important to me. And mine, I might add."

"Depends," the secretary of state said. "You're going to get a lot of enemies out of this. You're already going to get them, no matter how we play it after stirring this up. But if we can get all the data, you're also going to have some friends. Some very senior friends."

"Trust not in the friendship of princes," Mike said, still frowning. "I don't know why I even brought it up. I know I'm going to Lunari and I'll get the DVDs if at all possible. But I'm not sure it's going to be possible. Insertion and extraction is going to be a bitch. And we've got no intel."

"There's a possibility, there," Parais said. "But not for this discussion."

"As to getting paid," Mike said, shrugging. "The good senator from New Jersey owes me five mil if I find the girl. I pointed out to him that if his 'constituent' didn't pay up, he was going to be given the bill. Let him pay it."

"We'll talk," the President said, standing up. "You're going?"

"I'm going," Mike said, looking at the table. "God help me."

"He will," the President said, nodding. "His hand will be over you, Mike. I know it will."

"Thanks," Mike said. "Although I'll admit I'd rather have a B-52 loaded with JDAMs."

"You said you have data for us," Mike said when the President and most of his party had left.

"We've got a partial layout for the streets," Parais said, sliding over a DVD. "Also some data on the building but not the interior. I had an intel crew sweep for computer noise and there wasn't any. However, we know there is at least one computer in the building from information on the street. So . . ."

"It's shielded," Vanner said, sighing. "Which means they know how important this place is."

"There are at least twenty guards on duty at all times in and around the building," Parais continued. "And there are more than sixty working for the same clan in the area. All of them will come swarming at the first sign of a firefight. In addition, if it's apparent that it's not the regular authorities, such as they are, or another clan attacking, the other clans are likely to pile in. I'm not sure about reaction times, but you're looking at Mogadishu if it drops in the pot."

"We need more intel," Mike said, shrugging. "We need interiors. We need to know where the DVDs are. We need to know where Natalya is. We can't even be sure she's still there. What about a ground-pen sweep?"

"There aren't any tasked for that area at the moment," Pierson said. "I checked."

"Bob, the President just made a special effort to stop by," Mike said with a sigh. "Retask."

"That's not a simple action, Mike," Pierson argued. "I can't just pick up the phone and . . ."

"Yes, you can," Mike said, his face hard. "You pick up the phone, call your boss and say 'Hi, I need a ground penetration satellite retasked. Why? It's compartmentalized. But the President asked.' Do you really think he's going to ask the President if he really asked? And if he does, do you think the President won't back it? Hell, Bob, I shouldn't have even had to ask. We should already have the data."

"I'll see what I can do," Pierson replied with a sigh.

"I'll get it retasked," Parais said. "Easier and less questions if I order it. And you're right, this is a presidential directive mission. That's easily a high enough priority."

"Preferably, we need people inside," Mike added, looking thoughtful.

"Dracul?" Vanner asked.

"Not if there are that many guards," Mike said, shaking his head. "The lack of intel is what's getting me. But I'm not sure how to get someone in the club."

"We can get a girl in," Carlson-Smith noted. "The data from Rozaje included some internal e-mails of the clan. Girls go to Lunari from all over. All we have to do is pull a car up with the right words, drop the girl off and leave. The driver doesn't even have to be Albanian. Of course, that leaves her in a very bad spot. I'm not sure MI-6 has a female agent who would take that mission. Lunari is nearly as bad as Rozaje."

"That's not an issue," Mike said, distantly. "I've got one. I just can't figure out how to get the intel out. She won't have a way to send out commo and she won't be able to just up and leave. Even if she can develop intel, it won't do us any good."

"We might be able to offer some help," Parais said uneasily. "I was directly ordered to offer this technology but I'm not happy about it. It's highly classified."

"Get over the pro-forma protests," Mike said, his eyes narrowing. "What is it?"

"The tech is experimental," Parais said. "But we can internally wire a person for sound and video. Not very good video, but both. And it's almost untraceable. And for sure won't turn up on standard scanners."

"How the hell do you do that?" Mike asked, blinking.

"You hook it up to the optic nerve," Vanner said, watching the DIA secretary carefully. "You either preprocess there or send out a rough signal and process it somewhere else. I've read about the theory. Has it actually been done?"

"Not on humans," Parais admitted. "We haven't been able to find an agent that will permit the operation. It's not without risks. Blindness for one."

"You're thinking about inserting Cottontail?" Vanner asked.

"Yep," Mike said thoughtfully. "We'll need a doctor who's willing to carefully explain the risks. Where would you do this?"

"There's a special hospital in Virginia . . ." Parais said.

"Does she get Dr. Quinn?" Mike asked, laughing.

"Been there, have you?" Parais smiled. "That's actually

one of my charges. But that's where the procedure would take place."

"We're probably on short time here," Mike pointed out. "The Albanians know what they have and with Rozaje hit they're going to do something about it."

"The procedure is fairly noninvasive," Parais said. "At least from what I've been told. They go in through the nose for the video portion and there's only a very small implant in the mastoid for the audio. It's something like having a tooth pulled."

"I'll have to pitch it to Katya," Mike said, frowning. "If she goes for it, we'll drop her off on our way through with someone to keep an eye on her after the procedure. How long for full recovery?"

"A day or two at most," the DIA director said.

"What about . . . I dunno, security?" Mike asked.

"The transmitters are frequency hopping and use burst signal compression," Parais said. "Very hard to detect and they're encrypted transmissions. The data won't get compromised."

"I just hope the agent doesn't," Mike replied.

# ★ Chapter Thirty-Two ★

As soon as the unmarked plane landed in Vegas, Mike pulled out his cell phone and turned it on. Not surprisingly, he had a half dozen messages.

"Gurum, it's the Kildar," Mike said, walking over to the waiting minivan. He nodded at the driver as he entered and just hoped the guy actually knew where he was supposed to be going.

"Kildar," Gurum said, in a relieved tone. "I have arranged a meeting with a Mr. Robert Thomas and his partner Mr. Colin Macnee for this evening. In about an hour and a half. Are you going to be able to attend?"

"Probably," Mike replied. "Driver? Time to the hotel?"

"About twenty minutes, sir," the driver said.

"Probably," Mike repeated. "If I'm there in an hour, the answer is yes. You checked out Thomas?"

"Oh, yes, sir," Gurum burbled happily. "He was one of the people on my short list of potential distributors. I've had three other companies express strong interest in the line, but Mr. Thomas's company specializes in placing high-end beers in specialty stores and bars. I think that he is likely to be the best bet we have for a really good income from the product line."

"Sounds good," Mike said. "I hope to see you in an hour and fifteen or so."

"Oh, and both Daria and Colonel Nielson have been attempting to contact you," Gurum added.

"I've got them on my cell to call back," Mike replied, sighing. "By the way, have you seen Chief Adams?"

"No, Kildar," the brewery manager replied, puzzled. "I had assumed he was with you."

"No." Mike frowned. "I haven't seen him since we landed. If you see him, tell him to give me a call, okay?"

"Yes, Kildar."

"See you in a bit."

He hit the disconnect and looked at the other calls. One was a number he didn't recognize, one was from Nielson, another was from D.C. and the last was from Adams's phone. Ah-hah! The chief had finally checked in from whatever he'd been doing. He called that one first.

"Daria."

"Why do you have the chief's phone?" Mike asked.

"I've been setting up our return flight," Daria replied. "I borrowed it from him while we were still on the plane. He seemed more than willing to give it up. Mr. Hardesty had to return for another charter and there was a hold-up on ground transportation in Georgia. I was calling, though, to tell you that Colonel Nielson wants to talk to you and that we got a call from a number in Washington that refused to leave a message. They stated that they were calling for Colonel Pierson, though, and I took a number as well as giving them the number to your cell phone."

"Thanks," Mike said. "Do we have transportation? Wait; Hardesty had all our gear!"

"That has been handled," Daria said and he could practically hear the dimples. "I called OSOL and discreetly explained the problem. I suspect that the other call is about that."

"Thanks," Mike said, sighing. "I'm going to have to read Hardesty the riot act, though. I've got to call Nielson. If you see the chief, tell him to *call* me."

"I will, Kildar."

"Kildar Caravanserai, Obreckta speaking, how may I help you sir or ma'am?"

"Obreckta, this is the Kildar," Mike said, looking at his watch and doing the time in his head. "Is the colonel still up?"

"Yes, Kildar," Obreckta replied. "Please hold while I transfer you."

"Nielson."

"Jenkins," Mike replied. "What's up?"

"I dunno, you wanna tell me?" the colonel replied testily. "I think we should go secure."

"Scrambled. Again, what's up?"

"I got a call from the U.S. embassy stating that we were going to be receiving some 'training cadre' from the U.S. Army. You know anything about that?"

"Damn that was quick," Mike replied wonderingly. "Expect three SF teams or so and some Rangers. Officially, they're going to be training the Keldara. Unofficially . . . I'll talk about it when I get back."

"Okay," Nielson said, sighing. "I'll start working on bunking."

"The barracks is going to be cleared out," Mike said. "That's part of the 'unofficially.'"

"I need to hear this, don't I?" Nielson replied.

"Yep. But not over a phone. Even a secure phone. When I get back. Which will be on Tuesday or so."

"See you then."

He looked at the last number and dialed it as the minivan pulled into the reception area of the hotel.

"OSOL, Captain McGraffin speaking."

"Jenkins."

"Go scramble, please."

"Be aware that I'm in an unsecure area."

"Oh." The officer on the other end of the line paused for a moment. "Your materials are going to be sent to your home base via military transport. Clear enough?"

"Clear enough," Mike said.

"Your oh-so-efficient secretary informed us that she had already secured a charter aircraft to return your personnel. Do you need anything else?"

"Not at this time," Mike replied. "And I'm not sure about the wisdom of using mil craft for moving the materials. I'll discuss it at another time."

"Understood," McGraffin said. "Anything else?"

"Negative. Oh, one thing. I'm missing a man. My second in command, actually. Anyone heard from Adams on your end since we landed?"

"Uh." There was a pause as McGraffin clearly checked his paperwork. "Negative on that, Mr. Jenkins."

"Thanks," Mike replied, frowning. "Out here."

Mike hadn't even realized that he'd navigated his way to the elevator by instinct.

And he still wasn't sure who'd sent the driver.
Or where his second-in-command had got to.

# ★ Chapter Thirty-Three ★

"Kildar, it is very good you are here," Gurum said nervously as Mike entered the suite.

The penthouse was more of a two story town-home, much more spacious than any apartment Mike had ever owned. Daria had mentioned getting a deal on it, but he was pretty sure the penthouse was costing more than the convention space. With thick carpeting, original paintings on the walls and antique or designer furniture, it seemed far too luxuious for his needs. However, one of the Keldara girls had been over it for security and determined that the conference room, which was entirely interior with no external walls or windows, was set up very much like a secure room. And the rest of the security on the suite was similar. There was one door and anyone approaching the door had to traverse a long corridor for which there was a security camera. The suite was clearly designed for use by paranoid executives and movie stars, which made it well suited for Mike.

"What's the status, Gurum?" Mike asked, his brain still filled with the problems of the Lunari mission.

"Mr. Thomas will be here shortly," Gurum replied.

"But not on time. He just called and he's running a little late. I am thinking of starting with a bid of two euros per bottle, freight on board at P'Otly, ten euros for the keg."

"Let them open," Mike replied. "And go for everything the market will bear. We should have brought Mother Lenka with us; she'd screw them without their even recognizing it. And get . . . Greznya and Anisa up here right now. They're going to charm the socks off of these guys for us."

"Are you sure, Kildar?" Gurum asked. "Women aren't usually . . ."

"Gurum, you've done an excellent job," Mike said with a sigh. "But you really need a lesson in how to sell. If I had set it up in advance, one of the girls would be doing the entire sell and you'd just be there to close and do the paperwork. Get Greznya and Anisa right now. And Chief Adams if anyone can find him . . ."

"Mr. Thomas," Anisa said, as she waved the two businessmen through the door. "It's a pleasure to see you again. And this must be Mr. Macnee."

She'd barely had time to get dressed and fix her makeup but she knew she was looking good. She'd borrowed a short skirt, too short really, from one of the "rescue" girls and had purchased a pair of high heels during the mission. A light blouse, a small string of pearls and she was ready, as the Kildar had put it, to slay them.

"Call me Colin," Macnee said, smiling. He was a short man going bald who had opted for the shaved skull look. "You must be one of the Keldara booth girls I heard about."

"Watch her," Thomas said, jovially. "She's one of their militia girls, too. She's probably packing."

Anisa smiled thinly and shook her head. Now she was really ready to slay them.

"Not in here," she said, laughing as honestly as she could manage and showing them into the suite. "The rooms down the corridor are held by the Keldara. When you came down the corridor you were identified in advance and swept for weapons. Mr. Macnee is carrying a small clasp knife in his right pocket. You, Mr. Thomas, have a license to carry a concealed weapon issued by the state of Pennsylvania. You scored a forty-five out of fifty on your last qualifying shoot. Your registered handgun is a Sig Sauer .40 caliber. A very popular choice I might add. I prefer the H&K USP .45 myself, but the Sig is a nice weapon."

"As I mentioned, Anisa and Greznya are much more than just pretty faces," Mike said, walking over to the two businessmen and holding out his hand. "On the beer side, I use them for datamining and analysis."

"And in your other business?" Thomas asked, trying to get back in control.

"I use them for . . . datamining and analysis," Mike replied, smiling.

"How many enemies are in the building," Greznya said, slithering to her feet. She'd opted for one of the sleeve dresses. With her long legs and moderate bust, it worked very well. "What type of weapons. Location of information, hostages or targets to be extracted. That sort of thing. I'm Greznya, the intel team leader."

"All that stuff about a militia in the brochure is for real?" Macnee asked.

"Yes," Mike said as Anisa went to get them drinks. "It's for real."

"We can use that, you know," Macnee said seriously. "Beer drinkers tend to be more patriotic than the wine types. 'Every beer you drink helps in the war on terror, so drink up' sort of thing."

"Not that I hadn't thought of it." Mike said, smiling.

"You said they'd already had some combat action," Thomas replied as Anisa handed him a drink. He took a sip and then looked at it.

"Elijah Craig," Mike said, smiling. "I believe bourbon is your tipple?"

"Datamining," Thomas replied, shaking his head.

"Yes," Mike said. "And, yes, they've engaged in combat actions. Including ones that, minorly, made the news. Greznya?"

"AP picked up on the attack on our valley," Greznya said, sliding a printout of the AP wire across to the businessman.

"Were you there?" Macnee asked, leaning over to look at the sheet of paper.

"I was on the communications end," Greznya said.

"And intercept," Mike added. "We knew they were coming before they did. You see, we believe in doing our homework."

"And does that extend to the beer side?" Thomas asked, setting down the paper.

"In the main," Mike said. "We know we can get a distributor for Mountain Tiger. We just want the best distributor we can get. Frankly, you are high on the list, but not the top."

"In other words, we have to sell ourselves to you?" Macnee asked, smiling.

"You could put it that way," Mike replied.

"And the ladies are here to . . . ?"

"The ladies run the brewery," Greznya said, smiling. "Brewing is a woman's secret among the Keldara. And, thus, we're going to be making most of the money from it. So . . . say we're here representing the interests of the Keldara women," she finished, leaning back and crossing her legs.

"A brewery run by beautiful women that fights terrorism," Macnee said after he regained his voice. "My hands are getting sweaty just thinking about the marketing."

"Are you sure that's what's making them sweaty?" Mike asked, gazing at Greznya in surprise. He knew that if one of the Keldara mothers was present, Greznya would be halfway out of the clan.

"No," Macnee admitted. "What were you thinking of as terms?"

"Five euros per liter, delivered at P'Otly," Greznya said, smiling and batting her eyes. "We also will supply the special ceramic bottles for discerning customers."

"Out of the question," Thomas snapped after he'd actually processed the information. "We can't sell it for anything like a profit on this end at that rate! We'd have to charge ten dollars a bottle. No. More! That's . . . impossible."

"It is what is called an opening bid," Greznya said, smiling and recrossing her legs as she shifted on the couch. "I'm sure you have some reasonable counter . . ."

★ ★ ★

"Three euors per liter, freight on board in Georgia," Thomas said, shaking Greznya's hand and doing the same with his head. "We'll figure out a way to get the market to bear. Am I nuts?"

"If you are, so am I," Macnee said in a dazed tone.

"Contracts," Mike said, sliding them across the table. "They're taken from the standard contract that the AABA recommends. There's some wiggle room. And we'll supply the first ten thousand liters at one euro per liter along with six thousand ceramic bottles at fifty cents per bottle. You might want to look for a better supply on those, if they meet the Keldara standards."

"Will do," Thomas said, shaking his head again as he looked over the contract. For all the daze he appeared to display at the effect of the girls, more of whom had drifted in, all dressed to the nines as they found out that the negotiations were going on, he read the contract carefully. "We can do this. We will do this. And we're going to make lots of money doing it."

"You're sure?" Macnee asked.

"Yeah, I'm sure," Thomas replied. "We'll start the roll-out in New York. This September."

"Ah," Mike said. "No direct reference I hope."

"No," Thomas said. "But when we run the ads, we're going to have pics of police and firefighters with the beer. Between that and the pics of your spec-ops teams, the subtext will be clear. And we'll just let the point lie that the extra you're paying is supporting the War."

"And the girls," Macnee added, smiling at the group around him.

"We're getting a good price?" Anisa asked in Georgian.

She'd been snuggling up to Macnee but otherwise keeping her head down during the negotiations.

"Quite survivable," Mike said in the same language. "It'll mean, at a guess, about sixty euros per month per worker. A bit more for Mother Lenka and Gurum."

"Good," Anisa said, smiling. "I might actually be able to afford a husband."

"And not go through the Kardane?" Greznya said, looking over at Mike and winking.

"Oh, good point," Vanda said, grinning. "No one would want to avoid the Kardane now."

"So I save it for when we get married," Anisa added, shrugging. "Nothing says that you cannot enter into Kardane just because you can afford the price!"

"Oh, we so don't want to go there . . ." Mike said, sighing.

"What is this?" Macnee asked, looking at the cross-talk.

"I was explaining that we'd be able to keep the brewery running at this price," Mike said, shrugging nervously.

"There was more," Thomas said, grinning. "I could tell."

"You really don't want to know," Mike replied. "There's a lot about the internal workings of the Keldara you don't want to know."

"Anything that will affect the marketing?" Macnee asked.

"Hmmm . . ." Mike muttered. "The Keldara are very . . . conservative. The girls are more or less owned by one male or another . . ."

"We are not!" Greznya snapped.

"You're controlled by your father, who can . . ." Mike

said in English and then switched to Georgian. "Let me explain this as well as I can, okay?" he said to Greznya fiercely. "I know American customs and where there are going to be friction points, okay?"

"Okay," Greznya said, frowning.

"How old do you think Anisa is?" Mike asked Macnee as the girl leaned against him harder.

"I'd put her at about twenty," the fiftyish businessman said, shrugging. "I mean, that's a bit young . . ." he added, nervously fingering his wedding ring. "But I'm not planning on . . ."

"She's seventeen," Mike said, grinning as Macnee sat up and started to back away. "Don't let it bother you and it won't bother them. And what goes on in the suite, stays in the suite. But the point is that she's working as an intel specialist and she's a damned good one. Quite a few of these girls are married and the oldest is Greznya, who isn't by the way, and she's nineteen."

"Oh, my . . ." Thomas said, blinking hard.

"The Keldara grow up fast," Mike said. "Greznya is considered an old maid. Most of them get married around fifteen. These girls didn't have electricity in their homes a year ago. Now . . . well they're some of the best intel troops I've ever had the honor to serve with. Not to mention great models," Mike added with a grin.

"The girl in the pictures?" Macnee asked, frozen. "The redhead. How old?"

"Fifteen," Mike said, shrugging. "I checked the various laws; it's legal. She's dressed, so it's not child pornography. And you won't have to worry about a lot of information getting out about them, no matter how much interest. The

Keldara don't talk and the area they live in is a restricted military zone. The point to this brewery, and other things that I'm doing, is to get them an economic boot-strap into the twenty-first century; there's only so much I can do alone. They need to earn it so they understand where it comes from."

"Okay," Thomas said, looking at Greznya in even greater interest. "Where'd you learn to negotiate like that?"

"In the village market," Greznya said, shrugging. "When you have nothing, you learn to bargain for every kopek."

"I suppose there's that," Thomas said. "Well, this has been a fascinating evening, but if I don't drag Colin off, he's likely to get divorced and I can't afford that."

"Spoilsport," Macnee said, but he heaved to his feet with a sigh. "Ladies, it's been fascinating to meet you. I don't suppose we can visit?" he added to Mike.

"You, I can get through the checkpoints," Mike said. "Honestly, all that anyone who wants to get near the Keldara has to do is bribe the regular guards. But once you get to the area we enforce, nobody moves without my say."

"I think we'll leave the 'local warlord' aspect out of the marketing," Thomas said dryly.

"Please do," Mike said. "Among other things, there are various people who would like to put my head on their wall. And I mean that quite literally."

"Another thing to keep in mind," Macnee replied. "We'll be in touch with Gurum about delivery schedules. I'm sure you have other things to do."

"Such as talk to Katya," Mike said as Greznya closed the door. "Girls, it looks like we're in the clover. But I'm not done. If you ladies could clear the suite and somebody ask Cottontail to stop by. And has anyone seen Chief Adams . . . ?"

"You are joking, yes?" Katya said, her eyes wide as Mike finished explaining the plan.

"I am joking, no," Mike replied. "We'll talk with the doctors about it and if you absolutely say no, then the answer is no. But you won't be able to just walk into Lunari and back out. And even if you walk in, we won't know where you are. This way, we can track you constantly and be ready to pull you out."

"I agreed to do this for twenty thousand euros," Katya said, angrily. "But not to get cut on beforehand. I will probably get cut enough in Lunari."

"Do you want more money?" Mike asked, shrugging. "I will promise you this, if the surgery goes bad I will put you in a very nice place and set you up for the rest of your life."

"I won't be able to see it, yes!" Katya snapped.

"Tropical paradise, guaranteed," Mike said, seriously. "Servants and all the rest. How much do you want for this?"

"The same either way," Katya replied tightly. "If I do this operation, we are done. I get very much money and a nice place someplace warm. I'll make my own way from there."

"Done," Mike said. "There might be some requirements to tell them how things are going after the fact. Can you handle that? Among other things, it would mean that you'd have the U.S. government taking care of at least part of your medical."

"Probably," Katya said, frowning. "But I still want the tropical island."

"Agreed," Mike said, smiling. "So, to be clear, that's a yes?"

Katya paused for a long moment and then shrugged. "Yes."

"I'll point one thing more out, though."

"What?" Katya asked.

"You're going to be wired for sound and video the rest of your life," Mike said. "Admittedly, it will be a limited number of people that can access it. The U.S. government is probably going to be showering you with money to try to get you to do other ops. You're going to be the world's top super bug until they find somebody else crazy enough to do this. And with your looks and . . . training I'd be surprised if you couldn't get in about anywhere."

"Why don't you, then?" Katya asked, her brow furrowed.

"I'm a fighter, not a lover."

"And I'm a killer, not a lover," Cottontail pointed out, with a purely evil smile.

Mike was tapping his foot, watching the Keldara take down the last of the display.

The convention was over, the troops were packed, and he *still* hadn't heard from Adams. He was beginning to think that maybe the redoubtable former SEAL had run into a mugger or something. Maybe he should call the damned morgue. Or, hell, face it, the chief might have just decided that being around Mike wasn't conducive to long life and prosperity. Although he'd been making more money with Mike than he'd make doing virtually any job for which he was trained and prepared.

"Kildar," Gurum said, diffidently. "We have all the gear packed. It is time to go."

"Where in the fuck is . . ." Mike started to say and then stopped as he saw Adams wander around a set of booths that still hadn't been taken down. He was noticeably weaving and appeared to be in lousy shape. Mike wasn't sure what . . . Oh. Hell. He'd forgotten about Adams and Las Vegas. He shouldn't have, but that last weekend had been a *long* time ago. And, frankly, Mike didn't remember most of it.

"Been on a bender, Ass-boy?" Mike asked maliciously, as soon as he was sure that Adams was suffering from a hangover and not malaria.

"Oh, Go'," the chief replied, leaning up against a booth and stifling a belch. He scratched under a, apparently new, Hooter's T-shirt for a moment and contemplated the scenery blurrily. He also had picked up a pair of Bermuda shorts, somewhere, that were at least a couple of sizes too large. They appeared to be belted with string. "Wha' day is it?" The words were distinctly slurred.

"Monday," Mike said. "The day we're leaving."

"Good," Adams said, trying to stand to attention. "I ma' mo'ment."

"Is that all you have to say for yourself?" Mike asked, putting his hands on his hips. "That you made movement? You're supposed to be my second-in-command! You're not a fucking meat anymore, Chief!"

"How 'bout, 'Viva Las Vegas!'?" the chief replied and

belched again. "Or, 'I ha' a rea'y fuckin' good fuckin' ti'e'? Wha' I can rer'mem'er of it."

With that, the chief slowly slumped down the side of the booth until he was flat on his back on the convention hall floor. Then he began to snore.

"I'm tempted to send him home in the container . . ." Mike muttered.

# ★ Chapter Thirty-Four ★

"Mr. Jenkins," the doctor said, nodding and looking over at Katya. "And you would be, potentially, Patient Number 7194."

Mike had sent the rest of the Keldara back to Georgia along with Chief Adams, Vanner and Carlson-Smith, who seemed to be permanently attached to their collective hip until the mission was complete. He had stopped in Virginia, however, to stick with Katya for the procedure and ensure she was taken care of. He still wasn't sure where the hospital was; the drive had involved the normal closed van. Just "somewhere in Virginia" down in the flat-country. He couldn't place it within a hundred miles.

"Wow, lots of casualties, lately," Mike said, smiling.

"We do not, in fact, increment by patient," the doctor replied. Mike had to assume he was a doctor, since he said he was. But the usual plaques were distinctly missing from the bare walls of the spartan office. "Otherwise people could make a guess such as you just made as to casualty rates among black units. The total number of patients operated upon by this hospital is as secret as their individual identities."

"I like this place," Katya said, smiling in her friendliest manner at the rotund physician. "I am told of what is plan. Put in microphone and camera. In body."

"Not exactly a camera," the doctor said, pulling out some papers and moving around to the other side of the desk. "We're going to insert a small bundle of wires into your visual cortex, where the optic nerve intersects the brain. These, together with a microprocessor and a small transmitter, will decode the view that your eyes are sending to the brain. This procedure has been successfully demonstrated on everything up to and including chimpanzees. There has not, yet, been an attempt with a human. The technology is very cutting edge and, frankly, we haven't found anyone willing to undergo the procedure. You're aware of this?"

"Yes," Katya said, shrugging. "I am being paid much to do this mission and I need the . . . things."

"Very well," the doctor said. "However, I have to warn you of potential known side effects as well as possible unknown side effects."

"Go ahead," Katya said, sighing.

"There is a possibility of reduction or loss of sight," the doctor said. "We haven't actually had a patient who could tell us just how accurate their sight is and how it has changed. There are visual acuity tests for animals, but they're not entirely accurate. There is a possibility of long-term sight degradation. There is a possibility of long-term secondary cranial degradation. There is very little data on long-term brain implants available. Infection around the implantation site could cause cerebral damage, brain damage that is. Damage is also possible from the long-term degradation. There is a slight possibility of debilitating stroke. And as with any surgical procedure there are possibilities of death. Are you sure you wish to continue with the procedure?"

"Doctor," Katya said, strangely quiet, "I was raised in an orphanage in Russia with hundreds of other girls. I had nothing of my own until I was sold, straight from the orphanage, to a pimp who raped me when I was twelve. And he was not the first; I got my tits when I was eight and was raped soon after by the master of the orphanage. I have been beaten, raped, tortured and threatened with death all of my life that I can remember. I have been hungry and cold more times than I can remember. Death holds no fear for me. Nor does blindness. Or brain damage. I wish that I did not remember most of my life. And with this . . . devices, I will have great power. Many will wish to use me for their spy. If it works I will never be poor, or dependent upon men, again," she spat.

"Doc?" Mike said to the stone-faced physician.

"Yes?"

"Any other enhancements available?" Mike asked. "Hidden weapons? Poison fingernails? Jump jets in the feet? She'll take 'em all."

The doctor regarded him balefully for a moment and then cleared his throat.

"We're only authorized to provide the listed implants. The visual system does, however, have a biofeedback replay system that is potentially capable of enhancing long and short distance vision. It requires practice."

"Telescope eyes, cool," Mike said, grinning. "So she can get jump-jets in her soles?"

"There are other . . .. devices," the doctor said, shrugging. "But I'm not authorized . . ."

"Got an outside line?" Mike asked seriously. "I can get them all authorized. How long would she be down?"

"How much do you want?" the physician snapped. "I can't even tell you what they all are."

"Get me an outside line," Mike said, sighing. "I'll get you the authorization."

Katya looked over the long list in wonder.

"What is 'micrometallic skeletal enhancement'?" she asked, her eyes wide.

"You don't want that," Mike said, looking over her shoulder. "Unless there's been some radical breakthrough in nanotechnology they're sitting on, it would mean stripping off your skin and muscle to get it. On the other hand, you'd be bulletproof, to low velocity weapons, over most of your body. Jesus Christ. There aren't many of these that are listed as actually used. But the ones that are scare the hell out of me. At least the 'sonic transceiver' is listed as 'tested, stable.' But I was joking about the poison fingernails!"

"Where?" Katya asked.

"'Digital extremity chemical insertion device,'" Mike said, pointing. "It looks like a pretty nasty procedure, though."

"Worse than having someone stick a scalpel up your nose?" Katya asked.

"The pouch for whatever you want to give the recipient is in the palm," Mike pointed out. "You'll go around squirting cyanide all over every time you clench your fist. Not to mention injecting yourself."

"Use something that has an antidote, then," Katya said, grinning. "Antidote on one hand, poison on the other."

"There's bound to be problems with it," Mike pointed out. "Go for the 'subcutaneous nonmetallic puncture device.' Means you can carry a knife anywhere."

"I like the poison fingernails," Katya said. "I can use them on this mission!"

"I'm afraid that if you get the full upgrade, they're never going to let you out of their sight," Mike said with a sigh.

"'Subcutaneous injection, phys . . .' I'm lost again."

"'Subcu . . .'?" Mike muttered for a second and then shook his head. "It's a combat drug. I'm not sure which one; they've been playing around with them for a long time. Probably a temporary enhancement of strength and reaction time along with calming agent so you're less scared."

"I don't get scared anymore," Katya said, darkly. "I get angry."

"Perfect for you, then," Mike said.

"'Mas . . .'" Katya said, pointing to one line.

"Face job," Mike said. "Change your appearance."

"So I can look like a particular person?" Katya asked.

"You don't sing well enough to replace Jessica Simpson," Mike said, shaking his head. "It's for people who can't use their present face for whatever reason. Get a couple of the subcutaneous pouches. You can fit all sorts of stuff in those. And, hell, if you really want the poison fingernails . . ."

"Why thank you, Kildar," the girl said, smiling thinly.

"But I'm definitely getting you out of my house after

this," Mike said, grinning. "And you'll need that maseo-facial surgery if you think you're going to get back in."

"You don't love me," Katya said with a pout.

"I don't trust you," Mike replied with a smile. "You'd be surprised how much I like you. I'm not sure I'd go as far as love, but . . ."

Katya looked at him oddly for a moment, then shrugged.

"The audiovisual upgrade," she said, looking over the list. "Three subcutaneous pouches, the combat drug upgrade and the poison fingernails."

"I'll tell the doc."

"So do I get to call you by your real name?" Mike asked as Director Pareis came into the small, and distinctly secure, waiting room.

"Do I?" Pareis asked.

"I hope you don't even know it," Mike snapped.

"Come on, I'm the DIA director," Pareis said with a sigh. "And I've now officially stated that I'm uncomfortable with fitting this . . ."

"Russian whore," Mike finished for him.

"Foreign agent," Pareis corrected, "with some of the most advanced personal enhancement technology on earth."

"Including the tracker?" Mike asked.

"What tracker?" Pareis asked.

"Oh, come on," Mike replied, scornfully. "If there's not a GPS tracker on that girl I'm going to call the President as soon as I get out of here and tell him he needs to can you for being a complete moron. Cottontail is one dangerous bitch. And she's now going to be the most dangerous bitch on the planet. Once she gets those fingernails loaded I'm not going to want to be in the same room with her."

"It only transmits when a tickler signal comes from a satellite," Pareis admitted. "And I'll be surprised if even she can detect it."

"You've tested these things for interference, right?" Mike asked.

"As well as we can," Pareis admitted. "She'll need a day or two of testing and tweaking once she's out of recovery."

"And then we hie ourselves to wonderful Albania," Mike said, snorting. "I take it we got the overheads?"

"They'll be brought to you by officer courier as you're on your way home," the director said. "Along with an intel update. We still don't know if the girl is still there. They do ship them out, you know. Notably to Italy. And we've been afraid to put out feelers about her for obvious reasons."

"She's still there," Mike said. "I can feel it in the water."

"How you doing?" Mike asked.

The G-V was technically from a charter company, but it had been supplied by DIA so Mike figured it was something along the lines of Air America. The pilots were certainly reticent. Mike missed Captain Hardesty. Not to mention the stewardesses that had accompanied the flights over; he'd had to get his own drinks and it took some hunting and eventually resorting to forcing open a fixture with a screwdriver.

"You were right about the fingernails," Katya replied, holding up her hands. The palms showed a line of small puncture wounds. "But there is a valve. However, I start playing with it when I get upset . . ."

"Which is most of the time," Mike said, looking at her and smiling. "You'll just have to learn some restraint."

"I'm working on it," Katya said, blinking and shaking her head. "And I keep getting double images, one of them grainy. Like a bad TV set showing me what has just happened."

"You need to work on locking that down," Mike said, pulling out the sheets of paper, liberally stamped with "Top Secret," which were her post-op instructions. "No fever when we left, which is good."

"I'm sore in some odd places," Katya admitted.

"Odder than normal, I take it," Mike said, carefully taking her hand. "You'll get used to it. Are you going to be okay—"

"From all this?" Katya asked, withdrawing her hand. "Or on the mission?"

"Yes," Mike said, crossing his hands in his lap.

"I am going to get well paid," Katya said, smiling. "That is all that matters. Why this sudden show of concern, Kildar?"

"Do you think I didn't care?" Mike asked. "From the beginning? Did you think I was just one of the users in your life?"

"No," Katya admitted.

"I suppose that makes me one of the suckers, then," Mike said, snorting.

"Not that . . . either," Katya said, at least sounding honest. "So I don't know what you are."

"Because there are either users or suckers?" Mike asked.

"Yes," Katya admitted. "So, yes, I must accept that you are a sucker. Certainly for giving me all these gifts."

"Use them on the wrong person, and every agent on earth will have a termination contract on you," Mike pointed out.

"So I must find the right men to use them upon, yes?" Katya said, smiling and working her fingers. "I look forward to it."

"You've got real problems," Nielson said, gesturing at the map. "You realize that, right?"

"I know some of them, tell me the rest," Mike said, sighing and leaning back in his chair. He was glad to be back at the caravanserai; America had been almost a culture shock. The caravanserai really did seem to be home these days.

"I won't go over the tactical issues," Nielson said. "I've been looking at what you might call operational issues. The entire area around Lunari is controlled by the Albanian gangs. You've got multiple checkpoints to pass to even get to the town. And forget inserting on foot across the mountains. First of all, egress would be a bitch. Second, that's the center of the clan power. You'd have a fight on your hands, from all the Albanian clans, from, basically, the time you cross the border. And it's not only their turf, they'll outnumber you a few hundred to one. I don't see doing a land ingress and egress."

"Lunari is landlocked," Adams said. "You want us to fly in? The troops aren't trained in air-mobile operations. Or HALO for that matter."

"Training on helicopter insertion and extraction isn't all

that hard," Mike said. "But that begs the question; where in the hell are we going to get the helicopters?"

"More than choppers," Nielson said, gesturing at the map again. "You're dealing with multiple sovereign countries surrounding the area. I couldn't find one spot that I'd like to do an assembly and extraction through."

"I hope you're not just throwing this out as an insoluble problem," Mike said, sighing. "Because we can't use U.S. assets for this. Not a one."

"Not insoluble," Nielson admitted. "But it's going to be very expensive."

"How expensive?" Mike asked. "And what's your plan?"

"There is a group in Russia that supplies heavy lift choppers," Nielson said, tossing Mike a brochure. "They mostly work on relief operations and oil operations in remote areas. They went in with the Marines in Dali, which is where I first heard of them. When you said the Keldara were going to have to hit Lunari in force, I started looking at the problem and saw the solution pretty quick. And I've had some very quiet conversations with them about the problem. They're willing to provide enough choppers and pilots to get us in and out. But . . . they figure it's going to be a hot LZ. And then there's the problem of being identified. So they want two million, minimum, for the mission. Plus recoup costs on any aircraft lost on the mission, to be escrowed in a Swiss bank account controlled by a neutral third party. The vig on that is another mil. But there's more."

"Crap," Mike said, shaking his head. "Three mil for insertion? We need to get our own helicopters and crews."

"Maybe," Nielson said, shrugging. "But the rest is

expensive, too. You see, you can't take off from any of the countries around or nearby. Nobody is going to miss seeing a spec-ops group boarding military helicopters. And most of the area around has Albanians that are going to report it to the mob. Then there's just the diplomatic implications. So you're going to have to come in from the sea. You can't take off from Italy, which is the only place in range of a Hip helicopter, so . . ."

"We've got to lift from a boat," Mike said, sighing. "How much for that?"

"Three hundred thou," Nielson said, throwing the full budget brief on the table. "But that includes picking up the Hips, moving to Albanian waters, launch, recovery and taking the Hips back to Georgia."

"Well, even if I can get the senator to geek, that's it for a profit on the mission," Mike said with a sigh. "I think I'll call D.C. and tell them that I'd like a combat bonus. Because we are going to lose people."

"And we'll have to depend on these helicopter pilots not to fuck us?" Adams asked.

"You got a better plan?" Mike asked.

"Yeah, call some of the 'trainers,'" Adams said. "One to ride on each chopper and a group on the boat."

"Maybe," Mike said. "But we have to get started on this now. Nielson, get that portion moving right away. Vanner, tactical intel?"

"We got reads from ground penetrating radar on the brothel and the surroundings," Vanner said, shrugging. "So we've got an interior. The building is three stories of concrete with two stories of wooden addition on the top. There appears to be a basement as well—"

"Which is where the DVDs are going to be located," Adams predicted. "We're going to be fighting our way in and out."

"We can get the troops familiarized with the building by doing a mock-up," Mike pointed out. "But we still don't know where any of the targets are located for sure."

"The DVDs are likely to be in a safe," Nielson pointed out. "Anybody know how to crack a safe?"

"Not I, said Cock Robin," Vanner replied, shrugging.

"Gimme enough demo and I can move the world," Adams said, raising an eyebrow.

"We want them back intact," Mike said. "We need somebody who actually knows how to open a safe. Nielson?"

"One safecracker coming up," Nielson said, sighing. "We don't even know what kind of safe."

"Then find one who can think on his or her feet," Mike said.

"I'll take that one," Carlson-Smith said, smiling. "I'll simply give Drake over at MI-5 a call. I mean, he's the fellow who keeps an eye on fellows like that. And MI-6 has people who train in such as well."

"Thank you," Mike said. "What are the Italians going to say to a bunch of helicopters taking off for Albania? Or the Albanians for that matter?"

"The Albanians have shit for coverage on that coast," Vanner said. "They're not an issue. We'll have to stay out of Italian territorial waters until we're done. Or . . . I hate to suggest this, but we can take some copies of clips and present them to a couple of people in the Italian government. After that, I don't think they're going to say much at all."

"That's a very slippery slope," Mike said after a moment's thought. "Let's see if the Brits can convince the Italians to look the other way," he added, looking over at Carlson-Smith.

"It might help to have a pic at least of that Ital general . . ." Carlson-Smith pointed out.

"Do it," Mike said with a sigh. "But let's try to limit that. Otherwise we'll become a target just like Lunari. Adams, get started on the mock-up. Nielson, get the freighter moving and get those choppers down here. Russell will take point on training for insertion and extraction with the chief in overall charge of the tactical training. Mr. Carlson-Smith . . ."

"I suppose I have a plane to catch," the MI-6 agent said with a sigh. "I very much hope that the next time I come to visit that you do have your own helicopter. These roads are torturous."

"So does Vanner," Mike said, frowning.

"Say again?" Patrick piped up.

"We need to get Katya inserted, now," Mike replied. "You're going to take the Sawn intel team and monitor. You know what intel we're looking for. Turn over the shop to Lilia for the time being. Take a fire team of Keldara shooters from Team Sawn with you for security."

"So I'm going to be sitting in the woods for the next week or two?" Patrick asked. "Cool."

"Hell, no," Mike replied. "What gave you that idea?"

# ★ Chapter Thirty-Five ★

Katya stepped out of the car when she was told, her head down, and headed for the door, lifting her head just long enough to get a good look around. Camera above the door, one of two apparently into the same building, another camera there. More on each end of the street. Windows up the wall, barred. One guard on the door. That should be enough.

The two men who had driven her across the Macedonian border were hired thugs and had picked up some fringe benefits on the drive; she had a fading bruise on her cheek from her one protest about that. According to plan there was supposed to be a backup team out there, somewhere. But she'd anticipated getting hit. A lot. A slap on the face wasn't anything to cry about and she hadn't, just sucked him off as he'd told her to. She'd really wanted to jam her new nails into his scrotum and watch his face as he bled out, but she'd resisted.

She'd also resisted clenching her fists. The packet was loaded, although until she manipulated the valve in her palm it shouldn't squirt out. But she'd been told the poison was "fast acting" and didn't have an antidote. It was also unlikely that she'd be able to use it more than once.

She had been consigned to hell for at least a week. She needed to save it for when it would actually do some good.

But if they thought she was going to do this mission without just one slaver choking out his life at her hands, they were very stupid people indeed.

"Get inside," the man on the door said, opening it and moving to slap her.

"No, I'm going," Katya said, whining, ducking her head and scooting through the door ahead of the promised slap.

"This the new bitch?"

The room beyond was dark with only a single bulb hanging from the ceiling. There was a table with some men playing poker, a few girls sitting on laps and more men along the sides.

"Katrina or something," one of the men said, standing up and walking over to her. "Look up, bitch, I want to see your face. What's your name, bitch?"

"Katya," Katya said, quietly. "They call me Cottontail."

"Are you?" the man asked, pulling up her skirt and brutally ripping off her panties. "Hey, the carpet matches the curtains."

"Good looker," one of the men in the shadows along the wall said. "She's only going to make a few euros here, though. Send her on to Italy."

"We need to know that she knows her job, first," the man standing in front of her said.

"I am good hooker," Katya said, looking down at the

floor again and ignoring the torn clothes. "I was hooker in Ukraine. I know my place."

"We'll see," the man said, picking her up and throwing her on the table. "And we'll see how tight that pussy is," he added, unbuckling his belt.

"Just as tight as it was before you, Greva," another voice laughed.

Katya ignored it and thought about scratching. Just one little scratch . . .

When the last dick had pulled out of her ass, a man rolled her over and slapped her. There had been quite a few of those as well.

"I'm Boris Dejti and you are . . . ?"

"Katya," she whispered, working her mouth. There was only a little blood from a split lip, but she'd really like to spit. She also knew she'd be hit harder if she did.

"Go upstairs and find a bed," the man said. "Then get your ass out on the street. You owe me six hundred euros tonight. That's to pay off your debt. I bought you and if you want free, you have to pay me ten thousand euros. Of the six hundred, one hundred goes towards your debt, the rest is the interest. You owe me twenty euros a day for your bed, and ten euros a day for your food. Anything else you can keep. If you give it to me, though, it pays off your debt quicker. You understand?"

"Yes," Katya said, still quietly and keeping her head down. It was the usual deal with bastards like this, but even more usurious than usual.

"We're all friends in this town, we know whose girls are who," Boris continued, grabbing her hair and twisting her head up painfully. "You try to run, somebody in this town will bring you back to me. And then I'll take the skin off of your body in little strips, you understand?"

Just one little scratch.

"I understand," Katya whimpered. "I'll be good. I'll be a good whore."

"Get to work, bitch."

She hobbled upstairs, sore in a way that she'd almost forgotten. It was a soreness that soaked at the soul, like the foul taste in her mouth, a soreness in every pore of her being and certainly all three holes that would fit a penis. She'd also lost some of her muscle control in her mouth in the time with the Kildar. She hadn't had to constantly serve men, there. Her jaw ached along with the rest of her.

There were guards where the concrete steps gave out and the wooden ones started and she began to see a few girls around, looking out of the curtained rooms on either side of the corridor. They all looked very sick. She guessed that you'd have to be *very* sick not to work in this place. There were a lot of girls here. Finding this stupid Natalya bitch wasn't going to be easy.

She poked into rooms, seeing the few posessions of the girls by or on most of the matresses strewn on the floors, until she came to one about halfway down on the fifth floor. There was a mattress there, like the others with no sheets and plenty of stains. And a small blanket, all the concession to survival offered to the girls in these parts.

The other mattress in the small room had stuff by it. She knew that the girls would steal anything of value, even the least little cosmetics, which was why she had hardly anything. At some point she'd find a place to hide stuff down on the street.

No, she wouldn't have to. She wasn't going to be here that long. But should she anyway? Yes, stay in cover . . .

"Katya, you read?" Vanner whispered over the radio in her head.

"Uhmmm . . . ?" she hummed. She'd tried the subvocalization thing but wasn't really good at it, yet.

"We're in place," Vanner said. "Video and audio are coming through . . . surprisingly clear. You hang tough. The teams are on track to be here. Sorry there's not a damned thing I can do until then. But we're here."

"Hmmm . . ." Katya said, rolling her eyes. Vanner was such a dick. He-Man hero, hiding in some hotel. And watching everything that happened to her, but not feeling it. He was probably stroking off to the video.

"Just wanted you to know I was here," Vanner said.

"HMMM . . ." Katya practically screamed.

"Got it. I'll shut up."

She tossed her bag on the bed and went back down the stairs; she had seen a sign for a bathroom down there.

The place was filthy and stinking, no surprise. But it had some hot water and she washed her face and soaked the bruises for a moment. Then she slipped a comb out from under her dress and combed her hair, making herself marginally presentable.

Time to go hang it out on the meat rack.

"Mikhail," Vanner said, looking over at one of the bored Keldara security team. "Time to build the cover."

The team had inserted as individuals, each of the men bringing one of the Keldara girls with him along with their gear and taking individual rooms at the Hotel Albana. When they were all in place, the gear had been moved to Vanner's suite and everyone had gathered there and remained there, the girls taking turns monitoring Katya while the shooters just cleaned their weapons and were bored.

But if a group of men didn't get it on a little in Lunari, questions would be asked.

"So, how do I do this?" the team leader asked, setting down the SPR from which he'd been wiping imaginary dust.

"It's not that hard," Vanner said. "Go get your car, drive around town, pick up a girl and take her back to your room. Let nature take it's course after that."

"Don't worry, Mikhail," Greznya said, grinning. "What happens on the mission, stays on the mission. I won't tell your mother."

She was already late for the first pickings around lunch and there wasn't much traffic. And she had a lot of competition.

Girls were lined up along the street outside the brothel, waving at every passing car, shouting, screaming even. She watched as one walked right out into the road and tried to stop a passing Lada, with three men in it, by standing in front of it. The driver honked and maneuvered around her at which she screamed and punched the passenger side window, letting out a stream of profanity that even Katya found impressive.

Katya looked at the women along the street and despaired of ever finding this Natalya bitch. She was just standing there, her arms crossed, when a Fiat pulled to a halt and honked its horn. She didn't even realize it was honking at her until three other girls rushed over, leaning in the passenger window, and she heard the argument.

"No! The one behind you you stupid bitches!" the man shouted in English. "Get out of the way you ugly whores. That one! The blonde!"

Katya walked up behind the center girl trying to force her way into the car and calmly kicked her in the crotch. That area was just about as sensitive on a woman as on a man, not to mention being that girl's main source of income, and the girl let out a shriek and crouched back, falling over on her stilletto heels.

"I'm just who you want," Katya said, kicking the girl blocking the door handle in the ankle and opening the door. "I take very good care of you."

"You're fucking gorgeous," the man said, embarassedly wiping at his face when he actually drooled.

American from the accent, overweight but not gross and balding. And very excited. She'd seen worse. She leaned over and ran her hand over his crotch. Well, not that excited. This was going to take some time.

"I am very good for you," she said.

"You look . . . young," the man said. "Where am I going? Where am I going?"

"I have room," Katya said, shaking her head. She didn't know where the hangouts were in this town. Five minutes on the street and she was already picked up. Of course, after decent living with the Kildar, and the easy life in the brothel before that, she looked better than most of the street hookers in this town. Enough better that it actually frightened her for a second. But if Boris, the bastard, hadn't noticed anything she was probably safe.

"I've been in one of those," the man said with a shudder, looking around at the traffic fearfully. "And I nearly had my car stolen. They tore out the radio and you wouldn't believe what those assholes at the rental agency charged me to get it replaced!"

"You have hotel?" Katya asked, rolling her eyes. This was going to take extra fuck time and travel time and then she had to get back! Maybe she could work the hotel, but the security probably already had deals with other girls. Well, that was what blowjobs were for. "I can give you blow, here."

"Not here, it's not safe," the man said breathlessly.

Katya tried very hard not to sigh, the guy was such a . . . what was it Russell said, a "whiner"? Stuck in that hole in Georgia, servicing kopekless farm hands, she'd forgotten about tricks like this. The scared ones, the ones that were running from everything and completely out of their element. Sure enough, he had a wedding ring. He was probably over in Europe for "business" and somehow drifted to Albania.

"We'll go to my hotel," the man said, suddenly, turning left and nearly broadsiding a van. "Could you take your hand off my zipper? I'm sort of . . ."

"You need good thing," Katya said, sliding over and working more on the man's crotch. If she didn't he'd take forever to cum when they got to the hotel. He clearly hadn't had an erection in the last decade.

"How young are you?" the man said, suddenly, slowing the car down.

"I am not too young," she answered, not sure if he wanted some young thing or was afraid of her being "too" young. How young was "too" young? Was she "too" young when Ivan had raped her when she was eight? "But I am young enough to make it very good for you."

"Wait," he said, actually turning and looking at her. Since she'd gotten in the car, he'd seemed afraid of even that. "You're speaking English?"

"I speak little," she said, cursing. Fluent English, and she was fully fluent at this point, wasn't common among street whores. "How young you want me?" she asked, couquettishly, dropping her head and looking up at him from under her lashes. "I can be as young you want. I am very nearly virgin," she added, knowing that would get him off. Sure enough, he actually went from entirely flaccid to having a pulse.

"How young are you?" the man said, speeding up again and running a red light. Not that anyone paid any attention to them, anyway.

"I am just turn sixteen," Katya said, stripping an easy year off her age and picking one that Americans seemed to fixate upon. "I am old enough, here. There is no problem."

"Are you sure you're sixteen?" the man said, with an edge of disappointment as they pulled up at the hotel.

"When we get to the room, I tell you real age," Katya said coyly, smiling up at him innocently and batting blue eyes through lashes again. "I give you very good time and you give me good money, yes?"

"Yeah, yeah," the man panted. "But . . . I can't be seen going through the lobby with you . . ."

"Give me room number," Katya said, trying very hard not to sigh. "I meet you there."

Mikhail didn't like this particular "mission," but he felt he had to set a good example. Each of the team would have to move around town and meet and . . . spend time with the hookers that supported the local economy. There were a few problems with that in his case. The first was that he'd never picked up a hooker. The rest didn't bear thinking on.

He drove down the main boulevard in a surprisingly nervous state for someone who'd faced Chechens in battle. He thought that he had been fully trained for whatever he might encounter, but the American trainers had not really given him much advice on this particular skill. He could have killed some of the hookers lining the street and in many cases shouting at him. But he wasn't sure he knew how to talk to them. There should have been a training task on this. He'd have to bring it up when they got back. If they got back.

He knew he didn't want to pick up one of the hard-faced bitches that looked as old as his mother, and not nearly as pretty. They were mostly the ones that screeched from the sidewalk like crows and sometimes ran over and tried to pull his car door open. And some of the girls just looked . . . He couldn't imagine doing it with them. They were just . . .

Finally he spotted what he was looking for after about an hour of driving around and pulled over, waving at the girl.

The brunette practically ran to the door as he leaned over and unlocked it. She still had to hip-check another woman, one of the older ones, out of the way and tumbled into the passenger seat.

"Hello," the girl said, sliding over to lean against him. "I'm Tanya. I give you very good time."

"Mikhail," the Keldara said, putting the car in gear and trying to figure out which way back to the hotel.

"Hello, Mikhail," the girl said, sitting up. "Where are we going?"

"The Hotel Albana if I can find it," Mikhail said.

"I think you take a right up here," the girl said, sighing. "I've been there, once. Is nice. But it takes time to get there and back, so it will be more. I give you very good time for an hour for . . . fifty euros."

Vanner *had* told him that the girl should cost thirty or forty euros but he wasn't going to haggle. One of the reasons that he'd picked this girl out was that she looked as if she knew what she was doing but she didn't really look like a whore. He just couldn't haggle with her.

"Fifty is okay," Mikhail said, frowning. Vanner had told him to just submit an "expense report." He figured one of the women would know how to do that.

"Ooo, you're nice," Tanya said, running her hand over his arm. "You are going to like this very much."

Mikhail frowned for a second and then sighed.

"Is something need to tell you," he said.

"You want special service is more," Tanya said, not looking very happy. "In ass is ten euros. You want hit, is more."

"It's not that," Mikhail said, hurriedly. "It's . . . I've never done this before. Been with a . . ."

"Prostitute?" the girl asked then looked at his face and stopped. "Oh. Have never been with girl?"

"Don't laugh, please," Mikhail said desperately.

"Learn early not to laugh at men," Tanya said, still looking at him seriously. "You tell truth?"

"Yes," Mikhail said, frowning. "Where I'm from . . . is not much chance. Good girls . . . don't. Bad girls . . . leave."

"Oh," Tanya said. "Well, I show you good time. Will be okay, okay?"

"Okay," Mikhail said, smiling finally. "Thank you for not making fun of me. How did . . ."

"How did nice girl like me end up here?" Tanya said, sighing. "From nice boy like you."

"Excuse me?"

"Boyfriend," Tanya said, leaning back into her own seat. "I'm with him for . . . three months or so. He tells me has a friend can get me into Germany as maid. There is no work in Russia for me, so I say I'll meet friend. Turns out friend gets hookers for Albanians. Never see boyfriend again."

"That's . . ." Mikhail said angrily.

"Shitty, yes?" the girl replied with a bitter laugh. "I think, maybe he not know. I love him, yes? And he do this to me. But he must know. Sometimes think of what would want to do to him if found him again. Are not nice thoughts."

"I'll hold his arms for you," Mikhail said. "If you not want to do this . . ."

"I have to do this," Tanya said desperately. "Don't drop me off, please. I need to earn money. If I don't bring back money, I get beaten."

"Okay," Mikhail said, as they pulled up to the hotel. "We do this."

"You very nice," Tanya replied, snuggling back up to him. "You nice boy, nice man. I think I give you special service. I rock your world."

# ★ Chapter Thirty-Six ★

When the American answered the door he grabbed her and tried to kiss her on the mouth. Katya thought about it for a second and let him. He'd put on cologne and brushed his teeth. Americans. Like she cared.

"I am very good for you," she said, rethinking her strategy. If she walked back to the hotel, she'd probably be passing through a bunch of other brothels' territories. Which meant if she tried to pick up tricks, she'd get the crap beat out of her by the pimps that watched the girls. Paying for a taxi, unless this guy was incredibly generous, was out of the question. Even if he gave her the fare, she'd be better to pocket it and walk.

But it was at least a half hour walk back, if she walked fast. In heels.

So . . . and so.

"I give you good time," Katya said, pushing him back towards the bed. "And you give me money, please?" she practically sobbed. "I am sorry to ask, I am not good whore. I have only been whore for few days." She sat on the edge of the bed and started sobbing.

"What?" the man said, sitting up and patting her on the shoulder. "Really?"

"I am orphan," she sobbed. "I am thrown out of orphanage. There I learn English. Not so good, but I can understand, yes? I have nowhere to go, no one hire me. I must do this." She looked up, suddenly, and stared at him, fiercely. "I will do this with you, yes? You are good man, sweet and nice, a good American, yes? I will give you much sex, but, please . . ." She broke down and sobbed. "Please, I ask you not send me back out. I will give you sex over and over but Boris, he hit me if I not bring back enough! Please to help me!"

"How old are you, child?" the man said, pulling her up into his lap.

"I am . . . I am fourteen," Katya sobbed. "I am only whore a few days. Boris, he rape me and tell me I make money for him. He make me pay rent and I must pay him eight hundred euros every day! Yesterday, I only make sixty euros! He hit me much," she added, pointing to the bruises on her face and her cut lip.

"That's just . . . abominable," the man snapped. "Horrible! You can stay here, if you want. I'm going to be here . . . I'd planned on being here for a few days . . ."

"No!" Katya gasped in fear. "No! Boris' men, they find me. Find you! No, I will stay with you until is very late. But I must have money! I must . . . you are not . . . I must . . ." She broke down again.

"Look," the man said. "I'd planned on spending . . . quite a bit, here. You can have it. I don't really need . . ." He stopped and sighed.

"You need, yes?" Katya said, looking up with tears in her eyes. "I will. With you, I am very good for you, yes? And . . . you need. I feel you."

"My wife and I . . ." the man said with a sigh. "I mean, I love her, but she just . . . doesn't want to anymore. And I'm not going to . . . you can't just up and beat a woman because she doesn't want to have sex. So . . . I use a Kleenex and . . . well. Anyway, I was at a seminar in Italy and there was this . . . young lady. Like you but . . . not as young. And she . . . was very good for me."

Katya was fighting yawning and trying to keep the tears going at the same time. It was a tough call, but she managed it. The important part was to stare him in the eye and nod. Doing your nails was a bad idea. Save that for later when he was on top and wouldn't notice as long as you kept making lots of noise.

The long story of the man's journey to the most whore-infested town in Albania wound to a close and Katya jerked back to wakefulness, trying to remember what he'd said.

"Your wife is very bad woman!" Katya said, throwing her arms around him. "She should give you what you need. You are good man!" *I hope I can suck enough out of him for all this time. But if I play my cards right . . .*

"She's not a bad woman," the man said with a sigh. "She just doesn't understand how . . . what I need. And . . . she's not as good looking as she used to be. I don't want to leave her, though. So . . . here I am. In Lunari. It seemed like a good idea with a few drinks in me . . ."

"But I am good you," Katya said, standing up and lifting up her skirt a little. "I am take care you. But . . ."

"I'll pay you," the man said, reaching into his shirt and pulling out a secure wallet. "I'll buy you from him if that's what it takes!"

"Would not sell me," Katya said, pushing the money away and mentally calculating the bulge. If that was all he had with him, she was sunk. "This town, is not safe and safe at all same time. I know people make safe. But need money. You pay me, I stay near you most of time. Must go back so they know I not try to run. But I come for you. I show you town, we go to club. You pay me. I give you much sex, more sex than ever have in life. We get other girls, do it together if you want. Not much more money at all. I take very good care of you! But . . ."

"Would a thousand euros a day cover it?" the man asked, pulling out travellers' checks.

"I cannot do with those . . ." Katya said in real desperation. "But can cash at hotel?"

"I have some euros, too," the man said, handing them over to her. It was about three hundred, so far so good. Oh, shit, the mission. This would have been heaven if she was really one of the whores in the brothel. But she had a different mission. "And, yes, I can cash them at the hotel. And it has an ATM, but . . . if I hit that too hard my wife will wonder why."

"We take care of it," Katya said, seriously, but with a touch of innocence. "I take care of you and give you very good time until you leave. I am rock your world."

"Oh . . . wow!" Mikhail said, lying back on the bed.

"You come quick," Tanya replied, wiping the cum away from her mouth. "And lots. I think there is more there," she added, stroking his member. Sure enough, it started to pop back to life.

"I'm not sure . . ." Mikhail said, starting to sit up.

"I show you other way," the hooker said, standing up and pulling off her sheath dress. "You like my body?"

"You're very pretty," Mikhail admitted. She would only be average as a Keldara, but he'd never seen a Keldara girl naked so he had limited experience to judge. All he knew was that he wanted to do it again. And again and again.

"Come over here," she said, lying down on the bed. "You need condom."

"I've got one," Mikhail admitted, getting up quickly and digging through his bags until he found the foil packet.

"I show," Tanya said as he fumbled with the latex sheeth. "Is almost too small." She took the condom, placed the tip in her mouth and put it on that way. "You like?"

"Yes," Mikhail admitted. "What . . . where . . . ?"

"Come here," the girl said, pulling him over to her. "On top. Try not to put all your weight on me . . ." She started to spit on her fingers to moisten herself and realized she didn't have to, she was actually enjoying herself. "I get you there . . ." she added, guiding him down and in.

"Oh . . . wow," Mikhail repeated, starting to pump at her furiously. He looked up after a moment and stopped as he saw tears in the girl's eyes. "Are you okay?" he asked, starting to pull out.

"Don't," she said, digging her fingers into his buttocks. "Is good for me, too. You are very nice. I like. Makes me sad, though. I not be whore for very long. Is almost like boyfriend again."

"Only almost?" Mikhail asked.

"Actually, is better," Tanya admitted, grinning through

the tears. "Boyfriend was too small. I think you are rock my world."

Katya got out of the taxi, one of the last driving around Lunari, and twisted her spine to get it back in line, getting a full view of the front of the building. Two guards, more barred windows up to the fourth story, heavy steel door. The street was mostly deserted, though, at this time of night.

The man, he said his name was Tom and he was a neurosurgeon from Cleveland, Tennessee, had been as hard to get off as she'd predicted. But he still wanted sex most of the time and she'd given it to him. And he must have slept in, because he hadn't passed out until after three. It hadn't advanced the mission much, but it gave her some leeway. She had her money for the day, at least.

"You're late," the guard on the door growled. She was using the front entrance, which she'd never been through, because it was clear the others were closed.

"I have to make money, yes?" she asked.

"Get in," he said, irritably. "You're the last one."

Boris, unbelievably, was still awake, the bastard.

"Where the fuck have you been, bitch!" he stormed, walking up to her and smashing her to the floor with a hard slap.

"I have your money!" she whimpered, reaching under the dress and pulling out money. "Six hundred euros!"

"Let me see that," Boris said, snatching the money out of her hand and then reaching into her dress and fumbling around. "More, bitch? You have more!"

"I found a rich American," Katya said, stopping the

dissembling and standing up. "He thinks I'm fourteen and just broken in. My amazing skills at sucking him off being natural, I suppose. Six hundred for my debt, thirty for room I'm only going to use for a few hours and food I didn't eat, yes?" She reached out and calmly plucked a hundred euro note out of his hand. "This is for me, yes? If you hit again, American might not like my face. He wants me and sometimes other girl. Let me pick and he stays happy, yes? And you make your money. Is another hundred there is yours. Or . . . you can hit and tell me I'm stupid bitch and beat me up so I not look good . . . and tomorrow maybe I have six, maybe not." She shrugged and dared to look him in the eye.

"You've been around," Boris said.

"I said, I am whore in Ukraine," Katya said, shrugging. "Have been a whore for . . . five year. I know how to work men, how to suck them dry of money. I speak English, I speak Russian, I even speak fucking Georgian. No Albanian. But I spend some time here, suck my American dry, send him home happy to his fat wife and then you send me to Italy where I make you real money."

"Bring him to the club, tomorrow," Boris said, his eyes narrow.

"He doesn't like those shitty rooms upstairs," Katya said. "I will, but . . ."

"There are other rooms," Boris said. "Ten euros to rent. Clean sheets, red light, very nice. You didn't know?"

"No," Katya said, trying not to sigh again because then he would hit her. "You only told me to get out on the street and make you your money, yes? I have made you your money. I'll bring him to the club. But . . . he likes me. He likes girls like me. Let me find another for part of the time. There will be at least one here that will do. I'll bring him, introduce him, get him to buy pay-me drinks, yes?"

"You know the routine," Boris said. "But I think you're a little too smart for your own good."

"I bring you money," Katya said, shrugging. "Why you care?"

"Because you better understand that I own you, bitch," Boris snarled, grabbing her by the arm. "And I can teach you that without ever leaving a mark. Come with me."

He dragged her to the back of the club and into the men's restroom. It still hadn't been cleaned from the night and smelled of shit, piss and puke.

He kicked open one of the stalls and shoved her head into the fetid bowl of the toilet.

"Lick it clean, bitch," Boris snarled, shoving her head down. "You're no more than a fucking whore. And whores do what they're told. So lick that shit out of the bowl, bitch!"

Katya gagged but did what she was told, licking at the shit besmeared bowl. She tried to tell herself that she'd done worse, but when didn't come to mind. Yes, it did. There was a Japanese tourist in the Ukraine that had paid her to eat his shit. But she'd at least been paid. And that was a long time ago.

When Boris jerked her head up she was careful to look as meek as possible. He wanted her humiliated so she brought up some more tears and quivered in fear.

"Please," she whimpered. "I bring you money! I will!"

"You're damned right you will," Boris said, reaching into her dress again and pulling out her remaining hundred euro note. "And this is a fine for thinking you're smart! Now get your ass up to the room, bitch. And your rich American had better be in my club tomorrow!"

Katya kept her head down on the way up to her room. Light was apparently optional above the main club level and she kept stumbling over bumps and cracks in the floor with her heels as she made her way.

When she got there she saw that her stuff had been picked through but they hadn't taken her toothbrush at least. But she didn't have any toothpaste left.

She made her way back to the only bathroom she had found, other than the one on the ground floor and she wasn't going there any time soon. She brushed her teeth with the horrible soap that was on the sink and managed to get the last of the shit taste out then took a sketchy shower. The hot water had apparently been turned off as well.

That done she went back to her semen- and blood-stained bed, set her dress against the wall to avoid having it stolen and linked her fingers behind her head, staring at the ceiling.

So far, the mission was going better than she'd expected.

"Mikhail, do you have any idea what time it is?" Vanner asked grumpily.

"Yes," the team leader said. "I have problem."

"Come on in," Vanner said, waving the way into his bedroom. The intel team had set up in the main room and he'd taken one of the two bedrooms. He'd just gotten off of monitoring duty and had looked forward to a few hours of rest before Katya woke up. One of the girls was on duty to monitor when she was asleep, in case a serious security issue came up. But Vanda would get to sleep during the day. He wasn't going to get the chance.

"The girl I pick up . . . " Mikhail said as the intel specialist closed the door.

"Oh, crap," Vanner said, collapsing on the bed. "Don't tell me you've fallen in love with a hooker."

"She not want to be whore," Mikhail insisted.

"Mikhail," Vanner said, frowning. "We're on a mission here. We can't afford for you to go all John Wayne on us."

"What?" Mikhail asked, confused.

"You were supposed to just go out and get laid," Vanner replied, sighing. "Not fall in love with the girl. Look, most of the hookers in town aren't here because they grew up wanting to be hookers. In fact, you'd be hard pressed to find one that had that on her list of intended vocations. But that's what they are, now. What do you want to do about it? Where is she, by the way?"

"In my room," Mikhail said, worrying his lip.

"Damnit, they have a curfew," Vanner snapped. "Her pimp is going to come looking for her."

"She called," Mikhail said. "She tell them she is staying with her . . . trick and will bring money in morning."

"She needs at least . . ."

"Six hundred and thirty euros," Mikhail said, miserably.

"And I suppose you want me to cough it up," Vanner said. "The Kildar to pay for it."

"I will pay back," Mikhail said. "I not want her to get hurt. She is from Club Aldaris. That is target, yes?"

"Christ," Vanner said, sliding up the bed and leaning on the headboard. "Mikhail, you're supposed to be security for the suite. You think she can come in here with you?"

"No," the trooper admitted. "But . . ."

Vanner held up one hand and thought for a second.

"Okay," the intel specialist said, frowning. "You're on deck for security tonight. You're supposed to be in there now. So go tell her you have to go for a while, she can sleep there. Tomorrow you take her back to the club, she pays her pimp, then you two go back to your room. Get some rest, don't just screw all day because you're on duty tomorrow night, too. We'll see what we can arrange."

"Thank you, sir," Mikhail said, standing up.

"I want to meet her, tomorrow," Vanner added. "Maybe we can salvage something useful out of this."

"Yes, sir."

"Now . . . go!"

"Come," Mike said at the knock on the door.

"Kildar," Oleg said, entering the room and coming to attention.

"Sit, Oleg, what's on your mind?" Mike said, clearing the screen on his computer.

The helicopters had arrived and the Keldara had gotten started on that training. Most of them had never ridden in an airplane before and few had even seen a helicopter. But, as always, they were soaking up the information like so many sponges. And the majority already knew how to fast-rope for that portion of the entry.

Taking off and landing on the freighter, though, was going to be problematic. Mike intended to exercise in the Black Sea before they headed for Albania.

"Kildar, I am not sure how to say this . . ." Oleg said.

"If it's about that . . . Kardane thing . . ." Mike said.

"No, no!" Oleg replied, waving his hands. "It does, however, touch on the honor of the Keldara."

"Go ahead," Mike said, furrowing his brow.

"Before you came, we had problems with the Chechens," Oleg said, furrowing his own in thought. "They often came wanting us to give up our food, our mules . . . our women."

"And you fought them off at least once," Mike said. "I heard about that."

"But even then . . ." Oleg said and paused. "I should not be the one saying this, but the elders don't have the same . . ."

"Who was she?" Mike asked softly.

"My sister," Oleg said. "Elena. She was twelve."

"Oleg, it's a big damned world out there . . ." Mike said, then paused himself. "What are you asking?"

"There is going to be information in Lunari about . . . much," Oleg pointed out. "Greznya spoke to me. An Elena, a Georgian girl, was listed on one of the . . . hard drives you recovered. The one in Romania . . ."

"Oleg, she might not be in the same building," Mike said, sighing. "It's an astronomical unlikelihood that she will be. And, Oleg, you've seen the raw intel. That town is one fortress after another. If we can find and extract Elena, without compromising the mission, we will. And if we can't extract her, but we can find her, I'll move heaven and earth to get her back. Is she the only one?"

"No," Oleg admitted. "Catrina Mahona. She was taken . . . four years ago. And there was no record of her. But, Kildar, both of these women, they are . . ."

"Dead to the clan," Mike said, nodding. "I understand. They are soiled, untouchable. I'm talking to a school in Argentina that might take in the girls we've recovered, those that don't have some sort of life to go back to. I may send them some of the girls in the harem, as well. Would that do?"

"Kildar . . ." Oleg replied, his face working.

"Concentrate on the mission, Oleg," Mike said, his own face hard. "You've communicated your concerns to me. Let me handle it from here. You've got enough to worry about."

"You're not usually up this late, David," Senator Traskel said as he was led into the sitting room. The President was leaning back on the couch, his eyes closed, and pinching the bridge of his nose, while his chief of staff poured coffee.

"There were just too many things going on today to break off early," the President said, yawning. "And another long one tomorrow unless I'm much mistaken. What can I do for you, John?"

"I picked up a rumor that we have an operation going on in Albania," Senator Traskel said, sitting down and accepting the proffered coffee cup. "I hope that it's nothing that should have been discussed with my committee beforehand. Albania is a sovereign country, with a growing reputation in the UN . . ."

"Albania?" the President said, looking over at the chief of staff, quizzically. "You're talking about a special operations black operation? As far as I know, no American military operation is being planned for Albania.

I can't even imagine why we'd do one. I mean, it's a land that exports nothing but drugs and beaten-up prostitutes, which is good and sufficient reason for democratization. But it doesn't actively threaten the U.S., so we've more or less left it alone except for encouraging improvement. Through the UN, as a matter of fact."

"You're sure about that?" the senator asked. "I heard a fairly credible rumor that a company of American Rangers was going to be flying into a town in Albania to rescue some hostages. I didn't even know there were any hostages in Albania. If there were, I think the American people would be interested, don't you? I know that many things must be kept 'black,' as the military likes to put it. But some things need the sun shone upon them, don't you think?"

"I'm sure they do," the President said, smiling. "But as I said, there is no American military operation going on in Albania. No, wait," the President said as the senator started to protest. "I might be wrong. There are operations going on all over the world. It is possible that there is a group of terrorists there we're going after. Albania is primarily Muslim, after all. Let me check."

The President leaned over and picked up the phone.

"Grace? Could you call OSOL and ask them if we have an operation going on in Albania? Something about a company of Rangers? If so, I want to know, right away, what the nature and purpose of the mission is. Thank you." He turned back to the senator and shrugged. "As you know, OSOL has its finger on the pulse of every operation, black or white, that is done under any special operations umbrella including the blackest DIA operations.

If there's anything going on, they'll know it. In the meantime, what do you think of the Astros this year?"

"Your information was wrong," Traskel snarled into the phone.

"I don't think so," the man on the other end said. "A company of Rangers was sent to Eastern Europe. That's a fact. And another source said that there was a mission planned for Lunari using a company-sized force. There are people that don't agree with all these military adventures of this idiot in the White House. We talk. You know that."

"They're looking for the girl," the senator said, his face working. "And she's in Lunari. Get over there. You should have cleaned this up the first time. Clean it up now."

"Do you have any idea how many women are in Lunari?" the voice choked out.

"They're going to find her, so can you. And then finish it. No little games, you understand me. Finish her."

# ★ Chapter Thirty-Seven ★

"Katya," a female voice whispered in her head. "This is Nadzia, Team Swan. Good morning."

"Hmmm . . ." Katya replied as she brushed her teeth again. She'd traded a dollar she'd hidden in one of her pouches for some toothpaste and Lord did she need it. It was almost lunch time. Time to go look up "Tom" again. She had to look halfway decent. A heroine in a movie that's been roughed up but still looks like a model. . . . She ran her fingers through her hair and tossed it around to get just the right effect. If she only had some cosmetics, she could get it perfect.

"Additional mission. There are some Keldara girls that might be in the town. We have visuals of them. If we see one, through you, we'll redirect. Understand?"

"Hmmm . . ." Katya said, rolling her eyes. Great. Fucking Holier-Than-Thou Keldara. Nobody ever came for her when she needed it.

"You need to get more of a layout on the club. Use your American if you can."

"HMMMM . . ." *Teach me to suck eggs, stupid Keldara bitch!*

"I can see you're not a morning person."

Katya sighed angrily and finished brushing, then headed back down to the street. Supposedly, there was something resembling breakfast around here, but "Tom" had had some food in his room and that was enough to keep her going through the very short night.

But, first, she wanted to take a look around. Most of the girls were still just getting ready for the day, the lazy whores. Getting out early, looking fresh, would usually pick you up at least two or three tricks. All it took was getting out of bed. If she ran this place, there'd be a reveille.

But the fact was that there wasn't. So the girls were still getting up and she could see the faces.

It was all the way on the sixth floor that she found her. The girl was just finishing working on her hair using a bit of mirror on the wall. She was pretty sure it was the same girl, but she continued to stare, then hummed and finally sighed.

"Sorry, you're calling us aren't you?" a female voice said. "Yes, that appears to be the target. Find out what room she uses. Move into it if you think it will work."

She'd hatched a plan in an instant, but she wasn't sure how to tell the stupid Keldara. There was very little in the way of privacy. Later for that.

"Hello," she said, walking over to the girl.

Natalya looked at her fearfully, then around for support.

"I'm not going to put on you," Katya said, looking her up and down. The girl was young and fairly good looking. She'd look better with some cosmetics, no question. Could she swing this? "I have found a rich American. He wants two girls, even though he can barely get it up with one. And he likes young ones. But not to hit on, he is nice. You are pretty good. You want in?"

"Will I make as much as usual?" Natalya asked in a resigned tone.

"If you work with me, you will," Katya said, shaking her head. "More and with less work. You need to learn to be a good whore, though. He thinks I'm fourteen and barely touched. I'm not going to take him some dragged out whore. If you can't act, the deal is off. You speak English?"

"No," the girl said, still looking at her fearfully.

"Good," Katya said, the plan blooming. "Let me handle the talking, then. And don't tell anyone what the arrangement is. You'll get seven hundred euros a day. He uses traveller's checks. I know a man who will give me a special deal on them, so I'll cash them, alone."

"Ah, got it," the Keldara listener said. "We'll supplement. I'll get Vanner and tell him."

"We'll go down, you stay by the doors. I'll find him and we'll get together with him and tell him the deal. Yes?"

"Yes," Natalya said, her eyes wide. "But why are you being nice to me?"

"Who says I'm being nice?" Katya said, laughing evilly. "I'm going to let you do most of the fucking and I'll take most of the money. And because you're such a little mouse you won't try to double-cross me, will you?" She leaned forward and ran her sharpened nails down the girl's neck, lightly. "Will you?"

"You know," Vanner said, leaning back at the head of the bed and monitoring the grainy video take on his laptop. "If we were really just after the girl, we could pull her out like this. No muss, no fuss."

"Who would have thought they'd have her out walking the streets?" Nadzia asked, shaking her head. "That means something, but I'm not sure what."

"Well, whatever is important about the girl, the Albanians clearly don't know it," Vanner replied. "Upload that item. We might want to find an alternate plan to get the girl. One that is less likely to get her whacked."

Katya realized she had screwed up by not making special arrangements to meet "Tom" last night. But as soon as she stepped down to the street, she saw his Fiat cruising slowly along the boulevard.

"Tom!" she shouted as he pulled next to her. She ran over and leaned in the window, giving him a good solid French kiss. She hoped some day she'd get the chance to tell him how her night had gone. But not today, not after that kiss.

"He hurt you," Tom said, running his hand carefully over the fresh bruise on her cheek.

"It is okay," Katya said. "Men have hit me since I was very young. I am used to it. I told you I have friend," she said, waving to Natalya. "We will give you very good deal, but we must talk. And, if you don't mind, I would like to shower at your hotel. Would you scrub my back?"

"Do we have this set up?" Katya asked in Georgian when she was in the shower. The hotel water was at least warm, if not exactly clear. And hot didn't seem to be a setting. But there was some shampoo, thank God, and decent American soap. She scrubbed hard.

"It's set up," Nadzia answered. "Whenever you're ready to make the switch. It will be in the hotel."

"Good," Katya said.

"We're communicating with higher about extracting you and Natalya prior to the main op, less likely to get shot."

"That would be nice," Katya said dryly. "How long?"

"No more than four days," Lydia replied.

"I hope I can string him along that long," Katya said. "It's the best bet I've got for keeping close to the girl."

"You're doing fine," Nadzia said soothingly. "Just keep on like you have been."

"Being beaten, raped and having to service men?" Katya replied sarcastically. "You try it."

"I've got other skills," Nadzia said. "One of which is making sure you have your money to keep your pimp off your back."

"I'm done here," Katya said.

"Out."

"You talk to yourself, too?" Natalya asked dreamily.

Katya nearly had a heart attack until she realized the girl was never going to know the Keldara accented version of Georgian they'd been speaking. The dialect was practically another language.

"Sometimes," Katya said, wondering what the girl might have understood. "When I think I'm alone!" Should have made sure.

"Do you have voices?" Natalya asked in the same dreamy voice. "I have voices. They tell me that the bad man is coming."

"They are all bad men," Katya said, wondering if the

girl had implants like she did or if she was just crazy. Hopefully, just crazy.

"No, this is the real bad man," Natalya said. "He said that he would come for me. That he would let me wait and fear. But he didn't come back. And they sent me here, instead."

"Well, he's not here," Katya said. "But I am. And if you don't get out of damned bathroom you're not going to have to fear him because I'm going to kill you!"

"He seemed like such a nice man," Natalya said, as she closed the door. "So very nice. He had a nice face."

"Bingo," Vanner said as he replayed that portion of the tape. Of course, that also meant that he had to look at Katya's tits from an angle he'd never seen them from before. But he managed to keep his mind on work. "She saw the face of the guy who was impersonating Grantham."

"And he said he'd be back," Nadzia continued. "To kill her, later. But the Albanians had shipped her, already."

"So did he know that there was full audio/video in Rozaje?" Vanner mused. "Who did know, at that time?"

"The British government," Nadzia pointed out. "Maybe the American government as well?"

"Yeah, but who in the American government?" Vanner asked rhetorically. He turned to the satellite link and started typing. "Want to bet that Senator Traskel is on the list?"

"Who's going to do the plant?" Nadzia asked. "Two of the girls are out planting vids, I'm on deck and Vanda is sleeping."

"I've got an idea," Vanner said, smiling.

★ ★ ★

"Oh, this is very good," Mikhail groaned as Tanya humped him from on top.

"You are very good," Tanya replied, panting. "I think . . . toooo gooo . . ." She paused and gasped as there was a knock on the door. And then squealed as she was suddenly thrown halfway across the bed and Mikhail was on his feet with a pistol clutched in a two handed grip.

"What are you . . ." she asked, half in a whisper.

"Get down and be quiet," Mikhail replied, cat-footing to the door, apparently ignoring that he was entirely naked. "Who is it?"

"Vanner. Open up."

Mikhail uncocked the gun and looked around wildly, then snatched up a towel before opening the door.

"Smells like you haven't been getting much sleep," Vanner said in Russian as he walked in the room. "Where's the girl?"

"Here?" Tanya said, popping up over the far side of the bed holding her sheath dress in front of her.

"Get some clothes on," Vanner said and looked Mikhail up and down. "And you, Mikhail. But take the condom off first."

"We will both be very good to you," Katya said as she walked back into the room with towels wrapped around her hair and torso. The latter barely covered her pubic hair and was pulled down low on her breasts so she had his full and undivided attention. "But there are some things that we have to do for that deal."

"Okay," Tom said, breathlessly. Natalya hadn't even

waited for a suggestion and was fellating him rigorously. "Whatever you two want . . ."

"I have found man that will give me good deal on travellers' checks," Katya said. "I will cash them. Just once every day, eight hundred euros. And we must spend time at the club."

"I don't . . ." Tom started to say and then winced.

"We don't go to girls' rooms," Katya said, quickly. "There are nice rooms, only ten euros to use. And if you find other girls you like, you go with them, too. But you must buy us some drinks so Boris makes money or he will get angry." She brushed her cheek, lightly, and shook her head. "He was very angry that I come back so late last night. He think I run. If you want both of us, must keep him happy."

"Okay, okay," Tom said, groaning. "Whatever you want . . ."

"Move over, stupid one," Katya said in Russian, kneeling down in front of the neurosurgeon. "You don't know how to really give a man head."

"So you're Tanya," Vanner said when both of them had gotten dressed. She was a fairly pretty brunette, he had to admit. Not up to Keldara standards, but close.

"Yes?" she replied, looking over at Mikhail.

"You've probably figured out by now that Mikhail is not a farm manager here on vacation," Vanner said, smiling. "By the pistol, if nothing else."

"I . . . hadn't thought so before . . ."

"You want out?" Vanner asked. "Out from being a whore that is?"

"Yes," the girl said fiercely then paused. "But I cannot run. I would be beaten, killed."

"Not where we'll send you," Vanner said. "The Albanians won't be able to touch you. But to get out, really out, you need to help us."

"What are you doing?" Tanya asked nervously.

"You don't have to know," Vanner said. "All you have to do is what we tell you, when we tell you, exactly. And you don't talk about it. Not even to your girlfriends. If you do, you're going to get Mikhail killed, and yourself. Do you understand?"

"Yes," the girl answered.

"Okay," Vanner said, pulling out a metal packet and tossing it to her. "Put that in your purse. You're going to plant it for us."

"Now," Katya said when the doctor was laid out flat on the bed and Natalya was using up the hot water. "The money changer I found is near the hotel. I will go to him once per day, as I said. But we must go to the club as well. And I must sleep there late at night, so that they know all their girls are still in town. So, we must either come back here, later, to get the money changed or I change it now."

"You're just going to run, aren't you?" Tom said, sighing in regret. "Take the money and run . . ." he sang.

"No, Tom," Katya said, seriously. "Please, look at me. I will not run." *That's right, look right into these innocent blue eyes you sucker.*

"Okay, okay," Tom said, pulling out his money pouch and taking out the travellers' checks. "How much?"

"Eight hundred, please," Katya said, putting her hand

on his arm and leaning into him. "I promise. I am only gone . . ."

"Ten minutes," Vanner whispered. "Max."

"Ten minutes," Katya continued, stepping over his "max." "And Natalya stays here, yes? When she gets out of shower, she give you good time."

"Not as good as you, Katya," Tom said, handing over the endorsed travellers' checks. "Nobody is as good as you."

"I be back very soon," Katya said, standing up. "I do whatever you want. I play little girl, yes?" she asked, pulling her hair into ponytails.

"Do you have a schoolgirl outfit?" Tom asked, breathing hard.

"No," Katya said, pouting. "I not even have hair ribbons. Is all I have, what you see," she added, waving at her body.

"I could . . ."

"If you want send me shop," Katya said, smiling winningly, "I buy whatever you want. I be whoever you want. Any name you want, any girl you want. You do whatever you want."

"Can you . . . resist a little?" Tom asked.

"I be whatever you want," Katya said, slipping to the door. "Ten minutes."

"In ten minutes, with this much money, I could be on my way to Greece," Katya said as she strode down the hall. "This is the time for me to cut and run, normally. Where am I going?"

"Third floor," Vanner answered. "West stairwell."

She rode the elevator down to the third floor and

stepped aside for another whore who wordlessly boarded the elevator as she got off. Then she headed for the stairwell.

"Fire hose compartment on your right," Vanner said as she stepped into the stairwell. "Container under it."

She pulled the plastic container out and had a moment's trouble opening it. But when she did, a thick envelope fell out.

"Put the travellers' checks back in," Vanner said. "You can't hold onto them with Boris searching your dress every time you go back."

"You're getting off on this, aren't you?" Katya asked, slipping the checks into the box and replacing it.

"Only when you're looking in a mirror, honey," the former Marine said. "Seriously, you're doing great."

"Compliments get you nowhere," Katya said, stepping back into the hallway. "But the Kildar had better come through with the money or he's going to find out how badly I can scratch these days."

"Are we going to be okay?" Tanya asked when she got back to the room.

"We'll be fine," Mikhail promised. "As long as you don't talk about anything you do or are asked. Okay?"

"Yes," the girl answered.

"I'd like to go back to what we were doing," he added. "But we'll have to wait until later. How long have you been in Club Aldaris?"

"Three months," Tanya said. "Why?"

"Have you spent much time in the club?" Mikhail asked, pulling out some sheets of paper.

"Yes," she replied. "All the girls spend time working in club. Why?"

"Because I need to ask you some questions about it," Mikhail said, unrolling the sheets and pointing to a spot on the floorplan. "What is this room used for?"

"There, you see?" Katya asked when she came back in the room.

Tom was sitting on the bed, looking at Natalya, who was crouched in the corner, rocking.

"Is she okay?" Tom asked, nervously. "She came out of the shower and seemed just fine. Then she screamed and she's been over there ever since."

"Bad man," Natalya was muttering, appearing to draw on her leg with her finger. "Bad man's going to come . . ."

"Some girls, they don't do well here," Katya said, carefully. "I talk to her, I get her calm down. She still be very good to you."

"I like her," Tom said, his face twisted. "She seems so . . . fragile. So do you, but not like her. I wish I could take both of you away from here."

"It cannot happen," Katya said, sighing and approaching the rocking girl. "Natalya?"

"Bad man is coming," the girl was singing to herself. "Coming back for you . . ."

"Natalya!" Katya said, sharply. "There's no bad man, here. Is he the bad man?" she added, darting a glance at "Tom."

"No, not here," Natalya said, still drawing on her leg.

"Natalya, go suck on Tom," Katya ordered.

The girl quickly scurried across the bed and began opening the doctor's fly.

"She was worried she hadn't been good enough for you," Katya said, letting out a sigh of relief that sounded very real because it was. "That was all. She let it worry her too much. If you don't do well enough for the pimps, well, they beat you and other things."

"Oh," Tom said, shaking his head as the hooker began fellating him. "I don't think I can . . . you know, right now."

"Maybe we get some schoolgirl outfits?" Katya asked. "Some makeup? Am told can look very much like Britney Spears. . . . You want rape Britney?"

# ★ Chapter Thirty-Eight ★

"Kildar," Anastasia said, looking in the door. "Father Kulcyanov wishes to see you."

"Send him in," Mike said, trying not to sigh and clearing the screen on his computer. The operation had turned out to be almost nightmarishly complex and making sure all the strands were in place had become a day-by-day struggle. The last thing he needed was to deal with the often long-winded Father Kulcyanov.

It had ended up making more sense to move in stages. The freighter didn't need much in the way of modification for the mission so, since the one they'd hired had been in the western Med when the deal was made, it had headed directly for Albanian waters.

The helicopter company, Russkiya Heavy Lift, had often operated in and around Macedonia and Albania, supplying implementation forces and humanitarian operations. With a few words in the right ears, getting permission for the helicopters to pick up an "oil rig relief team" hadn't been hard.

The teams were, thus, to be flown into Hellenica airport, board buses and drive to the Greek coast, then be picked up by the choppers and flown out to the freighter.

The biggest hassle had been getting the equipment to them. This had required the services of another freighter and a mid-ocean transfer managed by Chief Adams.

Pulling it all together had been a constant struggle with logistics while maintaining security. Vanner had ended up going to Spain to arrange the freighter, Chief Adams had put more pages into his passport flying to Turkey and Greece to ensure the arms made it through, and even Nielson had had to fly to Germany for an updated intel brief. Carlson-Smith had smoothed the way in Greece and found a rather respectable looking fellow who knew an enormous amount about the safe industry. He had turned out to be unwilling to actually put his life in jeopardy, but he had determined the actual safe that the Albanians had installed, its location, and carefully drilled some of the Keldara women in the opening method.

And if it turned out to be the wrong safe, Mike was planning on using the chief's method and the hell with the contents.

Mike admitted that without the chief and Nielson, not to mention Carlson-Smith, he would have been lost. Hell, even Daria had been doing dog work keeping up with all the paperwork. She had a better ground-level feel for what was where at any time than the rest of them.

This level of organization and support was so far beyond his previous training he half the time had no clue what people were talking about in the, frequent, meetings. But he doggedly asked questions until he understood, came up with a series of checkpoints and times for people to make and then ensured they did. And Daria kept up with those without batting an eye.

Russell had turned out to be a keeper. The big former Ranger had apparently soaked up everything the U.S. Army had to tell about airmobile operations and had drilled the Keldara mercilessly. In less than a week he had every one of the teams fully trained on everything from fast-rope work to sling-lift. They wouldn't need the latter as far as Mike could tell, but it was nice that they were trained.

If things slowed down for a while he might just get a plane and start training them on parachute work. What the hell.

"Kildar, it is good to see you," Father Kulcyanov said, entering the office at a dignified pace.

"And you, Father Kulcyanov," Mike said, pulling a chair around to the coffee table in the office. "How are the crops?"

"They are well, Kildar," the elder replied as Anastasia directed one of the harem girls to lay out tea. "It is difficult with the young men all engaged in preparing for the mission, but we persevere. This mission is important to the Keldara and to you and we are your followers."

"And the Family is well?" Mike asked picking up one of the teacups and taking a sip.

"The Family is well," Father Kulcyanov said, sipping at the tea and nodding. "Well. But to support you and yours through the generations, we must increase, Kildar."

"I hope that all is well with the women?" Mike asked, confused.

"All is well," Father Kulcyanov said, nodding sagely.

"Women are a trial, but we must have them to support the home, yes?" He nodded at the girl who was still standing by in case the Kildar needed anything.

"And support the militia," Mike pointed out. "The girls on the mission were invaluable. The Keldara are amazing people."

"But to have more Keldara," Father Kulcyanov said, "we must have marriages, Kildar."

"Oh," Mike said, shaking his head. "This is the Kardane thing, isn't it? Thank you, Lida, that will be all," Mike added, gesturing with his chin for the girl to leave the room.

"The wedding is in only four weeks, Kildar," Father Kulcyanov said, regally. "You will be gone for two of those, at least . . ."

"And it's not a good idea to have the ceremony on the day before the wedding, huh?" Mike said. "Father, we are very busy—"

"We have secured the horses you requested," Father Kulcyanov said, ignoring the argument. "All is prepared, Kildar. When can you perform the Rite of Kardane?"

"Given what we're working with, here, the whole ritual makes me uncomfortable," Mike admitted. "But I think I can still squeeze it in. Hang on."

He walked to the phone and hit the speakerphone.

"Nielson?"

"Here, Kildar," the colonel said. "I'm up to my eyeballs, though . . ."

"When is a good day to close down the caravanserai for a whole night?" Mike asked. "Don't say 'never.'"

"After the mission?" Nielson asked. "I mean, we move in four days!"

"Not good enough," Mike said. "Give me a day. One night."

"Jesus, Mike," Nielson said but Mike could hear keys tapping. "Tomorrow looks best. I'll have to shift my flag down to the Keldara, though."

"Block out three hours in the evening for all the Keldara," Mike said. "And everybody in the caravanserai gets locked down. If they have to come and go, they use the back door."

"Will do," Nielson said. "What's this about?"

"It's a Keldara thing," Mike said. "I'll get back to you." He turned back to Father Kulcyanov and shrugged. "Tomorrow night?"

"Very well, Kildar," the elder said. "We will be prepared."

"And while I enjoy talking to you," Mike said, holding out his hand, "I am also up to my eyeballs in work. And now I must finish it faster."

"I will go and ensure that Lydia is prepared," Father Kulcyanov said, nodding.

"I'm more worried about Oleg," Mike said after the door was closed.

"Mr. Bezhmel?"

"Yes," the security specialist said, sitting down at the booth. He'd gotten a call from someone he occasionally did business with who had set up the meet in the Moscow hotel bar. No names as usual, which was just the way that the business worked. "You have the need of special security arrangements?"

"I have information that you need," the man, an American, said in Russian. Then he smiled. "And a special security need. You've been investigating the attacks on Rozaje and the Club Dracul?"

"Perhaps," Bezhmel said, shrugging.

"It is known that you work with the Dejti clan," the man replied, smiling still. "So I'll take that as a yes. You might be interested to know that the next target is Lunari, probably the Club Aldaris. Their mission is to extract this girl," the man added, sliding a picture across the table. "Her name is Natalya. And possibly to capture the DVDs from the Rozaje villa. This wouldn't be good, would it?"

"No," Bezhmel said, frowning. "Why are you telling me this?"

"Because I'm your friend," the man replied, then laughed quietly and shook his head. "God, I crack myself up. No, the reason that I'm telling you is that I need this girl killed before they get their hands on her. And this man . . ." he added, sliding another picture across the table along with a thick envelope. "No idea what name he'll be using but he'll be near Natalya. There is thirty thousand euros in there. If you kill both, there is another sixty thousand that will be forwarded to you. If you kill only one, that is your pay. If you kill neither . . . I'll expect a full refund. There are other security specialists in the world."

# ★ Chapter Thirty-Nine ★

Mike looked in the mirror and grimaced.

"I'm not sure about this," he said, shooting his lace cuffs nervously.

Mike still wasn't sure about the whole "Kardane" thing. For one thing, he had a *very* hard time wrapping his head around Oleg being comfortable with it. But since he'd agreed, he decided that it needed to be *right*.

Part of that was setting the mood. He could, of course, simply pick up Lydia in the Expedition, drive up to the caravanserai, have a good old time and then dump her back at her house. That, however, had far too "casual" a feel for what was an intensely important event. One point that Adams, of all people, had brought up was that the Rite of Kardane was a form of bonding between the Kildar and the Keldara; the Keldara, effectively, provided a maiden sacrifice and the Kildar, presumably, responded by being more closely bonded to the Keldara.

The Rite also provided genetic input. Anastasia had done some digging and found old records of the Kildars dating back to the Middle Ages. All of them had been "foreign" soldiers-of-fortune of one race or another, Kurd,

Greek, German, French and even British. All of them had attained the position by being superior fighters and commanders. So if Nature had anything to do with culture, the "genetic input" of the Kildars, through the Rite of Kardane, had added to the warrior component of the Keldara, bit by bit over the years.

But he still wasn't sure about his outfit.

"I am," Anastasia replied, smiling. "If you're going to do something, do it right . . ."

". . . Or don't do it at all," Mike said, sighing.

According to the Keldara elders, the Rite of Kardane hadn't been practiced since the time of the Tzars. And the last "true" Kildar had been a German mercenary who had started off as an advisor to the Tzarist Army and eventually worked his way into the nobility and been deeded with the Keldara.

Anastasia, traditionalist to the core, had pointed out that it would only be fitting to dress in a traditional, and formal, manner for the occasion. And she, again, had done the research.

Which was why Mike was dressed in a dark-green, short-waisted velvet coat and a white silk ruffled shirt with matching, very tight, dark-green trousers. The knee-high riding boots completed the ensemble.

"I feel like I ought to have a cap and ball pistol tucked in at my waist," Mike said, fiddling with the the lace at his collar. "You set?"

"Very much so," Anastasia replied, straightening out the lace. "By the time you get back, I'll have gotten dressed and be gone. Speaking of which, it's just about sunset."

"Right," Mike replied, pulling his jacket down to smooth out the wrinkles.

"Time to go."

Petro held open the front door of the caravanserai as Mike strode through. Mike, despite trying to remain serious about what was, after all, a very serious event, could not help but play the bars from "Pomp and Circumstance" in his head as he strode down the stairs.

Uncle Latif was holding the gelding by the mounting stand. Genadi had done a good job there. The gelding was an Orlov-Rostopchin "Russian Riding Horse," a breed dating back to 1845 and the premier riding horse of the Tzarist court. Flat black and about seventeen hands high, the beautifully proportioned gelding was trained for both dressage and "pleasure riding." According to Genadi, who it turned out had practiced in dressage at the university, he was both an easy ride and quite biddable with "a very smooth gait." The black leather saddle, with silver accoutrements, was almost invisible on the glossy horse's back.

Mike, however, looked at the horse in trepidation. He hadn't ridden in years. He'd *intended* to get some refreshers in riding before he did this, but the current mission had taken up virtually all of his time.

There was a smaller mare behind the gelding, a lead line running from her halter to the saddle of the gelding. The mare was a less common Braz Curly, a Russian warmblood that was a descendent of cavalry horses. "Gray" in horse terms, the mare was a beautiful, almost perfect, white, and her curly mane had been plaited with red ribbons. Despite being a warhorse descendent, the fourteen-hand mare was so placid as to appear drugged.

The toughest part of the whole operation had turned out to be finding the sidesaddle. Two had eventually been ordered from a company in Germany, a severely plain "training" saddle for Lydia and a much more ornate one for the night of the ceremony.

Mike looked the two horses over for a moment and then, realizing he was stalling, stepped up on the mounting stone, stuck his boot into stirrup, which was being held by Petro, and mounted.

The saddle didn't budge. Then again, neither did the horse. No sidling, no shifting. It was like mounting a warm, furry, rock.

Uncle Latif wordlessly handed him the reins and then stood back.

"Good night, Kildar," the Keldara said, bowing.

"Good night, Latif," Mike replied, settling in the seat. One thing that he did recall was that a horse wanted to know that the rider knew what he was doing. He took the reins in his left hand, gripped between two fingers and his thumb and slowly released pressure, giving a grip of his knees and a slight "click" with his tongue.

The gelding automatically started walking, the mare following placidly, and Mike, just to be sure, walked them around the courtyard as the two Keldara went back into the caravanserai. He'd been clear that he did *not* want anyone seeing him trying out the horse.

The velvet pants had a patch of suede on the butt and crotch and the first thing he noticed was that the patch made for a very firm seat. He'd always ridden in jeans before, which tended to slide a bit, and he found this a much more reassuring ride. The horse was also responsive but not overly so. One circuit around the courtyard was enough to give him the surety to head down the road toward the Family's enclave.

Actually, he sort of liked the outfit. Deep in Mike's scarred soul there was a peacock he vigorously suppressed; his normal mode of dress was jeans or shorts, depending on weather, and a T-shirt. For one thing, he really didn't feel he had the panache to carry off nice clothes. But when he had the chance to show off, he liked to. Hell, he even liked dress whites, which was something of a heresy among SEALs. He was pretty sure that didn't make him gay; he'd never had any interest in guys. But he was also sure that it wasn't something he was going to admit to Adams.

There was no choice but to walk down the switchbacks; a canter would have been impossible at the corners and a trot was, for the time being, out of the question. Besides, it was simply safer for the horses to walk down a slope. So, despite the fact that he was running behind schedule he carefully walked down to the road and then, as he reached the relative flats, broke into a trot, then a canter.

The gelding had an excellent canter, long, smooth and fast. However, looking back, he noticed that the mare was up at a gallop. Next time he needed better matched horses. Lydia had been riding, though. He'd have to ask her if she was comfortable with a gallop on the way back.

As he pulled to a halt by the Mahona compound, the door was opened by Mother Mahona, the senior lady of the Family. Mike drew a little comfort from the fact that she had a sober but not unhappy expression on her face.

One of the younger Keldara females was outside, waiting, and she took Mike's reins as the Kildar dismounted. Mike had insisted that the minimum necessary males be included in the ceremony. Mike straightened his jacket again and then marched over to the door, pausing at the entrance.

"I request the privilege of entering the home of the Mahona," Mike said, pausing.

"This roof is yours, Kildar," Father Mahona replied from within. "These walls are yours. This home is yours to enter."

Mike nodded, secretly sighing in relief; everybody was remembering their lines.

Mike walked in and looked around. The main room of the Keldara houses was usually packed with people; there was a bit of housing shortage among the Keldara that he kept meaning to rectify. However, at the moment the only persons present were Mother and Father Mahona, Father Jusev, the Orthodox priest from town, and Lydia.

The latter was wearing a white silk dress edged in seed pearls that looked not at all like most wedding dresses. It was cut down the front to reveal a rather startling amount of cleavage, stopped well above the knees and was form-hugging all over. She also was wearing a pair of white high heels. Normally, riding in high heels was damned near impossible, but with a sidesaddle it was much simpler. The outfit was, by Keldara standards, scandalous. One of the reasons that nobody else was present.

The girl was looking nervous but had the presence not to tug at the outfit as she awaited her lines.

"I am come to take my rights as the Kildar," Mike said, sternly, looking Father Mahona in the eye.

"The right of the Kildar is acknowleged by the Keldara and the Family Mahona," the elder replied, nodding. "The Kildar is reminded of his duty to the future family."

"I acknowledge my duty," Mike said, turning to Father Jusev, the priest. "I have come to take my rights as the Kildar."

"The right of the Kildar is acknowledged by the church," the priest said nervously. The fact was that the Orthodox church acknowledged no such thing. But Mike, despite the fact that he never attended, was the local parish's single largest contributor. Father Jusev was also aware that the Keldara weren't exactly Christian. Between the two facts, he wasn't about to stand in the way of the Rite of Kardane. "The Kildar is reminded of his duty of teaching," the priest added, swallowing nervously.

"I acknowledge my duty," Mike said, turning to Mother Mahona. "I come to take my rights as Kildar." His tone in this case was much less stern, intentionally.

"The right of the Kildar is acknowledged by the women of the Keldara," Mother Mahona said, smiling slightly. She was the only one who apparently found the ceremony humorous. "The Kildar is reminded of his duty of gentleness."

"I acknowledge my duty," Mike said, gently, then turned to Lydia, dropping to one knee and bowing his head. "My lady, I am come to crave a boon of you, one night of gentleness. May I have my time as is my right?"

"You may, Kildar," Lydia replied, nervously. "May you remember your duties in all things."

"I shall," Mike said, standing up and taking her hand. "I shall return with this daughter of the Keldara when the sun rises," he said, looking at the three. "I shall render my duty as tradition fits and no shame is had in this Rite."

"No shame, only duty," Father Mahona said.

"No shame, only duty," the priest intoned.

"No shame," Mother Mahona said, winking, "only pleasure."

Now *that* was off the script.

Lydia blushed scarlet but followed Mike out of the room.

The young Keldara girl was still holding the horses when Mike came out. She had unclipped the lead line and held both sets of reins. Mike first helped Lydia into the sidesaddle, not that she needed much help, then mounted and took the reins.

"Have fun," the girl said to Lydia, giggling, then ran around the side of the house.

Mike kept it down to a light canter up to the flats, then Lydia kicked her horse into a gallop and hit the first switchback at a run.

The gelding snorted and took off after the mare and Mike, working hard to keep his seat, gave the horse his head. However, when he drew up behind Lydia's mare, he reined back slightly, letting the mare set the pace.

After the first turn, which they took faster than Mike liked, the mare began to struggle and Lydia let her slow to a trot then a walk.

"That was fun," Lydia said, smiling over at him.

"Had you ridden before you started training?" Mike asked.

"Just some bareback on the plow horses," Lydia said, shrugging. "Not like this," she added, gesturing at the sidesaddle.

"Well, you've got a good seat," Mike said, smiling. "A better one than I do, to tell the truth."

"But you've got the better horse," Lydia said, grinning back.

Two of the girls from the harem were waiting when they reached the courtyard, both in "traditional" harem dress, including veils. They silently took the reins as first Mike, then Lydia, with Mike's hand in assistance, dismounted. Then they just as silently led the horses around to the stables.

"Are you okay?" Mike asked as they stood in front of the doors of the caravanserai.

"Yes," Lydia said distantly then turned to look at him. "I will admit that I am even eager." But her eyes had a shuttered look.

"But?" Mike asked.

"I worry about Oleg," Lydia admitted, turning back to the open doors. "Not for the long term, but for tonight."

"So did I," Mike said, taking her arm and stepping towards the door.

"Did?" Lydia asked.

"Oleg is . . . taken care of."

"Have another beer, Oleg," Sawn said, shaking his head. "And tell me what's been happening while we were gone."

"Nothing much," Oleg said, taking the mug from the other team leader and looking at it. "Training and more training."

"We'll need it soon enough," Padrek said, spitting through his teeth into the fire. "I've heard McKenzie muttering about this mission."

The team leaders were gathered around their own bonfire, taking a night off from training. Ostensibly it was a break so the teams didn't get too worn down before the mission. But everybody knew what the real point was; get Oleg good and drunk. The young man was superficially prepared for temporarily losing "his" girl to the Kildar, but it had to hurt.

"Hairy," Vil said, nodding. "But we'll get it done."

"To getting it done," Sawn said, raising his mug. "Hammer it, Oleg."

"I'm fine," Oleg said, sighing. "Just fine."

"You won't be if you br—" Vil started to say as there was a jingle of bells from the darkness beyond the fire.

All six team leaders looked towards the sound and then their eyes widened.

The woman, whoever she was, was wearing a blue harem girl's dress, transparent pantaloons, bikini panties and a blue midriff top. Lining every hem were small bells and more were on her fingers and toes.

The apparition moved sinuously into the firelight until she was sure she had the full attention of the group and then began to dance.

Somewhere in the darkness, a drum was being played, a beat that matched the human heart, as the woman sinuously glided in front of the fire until she was opposite Oleg. Spinning, bending and writhing, she appeared to dance only for him to the beat of the drum, until it abruptly stopped.

"The Kildar feared that you would be lonely this night," the woman said, huskily. "He has sent me for your pleasure and to teach you the arts of pleasuring a woman. I am for you this night, a proxy for your bride to be. Do you approve?" she asked, chuckling and kneeling down before him gracefully.

Sawn looked at his friend, who was sitting on the log with his mouth open.

"I think he does," Sawn said, grinning. "But you might have to give him a hand."

"Then I will," Anastasia said, taking Oleg's hand and pulling him to his feet. "Gentlemen, I will return him in the morning."

"Alive?" Vil asked.

The chuckles followed the pair back into the darkness.

Mike led Lydia upstairs to his private suite of rooms. As they climbed the stairs he could tell she was getting more and more nervous and he noted, with almost a chuckle, her surprise and shock when she was led to the kitchen.

"What, I'm supposed to cook, too?" Lydia asked, when she saw the food laid out on the counters and the pan on the stove.

"Not at all," Mike said, seating her on a bar stool where she could watch the proceedings. There were two places already set at the bar along with an unlit candle and flowers. He pulled a champagne bottle, one of three, out of a large bucket filled with ice and water and uncorked it. "You get to watch." He poured two glasses of the champagne and handed one to her. "Cheers."

"You can cook?" Lydia asked, surprised. "I don't mean . . ."

"Keldara men can't cook very much," Mike admitted, going over to the stove and taking down an apron. "But I learned to a long time ago. Lydia, we both know what this night is all about. But . . . hmm . . ." He took a sip of the champagne, tied on the apron and then poured some olive oil into the pan, working it around and then turning on the heat.

"In the U.S., we have a custom called 'dating,'" Mike continued, tossing precoated slivers of beef into the saucier pan. The sides were rounded and hammered so he could use it as a wok. "It's also a custom in about all big cities. Now, you're a country gal. The only people you know are the people of the Keldara and a few townspeople. But in the cities, girls don't know the men around them, generally, from birth. And the guys don't know the girls. So they have to meet *somehow*."

"I guess," Lydia said, crossing her legs and taking a sip of the champagne, then looking at the glass. "What is this?"

"Champagne," Mike said, not looking at her as he smiled. "Sparkling wine."

"It's good," Lydia said, taking another sip.

"Have more," Mike replied. "Anyway, where I come from, a guy meets a girl, however, and generally asks her out on a date to test the waters. They have dinner, maybe see a show and then, if the chemistry is right, maybe more. The bottomline from a guy's point-of-view is the 'maybe more' . . ."

"So I'd heard," Lydia said pointedly.

Mike turned to look at her and grinned.

"Different strokes," Mike said shrugging then getting back to cooking. "In the States, reasonably casual sex isn't that big of a deal. Different cultures and, trust me, I don't treat this evening casually. But the point is, when I was dating I was interested in getting the young lady interested enough to *really* test the waters."

"Were they?" Lydia asked, interested. "This wine is good, by the way. Dry."

"Makes you want to drink more," Mike said, looking over his shoulder again. "Go ahead. With the way that you Keldara drink, you're going to have a high tolerance. Anyway, to answer your question, a few. Okay, more than a few. But being a *good* date is the important point. There's a saying in the States: 'The way to a man's heart is through his stomach.'"

"We say something similar," Lydia said, giggling. "'Food makes the softer bed.'"

"Well, what I found out," Mike continued, slooshing some wine into the vegetable mix and setting a cover on it, "is that it's *really* the way to a woman's heart. Most men can't do much more than grill. So, instead of inviting a young lady out to an expensive restaurant, where you'd then have several other steps to getting to the point, I'd invite her to *my* place for dinner."

"I'd have said 'take me to the restaurant,'" Lydia said, then giggled again.

"Ah, but that's because you're a good girl," Mike said, looking at her and grinning. "I was very careful to only date nice girls. Do you know the difference between a good girl and a nice girl?"

"No?" Lydia said, pouring her third glass of champagne. Part of the requirements that Mike had laid down was, since there would be dinner involved, she hadn't eaten since lunch. The champagne also had more of a kick than she realized. He didn't want her to get drunk, but alcohol would tend to reduce her tension and that was a good thing.

"A good girl goes to a party, goes home and goes to bed," Mike said, turning back to the stove. "A nice girl goes to a party, goes to bed and goes home."

"That's terrible," Lydia said, laughing.

"Anyway, I'd invite a nice girl over," Mike said, stirring the vegetables, then adding some oyster sauce. The latter had turned out to be nearly impossible to obtain and he'd resorted to making it from scratch. However, he'd tried the recipe out in advance and the homemade worked fine. "Then I'd cook for her and wine and dine her, maybe watch a movie on video, and when it came time to close the deal, voila! There we were already in my apartment. No 'your place or mine,' no 'would you care for a cup of coffee.'"

"Sneaky," Lydia said.

"If you ain't cheatin', you ain't tryin'," Mike intoned.

"And if you get caught, you ain't a SEAL," Lydia finished, giggling. "So I should expect sneaky?"

"Up to you," Mike said, transferring the Chinese beef and vegetables from the pan into a serving dish. "But let's just have dinner, shall we?"

He'd already had rice prepared and he brought that out as well, setting it down at the bar. Then he shifted her over to her place, carefully holding her chair out and pushing it back in. The last step was to light the candle and turn out a couple of lights.

"This is interesting," Lydia said, looking at the food dubiously.

"I think you'll find it edible," Mike said.

Lydia picked out a bit of meat to start and then, with a look of surprise, took more.

As they ate they chatted about conditions among the Keldara and the condition of the farm. Every time that they got near touchy subjects, Mike carefully steered them away. He didn't want to talk about the previous mission, or upcoming ones, or where he was going with the Keldara. Light and easy was the tone of the evening. And he made sure he kept her champagne glass topped up.

As for sneaky, she'd missed the first "cheat." Mike had been careful to keep the wineglasses separated by at least an arm's-length. That was because her glass was at least twenty-five percent larger than his. Even if he matched her glass for glass, she was getting far more wine. And it was showing. The alcohol, and food, was making her less nervous as time went by.

"This is fun," Lydia said, sighing and setting down her fork. She'd eaten lightly, which was good. "There should be more things in life like this. But there is always too much work."

"That will get better," Mike said, wiping his mouth with his napkin. "You'd be surprised how much better. Dessert?"

Lydia had also never been exposed to chocolate cake. Certainly not the deep, rich chocolate fudge cake Mike brought out.

"Better to eat this by the fire," he said, grinning. "Bring your glass; there's more champagne out there."

He led the way to the parlor area, where a fire had been laid, and set the plates and his glass down, then flopped on the couch. The centerpiece of the coffee table was a heaping bowl of strawberries.

"This is nice, too," Lydia said, grinning happily and sitting down next to him. "I was thinking that you'd just . . . you know . . ."

"Nah," Mike said. "The idea here is to have fun. You can't have fun if you're worried sick about what's going to happen. And you shouldn't be. It's important, don't get me wrong. But it's also something natural and very fun. If it's done right, and I've rarely had complaints."

"I talked with Mother Savina about . . . it," Lydia said, nervously, her grin fading. "And Anastasia. I'm . . . it seems . . ."

"There is no way to describe it," Mike said, getting a bite of cake on his fork and holding it out to her. "Try the cake."

"That's good," Lydia said, her eyes wide.

"Alas, this I didn't do," Mike said, picking up a strawberry and offering it to her. "I don't bake well."

"You do other things well," Lydia said, taking a delicate bite of the strawberry while looking into his eyes.

"So do you," Mike said, for the first time in the evening actually getting horny. He'd been working the situation so hard *he* had forgotten to have fun.

She offered him a strawberry and he bit into it carefully, then got in a quick lick on her fingers that elicited another giggle.

They traded strawberries like that for a little longer and then Lydia, unexpectedly, took one in her teeth and leaned forward.

Mike took the bait, biting off his end of the strawberry and then following up with a kiss, flickering his tongue against her lips. Whether Lydia had ever had sex or not, it was clear that she had been, as his mother used to put it, "spooning." She had no problem with kissing whatsoever.

However, when Mike's hand crept up her leg, she tensed for a moment, then went back to the kiss. He slid his hand up the back of her leg, checking with his other hand on her arm. Goosebumps were always an indicator that a girl was getting turned on by caresses and she had plenty.

"Kildar," the girl said, huskily, drawing away and wiping at her lips. "I want . . . I think . . ."

"Don't think," Mike said, smiling. He took her hand and had her stand up. "But, yes, time to progress. Lydia, take off your dress."

The girl stood there for a moment and then, closing her eyes, lifted the dress up and over her head. It had a built-in bra so all she was wearing once she'd doffed it was her heels, panties, a garter belt and stockings.

"You are very beautiful," Mike said, taking a pillow off the couch and tossing it on the floor. "So, we progress. But before we get to other things, there is one thing that *I* require."

He stood up and cupped her breast, eliciting a shiver. She still had her eyes closed which made him almost chuckle.

"What do you . . . need?" Lydia asked, opening her eyes.

"There is a very old saying," Mike replied, pressing down on her shoulders so she knelt on the pillow. "'Stand before your god, bow before your king and kneel before your man.'"

"I was told about this," Lydia said, looking up at him. "But I have never . . ."

"I know," Mike said, unzipping his pants. "Later I will show you other things. But this I require. Later, I'll tell you why."

"Very well," Lydia said, softly, looking down. "I . . . would like to."

"And you will take it all in your mouth," Mike continued. He wasn't right up on her, but back a bit. "I take it you haven't seen a man undressed."

"No," Lydia said, uncertainly. "They *told* me about it."

"Your turn," Mike said, stepping forward.

Lydia slowly reached for his pants and then just as slowly pulled them down, an act that caused Mike to almost lose it. He stayed calm, though, while she considered . . . him.

Lydia cautiously held out one hand and touched him, tilting her head to the side to consider.

"It is bigger than I thought," Lydia said, nervously.

"And, frankly, Oleg is bigger than I am," Mike said. "Anastasia discussed what to do?"

"Yes," Lydia said, biting her lip and wrapping her thumb and forefinger around the base of his dick. Then she shifted forward on the pillow and took him in her mouth.

She had a bit of trouble getting the rhythm of hand and mouth together at first, but she quickly caught on.

Mike took her hair in his hand and sped her up. Again she got out of rhythm but soon got the feel for it, speeding up quite a bit.

Mike knew, though, that her neck muscles wouldn't hold out for long. However, being fellated by a delicious blonde virgin on her knees was more than enough for him. He quickly came into her mouth.

She stopped and gagged at that but he grabbed her hair and held her in place, pumping in and out to get the last drop.

"Catch it in your mouth and swallow," Mike said, gruffly.

"Yes, Kildar," Lydia said, after she'd swallowed.

"And now," Mike said, picking up her champagne glass and pulling his pants back up, "have a drink of champagne. It helps with the taste."

"It . . . wasn't bad," Lydia said, her brow wrinkling. She still swilled the champagne around.

"Orange juice," Mike said, picking up his own glass and having a sip. "It does something to the chemistry." He knelt down and kissed her. "Thank you."

"You're welcome," Lydia said, frowning.

"Now for the rest," Mike said, lifing her up to her feet and then into his arms. "You'll be fine," he added at the look on her face.

"I know I will be," Lydia said, still nervous.

"Keep ahold of that glass," Mike added, chuckling.

"I will," Lydia replied, smiling and then finishing off the champagne in it.

He carried her into the bedroom and laid her on the bed, sitting down next to her and picking a strawberry from the bowl by the bed.

"Strawberry?" Mike asked, grinning.

They replayed the strawberry game until she was smiling again. During it, Mike had managed to get rid of his boots, pants and shirt, sometimes with help.

Finally they were both more or less naked. Lydia still had her panties and shoes on but Mike was starkers. Lydia was starting to show some signs of nervousness, among other things trying to cover her lovely breasts, so Mike decided to take a detour.

"Roll over," he said, giving her a slap on the side and a smile.

"Why?" Lydia asked nervously.

"You'll like it, trust me," Mike said, more or less pushing her over.

When he had her on her stomach he opened up a jar and smoothed some of the massage cream onto her back. The cream was a mixture of almond cream with a bit of sesame oil, a trick that a former girlfriend who was a masseuse had taught him. She'd also taught him the proper way to give a massage so he started working Lydia's muscles with strong strokes from his thumbs, rolling them along the grain of the muscle in the girl's back.

"That feels good," Lydia said, sighing.

"Better if we had a massage table," Mike said, continuing to massage the girl's back and neck, then working downwards.

The massage, unfortunately, was counteracting the earlier blowjob. The point of that, besides Mike just *enjoying* it, was to let him blow off some steam. But Lydia had a truly gorgeous butt, rounded and firm, and while Mike wasn't planning on going for any back-door action, it was tempting as hell.

He massaged down her back and onto her ass, sliding her panties off in the process, then down the legs to her calves. Then he worked back up until he was up between her thighs and slid his fingers into her pussy. That elicited another surprised gasp, but she was also wet, which was a very good sign so Mike rolled her quickly over and pulled her head back by the hair.

He slid his tongue down the side of it to the juncture of her neck and shoulder, digging into that tender nerve point strongly and eliciting a moan. More goosebumps had built up on her arm, which was another good sign. The idea at this point was simply to keep her mind off of anything other than the moment. If she started to stiffen up it was because she was thinking about secondary concerns; what Oleg would think, what her family would think, the Keldara. He had to keep her mind centered on what was happening now to the exclusion of everything else. And that meant keeping up the stimulae so she *couldn't* think of anything else.

While he continued to stroke at her neck with his tongue, his right hand was busy, first playing with her nipples, which seemed particularly sensitive, then sliding down her side, eliciting a giggle at one point. Ticklishness was another good sign. It showed she had a degree of sexual nervousness that was on the good side. Girls who had virtually no tickle reaction were generally either asexual or just not into sex, period. That would make this evening rather trying. But Lydia had always had a natural sexiness that *had* to have some depth to it.

Finally his hand had crept back down to the bottom of

her stomach and he slid his fingers between her legs. They tightened for a moment as she half struggled to get away, then parted as his fingers did their magic. Some women got off on having their clit played with while others preferred penetration. From Lydia's reactions she was more of a penetration gal, so Mike slid his fingers in carefully, rubbing them along the clit as he did so.

He'd moved his mouth down to her breasts and found that the nipples were *definitely* an erogenous zone on Lydia. The combination of stroking and playing with her nipples had the girl writhing and panting.

The question at this point couldn't really be answered. Some women wouldn't orgasm without penetration while others rarely did *with* penetration. Without having experience with Lydia he wasn't sure which she would be. But the question was answered a moment later as the girl gasped and arched in a hard orgasm.

While she was still arching Mike quickly slid over and spread her, entering her quickly but as gently as he could. He could tell from the grimace on her face when the hymen was broken but he didn't relent, beginning to drive hard into her.

Lydia was clearly up for that, as her fingers dug into his ass and pulled him in, hard, as he stroked. Her eyes were closed and she was panting hard as he varied the rhythm, never letting her get bored with the action. She came again in less than a minute, then again almost immediately after with a scream of pain and pleasure.

The last orgasm was hard enough that Mike knew he had to stop for a second anyway. As he paused she opened her eyes and shook her head.

"I never knew . . ." the girl whispered.

"It's impossible to know," Mike said, kissing her on the forehead. "But I'm not done, yet." He paused for a moment and then grinned evilly. "I think that's enough of a rest."

"Oh . . . All Mother," Lydia whispered as he started again. "Oh . . . Gods . . ."

Lydia paused as she pulled the horse into the compound, biting her lip nervously. There weren't many choices. She could probably turn around and ride back to the Kildar and beg him to take her as one of his women. And there were . . . attractions to that. Attractions that worked hard against the fear of shame from the night before.

But, then, there was Oleg. They had been friends as children and even before they were betrothed she knew that she loved him. She would always love him, no matter what. And he had promised that he would not hold this night against her.

She finally loosened the reins on the gentle mare and let her continue into the yard, pulling to a stop not far from the front door. It was early for most people but she was surprised by the lack of activity around the house; it almost looked deserted.

However, as she stopped the front door opened and Mother Mahona came out with one of Lydia's female cousins, Nastya. Nastya held the reins as Mother helped Lydia down.

Mother Mahona's face was a picture. It was clear that she was glad that her daughter had returned, apparently unharmed. But that was combined with discomfort over the reason she had been out all night and curiosity at what the large leather satchel attached to her saddle contained. The case was tooled and formed leather with bright silverwork around the edges and it was heavy as Lydia undid the ties that held it to the saddle.

"Come in," Mother said, finally, leading the daughter into the main room of the house.

The first thing that Lydia noticed was that with the exception of Father Mahona, who was also trying to keep a welcoming demeanor, the only persons in the room were women. Most of them, furthermore, were Lydia's friends and peers, girls of her own age, a few married, most unmarried. She was secretly glad that Grand Mahn, Grandmother Mahona, wasn't in the room. The old fart had been going around for weeks with pursed lips and an angry look for the whole Rite, despite the fact that she was usually the first one to proclaim the superiority of anything old.

"Welcome home, Lydia," Father Mahona said, bowing to her slightly. "We welcome you once more to our fold."

The words had that suspiciously formal wording that sounded like the Kildar had written them. And made Father Mahona rehearse.

"I'm glad to be home," she said nervously, looking around at the group.

"Oh, bother with this!" Nastya finally snapped. "I want to know what is in the package! What is it?"

"I don't know, honestly," Lydia said, setting the suspiciously heavy leather case down on the kitchen table. "The Kildar told me not to open it until I got home. And he said we have to send the horse back, but the case is mine to keep."

"So what's in it?" Nastya asked impatiently. "Open it."

"Don't rush her," Mother Mahona snapped, but she was clearly curious as well.

Lydia broke the wax seal on the case, then opened it. Within, there were three more packages, one a blue silken wrap, one a soft suede purse that clinked and the last another silken package, tied with a silken cord, that was more or less rectangular.

Lydia opened the leather purse, first, dumping it out on the table.

What spilled from it was a waterfall of silver and gold coins that made everyone's eyes go wide. There was more money on the table than the entire Keldara made in a year.

"What's in the rest?" Nastya asked in a choked voice.

The rectangular package turned out to be cash, Georgian rubles tied around a thick stack of American hundred dollar bills. Lydia didn't want to think about how many dollars there were there, and dollars were much more stable than rubles, but the rubles had been fanned out so that it was clear there were five one hundred ruble notes. She snorted when she saw that. That was her official "price."

Lydia quickly undid the red ties from the blue silken roll and opened it. It turned out to be a jewelry wrap, containing a pearl necklace along with matching earrings and a bracelet. Contained within was a small note saying only "For your wedding."

"Oh, All Father," Nastya whispered. "I *so* want to be the Kardane Bride! Can we start making the arrangements now?!"

# ★ Chapter Forty ★

Mike clambered up the floating platform and onto the deck of the freighter, looking around cautiously. The sky was overcast but according to the weather reports it didn't presage bad weather.

Mike had ended up having to fly to Italy to clear up some diplomatic issues related to the photo that Carlson-Smith had carried. The very polite Italian intel chief they'd ended up doing most of the talking with was interested in what else might be in the trove. When told, politely, to fuck off, he'd pointed out that they needed the Italian acquiescence if they wanted to have the op go off. Otherwise, alas, an Italian coast guard cutter might just happen to be in the area.

So Mike had simply started listing some of the known quantities, avoiding names or other descriptions but listing the general levels associated with them. At which point the Italian government had, quietly, shit its pants.

Mike ended up in a five minute, very friendly, conversation with the prime minister, who had, as it turned out, had a rather longer conversation with the President. After which all the problems miraculously disappeared.

However, it had made him miss the choppers. Which was why he'd gone down to the docks near Brundisi and bought an offshore yacht. It had been a long time since he'd been on one of the larger and more powerful versions of a cigarette boat and he'd missed the feel of raw power. With nothing to do but get to the freighter in time it was the best time he'd had in months, including the sex.

But that pleasant idyll was over and as he stepped onto the deck he felt the mantle of command descend on his shoulders like a heavy cloak. Very heavy. Lead filled. Keldara were going to die on this op. He had to wonder if the damned thing was really worth it.

"Where we at?" Mike asked as the chief, followed by Daria, strode over.

"Troops are loading," Adams replied, waving at the groups of Keldara lined up to board the choppers. "All the secondary gear is onboard. The teams are dialed in. All we were really waiting for is you."

"I told you I'd be on time," Mike said as Daria waved two Keldara forward with his gear.

He stripped right on the cold deck, sitting on a coiled cable to pull on his pants. As he did he mused that this was a long way from his evening with Lydia. Who was, as a matter of fact, already in Lunari at this very moment, much closer to harm's way than he was. Not a good thought, all things considered.

"Vanner and the intel group is in place," Adams continued. "And the recon of the rally point is complete. So far it looks clear."

"We getting any take from Katya?" Mike asked.

"Lots," Adams grunted. "From what Vanner said her reception was not fun."

"As long as she lives long enough to give us a layout and location of the target, that's all that counts," Mike said.

"Things have since gotten better," Adams said. "She has a sugar daddy that's keeping her from getting bounced around too much and she's located the primary. She and the primary are keeping the sugar daddy happy, thereby securing the primary and getting a look at the club. She hasn't gotten much intel on layout of the club, but Vanner also picked up another source. That source has been a gold mine."

"Is he sure about the source?" Mike asked.

"What Katya has been able to confirm has all played out," Adams said. "The source looks genuine. Mikhail, the security team leader, has hooked up with one of the same pimp's hookers. She's seen more of the club than Katya and has filled in all the little blanks. We even know where the computer room is."

"Excellent," Mike said, standing up. One of the Keldara lifted his ammo harness into place and another handed him his SPR. "I'd say we're go."

"Agreed," Adams said.

"Gimme the maps and let's get this show on the road."

Katya listened to the music and tried not to ask what time it was.

Since the second day with her sugar daddy, they had mostly stayed at the club; the American neurosurgeon seemed to enjoy the atmosphere. Club Aldaris was like most such facilities in the world. There was a ground floor bar where the customers hung out and were propositioned by girls wandering the floor. In the center was the bar itself and on the back wall were three dance stages where the girls showed off their stuff.

Reception had been spotty all along. The combination of the thick ferroconcrete walls and the background noise had interfered with audio, and the video had been bad as well. So she also couldn't ask Vanner what the time was. It was time and past time to get out of the club and get ready to extract. But "Tom" was in the back with another girl.

She looked up as a man walked over to the table and looked them both over. He paid particular attention to Natalya, though, who was drawing on the table using condensation from the glasses.

"Come on, girl," the man said, reaching down and pulling at Natalya's arm. "I'm in need of some fun."

"Sir," Katya said, getting up and holding up her hand. "We are with another man. You should ask for someone else."

She glanced at Natalya who was frozen in her chair, looking at the man like a mouse looking at a snake.

"I just want this one little whore," the man said, dragging the frozen Natalya to her feet.

"Hey, buddy," Tom said, walking up behind the man and tapping him on the shoulder. "These are my girls."

"What, you own them?" the man scoffed.

"He's the bad man," Natalya said, so quietly it was hard to hear over the music. "He's come for me."

"Yeah, I rented them for the day," Tom said angrily. He'd been drinking steadily all evening and Katya was pretty sure he had to be drunk. “I bought ’em, they’re mine. So take your hands off of her.”

“I want this one,” the man holding Natalya said, reaching into his pocket. “I’ll pay you for her.”

“Wait,” one of the guards in the club said, walking over. “Is no fighting.”

“I don’t want your damned money!” Tom snapped, slapping the man’s wallet away. “Just get your hands off of my girl!”

“Katya, what’s going on?” Vanner asked.

“Problems,” Katya whispered. “Big problems.”

“So, why are we watching this?” Captain O’Keefe asked, watching the real-time video from the Predator drone.

“Because we care?” Pierson asked, shrugging. “In case there’s anything we can do to help?”

“Well, we can’t drop JDAMs on the town,” O’Keefe pointed out. “And we can’t send in a SEAL team to help out. And we can’t interdict with Tomahawks. So what exactly are we going to do?”

“Sweep around the edge of town,” Pierson said into the microphone. “You really think that the President isn’t going to want to know how it went down? And getting an after action report from Jenkins is like pulling teeth. So . . . we watch.” He paused and leaned forward, keying the communicator again. “Whoa. Head down Highway One. I think I saw . . .” He paused and blanched. “Zoom in on that group of buses. Get an angle from the side if you can.”

“That’s not normal,” O’Keefe said, leaning forward,

then looking up at another plot. "And they're already in the air."

"No, it's not," Pierson agreed. "And, yes, they are. Zoom in more on the windows."

"Crap."

"Kildar, Vanner."

"Go," Mike said, looking around the helicopter. The Keldara were as prepared for the mission as could be arranged, but he still was unhappy. As he watched, one of them reached into his blouse and pulled out a silver "cross"; the device was actually a hammer disguised to look somewhat like a Christian cross. The Keldara kissed the relic and replaced it in his blouse. For what we are about to receive . . .

"We have two major issues that have just come up," Vanner said, calmly. "The girls are still at the club and someone is trying to extract Natalya. Katya believes that it may be the person who was impersonating Grantham."

"Shit," Mike said. "You got a facial visual?"

"Yes," Vanner said. "I've uploaded it to Colonel Pierson. However, they have a Predator drone up and he has just informed me that there is a convoy of armed personnel headed for the town. ETA is about forty-five minutes."

"They'll hit us in the middle of the op," Mike said, thinking furiously. "Where?"

"They're coming in on Highway One," Vanner replied.

"So are we blown?" Adams asked.

"Any other indicators?" Mike asked.

"Nothing in the club," Vanner said. "Nothing in town."

"I don't think it's coincidence," Mike replied. "But we're still locked on the mission. I'll work on it. Good job. Tell Katya to stay with Natalya if at all possible. Time for her to use her toys."

"Roger," Vanner said. "I'm going to roll part of my security team to follow."

"Concur," Mike said. "Continue the mission. Adams?"

"Go."

"Get me Team Padrek."

"All I want is this one little bitch," the man snarled at the guard. "I'll fucking buy her from you!"

"She's bought and paid for, buddy," Tom snapped. "Get the fuck out!"

"Gentlemen, gentlemen," Boris said, walking over. "There is no need to argue about whores; there are plenty of whores."

"Then let him have others," the man said, reaching into his pocket again. "Here," he said, pulling out a thick wad of hundred euro notes. "Five thousand euros. Now I leave with her?"

"Now you leave with her," Boris said, nodding as he riffled through the money. "And you do what you want as long as she comes back alive."

"Fine," the man snapped, pulling her along with him towards the door.

"Hey!" Tom shouted. "I paid for her!"

"I give you money back," Boris smirked.

"I go with you, too," Katya said, stepping in front of the man. "I give you good time, you give me money!"

He paused and looked her up and down, then smiled.

"You want to go with me, too?" the man asked. "Okay, you want to play with the big boys, you can come along, too."

"Bitches," Tom shouted. "Nothing but fucking bitches! All you care about is the money!"

"Yes?" Katya said, laughing in his face. "So? And I was never fourteen!"

Tom snarled at her and started to draw his hand back, but then stormed out of the club.

"Now I go with you," Katya said, putting her hand on the man's arm. "And I show you what I can do."

"Where is she?" Mikhail asked as the Lada screeched to a halt in front of the club.

"Gone," Vanner snapped. "Looks like west towards Highway One towards the hills. We've picked her up on two vids so far, but in just a minute she's going to be outside our reception range."

"I'm on it," Mikhail said. "Keep an eye on Tanya for me."

"Tanya," Vanner said, as the girl opened the door. "We need a big favor. A very important, and dangerous, favor."

"Padrek," Mike said over the radio. "Change of mission. There is what looks like a reaction force headed for the town. Take the half of your team that was supposed to secure the Forward Aerial Assembly Point down Highway One about two klicks and block the road. Once the road is blocked I'll have someone pick you up. Try not to get engaged."

"Understood, Kildar," the team leader said.

"Your entry portion will shift to Team Oleg," Mike said. "Good luck. Try not to get your asses shot off."

"Where is Boris?" Bezhmel asked the guard inside the club as he hurried through the doors.

"In back," the guard said, indifferently. "We close."

"Let's hope not permanently," the security specialist said, hurrying across the almost deserted club. "Boris!"

"Ah, Yarok Ivanovich!" the Albanian said, smiling unhappily. "What do you want?"

"You know this girl?" Bezhmel asked, pulling out the picture of Natalya.

"Natalya," the pimp said, nodding. "What is so important about one little crazy whore? First two Americans fight over her, then you want her. She is gone."

"Gone!" Bezhmel shouted. "Gone where?"

"With American," Boris said, frowning. "You shout at me in my own club?"

"Fuck," Bezhmel cursed. "Look, there is an attack coming, but I have to find this girl. I have a group of soldiers coming to stop it, my people, former Spetznaz. They will take care of it but you must get your guards up, now! And I need to know where the girl has gone, now! You said she went with American . . ." Bezhmel said, pulling out the other paper. "Was he one of them?"

"The one she left with," Boris said, nodding and trying to catch up. "What attack?"

"The group that hit Club Dracul and Rozaje," Bezhmel said, putting the pictures away. "Where did they go? The man with the girl."

"I can ask around," Boris said. "They were in silver Mercedes. But . . . what attack?"

"My people will be here in about thirty minutes," Bezhmel said. "I need to find the others. East or west out of town?"

"Ask guards on door," Boris said, shrugging. "I go wake up my guards. I will make phone calls and see if anyone see them."

"Right, I'm out of here," Bezhmel said. "My second in command is Yevgenii. He will bring the soldiers here. The attack may come tonight but it may not. We need to surprise them."

"We will," Boris said, grinning. "We'll kill them all for Dracul and Rozaje."

"I've got to go."

"I'm getting something from her," Mikhail said. "Is it retransmitting?"

"Got it," Vanner said. "I'm trying to boost the gain. . . ."

# ★ Chapter Forty-One ★

"Where are we going?" Katya said, placing her hand on the man's crotch and rubbing it.

The Mercedes was very comfortable, with leather seats like the ones in the Kildar's Expedition but wider and softer. Some day, she would have a car like this one. Including the divider so the driver couldn't listen in.

"A place I know up in the hills," the man replied. "A quiet place where we can have some fun. Well, where I can have some fun," he added, grabbing her wrist and pushing her hand away. He twisted her arm up behind her back and leaned over to her ear. "There is a special kind of fun I like to have."

"You want do this, I need much money," Katya said, internally cursing as he twisted her arms behind her and cuffed them. "Please no hurt. I give you good time! No need hurt."

"We'll talk about that when I'm done," the man said, reaching into her dress and twisting her nipple, hard. "Well, just before I kill you."

"Oh, please don't do that," Katya said, sobbing.

"But it's what I like," the man whispered in her ear. "I

like to hurt little girls like you. I like to kill them. I'm going to do you just like I did that little bitch in Rozaje. I'm going to hurt you and hurt you more. Then I'm going to take you in the ass and strangle you while I keep pumping your ass till I come, bitch."

"Why you do this?" Katya whined. "Why you want Natalya?" As the man spoke she twisted her hands as if to get away. The valve at each joint at the base of the finger had to be pressed four times to open up the poison pouch. It was a laborious process. Fortunately, this jackass wanted to talk.

"It was so simple," the man said, laughing. "Just get a voice changer, put on a mask and I was Grantham. The bastard. He blocked my nomination with the last administration. I should have been the undersecretary for International Development but he brought up that shit from Nigeria as if little bitches matter! Well, I fixed him good. And now he's singing a different tune!" He looked at her and shook his head. "What does a little whore like you understand about anything. You're only good for one thing."

"You not need kill us," Katya whined.

"Try to figure out what Traskel has to do with it," Vanner said, suddenly. "And we've got a security team following you. Just hang in there."

"Please not kill me," Katya continued, trying not to snarl at the distant voice. "Who Grantham? I not know Grantham. I not know anything! Please don't kill!"

"Grantham's a senator," the man said, dragging her down so her head was in his lap as he continued to play with her body. He pulled her dress down and reached into a cigar holder, lighting up and then playing the lighter on her tit. "And you wouldn't understand anything about that anyway."

Katya let out a very real shriek at that and tried to struggle away.

"Please!" she begged. "Please not hurt me. I be very good to you. I suck good. I suck really good. I get you off good!"

"That's right," the man said, dragging her off the seat and onto her knees on the floor. "You suck me good and I might let you live. But if you bite . . ."

"I not bite," Katya promised. "I not scratch," she added, lying. "I be good to you, you let me live. Kill her if you want, I don't care. But let me live."

"I already made that mistake," the man said, looking over at the nearly catatonic Natalya who was huddled in the corner. "Kill the one bitch and let the other one sweat it out, waiting to die. But then my damned supervisor, the bitch who had my job, sent me to fucking Rwanda! And when I got back that little bitch was gone. But now she's here, and she can watch while you service me and then . . ."

"Mmmf," Katya answered as the man tangled his fingers in her long golden hair and shoved her down on his dick.

"That's right, I'll let you live if you suck me good," the man said as she began to fellate him expertly. "That's a good whore, you suck good. Fucking Grantham! Thinks he's so high and mighty . . . I needed Traskel, though, the fucker. He got Grantham to go on that damned trip. I got another one of you whores to slip a Rufie in his drink. He doesn't remember what he did that night, which wasn't much. Then the stupid bastards gave me that damned DVD and that was all I needed. That fucking Grantham is dancing to our tune, now. That's playing with the big boys! Between Grantham and Traskel, we've got Foreign Affairs and Judiciary sewn up."

He suddenly yanked her head back and reached down to pull both of her arms up with the shackles so hard she had to scream again.

"But do you want to know the best part," he said, leaning forward and whispering in her ear. "The best part is that with those two behind me, I can do this anytime I want. I can buy you little whores and hurt you and rape you and kill you and nobody is going to stop me."

"Please don't kill," Katya begged as the car pulled to a stop.

"Depends on how good you are," the man said, dragging her out of the car and over into the woods. "Get down on your knees and suck me so good I forget about hurting you."

"Give me one hand?" Katya begged. "I not hurt but can suck so much better with hand and mouth. Please? I take you all the way down. I swallow your cum. Not to kill me! Please!"

"Gunther," the man snapped, stepping back. "Get that other bitch over here so she can see this. I want her to watch every single second."

The driver dragged Natalya out of the car by her hair and into the woods, pulling her up so her back was to one of the trees and then wrapping a rope around the tree and her neck, tying her in place with it. The tree was far too thick for her to reach behind and untie it.

"Take me in your mouth, bitch," the man said, gutturally, dropping his pants and shoving his dick in Natalya's mouth. "Suck it!"

"Mmmf!" Katya replied, trying to wave her hands.

"You want one hand free?" the American asked. "Why?"

"I no bite," Katya whined, pulling back. "I no scratch. Can do better with mouth and hand, can suck and pump both. Is very good."

"Yes, it is," the man said, considering her carefully. He suddenly hit her in the face, hard, then when she was half unconscious on the ground quickly unlocked her right hand and then yanked the handcuff down, brutally, so that her left hand was locked to her left leg. "And like that, you're not going to be going anywhere," he added, yanking her back to her knees by her hair.

"Please, don't kill me," Katya whined, raising her right hand slowly up to his dick. "I'll be good. I won't talk. Just don't kill me."

"Do me good and I'll think about letting you live," the man said, laughing and dropping his pants to settle around his ankles.

"I'll do you good," Katya said, calmly, and then raked her fingernails down the inside of his thigh.

The man let out a shout of pain, punching her in the face automatically and then clamping his hand over the wound. The fast acting neurotoxin, though, caused the muscles in his leg to spasm and he fell to the side, his leg thrashing.

"What did you do to me, bitch?" the man shouted, starting to thrash in the leaves of the forest floor.

Katya wasn't listening. She had rolled with the expected blow and now was trying as hard as she could to get to the driver.

Gunther had been fully occupied in deep throating Natalya when he heard the shout, and when he tried to withdraw, Natalya reached down and grabbed his pants, tripping him.

The driver rolled sideways, crashing into Katya for a moment and then driving an elbow into her gut.

Katya folded over at the blow but as the driver started to get to his knees she rolled over to him and dug her right hand into his butt, then fell across him, pressing down on the palm and pumping the neurotoxin into the muscle of his ass.

Cottontail finally pushed herself to her knees and looked over at Natalya.

"It's finished," she said. "Now to get out of these . . ."

"Behind you," Natalya gasped. "The bad man."

The poison either wasn't as fast acting as she'd been promised or she hadn't gotten enough in the "bad man." The American had pulled a gun out of a shoulder holster and was waving it at her.

"I'm going to k-k-k-i . . ." he stammered, pulling back the hammer with difficulty. The pistol was waving like a branch in a high wind.

Katya turned away just as there was a shot and then flinched.

"I think he missed," she said, looking at Natalya who was watching wide-eyed.

"Hardly, lass," a British voice said from behind her. "I rarely do."

Katya turned her head the other way and her eyes widened as much as Natalya's.

"Tom?" she asked the man lowering the Walther PPK. "Tom?"

"Actually, the name is Charles," the man drawled in pure Oxford tones as he put the pistol away and pulled out a set of handcuff keys. "Charles Calthrop, MI-6. Pleased to make your acquaintance, Cottontail. It is Cottontail, isn't it?"

# ★ Chapter Forty-Two ★

"Vanner, what's the status on the primary?" Mike asked as the helicopter banked around a hill; the highly paid Russian pilots were earning their pay.

"Temporarily sort of secure," Vanner said.

"And what in the hell does that mean, exactly?" Mike snapped.

"You want the whole story, sir?" Vanner asked. "It's a long one. She is out of the box. She is currently unthreatened. She and Katya are colocated. I am attempting pick-up at this time. It got very hairy, but the situation is stabilized, I think. You want more?"

"Negative," Mike said.

"The bad news is that the club has been kicked over like an anthill," Vanner continued. "We've had a three hundred percent increase in external guards and the full force appears to be up at this time. You want to abort?"

"Negative," Mike said after a moment. "We'll continue the mission. Support force?"

"Still moving, still out of the box," Vanner said. "Boss, you do not, say again, do not have the element of surprise at the club. I've managed to insert some new surprises, but you are going in hot."

"Understood," Mike said, looking across the cargo hold at Creata. She was the youngest of the intelligence specialists, a tiny girl with birdlike bones and a narrow face framed by dark brown hair. She was so small and delicate that everyone in the Keldara called her "Mouse." She was also surprisingly adept with mechanical devices and had tested out to be the fastest and most knowledgeable in opening safes. She was sitting very calmly, holding a bag of tools that appeared to be at least two thirds of her body weight in her lap with her eyes closed and seemed to be either praying or going over the steps to crack the safe. Call it a mantra. "We'll still handle it. Out here."

Mike reached down and changed his radio to the setting for "all force."

"Listen up, troops," Mike said. "Primary is out of the box. They know we're coming. There is a heavy force coming in from the east. All the guards are up. We're going in anyway. The FAAP team is going to delay the heavy force. Primary recovery team now is added to front door. Entry and mission as planned. But it's going to be hot. Do the job and we'll get the hell out of dodge. That is all, Kildar out."

"Are you sure about this, boss?" Adams asked.

"I'm sure," Mike said. "We're going to get those DVDs and along the way we're going to fuck them all."

The fleet of birds banked over the last hill and then split, half the echelon heading down the main boulevard and the other half to the smaller rear street.

As they split, four Allouette helicopters increased speed and pulled away from the formation. Two braked to an out-of-ground hover five hundred meters from the club and pivoted sideways so that their troop doors pointed towards the club.

As soon as they were pointed, the two machine gunners in each of their doors opened fire.

The MG-240 was capable of spitting out over 1200 rounds per minute on continuous fire, but the machine gunners were, while newly trained, quite expert and held them to precise three- and five-round bursts. The combined fire tossed the guards on the front door of the club to their face, littering the sidewalk with bodies. This late at night, the only people on the street were the few remaining guards on the club so there were no complications from ladies of the evening.

The lead Allouette paused for a moment in an out of ground hover then, as the guards on the doors were reduced, slid forward in a deadly precise maneuver and paused opposite the club.

Intelligence had determined that the majority of the guards were barracked on the third floor. In each of the Allouettes were two RPG gunners, two assistant gunners and a sniper. As the Allouette slowly slid down the now nearly empty street, the RPG gunners began firing round after round into the barred windows of the third floor, filling the upper stories with deadly shrapnel. The backblast was directed out the other door of the stripped helicopter. In a few of the second and third story windows, figures briefly appeared. Those that were not currently being targeted by the RPG gunners were engaged by the Keldara sniper, whose precise rounds removed the majority of the threats.

As the helicopter working the front of the building was just about done with its run, one guard got smart enough to hurry to an upper floor and open fire on the helicopter with his AK-47. The majority of the 7.62x39 rounds flew wide, but two cracked into the turbine housing of the French chopper.

The Russian pilot saw about half of his lights go red in less than a second

"*Yob tvoyu mat,*" he shouted, killing the engine and dropping the hovering helicopter like a stone. "We're going in!"

"Where's Tanya?" Vanner asked.

"Second floor," Lydia answered, calmly. "Room Seven. It's interior."

"Tell Team Sawn when they clear the second floor to find her and extract," Patrick replied.

"We have response coming down Ordur Street," Greznya said.

"Got it," Vanner said, switching screens. "Blow det zones nine and nineteen . . ."

Yevgenii Kulcyanov grasped the fast-rope and slid down, hitting hard and then bounding to the back door of the club.

"Rig it," he said, not even looking over his shoulder to make sure Bran was behind him.

"Got it," the Keldara demo specialist said, slapping the charge on the heavy door. "Clear," he yelled, sliding down the wall to the side and then triggering the kilo of Semtek.

The remainder of the Keldara entry team had paused

out of the blast zone, hunkering down to take the blast on their armor. As soon as it went off, Yevgenii tossed a frag through the door, waited for it to detonate and then plunged into the smoke.

"Clear right!"

Padrek drifted through the dust from the destroyed main door and took up a position to the right of the door, sweeping around the mostly abandoned main club area. Abandoned by clientele, that is. There was heavy fire coming from the far side of the bar.

Padrek Ferani at 5' 9" was shorter than the average Keldara and darker as well, with brown hair and eyes that had a slight epicanthic fold, probably the result of a Mongol warrior passing through the area. But his frame was compactly muscled from years of farm work and the training the Keldara took for the tests of Ondah. That muscle had been further honed by the training regime of the Western instructors, as had an already fast mind.

Choosing the militia teams had, in the end, come down to something like choosing teams for ball in school. To an extent, the instructors had made sure that certain skills were passed around, but the team leaders had final call on who was in "their" team. And they'd tended to choose like-minded individuals.

Oleg was a born warrior, a true Viking descendent who tended to feel that peace could best be served by superior firepower. When he saw an obstacle, his choice was to smash it down. Vil was more subtle, preferring deception and quick movement, the rapier to the broadsword.

Padrek was one of the best Keldara at mechanisms, one

of the kids who had spent his whole life keeping the few bits of technology the Keldara posessed alive and kicking. He had the mind of an engineer, so when he saw a problem he tried to work it, to think "outside the box." As he surveyed the destruction, he was automatically processing actions both near and far in terms of combat time. And he sure as hell wasn't planning on a frontal assault.

Oleg would have tried to overwhelm with firepower. Vil would have tried a ruse.

Padrek tended to prefer technology.

One of the Keldara was down in the doorway and a blood trail denoted another that had been dragged out of the line of fire. The rest were hunkered down behind a barricade of tables, trading shots with the Albanians on the far side of the room. More of whom were pouring through a doorway that was *just* out of the Keldara's line of fire.

"Tch, tch," Padrek said, shaking his head. Team Padrek's primary instructor had been McKenzie, the Scottish former SAS NCO, and some of his manner had rubbed off. "This simply won't do, what? Krasa?"

"Go Padrek," the intel specialist replied. She was hunkered down outside the building, waiting for the club level to be cleared.

"You've got the detonation codes that Vanner sent, yes?" Padrek asked, consulting a piece of paper. "Could you give me a hit on number six and . . . eight?"

Creata waited as the eight members of the side entry team slid to the ground then stepped to the door. She looked over her shoulder and wasn't surprised to see the

Kildar giving her a thumb's up signal. She grinned at him, grabbed the fast-rope and slid into the alleyway.

As planned, she stepped to the far side from the door and huddled to the ground as Ivan and Mikhail squeezed her from either side, covering her from stray fire and random fragments.

"You don't have to lean in that hard," she muttered, barely able to breathe from the weight of the two. Oh, well, it was probably something like sex. Maybe some day she'd find out.

There was an explosion and then a series of shots, then Ivan stood up and yanked her to her feet.

"Stay between us, Mouse," he growled, running hard for the door.

"Tango down right." "Down left. Left clear." "Hallway clear." Another blast. "Door open. Descending." "Check fire, hallway. Main entry team in place." "Basement . . ."

Creata didn't stop in time and bounced off of Ivan's armor before being yanked to the ground by Ivan.

"What's happening?" she asked. She had been instructed to keep her radio off unless she absolutely had to use it.

"Too many guards in the basement," Mikhail muttered. "Secondary team going in." As he told her, there was a massive explosion from the level above.

"What was *that*?" Creata yelled.

"Padrek having fun," Mikhail replied, grinning.

"Up and at 'em!" Padrek shouted, standing up over the barricade and firing the MG-240 from the hip.

The detonation of the two IEDs the hooker had secreted in the staircase had blown the reinforcing guards out of the doorway like so much mangled meat. It had also seriously eroded the morale of the guards that had, successfully, bottled up the Keldara entry team. They stopped firing and turned to look at what had happened, giving Padrek the moment's respite he'd needed. Now the *Albanians* were suppressed as his fire, and the fire of the two SAW gunners on the team, filled the area around the bar with lead.

"Grenades," he yelled, continuing to snap out three- and five-round bursts, working back and forth along the top of the bar, sending the few remaining intact bottles up in an explosion of glass and liquor. "Now!"

As the grenades reached the end of their apogee he stopped firing and ducked; frags had no concept of who was friend or foe. There was a series of "cracks" and screams, then he was back on his feet.

"Follow me!"

Gregorii leapt over the black-clad body of a Keldara at the base of the stairs and took cover on the far side of the hallway as rounds cracked down the long gallery.

"Four, maybe more, on the south end," he said. "Twenty meters down."

"I'll cover," Yevgenii said, leaning around the corner of the stairs and spraying fire from his Squad Automatic Weapon down the length of the corridor.

Gregorii got down and low-crawled forward to the next doorway, reaching up and trying the door. Locked.

"Fuck," he muttered.

"Reloading!" Yevgenii called as the fire died.

Gregorii pulled his SPR around and began sending three-round bursts down the hallway, trying to keep the defenders at the far end suppressed. An AK was stuck around the corner and the trigger yanked, filling the corridor with bullets, one of which hit him on the armor.

"I need more cover than this!" Gregorii sang out.

Suddenly more than just the SAW was firing down the hallway and the AK was quickly yanked back.

"Thank you," he muttered, putting the barrel of the SPR against the lock and blowing it away with a couple of bursts. He pushed the door open with the barrel and then peeked around the corner. The room appeared to be clear so he slid through the door, tracking around for threats.

Well, not entirely clear. There was a girl huddled in one corner, chained to the wall. She looked as if she'd been beaten rather hard recently. And a nick on her leg was probably from a bouncer.

"Just stay there and be quiet," he said in Russian, gesturing her down. He leaned out again, carefully, given the amount of lead being thrown around, and checked the doorway at the end. Close enough. He pulled out a fragmentation grenade, pulled the pin and tossed it as hard as he could down the corridor.

Unfortunately, his aim was off and the grenade bounced off the edge of the doorway. He'd wondered why the instructors had been so insistent on accuracy and as he ducked back in the room he decided that now he knew.

"Fucker!" Yevgenii snapped as he jumped through the door. "You could have called grenade!"

"I figured you were hiding on the stairs," Gregorii replied, grinning.

"Just shut up and hand me a frag," Yevgenii said. "Grenade!"

★ ★ ★

"Grenades here, here and here," Anton said, pointing at the map as the Hip helicopter lifted off the road and into the darkness. "Run tripwires across the road. We'll drop trees from here to here. Then lay claymores as we retreat."

"We don't have any axes," Gena pointed out.

"Who needs axes," Anton scoffed, pulling a roll of det-cord out of his pack. "We've got demo!"

"Get them out of there," Mike said, tapping two of the Keldara reserve and pointing to the downed Alloutte as he stepped off the Hip. "Clearing status?"

"Ground floor clear," Adams said. "Two Keldara wounded, one dead. Clearing upper floors. Entry team has opened the basement, clearing at this time. Some resistance but they're handling it. More casualties."

"Oleg?" Mike said as he walked through the smoking entrance of the club.

"Reaction from all four directions," the security team leader replied. "Uncoordinate. Maintaining position. We're getting good reads from Vanner."

"Sawn?"

"Third floor . . ." There was a burst of fire in the background, then an explosion and the Keldara team leader grunted. "Second and third floor clear. We've picked up a primary per Vanner. Secure and pulling out. IEDs laid to cover."

"When you pull back, check with the basement team and see if they need any help," Mike said. "If not, go reinforce Oleg."

★ ★ ★

"Oleg! There are more coming down Dutris Street! We need help here!"

"How many?" Oleg asked, waving at the team with him and hurrying to the defense point on Dutro.

"At least twenty," Dmitri answered. "And they are giving each other covering fire now. A car tried to get past us as well."

Oleg turned the corner and hunkered down behind a stairway, peering over the top, then looking across the street at the defense team.

"We have them in a crossfire, now," Oleg said as he spotted figures moving down the far side of the street. "Juris, see if you can get onto one of the upper floors and give us cover fire. Jitka, set up your SAW and get ready for fun . . ."

"Make enough of a mess?" Creata asked, stepping over the body in the threshold of the room and looking around. The basement office's computers had been shredded by more than one grenade, but the safe on the far wall was impervious to fragments.

"More or less," Yevgenii said, grinning. "A little Mouse's nest, yes?"

"Genrich, Steppas," Gregorii said. "Start pulling out EEI. Mouse, we don't have much time."

"Got it," the girl said, hurrying over to the safe. "I'm going to be at least ten minutes," she added as she began pulling tools out of her bag.

"Understood," Gregorii said. "Safe room secure. Working on the safe . . ."

# ★ Chapter Forty-Three ★

"Creata's on the safe," Adams said, pulling off his balaclava and looking around the club. "Ten minutes. I say we get a drink. If Padrek left us any whole bottles."

"Who's she?" Mike asked, gesturing with his chin to a hooker being held by one of the Keldara.

"Tanya," Sawn answered. "She's an intel source that Vanner asked us to pick up."

"Vanner?" Mike asked, over the radio. "We giving rides to hookers, now?"

"You talking about Tanya, Kildar?" Vanner answered. "She's good people and we owe her; she laid in a series of IEDs that really saved Padrek's ass. Besides, Mikhail really likes her."

"Fine, fine, like, what-*everrrr*," Mike said. "So we're giving rides to hookers. What's the status with Oleg?"

"Pretty bad," Vanner admitted. "He's got a fight on his hands on all fronts."

"Sawn, this place secure?" Mike asked.

"Yes, sir," the team leader answered.

"Get everybody out there supporting Oleg," Mike said. "Keep a minimum security force back here."

"Yes, Kildar," Sawn said, striding away and talking to his radio.

"Creata?" Mike asked softly.

"Yes, Kildar?" Creata answered after a moment.

"How long?"

"I'm just beginning my drill, Kildar," Creata said. "Eight to nine minutes, minimum."

"Thank you, Mouse," Mike replied then looked around the room. "Stay here or go help Oleg?" he asked rhetorically.

"You stay here," Adams said, setting down his empty shot glass. "I'll go help Oleg Oh Kildar!"

"Works. Vanner, status on the primary?"

"Kildar," Vanner said. "Update on the situation with Katya. Still-unknown man pulled them out of the club over protests of the sugar daddy. Took them to area outside town with stated intention of killing them. Natalya recognized him as the 'bad man,' presumably the duplicate Grantham from Rozaje. Person explained most of the incident to Katya while gloating."

"And Katya is . . . alive?" Mike asked.

"Katya managed to scratch him and his driver," Vanner continued. "Was about to be killed, anyway, by the unknown man. The 'sugar daddy' prevented it. Turns out he's MI-6."

"Don't you just love it when a plan comes together?" Mike said. "Does he recognize the perp?"

"Negative," Vanner said. "I've uploaded a good face shot to Pierson; they're trying to run a match. He's apparently American State Department."

"Anything odd about this guy?" Mike asked, his brain twigging at something.

"Accent," Vanner said, immediately. "Pure Cambridge, Boston. Hah'vah'd, you know? 'Pah'k the cah'?"

"Wait," Mike said. "Run a check against the guy who first contacted me for the senator. He was a State Department brahmin . . ."

"Looking at the log . . ." Vanner said. "Wilson Hargreave Thornton. And now Google is our friend . . ."

"And?" Mike asked.

"Bingo," Vanner replied. "We now have one dead member from the Moldava Desk in the woods of Albania. Except he's actually in the Bureau of International Development."

"Connection to Traskel?" Mike asked curiously.

"He explained it all," Vanner replied. "Well, most. Enough. I'm sure we'll figure out the link, other than that they run in the same circles more or less."

"Got it," Mike said. "Look forward to the replay."

"That might be all we have," Vanner said. "I sent Mikhail after them to act as security but he was late. However, he's got a Land Rover following him according to Predator data. So somebody else appears to be after either Wilson Whatsisname or Natalya."

"And they're out of the box," Mike said, cursing under his breath. "We'll vector a recovery team in as soon as we egress this area. Tell them to either run like hell or stand pat, up to them. But we'll be up to get them soon."

"How is it there?" Vanner asked. "Oleg looks like he's getting pounded."

"Other than that, all good," Mike admitted just as there was a shot downstairs. "Check that. Gunfire. Out here."

★ ★ ★

Boris waited quietly in the safety room, cursing the bastards who had wrecked his club.

As soon as the explosions started upstairs, he had raced for the secure room in the basement. But even before he reached the stairs, he could hear gunfire from the side door and knew that they were under heavy attack. Probably too heavy for even his bloated guard force.

On reaching the basement, he'd ordered the guards to hold out as long as possible and then secreted himself in the "panic room." The room was concealed behind a set of shelves that contained some of the documents related to the wideflung network of whorehouses and street whores.

The room had been ransacked, but nobody, fortunately, noticed the carefully hidden door. After a few minutes frantic activity, the ransackers, mostly women, curiously, had left carrying almost every document and computer hard drive in the room. The exception was the woman working on the safe, and one bodyguard.

Boris would very much prefer it if whoever was attacking did not get the contents of the safe. Even if everything else was gone, he could rebuild from just what was in there, in money, drugs and especially his collection of DVDs. He wasn't sure, but he thought most of the attackers had gone upstairs. The rest of the gangs had to be attacking them from the outside. If he could just kill these two he might be able to make it out alive.

The problem was that the little whore of a safecracker was looking right at him. She'd started up the drill while the other women were in the room, then left it to drill as she chatted with the guard. All he needed was for her to turn around for a few seconds . . .

★ ★ ★

Creata was bored.

The first part of the mission had been exciting and scary. Three Keldara had been injured or killed trying to get to the basement office and she felt bad about that. But waiting to enter the corridor had been the most exciting thing she had ever done, except maybe fast-roping down to the alleyway.

Then running down the corridor and setting up had been exciting. She had had to carefully, but quickly, find the precise spot to start drilling. If she was off by half a millimeter, the entry wouldn't work. She'd carefully measured and then started the drill. After that, though, it got boring. Boring, boring, boring.

There had been two choices of drill, a mechanical or a laser. The laser drill was slightly heavier, but it had two advantages. It could detect when there had been a burn-through, and with the fine machinery on the far side of the outer plate Creata didn't want anything touching it but her, and it didn't have the problem of bits breaking or binding. It was a tad less reliable otherwise, but she had been careful to pad it for the entry and it started up without problem. Now all she had to do was wait for it to bore through to the tumbler assembly.

Bore.

Now she knew why the words were the same in English. They'd talked about this part in the briefing, and the Kildar had said that she'd get bored and then laughed. So she did, chuckling at the thought.

"What?" Ivan asked, frowning.

"I just figured out why the Kildar laughed when we

were talking about this part," Creata said. She'd propped her back on the safe, waiting for the bore to finish. Looking at it wasn't going to make it go any faster. "Any word on what's going on upstairs?"

"All four teams are pinned down," Ivan said, shrugging. "They've taken a few casualties. The only ones killed, so far, were Dimant back there on the stairs, Arkady opening the front door and Stanislav when the helicopter crashed. Oh, and the copilot of the helicopter. Bunch of wounded, though."

"I'm going as fast as I can," Creata said, shrugging.

"We know," Ivan replied, then grinned. "Although I have overheard some comments from upstairs. But they all know the timing. They're going to be okay."

"I hope they can extract okay," the girl said, biting her lip.

"The Kildar thinks . . ." Ivan said, just as the drill went into overrev.

"Through," Creata shouted, turning off the drill. "Quiet, now."

"Yes, ma'am," Ivan replied, grinning. But he keyed his mike and spoke into it softly.

Creata pulled the drill out of the casing carefully, rolling it to the side, then slid a doubled optical wire into the hole. One was for vision and the other one had a light. The interior was precisely as she'd been told it would be and she looked at the tumblers for a second.

"I can see the first number . . ." she muttered to herself, ignoring a faint click behind her.

The guard didn't seem to hear the faint click as the

shelves unlatched from the wall, and Boris held his breath as he slowly swung the door open. But, still, the guard, who was speaking softly into his radio, didn't seem to notice anything.

The guard was wearing heavy body armor so Boris slowly raised his pistol up to the level of his eye, took a two-handed grip and shot the guard just below the base of his helmet.

Creata turned around in shock as the whole area around her was covered in bloodspatter, only to find an unknown man, one of the Albanians from his looks, standing over the body of Ivan with a smoking pistol.

"Come away from there, girl," the man said, waving for her gently. "Come away and you won't get hurt."

"No," Creata said, scurrying behind the bulk of the laser drill. "They'll come for you, soon."

"But you're their safecracker," the man said, moving around to the side to get a clear shot. "Without you, they can't get in, can they?"

"I don't want to hurt you," Creata replied, keeping the drill between herself and the man. She had a very small body and could crouch behind it almost totally under cover. "Just go away."

"Ah, but I very much enjoy hurting little girls like you," the man said, stepping forward.

"You probably do," Creata replied and turned the laser on.

The fifteen megawatt chemical laser was designed to bore through one centimeter of 440 steel per second. Human flesh had about the resistance to it that butter had to a hot knife. It was nearly out of charge, but Creata only had to play it across the man's abdomen, 23 millimeters below his navel. The precise height that the laser had to be aligned to enter the safe.

Boris didn't even feel the pain at first: his legs simply collapsed under him as he felt something slither down them. He hit the floor on his face but retained his grip on his pistol and tried to raise it, only to find a small and shapely boot on his wrist.

"I really didn't want to hurt you," Creata said, pointing her own pistol at his face. "I simply wanted to kill you. Of course, I think that the disemboweling you just got is probably starting to hurt. Let me be nicer than you and make the pain go away. . . ."

Mike could see Ivan's body on the floor before he even got to the door of the basement office, but the shot that rang out was a surprise.

He skidded through the door, SPR up and pointed, just as Creata was putting her pistol away. There was a body on the floor besides Ivan's, an unknown Albanian with his legs tangled in intestines. His identity would probably forever be unknown, since he also had a bullet hole in the back of his head and his face was blown out.

"Oh, hello, Kildar," Creata said, turning back to the safe. "Do you think you could watch my back while I finish?"

"Of course," Mike replied, just as calmly. "I'll be as quiet as a church mouse."

# ★ Chapter Forty-Four ★

"Oleg," Juris called, tracking a moving figure and then stroking his trigger. The figure on the opposite roof fell, but two more dove past him and began peppering the window he'd shot through with fire. "We've got tangoes on the roof opposite. I have to pull out."

"I think we pissed these guys off," Jitka muttered over the radio.

"Their home turf," Oleg replied, scanning the street, then consulting his map. "They're very territorial are the Albanian clans. This is an affront to their honor. They'll keep coming, like ants to a picnic, until we've killed them all or the picnic's departed."

"Then I suggest we fold our napkins and go," Juris chuckled. "Could I get some cover on that?"

"Roger," Oleg said. "Dutris Street team, pull back by sections. Section one, move. All teams, fall back on the Club. Kildar, we are withdrawing by sections at this time. Request cover fire in and around the club."

"Oleg, this is Kildar," Mike whispered. "Everyone's with you. I'll get back to you on cover."

"Roger, Kildar," Oleg said as there was a scream in the background.

"Vanner," Mike said. "Who's out on the interdict mission and what's the status?"

"The area's rigged," Vanner said. "They're pulling back."

"Get two of the Allouettes to them," Mike said. "Have them provide cover fire for the withdrawal to the club. Begin moving all personnel to the evac point on the roof."

"Will do," Vanner replied.

"Die, you Albanian motherfuckers," Ionis muttered, stroking the trigger of his MG-240.

He'd thought flying in on the Allouettes had been scary. But that had worked out perfectly. Now, though, he and Stephan were under heavy fire, covering the retreat of one of Oleg's teams.

"Keep the ammo coming, brother," he muttered as Stephan clicked another hundred-round box into the linked belt that was feeding the gun.

"Keep firing, brother," Stephan replied, grinning, just as there was a whistling sound.

Ionis caught a brief glimpse of the RPG in the air before it impacted on the wall above him.

Oleg dashed across the street, ignoring the hail of small arms fire, and scooped up the MG-240.

"Dmitri! Sveryan! Grab Ionis and Stephan and get them under cover," the team leader roared, popping up over the stairway and hosing the far side of the street, holding the machine gun off-hand like a giant rifle. There was return fire, though, from every window it seemed and from the rooftop. He felt a round punch him in the armor and then another in the left leg. He ignored them and kept firing, both suppressing the fire from the far side of the street and drawing it so the team could withdraw. "Vagis! Juris! Somebody feed me!"

"Kildar, this is Sawn. We've withdrawn on Nevsk and Agayev. I'm shifting some forces over to Dutris, though. Oleg and his team are pinned there."

"Got it," Mike said, quietly. "I may have some support on the way. Get everyone withdrawn as fast as possible. Mouse is almost done. I need at least a fire team here in the building to make sure we get to the withdrawal point."

"Will do," Sawn said. "See you in Valhalla."

"Got it," Creata said, leaning back and twisting the handle. The handle moved for about a third of the way and then stopped. "Damn."

"What's wrong?" Mike asked. If they couldn't get the door open, the entire mission was for nothing.

"I thought I saw a fragment of metal in the tumblers," Creata said, standing up and walking over to Ivan's body. She calmly rolled him over and unshipped his SPR, then walked back over to the safe and hammered on the handle until it moved. "That's got it," she added, twisting it all the way to open and then opening the safe.

"Whoa," Mike said, blinking his eyes. "Sawn."

"Kildar, we've mostly pulled back to the club except for the group on Dutro. We have cover on their back, but they are under heavy fire."

"Okay, I need about . . ." Mike looked at the contents

of the safe again and then shrugged. "About ten guys down here. Some of the girls will do but I'm going to need strong backs."

"Roger, Kildar," Sawn said. "Will do."

"That is a lot of money," Creata said, pulling out one of the stacks of euros. "A lot of money."

"And the DVDs?" Mike asked, keeping an eye on the corridor.

"Here," Creata said, pulling out two audio storage boxes and lifting the lid on one. "In crystal cases, yes?" she asked.

"Check them," Mike said. "Vanner, what's the status on that Allouette?"

"Glad to see you!" Anton shouted over the rotor wash.

"You may not be," the pilot shouted back. "I know I'm not happy! See the machine guns?"

"Yes?" Gena shouted.

"They are to be used, yes?" the pilot said and then grinned. "As the Americans say, we are going Downtown."

"There is firing in town," Yevgenii Andrushkin said, looking over at Dmitri Balboshin. "And I cannot raise Yarok on his cell phone."

Yevgenii and Dmitri had been assigned to the same Spetznaz team, straight out of training, Yevgenii as a brand new lieutenant and Dmitri as an equally shiny senior private. And both had left the teams at about the same time, after an offer they couldn't resist from the Russian mafia. Since then, Yevgenii had risen on the paramilitary side of the mob, becoming a senior recruiter and leader of professionals in "wet work" while Dmitri had handled his personal security.

Yevgenii had reluctantly acceded to his former commander's request to form a large force for the Albanian mob. The Albanians and the Russians often clashed, but if there was a new anticriminal special operations team running around, Yevgenii felt it in everyone's interest to crush it as soon as possible.

That assumed that they could even get to the force before it completed its current raid. Yarok had said "soon" but not this soon.

"I could give a rat's ass about Yarok," Dmitri said, propping his SMG into a more comfortable position and fingering one of the frag grenades on his ammo vest. "We'd better get paid, though."

"We will be," Yevgenii said. "As long as we are not too late. Driver, hurry!"

"Yes, Mr. Kutkin," the Albanian driver said, nervously. "But this road is very twisty—"

"I don't care!" Yevgenii shouted, just as there was a crack from the roadside.

The small Keldara team had not had much time and they had only recently been through demolitions school. But the total of what they knew about dropping trees hadn't been discovered yet.

The explosion sequence was started by three grenades, their pins loosened and attached to wires spread across the road at waist height. As the first bus hit the wires, the pins were pulled and each of the grenades detonated.

Under the grenades, the trees that they were rigger-taped to had a triple wrap of detcord with two small charges of

Semtek wrapped in with it. The detcord detonated sympathetically from the grenades, detonating the Semtek in turn, and the base of the trees shot away from the road, bringing their crowns down like rockets.

But that wasn't enough for the busy Keldara. They had run more detcord from the primary trees to others along the roadway, along with stringing claymores on their trunks.

Before the first bus had even crashed into the obstacles suddenly dropped in its path, more trees were dropping into the road for over fifty meters, along with a hail of ballbearings that turned the buses into so many bleeding collanders.

"Oh, that was very cool," Gena said. The helicopter had pulled up high enough that he could see the entire road and they had added some flares so the scene was fully lit. The buses carrying the "reaction force" were twisted across the road every which way and three were on fire. Only the rear two buses appeared unscathed.

"Sawn, this is Anton," the fire team leader said. "The reaction force is . . . not having a good night. They will be late to the party."

"Good," Sawn said. "One good piece of news. How long to the town?"

"Perhaps three minutes," Anton said, cocking the door-mounted MG-240. "I take it you have more work for us."

"Yes," Sawn said. "Hurry."

Oleg had been hit two more times, but had only been able to pull back half the block. He knew he was bleeding too much, but he could barely take time to cram bandages on the wounds.

"Juris, you there?" Oleg called weakly.

"Above you, brother," the sniper replied.

"There are fighters on the roof over you," Oleg said. "Pull out."

"You don't have any cover, brother," the sniper pointed out. "I'll stay."

"Go," Oleg said. "Go now. That is an order."

"Going," Juris said after a moment. "But I thought I'd shoot the fellow about to drop a grenade on you."

"Thank you," Oleg said, stroking the trigger. He was almost out of ammo for the 240 and Sveryan, who had picked up the spares, had already been pulled back with a sucking chest wound. What was that song that the Kildar sang?

*"And in the fury of this darkest hour, we shall be your light,"* Oleg said, tracking a moving figure on the rooftop opposite and stroking the trigger. The machine gun spat out three rounds and then went silent. *"You've asked me for my sacrifice, and I am Winter Born . . ."*

"Oleg," Juris whispered. "Get up."

"Get out," Oleg replied. "Go."

"Not without you, brother," the sniper replied, targeting a figure on the far rooftop. The man seemed to stumble and then fell into the street but the single shot, even with the silenced sniper rifle, had attracted a hail of fire from all along the street. "Time to crawl."

"Bit hard to do," Oleg said, choking. "But, yes, we crawl . . ."

As they tried to leave the shelter of the stairs, though, rounds cracked all around them.

"Or not," Juris sighed. "Perhaps we stay here, yes?"

"I told you," Oleg replied, laughing redly. "You should listen to your brother."

"I would much prefer to be in the house, yes?" Juris said, leaning against the wall and trying to search for targets. "Having some of Mother Lenka's brew."

"I would rather be in bed with Lydia," Oleg said. "If you make it, tell the Kildar . . ."

"We will both make it, brother," Juris said, knowing he was lying. "But I will tell the Kildar . . ."

He paused as a body dropped from the window above, spinning to fire and then checking.

"You see!" the girl behind him said. "I told you it was Juris and Oleg! Here," she added, tossing him three boxes of ammunition for the MG-240. "Get to work, Juris. You always were lazy!"

"Elena," Oleg said, blinking his eyes in surprise. "Catrina? Is it really you?"

"I wondered how long it was going to take for you to find us," Elena said, making a moue. "I didn't expect it to be this long." She reached down and yanked off her stilletto heels, rubbing her feet. "I'm so glad to get those off!"

"We're not here for you," Juris said, slipping the ammo into the machine gun and opening fire. "Not that I'm not glad to see you, especially bringing ammo!"

"Oleg, Juris," Sawn said. "You there?"

"Here, Sawn," Juris replied. "We could use some cover fire."

"You're about to get it," Sawn said. "Get down."

"Tell whoever is firing to be careful," Oleg said, reaching up and pulling his sister in close as his eyes watered from more than pain. "We found Elena and Catrina."

"Found us, hell!" Catrina said, hugging Juris triumphantly. "We had to find you!"

The Allouette slid to a halt at the intersection of Dutris and Turla, behind the assaulting Albanians. As soon as the helicopter slowed, Anton and Gena opened fire.

The two MG-240s were firing down, suppressing or engaging everyone along the street as the Allouette slowly tracked back and forth. They started with the rooftops, firing from above and behind the attackers that had made their way up there, then started on those on the street.

The Albanians, caught in a crossfire from behind and above, didn't have many choices. Mostly, they died. Some ran into the buildings, a few managed to retreat under the helicopter, but they weren't much better off there. Efim and Vitaly, the other two members of the blocking team, had found a case of fragmentation grenades. Anyone headed for the helicopter found frags dropping on them from great height. Due to the timing of the frags and the distance to the ground, most went off before they hit. This didn't do the retreating pimps and guards much good, though, since that just meant the frags spread around better.

As the fighters near the helicopter were suppressed, the pilot slid the helicopter sideways down the road, letting the machine gunners and grenadiers engage more targets. However, it started taking fire from hidden riflemen in the windows of the houses along the street and backed off.

"Sawn, this is Anton" the team leader called. "What's the status?"

"Pull off," Sawn called. "All personnel recovered. We're beginning extraction. Come to the other end of Dutris and cover us as we leave."

"Got it," the pilot called, pivoting the bird up and around. "Will do."

"Anybody got any idea how we're doing?" Antoniya asked.

What was that line the Kildar used?

"Don't count your cards while they're sitting on the table," Sawn growled. "Just shag your ass."

# ★ Chapter Forty-Five ★

"So, you are MI-6?" Katya asked, confused, as the agent began uncuffing her.

"Yes," Calthrop said, grinning. "Lord Arnold thought you might like some backup."

"I never suspected," Katya admitted, rubbing her wrist and ankle as the cuffs came off.

"I had extensive amateur thespian experience at Oxford," Calthrop said, walking over to Natalya and cutting the rope around her neck. "I must say that my Sancho Panza was well regarded by the *Oxford Gazette*. I have a clipping around here somewhere . . ." he added, patting his pockets.

"I think we talk about it later," Katya said, wincing as she got to her feet. "There are things going on in town . . ." she continued just as a series of distant thumps carried over the night air.

"Ah, yes, your raid by the Keldara, what?" Calthrop asked. "And, of course, there are the two cars that appear to be coming up the hill."

"Oh, shit," Katya said. "Vanner, Vanner, can you hear me?"

"It's Lydia, yes," Lydia replied in her ear.

"We're okay, for now," Katya said. "But there are cars."

"The one in the lead is Mikhail," Lydia said. "The other is reported but who it is is unknown. A Land Rover. Definitely following you and probably hostile."

"It would have been nice to know that before now!" Katya snapped.

"You seemed a bit busy," Lydia said with a hint of humor in her voice. "The bulk of the force is engaged in the town or on other operations. Kildar says that you need to run, or fight, your choice, but hold on for a few more minutes until we can get some support to you."

"Understood," Katya said, looking around. "I think . . . run."

"I take it you're using that special thingy in your head," Calthrop said. "What do they say?"

"The lead car is a friend," Katya said, frowning. "The trail car is a Land Rover, probably hostile. The Keldara can't get free for a few minutes. So we're on our own."

"Then I agree," Calthrop said, holding out his hand and helping her to her feet. "We run."

"Mikhail."

"Go Lydia," the Keldara said, steering through a hard turn.

"Get ready to take a right."

"Is that the way to Katya?" Mikhail asked, confused. "I saw their lights above us.'"

"It will be."

"The other car is turning," Chito said, looking over at Bezhmel.

"Yes, but the Mercedes is up there," Yarok replied, pointing up the hill. "This road takes us up there. Keep going."

"Okay, the Tango One is still headed up the hill," Captain O'Keefe said, over the sat phone. "Sierra Two is headed down the side road."

"Got that," Lydia said, picking up the microphone. "Katya . . ."

". . . Turn right at the next intersection," Katya said, pointing.

"That's sending us back towards town," Calthrop said, braking to make the turn.

The big Mercedes was solid and a comfortable ride, but it was *really* lacking in acceleration and turning; the soft shocks made it turn *extremely* wide. He could already see flashes of light from the following Rover.

"We're meeting a friend."

Mikhail pulled the Lada backwards into the road and then bailed out, running across the small distance to the stopped Mercedes and tumbling into the back seat.

"Nice of you to join us, Mikhail," Katya said dryly. "Great security. I had to depend on the British for protection."

"I was doing my best," Mikhail said, jacking a round into the SPR. "But I was driving a Lada. What did you expect?"

"So was I, lad," Calthrop replied in Georgian. "Of course, I had a bit of a lead on you. Speaking of leads, we're losing ours with the Rover. Nice of you to park your car in the road, but I don't think that's going to stop them."

"Slow them down a bit, I hope," Mikhail said, shrugging and looking out the back window. "If not, well, we will die well."

"The only way to do that is *late*," Katya replied.

"Who the fuck would park a car . . ." Chito said, swerving the Rover around the parked Lada. He'd barely spotted it in time and had a seriously hard time keeping the SUV in control as it hit the verge of the road. But he managed after a moment.

"Someone trying to slow us down," Bezhmel replied.

How many in the car was the question. The American was dead; he'd seen the body as they drove past. He could take the credit on that one. All he had to do was take out the hooker, Natalya. Then he would be sixty thousand euros richer. But there was more than just the hooker in the car. At least one, probably more.

However, he had three fighters in the back of the SUV, himself and Chito. That should be enough to take out whatever was facing them.

"Hang on," Calthrop said, braking hard as he saw a switchback ahead.

The diplomat/assassin had taken the girls far up into the hills over the town but the current road was headed downward again. And the narrow, barely paved, road was descending in a series of nasty switchbacks that the big Mercedes dearly hated.

The outer tires dug gravel on the outside shoulder of the road, causing a burst of adrenaline through his system that hit like a hammer.

"That was too close," Katya said disapprovingly.

"Yes," Calthrop said through thinning lips. "But so are they."

"There," Bezhmel shouted, pointing to a narrow trail.

The switchbacks were not the only way down the mountain. At various points, local shepherds had driven their flocks straight down, generally just short of the switchbacks. Where the sheep and goats could go, a Rover could follow.

Chito hit the brakes and turned hard to the left, the front tires briefly leaving the ground and then thumping down.

The ride was bumpy, tossing the three gunners in the back around to shouted complaints. But the Rover debouched onto the road *ahead* of the speeding Mercedes as Chito braked it, narrowly, to a stop short of the far side of the road.

"Oh . . . shiiit," Calthrop shouted, slamming on the brakes and turning hard to the right.

As the Mercedes fishtailed across the road, Mikhail grasped a handhold and lowered the window on his side. As soon as it had more or less stopped he pointed his SPR out the window and opened fire.

"Fuck!" Bezhmel shouted as rounds began cracking into the SUV. "Out!" he continued, ducking and pushing on the driver so the idiot would bail out on the far side.

However, the duck had been fortuitous since it permitted the 5.56 round meant for *his* head to instead strike the driver in the right temple.

Chito's head snapped to the left as blood filled the interior of the vehicle and his body slumped in the same direction, tangled in the steering wheel and effectively blocking the door.

"Fuck!" Bezhmel shouted again, pushing at the body and trying to get to the door latch. "What are you fuckers in the back waiting for? SHOOT!"

"Out!" Calthrop yelled, bailing out on his side. He was somewhat surprised to feel the sharp strike of high heels in his back as Katya made her own time out of the targeted vehicle. Rounds were cracking through the air, and the car, before he could even get to his knees. But, in the meantime, the hooker had pulled Natalya from the back of the car and was already headed away into the darkness.

"Where are *you* going?"

"I am saving my life," Katya said, not looking back. "And hers, the *primary*, yes? You are going to help by killing as many of them as you can before you die."

"Oh, that is so bloody . . ." Calthrop said, rolling behind a wheel for cover as AK rounds began thumping into and through the car. The two girls, however, were already fading into the darkness. "Whorish."

He reached in with his right hand and drew the Walther from its shoulder holster, then shook his head.

"Not bloody likely," he muttered, reaching in to the other side and removing a Winchester .454 revolver. The weapon was a "pistol" only in technical description; the round it fired was similar in ballistics to a *very* heavy assault rifle. It also kicked like a mule. "Better. Right." He took a deep breath and then let it out, getting a good two-handed grip and licking his lips as the fire died from the back seat. So much for Mikhail. "Right. Bloody James Bond time, right? Get my double-O rating and everything. Right. They *so* did not cover this in recruiting. Mum was right; I should have been an actor . . ."

Bezhmel finally managed to get the door open and tumble to the road as the fire died down. But the first thing he saw was one of the shooters from the back seat sprawled on the road, his legs still in the backseat of the SUV.

There was only one of the former Spetznaz left alive, and he was clutching at one arm where a bullet had passed through the meat of the bicep.

"Move," Bezhmel said, waving him forward and plucking the AK from the hands of the dead fighter sprawled out the door. "I'll cover you."

"Right," the Russian grunted, hefting his SK-74. "I thought we were after a girl. Who are these guys?"

"I don't know," Bezhmel said, shrugging. "Probably the Keldara."

"Fucking Georgians," the former Spetznaz said, spitting and lifting up to stride forward. "Time for them to—"

Bezhmel was never to be sure what the former soldier thought it was time for. He had been watching the back seat but as the fighter lifted up Yarok saw a flash of movement through the back window and there was a tremendous report, as if someone had snuck along a .50 caliber sniper rifle.

The former Spetznaz trooper had just lifted up, also

watching the back seat, and was tossed backwards as if pulled by a wire. He hit on his back and slumped to the side, revealing a fist-sized exit wound from a round through the upper chest.

"Holy *Fuck*," Bezhmel shouted, aware that one, he was now entirely alone in this fight and, two, there was one *big* fucking gun on the other side.

One down, at least one to go.

Calthrop had never been in a gunfight. He'd been in one barroom brawl that he got out of as quickly as possible, and once had a mugger threaten him with a knife. But this was the first time he'd been in a gun battle and he wasn't sure of the rules. Well, the one thing he was sure of was that there *were* no rules.

But he'd watched quite a bit of the telly and movies. Actually, he blamed this whole thing on an addiction to James Bond movies, especially the early ones with Sean Connery. And while most of what he'd picked up from those, and other movies, was surely bogus, there was *one* trick he'd seen that might save his ass.

So he got down on his stomach, mentally working up the expense report for his clothes, and scanned *under* the car for targets.

There was one man apparently still standing on the other side. Calthrop could just see a knee past the left front tire of the Rover. He sighted on it carefully, pulled back the heavy hammer of the beastly weapon and pulled back on the trigger.

*"Bolgemoi!"* Bezhmel shouted at the tire by his side

exploded. Something hit him heavily on the hip, throwing him to the ground, but by the same token the Rover settled nearly to the ground, giving him more cover.

The round, however, was quickly followed by three more, each of which punched through not only the far doors but *both* sides of the Rover, sending spalling and ricochets off into the night.

"Fuck this," Bezhmel muttered, crawling to the dead fighter in the door. He patted at pockets until he came up with what he was looking for.

"Take this you goat-fucker," he muttered, pulling the pin on the grenade and tossing it as hard as he could in the direction of the fire.

Calthrop leaned against the tire and opened up the cylinder of the revolver, pushing out the spent rounds and quickly thumbing more in. Reload whenever possible. That bit was coming back from *very* distant classes in tactics.

As he closed the cylinder he heard a thump in the darkness beyond and looked carefully. When he saw the rolling sphere he remembered the *other* injunction that had been right up there with "reload."

"Oh, yeah," he said, trying to get to the *other* side of the wheel as fast as possible. "I was supposed to *move*."

On top of the crack of the grenade was a scream and at that Bezhmel leapt to his feet, running around the side of the Rover and sprinting towards the Mercedes while firing a stream of bullets from the AK held at his hip.

When he rounded the Mercedes he found that he

needn't have bothered. By the front tire was a sprawled body, a *very* large handgun not far from his outflung hand. In the backseat was another body, face down, one hand still on an SPR, the other slumped down into a floorboard awash in blood.

However, there were no women. Just the two dead men.

"Where oh where have my little lambs gone," Bezhmel whispered, setting the empty AK up against the side of the truck and drawing a Sig Sauer from his shoulder holster. "Oh, where oh where can they be?"

# ★ Chapter Forty-Six ★

"Hurry," Katya said, pushing the girl ahead of her down the twisting goat path. She'd heard one explosion and one more burst of firing and now all was quiet. She took that for a bad sign.

"I can barely walk," Natalya said, sobbing. "My feet are bloody."

"Your whole body will be bloody if you don't *run*," Katya whispered fiercely. She'd ordered the girl to take off her high-heeled shoes; they would be impossible on the narrow, steep, trails. But the ridge they were on was covered in rocks that had torn the feet of both of them to ribbons.

"Katya," Lydia said, calmly. "Situation report. It looks like Mikhail and the MI-6 man have both been taken down. The good news, such as it is, is that only one of the Russians is still alive. He's looking for you, but isn't directly on your track yet."

"How long until . . ." Katya panted, wincing as the rocks cut further into her abused feet. It was like the time that one pimp bastard had whipped her on her soles. But she was doing it to herself, which almost made up for it.

"At least seven more minutes," Lydia said. "I've made it clear that you're badly in need of support."

"Tell them to *hurry*," Katya replied.

"I have," Lydia said. "Let me remind you, the mission is to recover the primary."

"Yeah, I know," Katya snapped. "But I can't get my money if I'm dead."

They'd reached the second level below the switchback that the firefight occurred on and Katya stopped, winded, when they did. Natalya slumped to the ground, clearly willing to die rather than run anymore.

"This is no good," she muttered, looking up the hill.

"Katya," Lydia said. "He's found something. He's headed down the trail. The Americans say that he's following you, somehow."

"Tell them it's probably the blood from our *feet*!" Katya whispered fiercely. Looking up the hill she could see the flashlight, clearly. "We can't run anymore!"

"Then I suggest you figure something out," Lydia said with maddening calm.

"Easy for you to say," Katya said, looking around. There was a culvert, but since they were both trailing blood . . .

"Natalya," Katya snapped. "Get down on your hands and knees."

"Yes," the girl said in total resignation, doing as she was told. "I will die now."

"The hell you will," Katya replied. "I don't get my money if you die. Now, trying *not* to scrape yourself up and leave a trail, keep your feet off the ground and crawl into that culvert."

"Why?" Natalya said.

"Because I *told* you to, you little whore," Katya snarled. "Get. And when you're in there, crawl as far back as you can and *keep quiet.*"

Katya had retained her shoes, barely, by carrying them by the straps. Now she sat down and, wincing, donned them again. Once they were on and Natalya was climbing into the culvert, she started tottering down the road, painfully.

"Katya," Lydia said, with a note of confusion. "Predator says that Natalya has gone to ground and you are moving very slowly down the road. What are you doing?"

"Buying us time," Katya snarled. "Try to use it wisely."

Bezhmel spotted movement and turned off the torch, letting his eyes adjust for a moment. There, one figure.

He ran uphill on the road for a moment until he spotted a narrow trail and then took it as fast as he could without breaking an ankle. Part of the time he was on his ass, sliding down the steep hill, but he reached the road just behind the stupid little bitch tottering along on her high heels.

"Stop," he said, panting. The fight, and the chase, had worn him down; he wasn't in the same shape he'd been in when he left the service. "Stop," he repeated, turning the torch back on and spotlighting the little whore who was still trying to hobble away. He'd seen the blood, her feet weren't going to carry her far.

The girl turned around, wincing in pain from the light of the torch and held up her hands.

Not the right girl. But she would know where the other one went.

★ ★ ★

"Where's the other girl?" a man's voice barked from the far side of the light.

Katya screwed her eyes shut against the light and fell to her knees, head bent and hands covering her eyes.

"Please, sir," she begged, tears rolling down her face. "I don't know what is going on. I know nothing . . ."

"Where's the other girl, bitch?" the man said, coming closer. The torch was lowered and she could vaguely see his outline in the reflection. And the glint from a pistol that was centered on her forehead.

"She left me," Katya whimpered, pulling her hands away a little but still keeping her head down. "My feet, they were so hurt. She ran away, down the road . . ."

The torch came up and the man strode forward, looking down the hill.

"I don't see her," he said.

"She was there . . ." Katya said, reaching under her left armpit and pressing a valve four times in quick succession. Then she pushed, hard, on the small packet under her skin and let the drug take her.

She wasn't sure what was in it. The American doctors had talked about pseudo-adrenaline and oxidizers and steroids and man-made endorphins until her head was reeling with unfamiliar terms. But they had given her one demonstration under controlled conditions so she would know what to expect. All she knew was that the world seemed to slow down and she suddenly felt light, the pain of her muscles from running, and the pain of her feet, drifting away as if they were nothing. She also felt strong and graceful, as if she could dance off the face of the world and drift away into space.

Last, but not least, she felt angry. But, then again, that was how she always felt. And now she got to let it all hang out.

Bezhmel held the torch in his left hand and the pistol in his right, tracking back and forth down the road. The light from the torch was bright enough to clearly reveal the far switchback and there was no girl in sight.

He started to turn back to the little whore that had lied to him and got one brief glimpse of her rising up off the ground then . . . she seemed to blur.

Katya struck the man's gun-hand with the side of her fist, hard, spinning both gun and torch away down the hill. There was a complicated disarm she had been taught, but in the grip of the drug all she could think to do was smash. So she smashed.

She roundkicked upwards into the man's stomach, causing him to double over in agony at the drug-enhanced blow, then kicked him again in the face on its way down. She got a sick satisfaction from the crunch of bone and the splash of blood as his nose pulped. The second blow felt like it broke something in her foot, but she could care less. They'd told her that she'd only have thirty seconds, at most, under the full effects of the drug and she intended to make the most of it.

The little whore was supernaturally fast and so strong it felt like being hit by a professional kick-boxer. Bezhmel was trained in hand-to-hand combat, but this was like fighting a rabid mongoose. He had been taken totally off-guard and couldn't even start to defend himself as blow after blow came out of nowhere. . . .

Dropping her kicking foot and stepping forward, Katya actually turned her back to the man, then spun on one foot, driving the side of her clenched right fist into his right temple, then spinning back the other way for an identical blow to the left. That one was assisted by the fact that the man's head had been punched in that direction.

She punched down with one heel into his instep, driving the stilletto all the way through to the sole of his boot. Then, as he doubled over in agony at the pain, she punched up with her elbow to strike his jaw. She heard a crack, that time, that might have been neck vertebrae. She hoped not, she had more mad to get out. Hopefully it was just lots of teeth.

For now, in this time and in this place, she could let out every scrap of hatred seared into her soul. This man, this fucker that worked for the Albanians, he was every man who had ever raped her, every man who had ever beaten her, every man who had ever *touched* her. And she intended to take her full time, sped up as it was, on this one man. It might be the only chance she ever got.

Bezhmel was out on his feet. His eyes were blinded from the head-blows, a TKO in any boxing ring. But this wasn't boxing, and the woman clearly wasn't going to go for a simple technical. It was all that he could do to manage to stand, to try to raise his arms in pathetic defense, as insanely powerful blow after blow struck from the darkness . . .

★ ★ ★

Katya, feeling the effects of the drug starting to ebb, kneed the man in the groin, then punched into the solar plexus before he could even start to double over. Doubly bent, his neck was wide open and she drove one rock-hard, enhanced-strength, elbow blow into the back of his neck, dropping him to the ground.

The Kildar had told her that that was often a killing blow, but the man still was writhing in agony on the ground. Oh, well. That was easy enough to fix.

She raised one foot and drove the narrow tip of her hated stiletto heels into the top of the man's neck, just below the skull. The blow sunk the stiletto all the way up to the base. The man twitched once, much like a pithed frog, and then was still..

She looked up, startled, as a helicopter raised up from below the level of the road and slid sideways towards her. She had been so concentrated on the beating she gave the man, she hadn't even heard it approach. A spotlight suddenly came on, panning around until it caught her in its light. She had to shield her eyes, again, at the brightness.

The helicopter slid sideways, again, lining up its wheels with the edge of the cliff and Katya could faintly see movement behind the spotlight. She wasn't sure who it was, but she didn't really care anymore. She'd had her fun. If it was more of the Albanian motherfuckers, they could damned well kill her, but she was *never* going back into slavery.

"Hey, Katya," Killjoy said casually, walking out of the light. He was scratching under his armor and if he was perturbed at the sight of a woman standing on the back of a man's neck with her high heel shoved all the way through to his esophagus it didn't show. "Whatchadoin?"

"Your job, motherfucker," Cottontail replied, finally pulling her stiletto out of the man's neck. Even over the rotor-wash, there was an audible "pop." "About time you showed up. Reinforcements my ass."

# ★ Chapter Forty-Seven ★

Mike tossed the last bag of ill-gotten gains into the helicopter and waved Oleg and Juris by. He wrinkled his brow at the two obvious hookers helping the big team leader, but decided not to mention it.

"You gonna make it, big guy?" Mike asked the team leader, who was just about shot to shit but still limping along with the help of the sniper and the two girls, one of whom was carrying an AK.

"I will be at my wedding, Kildar," Oleg said, grinning. "And you had better be, too. And so will Catrina and Elena!"

"Glad to meet you," Mike said, making the connection.

"And you, Kildar," the one with the AK said, dropping a curtsey that slipped her dress up far enough to show pubic hair and then helping the team leader up the ramp.

"I'll be a monkey's uncle," Mike muttered as Adams ran up. "Well?"

"All accounted for," Adams said, not even pausing as he continued up the ramp of the Hip, which was hovering just off the roof of the club. "Hail and not hail. And, as you noticed, two recovered Keldara girls."

"Let's go, then," Mike said, stepping up onto the ramp. "Pilot, shag ass."

As the ramp started to close, he flipped up the safety switch of the activator and pressed the red plunger. The detonation was surprisingly muted. They couldn't blow the whole building, there were girls still on the upper floors, but the basement offices were well and truly trashed. As he looked around for a seat, though, he noticed a surprising number of unfamiliar female faces on the helicopter. Maybe they could have blown the whole building.

"Adams, we appear to have some stowaways," Mike said, sitting down on the floor since there weren't any spare seats.

"The basement rooms were being used as torture chambers for new girls or girls who had somehow really pissed the boss off," Adams replied, shrugging in unconcern. "And, of course, the troops had to run a gauntlet of girls as they headed for the roof. I guess a few somehow stuck to them. What did you expect?"

"Nothing less," Mike admitted, looking over at one of the girls who gave him a tremulous smile of hope. "Nothing less. They're the Mountain Tigers."

# ★ Epilogue ★

"Senator," Traskel's executive assistant said, looking through the door. "There's a Mr. Jenkins here to see you. He's . . ."

"Quite insistent," Mike said, shoving the door open and then shutting it in the secretary's face. "Hi, John."

"I thought you'd have the good sense to not meet me here," the senator said, picking up the phone.

"Oh, I think we can dispense with those games, Senator," Mike said, walking over to the desk and slamming the phone, and the senator's hand, down on the desk so hard they both broke.

"Jesus!" the senator roared, pulling his hand back furiously. "I"ll have you arrested for that . . ."

"Oh, I don't think so," Mike said, sitting down and tossing a packet on the desk. "You see, I found Natalya. And the bastard you sent to kill her. Who was stupid enough to talk about it. All of it, Senator. Top sheet is a partial transcript."

The senator leaned forward and gingerly opened the manila envelope with his unbroken hand; then started to read the transcription.

"There's no proof there," he said, hoarsely.

"There's enough to matter," Mike said. "The news media would be all over it like stink on shit, even if you are their fair-haired boy. Wilson Three-Names was a former aide. He's been definitely identified by a first-hand source as the man who both murdered a girl in Macedonia and attempted to frame Senator Grantham for it. And despite the voice changer, you can get a partial match. Between that and the confidential notes when you covered for him after that incident in Nigeria, which are easy enough to leak, you're toast. Don't even begin to try to fight this or you'll be facing charges as well as being out of government service."

"What do you want?" the senator whispered.

"You're leaving government service," Mike said. "Old war wound will do. You don't play around behind the scenes, either. No fundraising, no support for candidates, no quiet little deals, no lobbying. You are out. O-U-T. Out. Go teach or something, you're perfect for academia. And you don't have to work for your salary. Your wife will support you. But one glimmer of a hint that you're back in the power broker business and that entire file gets forwarded to every single news outlet on the planet."

"Fuck you," the senator snapped. "There's no way . . ."

"The Senate leadership have already seen that file," Mike said, grinning. "If you don't go, you're going to be removed from office. And then it will be all over the news. I'd imagine the President's party would even be able to pick up your seat after that debacle. Hell, I doubt that your party would be able to keep New Jersey. As it is, your party can appoint an interim and he'll probably be reelected."

"What are they going to do about Wilson?" the senator asked, deflating. "He'll talk. He's too much of a coward not to."

"He's already dealt with," Mike said, standing up. "He had a little accident in the Balkans. Bandits and such, you know how troubled it is over there. And if you try to fuck with me or mine, Senator, overtly or covertly, you'll be dealt with the same way. Oh, and you owe me five mil," he added. "The number for the bank account is in the file. Don't be slow on the payments. You don't want to deal with my collections department."

"What was the take from the whorehouse?" Pierson asked.

He and Mike had agreed to meet in a Georgetown bar after Mike's meeting with Senator Traskel. Mike had known he was going to need at least one drink afterwards. Although, the meeting with the Senate leadership had been more of a ballbuster all things considered.

"Damn near six mil," Mike said, shaking his head. "It turned out that the club was the central clearing house for most of the Balkans for that clan. Who ever knew that hookers could generate so much cash?"

"Not just hookers," Pierson said. "The gang was deep in the heroin business, apparently. Interpol sent us a very carefully worded but hearty thank you."

"Nice to know we're appreciated," Mike said, shaking his head. "And I kinda figured that when we found over six hundred pounds of the damned stuff in the safe. Which was why most of the Semtek and incendiaries were on top of it."

"Where are you going to start?" Pierson asked, changing the subject.

"Japan, I think," Mike replied. "They've got the most files after the U.S. You know I'm going to be the one most hated son of a bitch on earth after this. Shoot the messenger doesn't even begin to cover it. The U.S. Senate would love to bury me under the Capitol. Both parties. The leadership meeting was a real show of bipartisanship."

"You're also going to be one of the most feared," Pierson pointed out, chuckling. "The people in the know in those nations—and we're talking about *every* really *major* nation on earth—are not going to want to piss you off. Not after this. Forget saving Paris. The general outline of what you and the Keldara did is already making the rounds of the intelligence and military services, at least the high-level TS sections. As is the news about the files. And, believe you me, people are shitting their pants as they wait for you to turn up. Especially the ones that don't know, yet, if they're going to be getting a visit. Frankly, I'm not sure if they're more afraid of the files, or you personally."

"Well, I doubt they will ever love me. Most of them are hypocritical PC motherfuckers with not an ounce of brains between them. Bear witness that the French threw me out on my ass after saving their sorry asses. I'm never going to be well liked by 'the high and mighty' of Traskel's stripe." He stood up and tossed back his bourbon, then rolled the empty shot glass thoughtfully between thumb and forefinger. "Enough, I suppose, that they fear me."

"You, and your Mountain Tigers."

# ★ About the Author★

A veteran of the 82nd Airborne, John Ringo brings first-hand knowledge of military operations to his fiction. In addition to his nationally best-selling techno-thriller novels about Mike Harmon, his novels for Baen include the novels in the *New York Times* best-selling Posleen War series (*A Hymn Before Battle*, *Gust Front*, *When the Devil Dances*, and *Hell's Faire*), the Council War series (*There Will be Dragons*, *Emerald Sea*, *Against the Tide*, and *East of the Sun, West of the Moon*), the novel *Into the Looking Glass*, four collaborations with fellow *New York Times* bestselling author David Weber (*March Upcountry*, *March to the Sea*, *March to the Stars* and *We Few*) and three collaborative novels in the Posleen series: *Hero* (with Michael Z. Williamson), *Watch on the Rhine* (with Tom Kratman) and the *New York Times* best seller *Cally's War* (with Julie Cochrane).